CONTEMPORARY AMERICAN FICTION
AMERICANA

After writing this, his first novel, Don DeLillo went on to write eight more highly acclaimed novels: *Libra*, *White Noise*, *End Zone* (all available from Penguin), *Great Jones Street*, *Ratner's Star*, *Players*, *Running Dog*, and *The Names*. In 1985 he received the American Book Award for fiction for *White Noise*.

Don DeLillo

AMERICANA

PENGUIN BOOKS

PENGUIN BOOKS
Published by the Penguin Group
Viking Penguin Inc., 40 West 23rd Street,
New York, New York 10010, U.S.A.
Penguin Books Ltd, 27 Wrights Lane,
London W8 5TZ, England
Penguin Books Australia Ltd, Ringwood,
Victoria, Australia
Penguin Books Canada Ltd, 2801 John Street,
Markham, Ontario, Canada L3R 1B4
Penguin Books (N.Z.) Ltd, 182-190 Wairau Road,
Auckland 10, New Zealand

Penguin Books Ltd, Registered Offices:
Harmondsworth, Middlesex, England

First published in the United States of America by
Houghton Mifflin Company 1971.
Published in Penguin Books 1989

1   3   5   7   9   10   8   6   4   2

In preparing this edition for publication, the author has
made some cuts in the original text; there is no new material.

LIBRARY OF CONGRESS CATALOGING IN PUBLICATION DATA
DeLillo, Don.
Americana / Don DeLillo.
p.   cm.
Reprint. Originally published: Boston : Houghton Mifflin, 1971.
ISBN 0 14 01.1948 5 (pbk.)
I. Title.
PS3554.E4425A8 1989
813'.54—dc 19   88–39571

Printed in the United States of America
Set in Caledonia

To Barbara Bennett

PART ONE

1

Then we came to the end of another dull and lurid year. Lights were strung across the front of every shop. Men selling chestnuts wheeled their smoky carts. In the evenings the crowds were immense and traffic built to a tidal roar. The santas of Fifth Avenue rang their little bells with an odd sad delicacy, as if sprinkling salt on some brutally spoiled piece of meat. Music came from all the stores in jingles, chants and hosannas, and from the Salvation Army bands came the martial trumpet lament of ancient Christian legions. It was a strange sound to hear in that time and place, the smack of cymbals and high-collared drums, a suggestion that children were being scolded for a bottomless sin, and it seemed to annoy people. But the girls were lovely and undismayed, shopping in every mad store, striding through those magnetic twilights like drum majorettes, tall and pink, bright packages cradled to their tender breasts. The blind man's German shepherd slept through it all.

Finally we got to Quincy's place. His wife opened the door. I introduced her to my date, B.G. Haines, and then began counting the people in the room. As I counted I was distantly aware that Quincy's wife and I were talking about India. Counting the house was a habit of mine. The question of how many people were present in a particular place seemed important to me, perhaps because the recurring news of airline disasters and military engagements always stressed the number of dead and missing; such exactness is a tickle of electricity to the numbed brain. The next most important thing to find out was the degree of hostility. This was relatively simple. All you had to do was look at the people who were looking at you as you entered. One long glance was usually enough to give you a fair reading. There were thirty-one people in the living room. Roughly three out of four were hostile.

Quincy's wife and my date smiled at each other's peace earrings. Then I took B.G. into the living room. We waited for somebody to approach us and start a conversation. It was a party and we didn't want to talk to each other. The whole point was to separate for the evening and find exciting people to talk to and then at the very end to meet again and tell each other how terrible it had been and how glad we were to be together again. This is the essence of Western civilization. But it didn't matter really because an hour later we were all bored. It was one of those parties which are so boring that boredom itself soon becomes the main topic of conversation. One moves from group to group and hears the same sentence a dozen times. "It's like an Antonioni movie." But the faces were not quite as interesting.

I decided to go into the bathroom and look at myself in the mirror. Six framed graffiti were hanging on the bathroom wall. The words were set in large bold type, about 60-point, on glossy paper; they were set in a scripted typeface to look real. Three of the graffiti were blasphemous and three were obscene. The frames looked expensive. I noticed some dandruff on my shoulders. I was about to brush it off when a girl named Pru Morrison came in. She was from somewhere in Bucks County, just beginning to get caught up in the whirl of urban monotony. She stood facing me, her body flat against the closed door. She was all of eighteen and I was both too old and too young to be interested in her. Nevertheless I didn't want her to know about the dandruff.

"Thought I'd wash my hands."

"Who's that nignog?"

"Pru, I understand Peck and Peck has a special on riding crops this week. Why don't you run on over?"

"I didn't know you went out with nignogs, David."

I began to wash my hands. Pru sat on the edge of the tub and turned on the faucet just enough to cause a trickle. I wondered whether this was supposed to have a sexual connotation. Sometimes it was hard to tell about these things.

"I got a letter from my brother," she said. "He's manning an M-79 grenade launcher. He's in one of the roughest battle zones. He says every square inch of land is fiercely contested. You should read his letters, David. They're really tremendous."

The war was on television every night but we all went to the movies. Soon most of the movies began to look alike and we went into dim rooms and turned on or off, or watched others turn on or off, or burned joss sticks and listened to tapes of near silence. I brought my 16mm camera along. It was a witty toy and everyone was delighted.

"He says you can't tell the friendlies from the hostiles."

"Who?" I said.

"I hate your filthy rotten guts," Pru said.

"Quincy tells me you've got a new boyfriend, Pru. Texas A. and M. Some kind of junior cadet. Quincy tells me you met him through a computer dating system."

"That lying bastard."

"Your own cousin, Pru."

"You've got dandruff," she said. "I can see it on your jacket. Dandruff!"

Quincy was in rare form, telling a series of jokes about Polish janitors, Negro ministers, Jews in concentration camps and Italian women with hairy legs. He battered his audience with

5

shock and insult, challenging people to object. Of course we were choking with laughter, trying to outdo each other in showing how enlightened we were. It was meant to be a liberating ethnic experience. If you were offended by such jokes in general, or sensitive to particular ones which slurred your own race or ancestry, you were not ready to be accepted into the mainstream. B.G. Haines, who was a professional model and one of the most beautiful women I have ever known, seemed to be enjoying Quincy's routine. She was one of four black people in the room—and the only American among them—and she apparently felt it was her diplomatic duty to laugh louder than anyone at Quincy's most vicious color jokes. She almost crumpled to the floor laughing and I was sure I detected a convulsive broken sob at the crest of every laugh. She needed more practice, I suppose. All evening, in fact, she had been smiling at everyone who approached and responding with grave nods to all the social insights directed her way by the scholars in the room. It was confusing. Finally I reminded her that we were supposed to be polite to her, not the reverse. Then I added a brief lecture on the responsibility she had toward her people. She speared a passing hors d'oeuvre and became elegant again.

It was almost over. A few people had already left. It was just a cocktail party and small groups were forming for dinner. In a corner of the room Quincy's wife was doing a modified cocktail version of what we referred to as her karate striptease, a dance she said she had learned on their trip to the Orient.

In a little while I would ask B.G. where she wanted to eat. She would suggest that I decide. We would go to a small French restaurant way over on the West Side, on the rim of no man's land, where the wind blows cold off the river and the low bleak tenements breathe decay; and where, at this time of year, there is a sense of total emptiness, of a place that has been abandoned before the boots of war. No one could live there but torn cats and children with transparent bellies, and those distant lights, crackling over Times Square, belong to another city in another age. B.G. would order the frogs' legs. I would try to impress her by speaking French to the waiter with the warmth and intimacy of a hero of the Resistance greeting an old comrade-in-arms. The waiter would despise me and B.G. would see through my bluff. There would be nothing to do but finish the evening with one of those chain-smoking conversations about death, youth and anxiety. I remembered that I no longer smoked.

"Where would you like to eat?" I said.

But she didn't hear me. She was talking to a man named Carter Hemmings. Although Carter was thirty years old, or two years older than myself, he was one of my subordinates at the network. I was always very conscious of the ages of men with whom I worked. What I feared most at the network were younger men who might advance to positions higher than mine. It was not enough to be the best; one had to be the youngest as well. My secretary, through some tidy espionage, had been able to learn the ages of all those men whose levels of responsibility were comparable to my own. When she told me that I was the youngest by a full year and three months, I took her to Lutèce for dinner and got her a fifteen-dollar raise. Carter Hemmings was afraid of me. For this reason, and also because it was a time for holiday compassion, for prison reprieves and military truces, I did not interrupt his conversation with B.G. Instead I got myself another drink. Only about a dozen people remained. Sullivan, in her gypsy trenchcoat, stood against a wall. It had been foolish of me to invite her; she looked tense. A Pakistani who worked at the UN was facing her. He held a drink in one hand and an ashtray in the other. Sullivan seemed content to flick her ashes to the floor. I stood directly behind him and tried to get her to laugh by making swinish faces. She slipped her right foot out of her shoe and then, with exquisite nonchalance, tucked her leg way up behind her against the wall so that it disappeared, storklike, behind the shroud of her trenchcoat. She remained that way, on one leg, a cryptic shoe moored beneath her.

Whether on purpose or not, Sullivan always made me feel totally inadequate. I was drawn to her, terribly.

"Because I am a Moslem," the Pakistani was saying, "I do not drink. And yet I feel I must maintain a glass in my hand, or the others, perforce, will think me too solemn and undeviating an individual. We Moslems are very strict in the matter of alcohol, dress and the carnal relations. Perhaps you are tired of these people and would like to go to your flat. May I offer to accompany you? My Plymouth Fury is parked directly across the road. Where do you live?"

"In the hearts of men," Sullivan said.

I moved in on them. The grandfather clock began to chime. I looked at the Pakistani and moved my lips, without speaking, to give the impression that my words were being drowned out by the clock. After eight sustained chimes it was silent and I picked from my thoughts, in mid-sentence, a meaningless travelogue of Switzerland, and continued it aloud. He looked at his glass and then at the ashtray, trying to decide which might be more safely placed on top of the other. He was in unknown territory and wanted to have at least one hand free. Then Quincy came over and began to talk about a new mega-drug he had taken the week before. And the whole scene dissolved before any of us could find out what it was all about.

I went out on the terrace. Automobiles were moving across Central Park, ticking red taillights trailing each other north and west toward the darkness and the river, headlights coming this way, soft orange, the whistling doormen. The park's lamplights were dull cold steady silver. I was wasting my life.

Everybody called her by her last name. She was a sculptor, thirty-seven years old, unmarried, a tall woman who seemed by her manner or bearing or mere presence to change a room slightly, to make it self-conscious. Sullivan had the kind of face and body which inspire endless analogies and I will try to keep them to a minimum. At parties, appearing in a plain loose dress, flat heels, no makeup, hair long and lifeless and uncombed, she was the woman who was invariably described within good-natured coveys of people as strange, different, curious, remarkable. At such parties, as Sullivan would stand listening to some desolate man describe the ritual terrors of his life, or sit alone patting the swept waist of a guitar, I would hear people speculate on her ancestry. Many seemed to think she might be an American Indian. Others thought her origins were Catalonian or Polynesian or Dead Sea. Once I heard an admiring woman describe Sullivan's face as pre-Columbian. To me, she was simply homely. (One's vengeance, of course, had its sour politics to play.) Her hands were long and grimly knuckled. Her dark eyes seemed trained to remain unamused by whatever passed before them. Her narrow nose, a fencer's nose somehow, had a tendency to flare unexpectedly, sniffing disaster in someone's commonplace remark. In all, she was a lean hard over-boned woman. Men were always telling her how very much they wanted to go to bed with her.

I went back inside. Quincy's wife was sitting on the sofa now, stirring her drink with a toothbrush. Pru Morrison had apparently left. Quincy and two women were sprawled on the floor in front of the TV set. The two women were employed at the network, as was Quincy. One of the women made notes of what he said as he watched the program. I looked around for my date. Sullivan, still roosting on her left leg, was talking to a man who looked like a quonset hut. I began swinging my arms chimpanzee-style and executing heavy little hops. At the same time I inserted my tongue over my upper teeth and gums to create a bulge in the area between nose and upper lip. I hunched way over until my hands dangled below my knees. Sullivan gave me a brief look. Then the man took her glass and went into the kitchen. I straightened up and went over.

"What happened to your ashtray?"

"He had to get back to the office," she said. "Sudden crisis on the subcontinent."

"I should be at the office myself. Everybody's bucking for

9

my job. It's a contest to see who stays later. Guy named Reeves Chubb sleeps in his office about three nights a week. His desk is full of dirty shirts. We don't go in there for a meeting unless his secretary sprays the place with air-freshener. But I'm holding my own. I may even take a vacation one of these days."

"Skiing? All those nymphs in titty sweaters."

"I don't know," I said. "I'd like to do something more religious. Explore America in the screaming night. You know. Yin and yang in Kansas. That scene."

"Maybe I'll come with you," Sullivan said.

"Seriously?"

"I'd like to do it, David. I really would."

"I have to go out West anyway in a few months to do a documentary on the Navahos. I thought I'd take my vacation a couple of weeks before that and spend the time driving out there."

"We can take Pike with us."

"Sure," I said. "He can get somebody to run things for a while."

"We'll let him map out our route. We'll give him a battle-field commission. He'll like that."

I felt good. It was a good idea. The man came back with their drinks. We were introduced and then I went looking for B.G. Haines. The bathroom was empty. I went into the bedroom and examined the coats on the bed. Her coat wasn't among them. I looked in the closet and it wasn't there either. Then I went into the kitchen. It was empty too. I stood there awhile. Then I opened the refrigerator door and took an ice tray out of the freezer. There were four ice cubes left. I brought up phlegm from my throat and spat on each of the cubes, separately. Then I slid the tray back into the freezer and shut the refrigerator door.

I went back to the living room. Sullivan was still talking to the round gray man. I couldn't take my eyes off that empty shoe.

2

I was an extremely handsome young man. The objectivity which time slowly fashions, and the self-restraint it demolishes, enabled me to make this statement without recourse to the usual modest disclaimers which give credit to one's parents or grandparents in the manner of a sires-and-dams book. I suppose it's true enough that I inherited my mother's fine fair skin and my father's athletic physique, but the family album gives no clue to the curiously Grecian perspective of my face. Physical identity meant a great deal to me when I was twenty-eight years old. I had almost the same kind of relationship with my mirror that many of my contemporaries had with their analysts. When I began to wonder who I was, I took the simple step of lathering my face and shaving. It all became so clear, so wonderful. I was blue-eyed David Bell. Obviously my life depended on this fact.

I was exactly six feet two inches tall. My weight varied between 185 and 189. Despite my fair skin I tanned unusually well. My hair was more blond than it is now, thicker and richer; my waistline was thirty-two; my heartbeat was normal. I had a trick knee but my nose had never been broken, my feet were not ugly and I had better than average teeth. My complexion was excellent.

My secretary told me once that she had overheard Strobe Botway, one of my superiors at the network, refer to me as being "conventionally" handsome. We had a good laugh over that. Strobe was a small, barely humanoid creature who had the habit, when smoking, of slowly rotating the cigarette with his thumb, index and middle fingers, as Bogart did in an early film of his. Strobe hated me because I was taller and younger than he was, and somewhat less extraterrestrial. He talked often of the Bogart mystique, using Germanic philosophical terms which nobody understood, and he subverted many parties by quoting long stretches of dialogue from obscure Bogart films. He also had his favorite character actors, men whose names nobody could ever connect with a face, men who played prison wardens for seven consecutive movies, who were always attacking Japanese machine-gun nests with a grenade in each hand, who were drunkards, psychotic killers, crooked lawyers, or test pilots who had lost their nerve. Strobe seemed to admire the physical imperfections of people, their lisps, scar tissue, chipped teeth; in his view these added up to character, to a certain seedy magnetism. His world was not mine. I admired Humphrey Bogart but he made me nervous. His forehead bothered me; it was the forehead of a man who owes money. My own instincts led me to Kirk Douglas and Burt Lancaster. These were the American pyramids and they needed no underground to spread their fame. They were monumental. Their faces slashed across the screen. When they laughed or cried it was without restraint. Their chromium smiles were never ambiguous. And they rarely had time to sit down and trade cynical quips with some classy society dame or dumb flatfoot. They were men of action, running, leaping, loving with abandon. When I was a teenager I saw Burt in *From Here to Eternity*. He stood above Deborah Kerr on that Hawaiian beach and for the first time in my life I felt the true power of the image. Burt was like a city in which we are all living. He was that big. Within the conflux of shadow and time, there was room for all of us and I knew I must extend myself until the molecules parted and I was spliced into the image. Burt in the moonlight was a crescendo of male perfection but no less human because of it. Burt lives! I carry that image to this day, and so, I believe, do millions of others, men and women, for their separate reasons. Burt in the moonlight. It was a concept; it was the icon of a new religion. That night, after the movie, driving my father's car along the country roads, I began to wonder how real the landscape truly was, and how much of a dream is a dream.

Strobe died in the middle of a meeting. He had a heart attack at his desk. He is conventionally dead. But he would have been happy to know that his reaction to my physical traits was shared by others at the network. Hidden energies filled the air, small secret currents, as happens in every business which thrives in the heat of the image. There was a cult of the unattractive and the clever. There were points scored for ruthlessness. There were vendettas against the good-looking. One sought to avoid categories and therefore confound the formulators. For to be neither handsome nor unattractive, neither ruthless nor clever, was to be considered a hero by the bland, a nice fellow by the brilliant and the handsome, a nonentity by the clever, a homosexual by the lunatic fringe of the unattractive, a bright young man by the ruthless, a threat by the dangerously neurotic, an intimate and loyal friend by the alienated and the doomed. I did my best to keep low. I moved quietly close to walls and up and down the stairwells. A small incident confirmed the value of these tactics. It happened one day, after lunch, when I found myself crossing Madison Avenue stride for stride with Tom Maples, a young man who had joined the network at roughly the same time I had. We exchanged the usual cautious pleasantries. When we reached the sidewalk, a lovely teen-age girl wearing pink eyelashes asked me for my autograph. "I don't know who you are," she said, "but I'm sure you must be somebody."

Her smile was rather winning, and blithely I signed her fold-out map of the subway system, thinking Maples might be amused. He avoided me for the next six months. After that I did my best to be exceedingly humble and withdrawing. I felt it was essential to the well-being of others.

It's time now to run the film again. I mean that quite literally, for I still have in my possession a movie made in those years, and many tapes as well. There isn't much to do on an island this remote and I can kill (or rather redistribute) a fair amount of time by listening to the soundtrack and taking yet another look at some of the footage.

I went down the corridor to my office. My secretary was at her desk eating a jelly donut and writing a letter. Her name was Binky Lister. She was a cheerful girl, a few pounds overweight in a pleasant way. She was having an affair with my immediate superior, Weede Denney, but continued to be a trustworthy secretary, which means she lied on my behalf and defended me on all counts against charges made by the secretaries of men who feared and hated me. She followed me into the office.

"Mr. Denney wants you for a ten o'clock meeting."

"What's it all about?"

"He doesn't tell me everything for chrissake."

"Don't get mad, Binky. It was just an idle question."

Standing there she crossed her ankles awkwardly, a sort of non-facial pout. I sat behind my enormous desk and at once imagined myself naked. Then I pushed the chair back slightly and began to revolve in a magisterial 180-degree arc, surveying my land. The walls were covered with blow-ups of still photographs from programs I had written and coordinated. My bookcase was full of bound scripts. There were plants in two corners of the room and a dozen media periodicals arranged neatly on the end table. The ashtrays were all from Jensen. I had a black leather sofa and a yellow door. Weede Denney's sofa was bright red and he had a black door.

"What else?" I said.

"A woman called. She didn't leave her name but to tell you the frogs' legs weren't as tasty as usual.

"My life," I said, "is a series of telephone messages nobody understands but me. Every woman I meet thinks she's some kind of Delphic phrasemaker. My phone rings at three in the morning and it's somebody stranded at some airport calling to tell me that the animal crackers have left the zoo. The other day I got a telegram—a schizogram—from a girl on the Coast and all it said was: MY TONSILS WENT TO A FUNERAL. Do you ever send messages like that, Bink? My life is a telex from Interpol."

"If it's all so annoying, why did you smile when I told you about the frogs' legs?"

"It was good news," I said.

I went around to Weede's office. He was sitting in his restyled barber chair. For a desk he used a low round coffee table made of teak. Across the room was his three-screen color TV console. The barber chair, being an eccentricity permitted someone in Weede's position, hadn't bothered me much, but the coffee table was a bit frightening, seeming to imply that my titanic desk was all but superfluous. Weede was a master of the office arts, specializing in the tactic of reaction. Some time after I had joined the network, a subordinate of Weede's named Rob Claven decided to decorate his office with exactly fourteen of his wife's paintings. It was a fairly horrifying sight. Weede didn't say a word. But a week later a few of us, including Rob Claven, went to a meeting in Weede's office. What we saw startled us. All the paintings and old schooner prints had vanished and in their place was hung a single eight-by-twelve-inch reproduction of a detail from the Sistine Chapel. The almost bare walls were Rob Claven's death sentence. The Michelangelo was the dropping of the blade.

Finally Weede nodded me out of the doorway and directed me to the blue chair. He did this with a movement of hand or eye so close to imperceptibility that even as I sat down I

ـ ould not determine how I knew that I was supposed to sit in the blue chair. Reeves Chubb was already there, smoking one of his mentholated cigars. Weede told us an anecdote that concerned golf and adultery. Within a few minutes five more people entered, one a woman, Isabel Mayer, and the meeting began.

I looked out the window. Men in yellow helmets were working on a building that was going up across the street. They weaved in and out of its hollow bones, shooting acetylene, and catwalked over shaky planks. Strangely they did not seem to move with any special caution. Perhaps they had come to terms with the fear of falling. They had probably seen others fall and despised those deaths for the relief that followed the shock, a relief that must have risen with the wind, floor to floor, up the raw spindling shanks of the building. What could you do but go quickly to a dark bar and drink three burning whiskies? At one level two men squatted, riveting, and another, a level above, jumped from plank to plank, his arms held out slightly, hands at hip length. In mid-jump, at a certain angle against the open side of the building, he had the sky behind him, a rich and early blue, and they were framed in girders, man and sky, for what seemed an impossible second. I could see the riveters and the man jumping but they could not see each other. I watched for a long time, simultaneously trying to map the office voices and make them mean something. Then another man appeared from behind a girder, a tall man whose pants did not quite reach the top of his workboots. He stood motionless for a moment, hand canted against the rim of his helmet, shielding his eyes from the sun. He seemed to be looking at us. Then he lifted his hand above his head and began to wave. He was looking right at me, waving. I didn't know what to do. The cool voices clicked, measuring, compromising, destroying, pressuring. I felt he had to be acknowledged. I didn't know why but I felt it had to be done. It was absolutely imperative; a sign had to be given.

"Look," I said. "Look at that man over there. He's waving at us."

"Look," Isabel said. "He's waving. That construction worker. Do you see him, Weede?"

Then we were all on our feet, all eight of us, crowding before the window, waving back to him. It was exhilarating. We were all waving and laughing. Weede began to shout: "We see you! We see you!" We shoved each other to get more room. Isabel was trying to climb onto the wide radiator shelf that edged out from the bottom of the window. I helped her up and she knelt there, waving with both hands now. The sky was cloudless. We were laughing uncontrollably.

We finished the meeting in high spirits. Weede suggested we all go to lunch together. Reeves Chubb begged off, saying he had a lot of work to get done, and I knew that sooner or later Weede would make him suffer for that little bit of white-wash. We went to the Gut Bucket, a nouveau speakeasy with spittoons and sawdust where you paid $4.50 for a hamburger. It was full of network people, actors and models. There were hundreds of photographs of George Raft on the wall. We sat at a circular oak table. Nobody said anything for fully three minutes. Then the waiter came and took our orders.

Across the room a very attractive couple sat drinking. Their legs touched beneath the table. I stared at the girl, trying to catch her eye. All I wanted was a brief smile, nothing more. It would have pleased me a great deal. There was an energy in me which demanded release in these small ways. To thieve one smile from that man's afternoon. I hoarded such ego-moments, remembering every one. The nod. The pretty smile. The deep glance over the tip of the cigarette. Anything more would have been too much. I didn't want to cause any pain.

"Good meeting," Weede said. "Are we agreed on that?"

The waiter brought the food before we were finished with our second drinks. The place was filled with fantastic women. Weede told us about his camera safari in Kenya. He and his wife, Kitty, had spent a month there in the autumn. He said that we all had to come up to his apartment and look at the slides some time. At the network, people were always making vague invitations. Someone you hadn't seen in months would materialize in your doorway, a seraphic image above your morning coffee. "Let's have lunch some day," he'd say, and that would be the end of him. Or one of your superiors, lifting his soapy head from a washroom basin, would squint in your direction and mumble: "When are you going to come over and have dinner with Ginny [Billie, Ellie, Sandy] and me?" Genuine invitations were usually delivered in secrecy, either in confidential memos or behind closed doors.

Weede excused himself before dessert arrived and he left in an atmosphere of unbending silence. We all knew where he was going—to the Penn-Mar Hotel on Ninth Avenue, where Binky would be waiting for him. They met every Thursday for an hour or so. After he'd gone Isabel decided to order a brandy and we joined her. She was a short mashed woman of forty-five or so. Four months earlier, at a party aboard a tugboat repeatedly circling the Statue of Liberty, she had gone around telling everyone she had dropped one of her pubic hairs into Mastoff Panofsky's scotch and soda. Everybody was afraid of her. There was no logical reason for this; her job, in some obscurely defined way, dealt with fashion coordination, and she was not competitive with anyone in the entire network. Yet we all went to shameful extremes to prove our friendship and loyalty. It may have been that we sensed a dangerous feline perversity. Competitive or not, she seemed to be a woman who might attack at any moment, making no concessions at all to the etiquette of office combat. Now she began to tell us about the graffiti in the ladies' rooms of various restaurants around town. She hit the table after each recitation. The brandies came and we talked about the winter schedule, agreeing it was first-rate. A very tall girl wearing candy-cane trousers walked across the room; her legs seemed joined directly to her shoulders. Then Reeves Chubb came in. He saw us and waved. He dropped into the vacated chair with a burst of relief that seemed worthy of some historic moment, as if he had been gouging through a rain forest for months before finding us, the lost battalion.

"Did I miss Weede?" he said. "Guess I missed him, damn it. Thought I'd come down for a quickie before tackling that China thing. What's everybody drinking? I just heard Phelps got the ax. He doesn't know about it yet so don't say anything. They'll probably wait until after the first of the year. Paul Joyner thinks he's next. His door has been closed all morning. Hallie said he's been calling everybody he's ever known since high school. But he's been saying he's next for the last eight years. I guess he figures if he says it, it won't happen. Reverse jinx. The last few weeks have been hell on wheels. I've been in the office every weekend this month. If there's no letup soon, my child bride says she's going home to mother. Did you read where MBO is using re-cons for the depth skeds? I ran into Jones Perkins on my way down. He said Warburton's got some kind of rare fatal blood thing. I'd love to go to Aspen for the holidays but I don't see how I can swing it. My secretary's going though. I don't know how they do it. Hallie's going to Europe again in the spring. Have you heard what Merrill did, that perfect ass? Which reminds me. Blaisdell told me he saw Chandler Bates' wife in San Juan last weekend. Hanging around El Convento with some tacky scuba type. Isabel, those are the most stunning gloves. If I don't take a vacation soon, you're going to walk into my office and see nothing there but a heap of ashes. What's everybody drinking?"

We went back to the office. In the early afternoon it was always quiet, the whole place tossing slowly in tropical repose, as if the building itself swung on a miraculous hammock, and then the dimming effects of food and drink would begin to wear off and we would remember why we were there, to buzz and chime, and all would bend to their respective machines. But there was something wonderful about that time, the hour or so before we remembered. It was the time to sit on your sofa instead of behind the desk, and to call your secretary into the office and talk in soft voices about nothing in particular— films, books, water sports, travel, nothing at all. There was a certain kind of love between you then, like the love in a family which has shared so many familiar moments that not to love would be inhuman. And the office itself seemed a special place, even in its pale yellow desperate light, so much the color of old newspapers; there was the belief that you were secure here, in some emotional way, that you lived in known terrain. If you had a soul, and it had the need to be rubbed by roots and seasons, to be comforted by familiar things, then you could not walk among those desks for two thousand mornings, nor hear those volleying typewriters, without coming to believe that this was where you were safe. You knew where the legal department was, and how to get a package through the mailroom without delay, and whom to see about tax deductions, and what to do when your water carafe sprang a leak. You knew all the things you wouldn't have known if you had suddenly been placed in any other office in any other building anywhere in the world; and compared to this, how much did you know, and how safe did you feel, about, for instance, your wife? And it was at that time, before we remembered why we were there, that the office surrendered a sense of belonging, and we sat in the early afternoon, pitching gently, knowing we had just returned to the mother ship.

There was a phone ringing in the corridor. Nobody bothered to pick it up. Then another one began ringing. I walked slowly around my office, stretching as I went. I tried to remember whether Burt or Kirk had ever acted in an office film, one of those dull morality tales about power plays and timid adulteries. I noticed a memo on my desk. I knew immediately, from the brevity of the message, that it was another of the strange memos that had been appearing at irregular intervals for over a year. I picked it up and read it.

To: Tech Unit B
From: St. Augustine
And never can a man be more disastrously in death than when death itself shall be deathless.

Nobody knew who sent these memos. Investigations had been made, people questioned, but nothing came of it. Whoever sent them had to overcome two difficulties. He had to get into the multilith room and run off enough copies for our entire sub-section without being discovered. And he had to distribute the memos, one by one, to every desk and office in the area. The multilith operators had been cleared of any suspicion and so had all the mailboys. No one had ever seen these particular memos delivered; they simply appeared, either in the morning or the early afternoon. This was the first of the St. Augustines. Previous memos had borne messages from Zwingli, Lévi-Strauss, Rilke, Chekhov, Tillich, William Blake, Charles Olson and a Kiowa chief named Satanta. Naturally the person responsible for these messages became known throughout the company as the Mad Memo-Writer. I never referred to him that way because it was much too obvious a name. I called him Trotsky. There was no special reason for choosing Trotsky; it just seemed to fit. I wondered if he was someone I knew. Everybody seemed to think he was probably a small grotesque man who had suffered many disappointments in life, who despised the vast impersonal structure of the network and who was employed in our forwarding department, the traditional repository for all sex offenders, mutants and vegetarians. They said he was most likely a foreigner who lived in a rooming house in Red Hook; he spent his nights reading an eight-volume treatise on abnormal psychology, in small type, and he told his grocer he had been a Talmudic scholar in the old country. This was the consensus and maybe it had a certain logic. But I found more satisfaction

21

in believing that Trotsky was one of our top executives. He made eighty thousand dollars a year and stole paper clips from the office.

I sat at my desk and with a ballpoint pen traced the outline of my left hand on a blank piece of note paper. Then I called Sullivan but she didn't answer the phone. I walked around the office some more and looked out into the corridor. Many of the girls were back at work, unhooding their typewriters and storing squalid Kleenex in the bottom drawers of their desks where it would rest with old love letters, rag dolls, and pornographic books their bosses had given them in the spirit of the new liberalism, and also to see if anything would happen. I closed the door. Then I unzipped my pants and took out my cock. I walked around the office like that for a while. It felt good. I put it back and then filed Trotsky's memo in the folder that held all of his other work as well as some poems I had written in the office from time to time and some schizograms from girls I knew. (HELLO FROM THE SCENIC COAST OF NEBRASKA.) I opened the door. Binky was at her desk. She took a sandwich and a paper container out of a white bag. The sandwich, when she unwrapped it, looked wet and gummy. There was something very touching about that moment.

"Welcome back to the big rock candy mountain."

"Hi," she said. "I spent two solid hours at goddamn Saks without buying a thing. And now I'm about to eat a Coca-Cola sandwich. Merry Christmas."

"Trotsky struck again."

"I saw it," she said. "I still think it's you."

She knew that would flatter me. Often she said things that seemed intended to do me some good. I never knew why. In many ways Binky was a good friend to me and I used to wonder what would happen if I tried, in the jargon of the day, to complicate our relationship. Once, working late in the office, she removed her shoes while taking dictation. The sight of a woman taking off her shoes has always stirred me, and I kissed her. That was all, a kiss between paragraphs, but maybe it wasn't mere tenderness which made me do it, nor a desire to challenge the blandness of our attachment. Maybe it was just another of my ego-moments. It was only several days before that I had learned about Binky and Weede.

"Come on in," I said.

She brought her lunch with her and we sat on the sofa.

"Phelps Lawrence just got bounced," she said.

"I heard."

"There's a rumor that Joyner's next."

"Joyner started it," I said. "It's part of his survival kit. If he's not careful it's going to blow up in his face one of these days."

"Jody thinks it's the beginning of a purge. There's been a rash of confidential memos. She thinks Stennis might be forced to resign. But keep it quiet. She made me promise not to breathe a word."

"I've noticed all the closed doors. Sometimes I think they close their doors just to frighten us. Everybody knows closed doors mean secret discussions and secret discussions mean trouble. But maybe they're in there watching guitar lessons on Channel 31."

"Grove Palmer is getting a divorce," Binky said.

Suddenly I realized that I hadn't brushed my teeth after lunch. I kept some toothpaste and a toothbrush in my office and always brushed my teeth after a lunch that included a few drinks. The washroom after lunch was always full of men brushing their teeth and gargling with mouthwash. There were times when I thought all of us at the network existed only on videotape. Our words and actions seemed to have a disturbingly elapsed quality. We had said and done all these things before and they had been frozen for a time, rolled up in little laboratory trays to await broadcast and rebroadcast when the proper time-slots became available. And there was the feeling that somebody's deadly pinky might nudge a button and we would all be erased forever. Those moments in the washroom, with a dozen men sawing away at their teeth, were perhaps the worst times of all. We seemed to be no more than electronic signals and we moved through time and space with the stutter and shadowed insanity of a TV commercial.

"What's happening with your Navaho project?" Binky said.

"Quincy keeps jamming up the works. I'm going to talk to Weede and see if I can get to work on it alone. But don't mention it to anybody."

"David," she said.

"What?"

"They may drop 'Soliloquy.' "

"Are you sure?"

"The person who told me said the crappy sponsor wasn't interested in renewing."

"Why not?"

"The person didn't say."

"There's always the Navahos," I said.

"David, I think it's the third or fourth best show on TV."

"Soliloquy" was a series I had worked out on my own. It was the first major thing I had done since joining Weede's group—a small, elite and experimental unit put together for the purpose of developing new concepts and techniques. The rest of the network despised us because of our relative freedom and because of the industry prizes we had won for our warcasts, which were done independently of the news division. "Soliloquy" had won nothing. Each show consisted, very simply, of an individual appearing before the camera for an hour and telling his life story. I wanted to ask her what else Weede had said about the series. But that wouldn't have been fair. She had already taken a chance in telling me as much as she had. Just then Weede went by my office, moving swiftly, head down, body tilted forward as if on skis. He always came back to the office at least half an hour after Binky on Thursday afternoons; this maneuver, obviously, was an attempt to avoid suspicion. I liked to think that he walked around the block five times during that half-hour, or stood in a phone booth in the lobby and pretended he was talking to someone, moving his lips over the mouthpiece, perhaps actually speaking, carrying on a normal businesslike conversation with the dial tone. And he always walked by my office very quickly, then tried to avoid me for the rest of the day. He must have possessed an extraordinarily complex sense of guilt. I think he was afraid of me on those Thursdays. But on Friday morning he would come looking for me, breathing smoke and vengeance, as if I were the engineer of his guilt.

Binky went back to her desk. I loosened my tie and rolled up my sleeves. I had managed to deceive myself into believing that people would be deceived into believing that a man so untidy (in an atmosphere so methodically spruce) must be driving himself mercilessly. The phone rang. It was Wendy Judd, a girl I had dated in college. She was living in New York now, having traveled for a year right after she divorced her husband, one of the top production people at either Paramount or Metro.

"I'm dying, David."

"Don't generalize, Wendy."

"New York is vicious. Listen, before I forget, can you come to a dinner party tomorrow night? Come alone. You're the only one who can save me."

"You know I go bowling with the fellas on Friday night, Wendy."

"David, please. This is no time for jokes."

"Our team is called the Steamrollers. We play the Silver Jets for the all-league title tomorrow. Winner gets a cup with a naked Greek bowling ace embossed on the side."

"Come early," she said. "You can help me toss the salad. We'll talk over old times."

"There are no old times, Wendy. The tapes have been accidentally destroyed."

"Eightish," she said, and hung up.

Outside, the girls were hammering at their little oval keys.

I went for a walk. Everybody was busy. All the phones seemed to be ringing. Some of the girls talked to themselves while typing, muttering *shit* whenever they made a mistake. I went around to the supply area. The cabinets were the same color as troops in the field. Hallie Lewin was in there, leaning over a bottom drawer. There is no place in the world more sexually exciting than a large office. It is like a fantasy of some elaborate woman-maze; wherever you go, around corners, into cubicles, up or down the stairwells, you are greeted by an almost lewd tableau. There are women standing, sitting, kneeling, crouching, all in attitudes that seem designed to stun you. It is like a dream of jubilant gardens in which every tree contains a milky nymph. Hallie saw me and smiled.

"I heard Reeves Chubb got canned," I said.

"Really? I had no idea he was in trouble."

"Don't breathe a word."

"Of course not."

"Hallie, you've got the sweetest little ass I've ever seen."

"Why thank you."

"Not a word about Reeves now."

"I promise," she said.

I went around toward Weede Denney's office. On the way I saw Dickie Slater, the sixty-five-year-old mailboy, standing behind Jody Moore's desk rubbing his groin. When he saw me he grinned, man to man, and kept rubbing. Jody was on the phone, speaking Portuguese for some reason. I turned a corner and saw James T. Rice running down a hallway at top speed. I had no idea what I wanted to say to Weede. I was upset about the series being dropped and I felt venomous. In similar situations I usually reacted as a child might react after he has been disappointed or rebuked, with a child's petty genius for reprisal. I told bizarre and pointless lies. I broke my typewriter. I stole things from the office. I wrote snake-hissing memos to my subordinates. Once, after an idea of mine had been criticized by a senior vice-president named Livingston, I went back to my office, blew my nose several times, and that night sneaked up to Livingston's office and put the soiled handkerchief in the top drawer of his desk.

Weede was standing in the middle of his office, deep in thought, one hand absently grooming his bald head. He looked at me carefully.

"Can't talk to you now, Dave; wires are burning up; see you first thing in the morning."

On the way back to my office I stopped at Binky's desk to talk some more but she looked busy. I went inside and dialed Sullivan's number again. She was there.

"Utah," I said.

"Hello, David."

"Montana, Wyoming, Nevada, Arizona."

"I didn't see you leave last night. You abandoned me to all those keening necrophiles."

"Steamboat Springs, the Sawtooth Mountains, Big Timber, Aztec, Durango, Spanish Fork, Monument Valley."

"I hear America singing," she said, but not as if she meant it.

"I know a guy with a camp trailer. He's living in Maine somewhere. We can pick him up and then all head west in the camper."

"All I need is an hour's notice."

"Blasting through New Mexico in the velvet dawn."

"I'm late for an appointment," Sullivan said.

I tried to get some work done. It was dark now and I went to the window. Looking south, from as high as we were, I could see the stacked lights extending almost the entire length of Manhattan, and that delicate gridiron tracery in the streets. I opened the window slightly. The whole city was roaring. In winter, when the darkness always comes before you expect it and all those lights begin to pinch through the stale mist, New York becomes a gigantic wedding cake. You board the singing elevator and drop an eighth of a mile in ten seconds flat. Your ears hum as you are decompressed. It is an almost frighteningly impersonal process and yet something of this kind seems

27

necessary to translate you from the image to what is actually impaled on that dainty fork.

I strolled around to Carter Hemmings' office. He was at his desk, smelling the nicotine on his fingers. When he saw me he tried to neutralize the flow of panic by standing up, absurdly, and spreading his arms wide, an Argentinian beef baron welcoming a generalissimo to his villa.

"Hey Dave," he said. "What's happening, buddy?"

"I understand Mars Tyler got the sack," I said.

"No kidding. No kidding. Jesus."

"There's a big purge on. The tumbrels are clattering through the streets."

"Sit down," he said. "I'll get Penny to order some coffee."

"Can't spare the time, Carter. All the circuits are overloaded. How's that laser beam project shaping up? They're starting to put pressure."

"I'm trying to hammer it into workable form, Dave."

"Have a good time with B.G. last night?"

"I didn't know you knew her, Dave."

"Slightly," I said.

"Beautiful girl. But we didn't really hit it off. Dinner. Then I took her home."

"Weede was talking about you during lunch today. He's a curious man, Weede. Sometimes given to rash judgments. Better get cracking on that laser beam thing. I'll be in early tomorrow to take a look at it. Weede'll be in early tomorrow too. We're all coming in very early tomorrow. Have a nice evening, Carter. Say hello to your wife for me."

"Dave, I'm not married."

I went back to my office. Binky was in there trying to straighten out my files. It was almost time to leave. I fixed my tie and buttoned my shirtcuffs. In the corridor all the phones were ringing. I wondered who Trotsky was.

3

People leaned into the traffic, scouting for cabs. Thousands of men hurried toward Grand Central, moving in broken strides, dodging, marching down deep corridors, emptying into chambers, the warm trains waiting, long darkness, newsprint on every finger, the fight against sleep. I liked to walk home from the office because it made me feel virtuous.

The crowds didn't begin to thin out until I got south of Forty-second Street, and traffic was bad all the way. Below Forty-second, people were able to choose their own pace and yet here the faces seemed gray and stricken, the bodies surreptitious in the scrawls of their coats, and it occurred to me that perhaps in this city the crowd was essential to the individual; without it, he had nothing against which to scrape his anger, no echo for grief, and not the slightest proof that there were others more lonely than he. It was just a passing thought. I got home, turned on the TV, undressed, and got in the shower.

I was living then in an apartment overlooking Gramercy Park. My ex-wife lived in the same building. The arrangement wasn't as strange as it may sound—it wasn't even an arrangement. While married we had lived in a larger apartment on the other side of the park. From a friend I learned of the vacancy across the way and it seemed sensible to move in since my wife had just left me and there was no need for such a large place and no point in paying the higher rent. She lived in the Village for a while, taking ballet lessons, courses at the New School, instructions in macrobiotic nutrition; she also joined a film society and began going to an analyst. She invited me down to dinner one evening and said finally, over coffee, that her new life wasn't working out too well. The activities were not very involving and her gentlemen friends seemed able to discuss nothing more important than their season tickets to hockey games, football games and the Philharmonic. She missed Gramercy Park, she said; it was one of the last civilized spots in an ever-darkening city. Some time later an apartment became available in my building. I told her about it and she took it sight unseen.

She was a pretty girl, blond, with small breasts and a cheerleader's bounce. Meredith Walker was her name. We had met at a country club dance in Old Holly, the Westchester town where I was raised. I was nineteen then, home from college for summer vacation. Merry had been living in the town for only a few months. Her father was an Air Force major who had been assigned to head an ROTC detachment at a small college nearby. She said the family had been moving from place to place all her life. She was eighteen and didn't know what it was to have a home. I can remember that night well, a perfect August night with a warm wind raking the tops of the big oaks, with lawn sprinklers hissing and the silver couples standing near the trees, the men in white dinner jackets and their girls in chiffon and silk, each couple sculpted in the dim light, almost motionless, and the distances between them absolutely right so that the whole scene obeyed an abstract calculus of perspective and tone, as if arranged for the whim of a camera. A girl walked across the grass, then quickly whirled, shrieking, as the spray from a lawn sprinkler touched her arm. The laughter of her friends on the warm night was like a knife-chime on delicate glass and it seemed to take a long time to reach us. Merry and I were standing on the veranda. There were fireflies and music, a lazy samba, a foxtrot. Merry looked beautiful. We talked quietly and held hands. Once again, as on so many occasions in my life, I was stirred by the power of the image.

We went to my car and drove to the amusement park at Rye. There, in tuxedo and evening dress, we rode the dragon coaster four times and then returned to the country club. We danced for a while. I experienced a pleasant sense of self-awareness on behalf of both of us. We were being examined by the older couples, our parents' generation, and it was clear from their glances and the tone of their whispered remarks that we were regarded as something special. Later we met each other's parents and then her parents met my parents in one of those slapstick ballets of mistimed lunges, delayed handshakes and profound eye-averting silences. My mother ended the last of these silences by telling us about the dances she had attended in Virginia as a very young lady. We all smiled and looked over her shoulder, trying to spot the Rappahannock. I ladled out two glasses of punch and took Merry back out on the veranda. She told me about some of the places in which she had lived and about the unreal nature of life on a military base; it was life without a future tense, she said, and there was always the feeling that you would wake up one morning and find that everyone had left except the women and children. She was happy that her father was now assigned to a college and she hoped they would be able to stay in Old Holly for a few years at least. I was getting bored. In the past, she said, the closer they lived to military base the more difficult it had been for her mother to stop drinking. But things were better now and Merry was fond of Westchester. She said it had substance.

I went back to school in southern California. After Christmas, Merry went to London for an extended visit. She stayed with a cousin, Edwina, and her husband, Charles, who was English. She loved London rain or shine; she loved the parks, the theater, the pubs, the policemen's hats. Her letters were brisk and full of detail—names, numbers and historical dates. Americans cannot keep track of the centuries. Those were the days when I used to wonder who the Pre-Raphaelites were, when did Galileo live, was it Keats or Shelley who drowned. Meredith's letters gave me a bearing on the English scene at least and I used to study them diligently, memorizing all the kings and their dates, all the hilarious battles, as if her next letter might include a tricky little quiz. Such study was one of the duties of earnest young love; besides, in an odd statistical way her letters were charming, not very different from the epitaphs in Westminster Abbey. My own letters were long, poetic and unpunctuated, well stocked with sexual imagery. I felt that the six-thousand-mile distance between us permitted me some license. I enjoyed printing the words AIR MAIL in bold block letters with my Venus 4B drawing pencil.

The campus was at the edge of the desert. There was an artificial lake where I went swimming almost every evening, often in the company of Wendy Judd. In the morning I did push-ups before going to class. There weren't many classes. Leighton Gage was a small, expensive and very modern liberal arts college. (We had theology of despair in a palm grove.) In the afternoon I drank Coke and wrote poetry. I thought about Meredith a lot, her flawless nose and perfect teeth. Using fellow students as actors, I made a thirty-minute film for my junior thesis. It was about a man who goes into the desert and buries himself in the sand up to his neck. A bunch of Mexicans come along and sit in a circle around his head. My film instructor, Simmons St. Jean, said it was the most pretentious movie he had ever seen, but that pretentiousness wasn't necessarily bad.

My mother died in April and that summer Merry and I were married in the Episcopal church in Old Holly. I tried to stop smoking. We went back to Leighton Gage together for my senior year. I wanted only to relax, to learn to read the mind and body of my mate, to keep away from Wendy Judd, who continued to hunger after my shadow, my image, the thrust and danger of my car. I wanted to free myself from that montage of speed, guns, torture, rape, orgy and consumer packaging which constitutes the vision of sex in America.

Merry's tight little body unclenched and I swam in and out with joy. Nights in the Sugar Bowl. Faint pale petal-scent of the Pasadena Rose Parade. We spent plenty of time together. During senior year at Leighton Gage it was necessary only to pay the tuition and register. You went to a few classes every week, if you wanted to, and the rest of the time was devoted to researching your major interest. Merry and I explored the desert and I did a lot of filming. I was using a Beaulieu 8mm camera then, the S2008 to be exact, with non-detachable pistol grip, automatic exposure control, an Angenieux zoom lens— all in all, a clever piece of optical mechanics that had set my father back almost seven hundred dollars. The possibilities of film seemed unlimited. Through the camera lens passed the light of a woman's body. I felt I could do things never done before. A hawk glanced off the sun and I plucked it out of space and placed it in the new era, free of history and death. I made a forty-five-minute film about underwear. The college gave all student filmmakers in senior year the use of its sound equipment and this was my first talkie. Merry was in the film. She and five of my friends, male and female, sat around my room in their underwear and talked about the different kinds of underwear they had worn since childhood. Simmons St. Jean said it was refreshing but stupid.

After I graduated we returned to Old Holly and moved in temporarily with my father. It occurred to me that I had fifty more years to live on the earth and not the slightest idea how I would spend them. My father took care of that. After a one-week period of grace, during which I was supposed to be resting up from my four study-crammed years at college, he began telephoning business associates. My father was an account supervisor in a large advertising agency. He was directly responsible for twenty-two million dollars in billings. It took him only till Wednesday. He came home and gave me a choice of three jobs, two in advertising agencies, where I would start either in the training program or as a sort of micro-assistant in the broadcasting department, and one at the network, where I would have to start in the mailroom. I took the network. I felt it was important to avoid following too closely in his footsteps. Merry agreed. Independence is everything, she said, especially when you're just starting out in life.

Merry and I took the large apartment on Gramercy Park. My job paid very little and I had to borrow from my father. But I began to come along, getting out of the mailroom in only four months, which they told me was close to the record. We had a good time in New York that first year. We made quite a few friends and we were a popular couple. Merry got a secretarial job and we left for work together in the morning and then met in the lobby of her building every evening so that we could go home together. We told each other everything that had happened to us during the day, although there wasn't much to tell. On Sunday afternoons some friends would come over and we would stir up a huge creamy bowl of the drink-dessert we had concocted, the Spontaneous Abortion— gin, vodka, scotch, rye, brandy and a half gallon of cherry vanilla ice cream. Merry clipped recipes from the ladies' magazines and we would cook together in the evening; when we ended up with something charred and inedible, which was fairly often, we would go laughing around the corner for a hamburger and chocolate shake. In some deep shaft in my being a black machine began to tick. Merry bought some striking clothes with the help of an allowance her father gave her. She had the right figure for the kind of condensed clothing everybody was wearing then. We were always very conscious of what we wore and there were no rules to worry about. One way or another, everything we wore looked great. We saw all the new movies and went to a lot of parties. We seemed to believe that everything we did was the most wonderful thing that had ever been done. We wore certain clothes to certain movies. Grays for black and white. Boots, leather, chino, flag shirts and the like (our pre-acid gear) for Technicolor. Dressing, we matched each unmatching item with great care and spent several minutes assuring each other that we were ready for the waiting line at Cinema I. Each movie we saw was the greatest. Merry would talk about it constantly for two days and then forget it forever. There was no time for remembering things because something else was always coming along—another great movie, a great new pub or restaurant, a great new men's shop, boutique, ski area, beach house or rock group. I took an army physical and edged out a narrow escape thanks to my trick knee and a chronic cyst at the base of my spine. The action was really just beginning then and they were fairly selective about the young men they tapped for immortality.

Soon I was no longer content merely to make love to my wife. I had to seduce her first. These seductions often took their inspiration from cinema. I liked to get rough with her. I liked to be silent for long periods. The movies were giving difficult meanings to some of the private moments of my life.

Meredith was strongly influenced by British films of the period. She cultivated a sort of corporate unpredictability. Walking with me on the street she would suddenly release her hand from mine and skip away into some fantasy sequence. When we shopped together she stole things, one or two small useless items, hiding them in her sweater and making jokes about looking pregnant. At the Metropolitan Museum she told a guard I had tried to molest her in the Egyptian Tomb; this was the first of many such quaint harassments of people in minor positions of authority. Once we saw an old lady in Central Park selling flowers. Merry asked me to buy two dozen mums and then led me to the small bridge at the southeast end of the park. We stood on the bridge and dropped the flowers in the lake, one by one, as the ducks circled in the violet haze. It was all there but the soundtrack and I could imagine a series of cuts and slow dissolves working in Merry's mind.

At work I dressed in the establishment manner, which, granted, was not without a touch of color, the establishment having learned that every color is essentially gray as long as everyone is wearing it. So I did not hesitate to show up for work in an orange tie, but never more orange than the orange others wore.

Once out of the mailroom, I began to learn more about fear. As soon as fear begins to ascend, anatomically, from the pit of the stomach to the throat and brain, from fear of violence to the more nameless kind, you come to believe you are part of a horrible experiment. I learned to distrust those superiors who encouraged independent thinking. When you gave it to them, they returned it in the form of terror, for they knew that ideas, only that, could hasten their obsolescence. Management asked for new ideas all the time; memos circulated down the echelons, requesting bold and challenging concepts. But I learned that new ideas could finish you unless you wrapped them in a plastic bag. I learned that most of the secretaries were more intelligent than most of the executives and that the executive secretaries were to be feared more than anyone. I learned what closed doors meant and that friendship was not negotiable currency and how important it was to lie even when there was no need to lie. Words and meanings were at odds. Words did not say what was being said nor even its reverse. I learned to speak a new language and soon mastered the special elements of that tongue.

In a curious way I liked my job—in the beginning, at least. It made me think and see as I had never done before. In those early days I visualized my mind as a dark room with many doors. I functioned best with several doors open. Sometimes I opened more doors, let in more light, risked the truth. If anyone seemed to perceive a distant threat in my remarks or actions, I closed all the doors but one. That was the safest position. But usually I kept three or four doors open. The image of this room was often with me. When I spoke at a meeting I could see the doors opening and closing in my mind and soon I arrived at the point where I could regulate the ebb and flow of light with absolute precision. I got a raise and then another. I became involved in the actual production of shows. Meanwhile, life with Merry went on the same way, a blend of jump-cuts and soft-focus tenderness. But something else edged in, a whisper of desperation. I'd come home late and find her sitting on the floor wearing a sombrero and trying to write a haiku. It pained me to learn that she did these things even when she was alone. She bought many funny hats during this period and wore them everywhere—sombreros, jockey caps, straw boaters, a wool seaman's hat, a wide-brimmed mata-hari, a fez, a baseball cap. The black machine ticked.

"Let's do something mad tonight," Merry would say.

But there was nothing left to do. We tried to rediscover the spontaneous joy of that roller coaster ride. We even went back there once, a pair of veterans returning to the Normandy beaches, but it rained that night and we sat in the car in the parking lot and watched the high white lights go out. Feeling it was a time for final gestures, for the ultimate convolution, I made clumsy love to her in the front seat. The motor was running, wipers working, radio caught in a buzz between stations, and we bumped through all these sounds as through an interstellar pocket in deepest space.

The first girl was Jennifer Fine. I realize there is nothing more dull than another man's chronicle of infidelity and in many ways that first affair of mine was a dullard's dream; it differed from most only because I was not a commuter and did not have to adapt my orgasms to the disciplines of a train schedule. Yet a few words must be said here about Jennifer Fine if only to show what happens to people like myself when they are given something like love and asked for nothing in return but a recognition of the other's need for some elemental form of gentleness. She was a dark girl with large brown eyes. She worked in the research department of the network. We had met there when I was a mailboy, and she had seemed lonely and interesting. Once I realized that Merry and I could not remember our lines, I looked up Jennifer's extension in the network directory. She was the one, I decided, who would guide me into the vortex of the cliché.

We met for a drink in one of those oxblood pubs on the East Side where the laughter and tinkling chatter seemed canned, subject to volume control. I established a format by showing up five minutes late, knowing that Jennifer would arrive precisely on time; that was the kind of girl she was. We ordered drinks and talked cheerfully for a few minutes, mostly about network people we both hated. Then we lapsed into a massive silence as if suddenly realizing that all possible communication between us had been exhausted in ten routine sentences. I knew I was going to like Jennifer. I liked the way she held to her silence. In that movie-set atmosphere she seemed a librarian-mystic. Her face was thin and not quite pretty (but at the same time almost beautiful) and it was partly concealed by her long hair; purposely, I thought, as if the face sought refuge from time to time. Her hands could not keep still and there was evidence of fingernail-biting. She looked into the empty ashtray. I put my hand beneath her chin and raised her head, soft eyes shifting, two spoonfuls of tea. It wasn't long before I was discussing how important it was to take certain precautions. I was a married man, after all, and we might easily be seen by someone from the office. I outlined a series of procedural measures covering lunch, drinks, dinner, inter-office phone calls, office parties and so forth. I did this not because I really cared whether someone might find out but because intensity and suspense are fundamental to the maintenance of a successful affair.

The following evening, once more arriving separately, we met for dinner in an Indian restaurant on West Forty-ninth Street. A spectacular woman wearing a sari took our order.

Jennifer and I had a long talk. She was afraid of everything—subways, strangers, high buildings, the number nine, plastic, smoke, airplanes, snow, pigeons, insects, parties, cabdrivers, elevators, suburbs, Bergman films, Spanish cuisine, men in Gucci loafers. After dinner we walked through Central Park, emerging in the West Eighties, and headed toward her building, a summer evening, bald men sitting on orange crates with handkerchiefs on their heads. Two squad cars and an ambulance were parked halfway down the block. It was still light. Children played and a dog moved across the shadow of an old man's cane. We came to her building and went upstairs, saying nothing, both feeling the tension generated by the sound of our footsteps on the dark staircase. It was a small neat apartment. The bathroom smelled of lemon and mint. When I came out she fled to the kitchen alcove to make drinks. I sat on the sofa bed and we talked across the room, balancing the celebrated dangers of the West Side against its lower rents. So this is the extramarital life, I thought.

"I'm making you a gin and tonic. It's too late to protest."

"Nice apartment," I said.

"Do you think it's too conventional?"

"It's so conventional it transcends convention. It's like a premature artform. A room in a museum a hundred years from now. The American Wing."

"I really should get an air conditioner."

"They're expensive, aren't they? We had to pay a small fortune for ours."

"It's terrible, isn't it?"

"Mind if I take off my jacket?"

"Of course not," she said.

"There, that's better. Maybe I can open that window a bit more."

"It's stuck. It's been stuck ever since I moved in."

"How long have you been living here, Jennifer?"

"It'll be two years in October."

"Is this a rent-controlled building?"

"David, before you make love to me, promise you'll call me again."

Girls like Jennifer carry with them through their lifetimes an empty cup into which a man must pour his willingness to be responsible. They ask only that, to be taken seriously. I left her apartment at two in the morning and returned three evenings later. After several months I began to realize how much I meant to her. Of course, like all filmgoers and dabblers in adultery, all students of the cliché, we had discussed the importance of keeping our relationship at a low emotional level. But all this time I had been trying, almost desperately, to make her fall in love with me. Once I was sure she had, I began my retreat. I saw her less often and when we were together I was moody and evasive. Jennifer knew what was happening and it hurt her deeply; she was not just another of those neurotic rag dolls, so indigenous to New York, who fed on rejection as if it were a nipple. In bed I was treacherous, playing private games, teasing along the edge of fetish and violence. One night, the next to last, I swung off her, got out of bed, turned on the radio, reached for a pack of cigarettes and lit one quickly—all the things, it seemed, I had been looking forward to while we were making love. Then I put on my tapered shorts and sat in an armchair.

"Do you have to leave right away?" she said. There was no tragedy in her voice and no plea; she simply wanted to know, to confirm.

"She's been complaining about all the late nights. She thinks they're working me too hard."

"Before I forget, next Tuesday is off, David. My sister is getting married and we have to rehearse. I go to Brooklyn for weddings and funerals. Is Wednesday all right?"

"I guess so. I'll have to let you know. I saw you on Park Avenue today."

"When?"

"Lunchtime. We walked right by each other."

"Why didn't you stop me?"

"You weren't alone," I said.

"David, that was my future brother-in-law. And this is the third or fourth time you've mentioned something like this. You know I'm not seeing anyone."

I put out the light. Then I turned up the volume on the radio. Sound filled the room, huge noise, bass and drums booming out of the speaker, beating and scratching, then the sting of a fierce needling trumpet. In the darkness that trumpet had a deeper beauty, filling space, leaving time behind, a difficult sound departing and returning, and I did not feel I was in a room with four walls. A note hung at eye level, dim speck on the railroad horizon, then vanished into a long silence shaded by the revving bass. I went to the bed and sat there, still smoking, legs draped over her belly, crosswise, my back to the wall. A boyfriend for Jennifer. What a gift-wrapped piece of luck he would have been for me. Whatever guilt I felt was set around a picture of Jennifer, alone and wounded, and had nothing to do with my stock betrayal of Meredith. To Jennifer I remained unrevealed. I refused to give her any sense of myself and I can only guess the reason, that I needed every ego-scrap, that I feared my own disappearance. To say I took advantage of her love would be much too mild an indictment. What I did was worse. I did not take advantage of it; I did not even acknowledge its existence. I pretended to believe that I was just another season in her life, in no way exceptional; there had been others and there were surely more to come the moment I went my way. Then her body shifted beneath me, hunting a beat, and the four walls returned. I had an early meeting the next day.

"It's getting to be time," I said.

"David."

"It's getting to be time to go. Time to wrap it up, folks. Be back tomorrow night on behalf of the Bell System—communications for home, industry, and four-fifths of the universe—with another installment of whatever it is we've been doing here, brought to you courtesy of the first family of

41

telephones and electronics since time began and life crawled forth upon the land where it has remained ever since with an asterisk for the Ice Age. What time is it? It must be after two."

"Fascist," she whispered, once, twice, again, a clear brilliant fury in her calm voice.

I saw her alone one more time. I wanted to make perfect love to her. A final touch. But she would not even let me see her home. All she wanted was a book I had borrowed.

There were several other women, girls, during my affair with Jennifer, and there were many afterward. It was simpler with them and at times I was even more the fascist but they let me get away with it, either because they had no choice or because they liked it that way. I was very fond of Jennifer. She is the only one who remains more than a memory of slideout beds, indifferent dawn departures and that hellish feeling of having left something important behind me in one of those indistinguishable rooms.

Meredith found out of course; they always find out. It brought us closer together. I came home late one night. She was in our yellow bed, sitting up like a daisy.

"I've discussed it with mother," she said. "I'm leaving you."

"Will you go back to Old Holly?"

"Dad has been re-assigned. They're going to Germany. For a while I thought I might go with them. But I've decided to stay in New York."

"Maybe I'll go with them," I said, a remark that was supposed to imply that I liked her parents, that I wanted to hide my shame in a foreign country, that I had not lost my sense of humor.

"There's some cold lamb in the fridge."

(What a game kid, I thought.)

"No thanks. Quincy and I took a break around ten and had some dinner at Asia Minor, that place I told you about where Walter Faye punched the waiter. Walter Faye's the one with the wife who's from Brazil who invited us out to Greenwich that weekend we couldn't go."

"And then you both went back to work until half an hour ago. You and Quincy. All alone up there in that big shiny building. Remember how you used to tell me what a strange feeling it was to be there at two in the morning? The only one in the whole building. You said you felt like an astronaut ready to blast off. Why bother sticking to the story at this late date?"

"It's hard to admit things to you, Merry," I said. "I don't mean to sound condescending but it's like explaining death to a child."

"Thank you," she said.

"You look all scrubbed and fresh. You really do. Terrific."

"I think I'd like to go to sleep now."

"Can we still be friends?" I said.

She went to Mexico for the divorce. I took her out to the airport and met her when she returned. I was twenty-three and she was twenty-two.

I stepped out of the shower. I could hear the weather report on TV, which made me think of a friend of mine, Warren Beasley, who used to be a weatherman. I dried myself, hitched the bath towel around my waist, went to the phone and could not remember who I wanted to call. I looked at the TV screen for a moment and then found myself in a chair about a foot away from the set, watching intently. I could not tell what was happening on the screen and it didn't seem to matter. Sitting that close all I could perceive was that meshed effect, those stormy motes, but it drew me in and held me as if I were an integral part of the set, my molecules mating with those millions of dots. I sat that way for half an hour or so. Then a commercial came on, one I had seen and heard dozens of times, and I got up quickly and walked around the room, feeling numb and sleazy, the way an awakening man feels when he realizes he passed out drunk on his host's sofa the night before. I went over to the coffee table and checked my mail. There were some bills and five or six Christmas cards. One was from a girl in Denver; she had written: WHEN YOU FEAR ENOUGH TO FEND THE FURRY BEAST. Another was from my sister Jane, who was living in Jacksonville with her husband, Big Bob Davidson, and their three children. It wasn't a Christmas card in the usual sense; it was closer to a family newsletter, the kind Jane sent every year at this time. It was mimeographed on a standard piece of bond paper; there was a magazine cutout of a sprig of holly pasted to the top of the page.

Merry Christmas from Florida,
    As I sit down to fill you in on another year in the Davidsons' busy life, I can't help but wonder if we haven't all been short-changed. There simply couldn't have been 365 days to this year.
    To start with, we adore Florida. We try to take full advantage of the sun, the beach and the mild climate. This casual, informal living suits we Northerners just fine. With all the sunshine favoring our fair city, the little people (Vaughn, 6; Blair, 4; Sue Ann, 2) are free from colds and sore throats all year round.
    In April, we made a whirlwind trip to Big Bob's beloved Philadelphia where we spent a zany day with the whole Davidson clan gathered to greet their wandering hero. What a memorable day that reunion was, particularly for Bob, who, I feel compelled to report, had more than his share of the ample liquid refreshment on hand. Then we scooted up to Old Holly, in Westchester County, where we visited with my Dad, who is still "knocking them dead" on Madison Avenue, and my dear "little" brother David. It was such a pleasant visit, but also sad, with the memory of Mother still lingering like notes from a far-off flute in that big old house. But David cheered us up with a gala day in the city, capped by a visit to his office in midtown Manhattan. We met many of his associates and even one or two TV "celebs." Bob was mighty impressed!
    Summer was a fun time in Jax, but also hectic. We had quite a few cookouts on our modest patio and I drove the "three mus-

keteers" over to the beach almost every day. We had a hurricane in September with many killed. Then it was time for Vaughn to go into first grade. Our little "scholar" combed his hair and put on a brand new suit for the occasion. However, just last week Bob had to rush him to the hospital for surgery to correct some kind of congenital problem. I hope I will have good tidings on this subject next year at this time.

Bob and the children join me in wishing everyone a joyous Christmas and a very prosperous New Year.

Her signature, *Jane Davidson*, was at the bottom. At my father's house in Old Holly, where they spent most of their visit, they never got out of their tennis sneakers and khaki shorts. This was a new Jane to me, this long-striding American man-woman. When we all lived together in Old Holly, I had never thought of either of my sisters—Mary was the other— as being anything less than feminine. Now here was Jane as co-captain of a roller derby team. They ate nothing but hamburgers, frankfurters and potato chips. Big Bob always seemed to be on the floor wrestling with the kids and their dog while Jane ran up and down the stairs like Babe Didrikson Zaharias, two steps at a time and a shitty diaper in her hand. My father, whose fantasy life (I suspected) was a curious blend of the dusty vast splendor of longhorn aristocracy and the faultless breeding of English dukedom, viewed this panorama with glacial disdain, one suede elbow resting on the mantelpiece, his stately manor stance, and a putrid cheroot in his mouth— Charles Bickford in a boundary war with some effete sheep rancher. But he managed to remain calm and an hour after they had left he confessed to a distant loneliness. He was a complicated man, often coarse in speech and manner, unintentionally comic at times, yet possessed of genuine insight— a good man, I think, beneath the snarl and brawl. Evidence of his fantasy life, manifested mainly by the clothing he wore and the books in his library, did not seem apparent to anyone but myself, and it may well be that I sought to dilute the force of his reality, the powerful effect on me of the very fact of his presence, by mixing some giddy daydreams into the jug. My father had served in the Pacific during World War II. He came back with some shrapnel in his chest and a lot of medals. He kept the medals hidden and never talked about the shrapnel but I knew that both were there. We had a long talk about sex and death and I drove back to the city even faster than usual.

I remembered who I wanted to call. It was Pike. I told him I had something important to discuss and we decided to meet at Zack's Bad News, a small bar in the East Village where he spent a lot of his time. I shaved, sprayed on some deodorant, ferreted some food particles out of my teeth with dental floss, then sandblasted with the electric toothbrush and gargled with mouthwash. I put on a pair of green chinos with slash pockets, my mandarin opium-shirt and Tobruk desert boots. Then I slipped into the stained leather Montana grizzly-hunting stud-coat I had just bought at Abercrombie's. I decided to walk down to Zack's. It was cold and the wind came around corners carrying the smell of snow and a faint intimation of evergreen from the Christmas tree stands. On Third Avenue the buses went by in packs, lit up like operating rooms, each window containing several moribund heads. A few yards in front of me was a man with a transistor radio. He held it to his ear and crossed the street with no regard for traffic. I walked behind him for five blocks and he didn't lower the radio once. I moved alongside him. He was listening to a weather report and talking to himself, or talking back to the radio. He was much younger than I had expected, a boy of about fifteen, very round and blotchy in appearance, secret eyes peering out of the baby fat, and he had the slightly retarded look of incipient genius—that crowlike scratchy cunning of the city's ragpickers and bottle-savers, those evolutionary masters of survival. The boy looked at me.

"Snow bulletin," he said.

I never liked to get too close to such people. I crossed Third

Avenue quickly. I had gone less than a block when I heard him shouting to me. He was standing on the other side of the avenue near a lightpost, hands cupped to his mouth and the radio tucked into his armpit, calling to me, his bulky figure vanishing and reappearing, a slide presentation, as the cars and buses passed between us.

"It's on the way," he shouted. "They just announced it. It's heading this way. We should get it any minute. Three inches by midnight. All motorists are warned to keep off emergency routes. The mayor says don't drive unless it's absolutely necessary. It'll be here any minute. Three to four inches. Snow! Snow! Snow!"

Zack's was an unusual place. Only on rare occasions were any of the local anomalies present—Zoroastrians, Zen cowboys, soothsayers and the like, or lost children looking for Ames, Iowa—and they never seemed to stay very long. It didn't draw any of the area's ethnic or subculture groups and it certainly wasn't vibrating with laughter and political talk, that graduate school atmosphere of elbowing jocularity. Zack's was one of the quietest places in New York. Most of the regular customers appeared to be crazy. They just sat and drank, mumbling to themselves. Every so often one of them would sing a totally incoherent song, a private hash of lullaby and talking blues, the kind of song heard nowhere else except on a subway at three in the morning. The place scared me a little.

Pike was sitting at his unofficially reserved table with a young girl I had never seen before. Pike was close to sixty. His full name was Jack Wilson Pike and he called everybody Jack. He had fine blue eyes, a disappearing chest and the leisurely belly customary in a man his age. I had met him through Sullivan, who once said that he was as American as a slice of apple pie with a fly defecating on it. She also said he had saved her life once, though she didn't state the circumstances. The girl wore an old chapped leather windbreaker which I recognized as Pike's, his aviator raiment.

"How do you like my waif?" he said.

The girl hit him on the shoulder.

"He says I'm his waif. He's an Air Force colonel and I'm the waif he like rescued from a burning building. The one his own planes bombed. We haven't come to the part of why he was hanging around in the streets while his own planes were dropping bombs."

"I was a spy," Pike said. "I was an advance man. I parachuted in at dawn so I could set up the bombing coordinates. They dropped me in with nothing but a shortwave set and a bowie knife. No guns, they told me. A single shot and the whole countryside would be alive with troops. If you have to kill, they told me, use the knife. It's quick and it's quiet."

She gave him a backhand to the ribs. Pike asked me what I wanted to drink. He seemed drunk himself, or well on the way, and in an hour or so his head would tumble to his chest, and his entire upper body, with the sad and ponderous majesty of a dynamited mountainside, would pitch toward the table. He returned from the bar with two drinks.

"I have news," I said.

"The lady told me."

"What do you think?"

"Drop me off at Miami Beach."

"Due west, Pike. Into the great white maw."

"The great white maw and her sister Katy. A man can get killed out there at this time of year. Ask Gash here. She hails from Wyoming, the equality suffrage state. Tell him about the elk herds, booboo. How it gets too cold for even an elk to tolerate. That's where I draw the line, at fur-bearing animals. When it's too cold for them, count me out."

"I'd like to live in a big wet greenhouse," the girl said.

"Blizzards," Pike said.

"They want blizzards," I said. "The network wants blizzards. We want to show how much progress the Navahos have been making and if we can get a blizzard at the same time the show'll be that much more interesting. Airlifts by helicopter. Makeshift hospitals."

48

"You'll garner the industry's choicest awards. But count me out."

"Look, that part of it is beside the point. We'll just drive out there, that's all, just for the hell of it. We won't be going for a few months so the weather's bound to be a lot better than it is now, even out there. I think we can pick up a camp trailer in Maine. And we'll just go. You can map out the route. It won't cost us much. Food and gas. And I'll spring for the gas."

"Ask Jack if he's ever driven cross-country before. Ask him if he knows how boring it can be in the deepest contiguous sense of that word. I've done it a number of times, windshield wipers beating in my brain."

"Look, my last two years in college I took my T-Bird out and back. It was terrific. I stopped only to sleep and eat. This time we'll go slower. We'll stay off the superhighways. We'll discover all the lost roads of America. I'm bringing my movie camera. We'll get it all on film. Your spiritual father, Pike. You've always talked about meeting a cougar. Well, he's out there, crouched on some big brown rock, swishing his tail."

The girl wasn't drinking. I couldn't figure out the connection between them. She was about one-third his age and seemed very attached to him but in a way I could not quite define. Her blankness intrigued me. She looked almost alluring in Pike's windbreaker, small and dumb and tentative. I felt a need to know more about her, to fill out that incomplete image. Only completed could it begin to tell me whether I had a further need to demand from it some small recognition of my galvanic potentials as a man. I remembered the attractive couple in the restaurant during lunch that same afternoon, legs touching beneath the table. Pike was beginning to fade.

"Why are you driving when you can fly?" she said. "Don't you love to fly? I love it. It's the sexiest thing there is."

"This is a religious journey," I said. "Planes aren't religious yet. Cars are religious. Maybe planes will be next."

"Planes are sexy."

"That's right, the way cars used to be. But cars are religious now and this is a religious trip."

Something stirred.

"He's out there, you say, swishing his tail. I've always wanted to confront a cougar face to face without bars between us. Something might happen. We might feel some kind of flow between us. It's hard for a layman like yourself to understand that. But getting up face to face with a gorgeous steaming beast like that. It's a mystical thing, Jack. A mystical thing. The cougar. The mountain lion. The catamount. The puma. I first saw him in a zoo when I was no more than ten. Even then I felt a bond between us. I'd like to confront him face to face. No iron bars. Something might happen."

"We'll go up into the Rockies," I said.

"I'd like to confront him before I die."

"We'll go up into the Rockies. That's where he is, crouched in the shadows, maybe waiting for an epiphany of his own. You get a battlefield commission. Sully said so. And you can map out our route."

"I have to do peeps," the girl said.

"The head's back there."

We were silent until she returned; she punched him on the back when she sat down. Then Pike said to me:

"What runs faster, a greyhound or a cheetah?"

"I don't know. I have no idea."

"Think about it. There's no hurry. Take your time. Greyhound or cheetah?"

"I'll have to guess," I said.

"If that's the best you can do."

"I say a greyhound runs faster."

He hit the table and gazed off into the wings, a look of ineffable disgust on his face.

"Tell him, cootie."

"A cheetah," she said.

"How do you know?"

"Cheetah goes seventy miles per," Pike said.

"How do you know how fast a greyhound goes?"

"No living thing, man or beast, can top seventy. Cheetah's the only one. Cheetah goes like the wind."

"Have they ever been matched in a race?"

"Greyhound's never been clocked above thirty-six. Why, a gazelle could trounce a greyhound. I can name any number of animals prepared to demolish the famous greyhound. Gazelle. Pronghorn antelope. Jackrabbit. Any number. Damn but you're stupid."

Pike was fascinated by animals. He liked to promote theoretical races, fights and tests of strength. His facts were often shaky but his convictions were deep and abiding. Nobody who tried to dispute the result of one of his epochal races or snarling culture-circled battles ever got very far. Pike would present a series of what he referred to as verifiable facts and documentations. His face would tense with rage and pain as he tried to demonstrate the obvious truth to his opponent. I don't know what theme he had found in the animal world that moved him to such emotion, maybe just innocence, the child's, the old man's enchantment with an undefiled life and the purest of deaths. Pike was a living schizogram, as were Sullivan, and Bobby Brand, whom I have yet to introduce, and my father and departed mother, and perhaps myself. He was almost gone now. His voice was thick and seemed to overlap itself, words sticking to his tongue. He lit one cigarette while another still burned in the ashtray. Soon I would learn what I could about his teen queen, the abstract cartoon he had rescued from footsteps and rain.

"Why is it you keep your hands under the table all the time?" I said. "You bring them up only to give Pike one of those tender clouts. Then down they go again. What's under the table that's so interesting?"

"Dorothy Lamour and the squid people."

Pike snorted and softly collapsed. I went to the bar and ordered another drink for myself. Zack put down his newspaper and removed the thick spectacles he wore. He poured the drink, then lifted the wet five, sponged down the bar, gave me change and went to sit in a folding chair beneath an overexposed photo of a bridegroom and best man outside the St. George Hotel in Brooklyn.

"What's that?" she said.

"Scotch."

"It's real neat to watch. The ice shines and there's like things going off. Little explosions all over."

"Why do you want to live in a greenhouse?"

"I want to live in a big wet greenhouse with hair growing in it. There'd be like doll's hair and doggy hair growing in all the pots. That would be neat. And anybody who wanted to be there could be there. John and Paul and Mick and the Doors and the Airplane and Bobby and Buffy. We'd all smoke and there'd be lots of audio-visual hardware. Then we would all eat hot fudge sundaes. That would be the neatest thing in the whole world."

"How did you meet Pike?"

"I was at Elephantiasis with a boy from NYU. The vibrations were bad. I was stoned on hash and I weighed about a zillion pounds. It was like being in the back of the blue bus. Then dada came over and bought this boy about a dozen drinks and he went to the toilet and never came out. Then dada took me to his room and we ate a whole Sara Lee chocolate cake and drank a big thing of milk. It was wild."

"My name isn't Jack, by the way. Not that I mind being called Jack. In a way I like it. It's like some wonderful Far Eastern theology where all the minor deities have the same name as the big guy. You make me feel guilty because I drink. Where do you live, by the way?"

"I stay with Lee, Jemmy and Kit."

I reached over and unzipped the jacket. My hand touched her cool breast. I was aware of a small movement behind the bar and I knew that one of Zack's shotglass eyes had lifted from the newspaper. I edged in closer, wedging her knee between my legs. My hand went up from her breast to her neck and face and when I kissed her there was a message returned from that humid mechanical mouth which let me know that whatever we did, here or later, was a matter of the vastest indifference. I did not bother drawing the jacket together and she did not bother noticing.

"Let's get out of here," I said. "We'll go to my place."

"We have to take him home."

"He'll be all right. He gets like this all the time. I have almost a thousand dollars' worth of stereo equipment."

"When I get real high I can feel the space between sounds."

"Let's go," I said. "We'll get some dinner if you like and then go to my place."

"Can he come?"

"He can take care of himself."

"We painted a circle in the middle of our room. We all sit in there when we smoke. It's real great."

"What else do you do?"

"Whatever we want," she said.

"But what?"

"You can do whatever you want."

"But can't you be more exact? I want to know exactly what you're talking about."

"It's simple. It's so simple. You can come back with me if you want. We have some stuff. But first we have to take him home."

I moved back away from her and finished my drink. Heaving slab of cougar-meat. Would I have to help undress him? Pluck off his weary socks with fastidious fingers and tuck him snoring into his army cot? Few things are more depressing than the sight of a drunken friend who happens to be twice your age; so many illusions are tested. He made a noise, then another, small dogs barking in his throat. His head rested on his left forearm. The hair at the back of his neck was light brown and gray. I put my arm over his shoulder.

"What color is the circle?" I said.

"It's red. It's a big red circle and we all sit inside it. You

53

can come if you want. Anybody can come who wants to. You and me and him. We can all go."

I leaned across and zipped up the jacket. I liked her. I had no desire to trample her. She was delicate and trusting, beautiful in her blank way, and my words could not reach the spaces she felt between sounds. But these facts did not give me the right to trample her. Communications theorist and emperor of stereo. I gave her fifteen dollars—for food, I said.

"No, I can't go," I told her. "We'll take him home and that'll be it for the night."

Then I smiled at her foolishly and she answered with the unembellished look of a feeble nun who has begged successfully for money and found no hand quite willing to touch her own.

You can tell something about a woman by listening to her footsteps on a flight of stairs. As she climbs toward your landing and takes the level walk past your door and then begins to climb again, you can say with some assurance whether she is shapely, impulsive, churlish, simpering, tired, witty or unloved. It is interesting to speculate on the curve of her ankles, how her apartment is furnished, whether or not she believes in a supreme being.

The footsteps I heard that night, that early morning, were those of my ex-wife, Meredith, who lived one floor above me and across the hall. As she went by my door I thought I detected a slight hesitation in her stride. I did not move from the chair nor lower the book I was reading. She climbed the next flight slowly, and in the absolute stillness of the building at that late hour the sound of her key in the lock was enough to break one mood and bring on another, and the soft closing of her door was not unlike that breath of sensuality heard between the silences of sleepless nights in rain falling, in voices on the street, in darkness vibrating to the resonance of every small sound. I waited fifteen minutes, then went upstairs. Meredith squinted out at me through the peephole,

54

then opened the door. She was wearing the parrot-colored housedress her parents had sent from Turkey, where her father was now stationed, tending an undisclosed number of tumescent missiles. She had a wonderful tan.

"How was Puerto Rico?"

"I had a marvelous time, David. You really should go down there for a week or two. Sit down. I'll get you something."

"I heard you go by my door. I was having trouble sleeping so I thought I'd come up for a minute or two."

"I went out with the most awful man in the world tonight. All he could talk about was his eight-speaker stereo system and E-type Jaguar."

She brought the drinks over to the sofa and sat next to me. Even though I saw her often during those years I was continually surprised by some of the changes in her outlook and personality since our divorce. She was much more the New York woman now, informed, purposeful, hard to impress. Gone were the cute enthusiasms of the teen-age bride, those sudden flings into space which seemed, so I thought, to be the outer extensions of a childhood marked by wandering. But with the new sophistication there was a concomitant nameless threat. Meredith was not so secure in her maturity that she did not suffer those periods of despondency and doubt which seem to weave through the lives of self-reliant women. She worked as a secretary to the art editor of a newsmagazine. It was a simple enough job, requiring typing and dictation skills, no more than rudimentary intelligence, and yet it prompted her to explore all the museums and art galleries of the city and to spend most of her vacations, and almost all her money, rummaging through the abbeys and chateaus of Europe, all those tourist bins patrolled by guards who look as though they have just deflowered their own daughters. One summer Merry and I had met by prearrangement in Florence, in some bell-swinging piazza, and sipped our orange drinks, so curiously reminiscent of an Eighth Avenue Nedick's, as the tiny invertebrate cars raced by our table, each driver pursuing

55

his private Grand Prix. Meredith's eyes blazed; her arm swept across that vista of stone warriors, philosophers, noblemen and extras. "What meaning!" she cried. "What stupendous meaning!"

"What do you hear from your folks? It's hard to believe they spent four full years in Germany. It went by like that."

"They're both fine," she said. "They want me to come over in the spring and if I can manage it I'd love to go. All those mosques."

"Turkey is a blending of several cultures, I understand."

"So mother says. Incidentally, I dreamed about you last night, David."

"Did you? Did you really?"

"We were sitting in the living room of the house in London where I stayed with my cousin Edwina that time."

"What were we talking about? Do you remember what I said?"

"I don't think we were talking about anything."

"I take it we were fully dressed. Or you would have mentioned something."

"Yes."

"What were we wearing?" I said.

"I don't remember."

"And we were sitting, not standing or walking around."

"I'm sure we were sitting. I was near the window. I was looking out on Lennox Gardens. And you were on the other side of the room."

"What was I doing?"

"You were just sitting there," she said.

"We must have been doing something. We must have said something to each other."

"I don't remember, David."

"Try to remember. It's important."

"Why?"

"Because there might be some kind of clue there. I mean it's not as though I strayed into a labyrinth. It's all part of some design. You put me in your dream and it's important for me to know what mission I was assigned. It's a kind of reprieve to enter someone else's sleep. The dream can tell you that you're not guilty after all. It's like a second chance. There's some kind of valuable clue in there someplace. Now try to remember what we did besides just sit there. Try to remember what we said to each other. It's important."

"I've told you all there is. If there's anything more I'm afraid I've lost it."

"I guess I'm making too much of it," I said. "Okay, let's hear about Puerto Rico and all the fascinating men you met down there."

She put the glass to her lips, looking at me over its rim. Then she decided to tell me.

"There was one. There on business. Extremely nice. You'd like him, David. Dry sense of humor. Very athletic. A photographer. There on assignment for *Venture*. He was born in Germany, which gave us something to talk about right away, my parents having been there and all. He lives in a converted farmhouse near Darien. Very married. Three sons. You'd just know that someone like Kurt would have all boys. That's the type he is. Athletic. Outdoorsy. Tweed and leather. But very married. We enjoyed each other's company. That was all. Nothing can possibly come of it."

This police-blotter description, meant to conceal the way she felt about him, had precisely the opposite effect; so precisely, in fact, that I wondered whether she had planned it that way. The stratagems of marriage sometimes seem refreshingly artless next to those of ex-marriage. She poured two more drinks and we talked further about Kurt. Meredith liked to confide in me. After some early hedging for form's sake, she would tell me about each of her romances with what seemed to be complete honesty. I enjoyed these discussions. They seemed to generate a real warmth between us, a fine, old and mellow heat, brandy by a fireside. I gave her genuine sympathy and some good advice and when my turn came, as

57

it always did, to stand by that cheery fire and lift that grand old snifter and sing of my own true loves, I told nothing but lies. It was very entertaining. Soon I began to understand the attraction of pathological lying. To construct one's own reality, then bend it to an implausible extreme, was an adventure even more thrilling than the linguistic free falls of the network. I think I went at it fairly well for a novice. I learned that in an atmosphere of seclusion, intimacy, motel-confessional, no lie is too gaudy, no cliché too familiar, no side-trip of the imagination too dramatically scenic. Beyond sheer entertainment value there were exactly ten reasons for lying to her. (1) The manic quality of these stories provided a nice balance to Merry's conventional episodes of the heart and lower glands. (2) The night was swarming with serious young people telling their troubles to each other and I preferred to stand aside from all this empathy and slush. (3) The telling of needless lies to a loved one, or former loved one, stimulates in the liar a complex feeling of regret, guilt, superiority, pity, tenderness and power—a compound I would take downstairs with me and analyze like a vial of splendid chemicals. (4) The fabulist in me, lurking just below the water-line, welcomed the challenge of topping each new lie and looked forward to some distant nexus of perfection, the super-union of all lies into one radiant and transcendental fiction. (5) Related to (4). Man's amoebic inching thrust toward godlike creativity. (6) Being beyond gravity, weightless, in a dream assembled by one's own hands. (7) The sexual excitement aroused in both of us. (8) Boredom. (9) I put something of myself into some of those stories and hoped, in vain as it turned out, to arrive at a definition, one disguised of course by the surrounding absurdity—a definition of myself without the usual anguish such readings entail. (10) There was really nothing to tell her in the way of troubles, romantic or otherwise. The only problem I had was that my whole life was a lesson in the effect of echoes, that I was living in the third person. This would have been hard to explain.

"The dream, David. I just thought of something. Maybe the clue is that we were just sitting there."

"The way we're sitting here."

"Maybe that's it. Maybe I was repressing something."

"Maybe that's it," I said.

Then, right on cue, she went to the window like Olivia de Havilland, so gracefully ill.

"It's still snowing," she said.

Communication between us was extremely precise. For a moment I thought of all the old Burtian and Kirkesque characteristics, the clenched emphatic fist, majestic teeth, angry hand brushing the hair, the surprise of a colossal smile, a smile as rich and full as a field of sun-cut Kansas wheat, and then a touch of passionate sadness, low flame in the eyes. Kirk as Van Gogh. Burt as the Birdman of Alcatraz. It was a comfortable feeling to be back in the simpleminded past. I noticed two new prints on the wall. I couldn't identify the artists but their subject was the same, expressionistic Germany, thick black plague and guilt, and I felt almost sure she had become interested in German painting because of her photographer friend, the man's man of the great outdoors. I moved toward her and the moment my hand touched her hip, loose and soft and lazy inside the housedress, I thought of the girl I had said goodnight to only several hours before, and of the circle she would resume with her sisters or brotherly lovers, the circle I had been afraid to enter. Meredith nude by the window was a known quantity. I took off my shirt.

Minutes later we were in bed and there was the feeling of a strange conspiracy. There was gratitude between us then, communication, mutual willingness to honor our conspiracy. And at the end, the fevers of our breaths mingling, what I knew more than anything was the feeling of coming back to an old and affectionate house. It was the twenty-first time we had made love in the five years since our divorce.

I carried in the portable TV and we watched a movie for half an hour or so. It was one of those old English films in which people are always promising to meet at Victoria Station the moment the war is over. She fell alseep then, on her belly, one leg draped over my thigh, her all-American ass classic and twinkling, campus-worthy as ever. My head went to one side and I was just beginning to go to black, in network parlance, when I heard footsteps in the hall below and the sound of crinkling paper. I knew that the journalist who shared the second floor with me was sneaking across the hall to put one of his garbage bags outside my door. Whenever he had just one bag for the janitor's morning pickup he left it by his own door; more than one bag, I got the surplus. I imagined his thin dry figure, in Punch-and-Judy pajamas and brown peeling slippers, hunching its way along the wall, teeth clamped tight and face all knuckled up. There are things nobody understands. In the last analysis it is the unseen janitor who maintains power over us all.

I slipped out from under her leg and turned off the TV. I went naked down the stairs, carrying my shoes and clothing. I wanted to wake up alone; it was a characteristic of mine, which many women learned to despise down through the years. My apartment welcomed me, dim and silent, the red-wine flavor of paintings and rugs, the fireplace and oak paneling, the black leather upholstery, old and comfortably cracked, the dull copper mugs on the mantelpiece and the burnished ale tone of the desk lamp—all warm and familiar and needing no acknowledgment, all reminding me that solitude asks no pledges of anyone. I took a shower and went to bed.

4

Weede Denney's head, prematurely bald and freckle-brown, repeated the suave circular bareness of his coffee table. It was as though the office decorator had devised them both, head and table, in a triumphant demonstration of ideal harmony between an executive and his furnishings. He stood for a second, dipped his knees slightly—something my father always did when his underwear got stuck in some netherland crevice, instructing me, a mere boy, that this was the civilized alternative to manual extrication, that boorish hobby of the underprivileged and the insane—and then sat down again in the black and ivory barber chair, refreshed and jacketless, his steel-drum chest eliminating any slight pleat or wrinkle from the muted blue shirt he was wearing. It was nine sharp, time for the Friday review, and we were all there, with pencils and note pads: Richter Janes, Mars Tyler, Walter Faye, Jones Perkins, Grove Palmer, Paul Joyner, Quincy Willet, Ted Warburton, and Reeves Chubb, who was wearing the same shirt, tie and suit he had worn the day before. Weede's secretary came in and took coffee requests, a process that consumed at least five minutes, most of them devoted to a mass clarification of Reeves Chubb's order, which included a large coffee, black, one sugar cube; a cream puff but not the kind with chocolate frosting; a fruit cup without the cherries if that was possible; and a packet of mentholated plastic-tipped cigars. Weede's face tightened somewhat during this scene and when it came my turn to order I graciously declined, saying I had already eaten my breakfast, and was rewarded for this lie by a rare Weedean pope-nod.

"Let's begin," he said. "Grove, I think we'll start with you. Ratings on the warcasts are way down."

"I've been in Tripoli," Grove Palmer said.

"Of course you have. No inference meant or intended. But the problem is there and we have to face it. Pressure is being exerted."

"I'm in favor of live satellite pickup. I've been in favor of live satellite pickup since my pre-Tripoli days."

"We'd never get permission," Quincy said.

"Don't bet on it."

"It's ghoulish," Warburton said.

"As Weede says, the problem is there and we have to face it. They're exerting pressure. I say let's exert pressure in return. Hepworth bought the half-hour for impact frequency. I say let's give it to him. I think we can get clearance for certain battle zones. Obviously you don't want to use tight shots if you can help it. And in any kind of live situation you don't want to use the kind of hard rock background we've been into. But in the brief time since my return from Tripoli, I've done some exploratory work and I think we can get clearance in zones where the tide is in our favor."

"It's ghoulish beyond belief," Warburton said.

Warburton was the oldest man in the room and, as such, had assumed the position of tribal conscience. This was done with the unspoken approval of everyone. He was the eldest among us, the most informed, the tallest and grayest, the least feared in terms of power potential, idea smuggling and sheer

62

treachery for its own sake, and, as everyone had undoubtedly heard in the twenty-some-odd hours since Jones Perkins passed the word to Reeves Chubb, the victim of a rare blood disease. Nobody ever paid the slightest attention to Warburton's pleas on behalf of humanity and good taste but we all felt, I think, that he was indispensable. He elevated our petty issues to a cosmological level and by so doing made it easier for us to ignore the whole thing on the grounds that we weren't qualified to deal with such high moral questions. It was nice to have Warburton around. He was so tall and gray and dignified. He rounded out the group photo we carried around in our calfskin heads. Without Warburton, we might have been a delegation of insurance salesmen at the annual get-together in Atlantic City—top men, of course, each a member of the million-dollar club, but still insurance agents; with Warburton (third row, center), we were the United States diplomatic mission to the Court of St. James's. Weede Denney referred to him both privately and publicly as his secretary of state. This remark was always accompanied by one of Weede's breathsucking chuckles, meant to indicate he was well aware that the joke was really on him. As the meeting began to melt away in my inner ear—drone-fests, I called these Friday affairs—I jotted down my version of the memo Weede would compose when poor Warburton died.

Re: Theodore Francis Warburton

It is always a sad occasion to lose an old and trusted employee. Theodore Francis (Ted) Warburton was more than that. He was a valuable friend, an invaluable advisor, a staunch advocate of the basic decency of man. Such qualities are rare today. I, for one, consider his passing a great personal loss. It is not often that we come across a man who possesses Ted's humanistic approach to the problems of our age. His untimely death diminishes all of us. I know everyone joins me in wishing his widow the very deepest of sympathies. No man is an island. We owe God a death. The torch has been passed. Ave atque vale.

"Let me ask you this," Mars Tyler said. "What's wrong with Grace Tully?"

"Old image," Walter Faye said.

"Exactly my point. Exactly what we need."

"Her appeal is vegetable. The vegetable kingdom cherishes her. She's their vegetable queen. Look, they're sitting there with twenty-two pounds of the Sunday *Times* spread all over the floor. The man is about forty-seven years old, wears glasses, never buys a paperback book that costs less than two and a quarter. He's leafing through the special men's wear section, having fantasies about a gold mohair dinner jacket. The woman is sitting there with the magazine section, wondering why the fuck somebody doesn't call them up and invite them over for whisky sours because it's so goddamn boring hanging around the house reading about ghettos and urban sprawl. That's the vegetable kingdom."

"Apropos of nothing," Paul Joyner said, "I understand Grace Tully makes it with anybody and everybody—man, woman or beast of the field."

"Let me ask you this," Mars said. "One, how does the vegetable kingdom differ from any other segment of the audience? Two, I still don't see why Grace Tully and her old image, as you call it, isn't exactly what we need for this particular sector as you yourself defined it. Three—we'll come back to three."

"The vegetable kingdom sits and stares," Walter said. "The animal kingdom just scratches. Basically it's as simple as that."

"There's something counter-productive about this discussion," Quincy said.

"Point well taken," Weede said.

"What was three?" Walter said. "You said there were three points."

"Let's come back to this," Weede said. "I want to generate a little heat on the Morgenthau thing."

"The Morgenthau thing is just absolutely fine," Jones Perkins said.

64

"What about Morgenthau himself?"

"What about Morgenthau himself," Jones said. "Well, he has just about made up his mind to do it and get it done and the hell with the haircream people."

"But has he definitely committed?"

"I would say he has just about definitely committed."

"In other words we have rounded the buoy."

"Weede, I would go even further than that. I would say he has just about definitely committed."

"Would you say in your own mind that the haircream people do or do not enter into it?"

"The haircream people definitely do not enter into it as far as I can see at this juncture, pending final word from Morgenthau himself when he returns from the islands."

"Which islands?"

"Which islands," Jones said. "I'll get on that right away."

"Let's move to World War III," Weede said.

"Apropos of Grace Tully," Joyner said. "I have it on good authority that back in the old days she used to make it with some of the biggest names on the Coast. Both coasts in fact."

"Let's get together," Weede said. "What I want to know at this juncture is whether the World War III idea is any more viable than it was a week ago in the light of recent developments on the international scene."

"At this juncture," Richter Janes said, "the World War III idea is about forty percent less viable than it was a week ago."

"That's what I wanted to know."

"What I want to know," Walter Faye said, "is why we can't show the toilet bowl in the effects-of-solitude prison thing. We can show toilet bowls in prime time. Why not in the afternoon is what I want to know."

"Kids might be watching," Weede said. "And I don't think the subject is germane at this point. I can't imagine any idea conceived by this unit which would necessitate the on-camera appearance of a toilet bowl. Besides, if we're not going to show the thing in use, there's no reason to show it at all. I believe it was one of the Sitwells who said if there's a gun hanging over the mantelpiece in act one, it had better be fired by the final curtain. Or words to that effect."

"Why can't we show the thing in use?" Walter Faye said. "Just once I'd like to see somebody on TV take a tremendous steaming piss. It could even have dramatic justification. We could think up some reason to make a pissing scene necessary. Maybe our protagonist has to get some poison out of his system; or, if it's a documentary about some disease of the liver or bladder, we could actually evoke some sympathy for our guy by showing how painful it is for him to take a simple piss. I wouldn't care where the camera was. We could stay on his face. The important thing is the *sound*. If we could just get that sound on the airwaves, just once, I honestly think we could take credit for expanding the consciousness of our nation to some small degree."

"Yes," Weede Denney said. "It would be almost as good as Ruby shooting Oswald."

The room relaxed, appreciating the jagged wit of this remark, and we all painted one more kill on Weede's already impressive fuselage. He lowered his barber chair two hydraulic notches and reached for the pack of cigarettes on the coffee table. Mrs. Kling, his secretary, came in then with a large breakfast tray and began distributing the coffee. I watched the construction workers in the building across the street. Richter Janes was sitting next to me, waiting for the coffee to reach him.

"Most of the high-steel men in this city are Mohawks," he said. "They all live out in Brooklyn someplace. There's a whole colony out there. They specialize in the high dangerous stuff. Any building more than thirty stories, you know those are Mohawks you see up there."

"It must have something to do with their inherent catlike agility and superb sense of balance," I said.

We were whispering for some reason.

66

"There was an Indian in my fraternity back at school. Nicest, quietest guy you'd ever want to meet."

"What was his time for the hundred?"

"Let's break bread some time," Richter said. "I'd like to pick your brain on a project of mine. I've been hearing good things about you."

"From whom?" I said.

"Word gets around," he whispered mysteriously.

Mrs. Kling left and the meeting resumed. At the network, people were always telling other people they had heard good things about them. It was part of the company's unofficial program of relentless cordiality. And since our business by its nature was committed to the very flexible logic of trends, there always came the time when the bearer of glad tidings became the recipient. Each of us, sooner or later, became a trend in himself; each had his week-long cycle of glory. Richter Janes' remark suggested that this might be the beginning of the David Bell trend. Richter himself had been a trend only a few months before; during his trend, which lasted a week or so, people popped into my office or sidled up to me in the corridor on a number of occasions to comment on what a good job Richter Janes was doing, how many good things they had heard about him, and how they had told him, just that morning, about some of the good things they had heard. I was never able to figure out how these trends started, who started them, or how the word spread. They seemed spontaneous enough and I found it hard to believe that top management would devise the whole thing, designate a trend-man of the month, someone whose morale needed boosting, and then instruct paid trendsetters to make spot remarks and chance comments concerning the good things they had heard about him. Up to that point I had never been a trend and had never felt any particular need to be one. Almost everyone sitting in Weede's office at that moment had been a trend at some time or another, but never, as far as I knew, more than once. In a given year there were usually nine or ten trend people. The trends ended as they had begun, with mystifying suddenness, and the person who had just been trendexed seemed a bit forlorn when it was all over, the gloss and neon gone, the numbers filed away, all the screens snowing and the airwaves bent with static.

"Quincy and Dave," Weede said. "Ball's in your court."

There was fatherly amusement in his voice. Apparently the destruction of Walter Faye had put him in good spirits. I had no idea what I was going to say since I had accomplished absolutely nothing all week. I thought I might simply paraphrase my remarks of the previous meeting, hedging and improvising as I went along, but there wasn't much chance of making that kind of escape. It had been tried hundreds of times and everyone was familiar with the clawprints and scent.

"Quincy, why don't you start the ball rolling?" I said.

"The Navaho project."

"The Navaho project," I said.

"There are long- and short-range problems," Quincy said. "Who's going out there, for how long, and will the Indians cooperate? I've been in touch with the Bureau of Indian Affairs."

"We both have."

"They'd like to know more before they commit."

"The Indians don't want pity," I said. "They want dignity."

"I got the same impression. We must have talked to some of the same people."

"They don't want pity in any shape or form. They want dignity. I think Richter can tell us more about that. Richter actually knows an Indian. Old fraternity brother."

"We're not actually in touch anymore. It's been more than fifteen years since college and I didn't really know the gentleman all that well. He was a nice quiet boy. I definitely remember that much about him. He was five-ten or eleven, weighed about one-sixty, lean as a whip, not an ounce of fat on him. He wasn't actually copper-colored if I remember correctly. If I remember correctly he was actually only three-eighths Indian. Three-eighths or four-eighths Indian. Crow I think he was. Crow or Blackfoot. But he was definitely one of the nicest, quietest fellas you'd ever want to meet. That much I'm sure about. It's absolutely vivid in my mind."

"Would you say this man wanted pity or dignity?"

"Dignity, Dave. There's not the slightest doubt in my mind. It was definitely dignity."

"Go, Quincy," I said.

"The thing of it is: Who's going out there, when, and for how long? If we want blizzards we want to get cracking. We want to get this thing nailed to the mast before any more grass grows under our feet."

"I've been in almost constant touch with the weather bureau," I said. "I'm trying to pin them down on some kind of long-range forecast for that sector of the country."

"What sector?" Jones Perkins said.

"Where the Navahos are."

"Where are they?"

"Quincy, you're the geography expert."

"Look, it's not as though we'll have any trouble finding them. The reservation is bigger than some states. It's even bigger than some countries, some of the smaller postage-stamp kingdoms in Europe. There's no doubt in my mind that it's bigger than Monaco for instance."

"Central Park is bigger than Monaco," Reeves Chubb said.

"Cocksucker," Quincy muttered.

"It's out around Arizona, New Mexico, Utah and/or Colorado," Paul Joyner said. "I happen to know that for a fact."

"Right," I said. "And as I understand it the area has some fine cliff dwellings and pueblo ruins that we can use as natural backdrops. Monument Valley, in point of fact, lies right within the boundaries of the reservation, or so I've been led to believe. It's a stark, beautiful, moonscape-type place."

"Why do we want blizzards?" Warburton said.

"We want to show that despite all the problems, they're making progress. Blizzards are one of the problems."

"I shouldn't have thought you'd need a blizzard. Poverty and disease speak eloquently in their own right."

"It can't do any harm," Quincy said.

"Ted may have a point," I said. "The other major thing that pertains to me directly is the 'Soliloquy' thing. Everything is fine on that score. The show has been an airtight lead-pipe cinch from the very outset. Critics have loved it, by and large, and mail has been running four-to-one pro."

"I've never liked that title much," Reeves Chubb said. "It's pseudo something or other. I brought it up at dinner the other evening. We have some house guests out and I wanted to get their thinking on it. I taped the whole discussion in case you, Dave, or you, Quincy, wanted to hear it. They're an extremely well-informed couple. Kate and Phil Thomforde. He's done things with McAndrew at Amherst."

"Weede thought up the title."

"Did I?" Weede said. "One of my less resounding successes apparently, at least as far as Mr. Chubb is concerned. Regrettably, Dave, I don't think the program will survive. Sometimes it's difficult to break new ground without getting dirt in somebody's eye. The sponsor has chosen not to renew and there's been no interest elsewhere. Dave, you know I always go to bat for my people and I assure you this instance was no exception. I tried my damnedest to get Larry Livingston upstairs to convince Stennis to let the network pick up the tab. Livingston said quite frankly—and you have to admire his honesty—that the show is a crashing bore. He said there was no point in seeing Stennis about it because Stennis—and this mustn't go any further than this room—Stennis has problems of an entirely different kind. The show was good. I say that unequivocally. But Chip Moerdler over at Brite-Write said it wasn't selling any ballpoint pens. In this business you have to learn to expect disappointments. But don't go away mad,

David. We have every intention of putting your not inconsiderable talents to further and better use. I'll be telling you more about this as soon as the Navahos are in the can."

"Chip Moerdler is a thundering ignoramus," Warburton said. "I've had dealings with that man. He wouldn't know quality if it struck him a blow in the solar plexus."

"Well and good," Weede said. "But you can't argue with a sales chart. Now I think we had better press on. There's one more bit of business that concerns you, Dave. That's the laser beam project."

"I've given Carter Hemmings a free hand with that. He seems to be something of an expert on the subject and I thought it was about time he got his feet wet. He's several years older than I am, you know, and sometimes it's best, for the sake of a man's morale in a case like this, to let him develop something on his own. It's always somewhat embarrassing for me to explain to Carter why he isn't included in these Friday meetings of ours. His impatience is understandable and I'm sure it won't be long before he joins us in solemn conclave. At any rate, Weede, Carter said he's got the laser beam thing hammered into top shape. When I spoke to him last evening he said he wanted to see you about it first thing in the morning. He said it's in absolutely stunning shape. Virtually ready to go."

"He didn't talk to me."

"I guess I'll have to resort to pressure."

And then, for no reason at all, I slid my foot several inches across the rug, and kicked over the empty coffee cup beneath Richter Janes' chair. I put my heel on it and crushed it. Nobody seemed to notice. I felt sick and exhausted. I wanted to be back in Meredith's warm musky bed, lost in the hollow of her breasts, swimming through fish-silver rooms, fathomless, deep in the shipwreck of sleep. I wanted to be with Sullivan in some lunar western wilderness, listening to Mingus on the car radio, and Ornette Coleman with his paintbrush horn, and Sullivan's arms crossed on her chest in sarcophagus fashion, her invisibly taped features; going flat-out across the northern plains, climbing, Bartók in the Rockies, cowboy songs and the nasal grassy drawl of banjos, and there is Oregon, the seal-slick distant sea. That's what I wanted. But I sat in Weede Denney's huge office, in the blue chair by the window, feeling sick and exhausted.

"Now it's time to hear from our resident China-watcher. Look smart, Mr. Chubb. How is the China thing coming along?"

"Weede, it's shaping up as the best public affairs series I've ever been involved in. I've already discussed it with seven or eight top people in the State Department. I've got calls in to six universities and two foundations. I've been putting in nights and weekends. My secretary has some kind of female thing and I've had to borrow Chandler Bates' secretary from time to time. The material is rolling in. Did you know that China had mastered most of the arts and sciences at a time when the Europeans were still combing fleas out of each other's hair? My wife thinks I'm working too hard. This is a big opportunity for us. China is a riddle. It's an enigma. Everything is being typed up. Mao Tse-tung and his followers walked six thousand miles to a mountain stronghold when what's his name was chasing them. The Chink with the wife who went to Wellesley. As soon as all the stuff is typed up and proofread and mimeoed, I'd like to get everybody's opinion on how it looks. Chandler Bates' secretary is slow so I don't know when it'll be ready. I'm very excited about this series. The Yangtze River is three thousand four hundred and thirty miles long."

"What's the series going to be about?" Warburton said.

"The whole big thing. China inside out."

"Will it say something we haven't already heard countless times?"

"There's a very real prospect of some exciting filmclips."

"Taken from a tall hill in Hong Kong, no doubt."

"The series will have a definite viewpoint. The stuff I'm getting typed up points that out very clearly."

"Points what out?"

"That a viewpoint is necessary."

"What viewpoint?"

"Yeah, what viewpoint?" Quincy said.

"I'm working on that with the State Department. They've been extremely cooperative."

Warburton said: "I'd like to quote Kafka at this juncture. 'Every fellow-countryman was a brother for whom one was building a wall of protection, and who would return lifelong thanks for it with all he had and did. Unity! Unity! Shoulder to shoulder, a ring of brothers, a current of blood no longer confined within the narrow circulation of one body, but sweetly rolling and yet ever returning throughout the endless leagues of China.' That, I submit, is your viewpoint."

"Ted, that's wonderful," Weede said. "I think you've really given Reeves something he can sink his teeth into. The part about unity-unity is splendid. It encapsulates all the surging drama of a land mass whose people we can only guess at. Where did you buy that tie?"

"It really sings, Ted. Maybe your girl can type it up for me. That part about the endless leagues of China is almost as good as unity-unity. Might be a title in there somewhere."

"Might indeed," Weede Denney said.

The meeting droned on. I watched Warburton's face. No, I could not have mistaken the flicker of mirth that worked at the corners of his mouth. I settled into the twilight, the lagoon, the mineshaft. A pigeon crossed the window ledge, nodding insanely, a fat prim spinster out for a stroll in Providence, Rhode Island, and then a distant boom of demolition sent it cracking into the air. I felt a tremor of pain at my temple. I tried to think of the Christmas shopping I still had to do. I would spend all day Saturday shopping for gifts and wrapping packages. I would buy something for Meredith and her parents; for my father; for Sullivan; for Binky; for my sister Jane and her children in Jacksonville; for three girls I had been seeing on and off; not for B.G. Haines; not for my sister Mary unseen and unheard from in years. I would take extra time and care wrapping the packages intended for Merry's parents and for Jane and her children. (The concept of distances has always stunned me—meridians, latitudes, international date-lines; swinging with the arc of the earth, while I am forever stationary, all distant places seem elusive to me, sliding away and under, hard to get mail to. For this reason I have always tended to be over-reverent toward parcels which are destined to travel hundreds or thousands of miles, as if they were carrier pigeons taking secret messages to the plucky guerrillas in the hills.) Then I had a mental picture of my sister Mary. She is sitting in a laundromat in Topeka, Kansas. She is smoking a kingsize filtertip cigarette and waiting for the clothes to dry. She is wearing a gray cotton dress. There was no reason for me to think of her in that particular city or state or place of business, in that gray and whitewashed hell, clothes spiraling like mechanical embryos in experimental bellies, and yet I felt it was a true vision broadcast to me in some extrasensory way. It made me unaccountably sad. The entire left side of my head was radiating with pain. There was another explosion several blocks away. The voices buzzed in and out of dark hives. I looked at his face again. Then, suddenly, it struck me, with all the mindblazing beauty of a brilliant astronomical calculation. Warburton was Trotsky.

"I believe that covers everything," Weede Denney said. "I'm taking a big silver bird to the Coast this afternoon. I should be back Wednesday. Any problems, Mrs. Kling knows how to reach me. Have a nice weekend and a pleasant Christmas."

"Officially sanctioned," somebody said as a footnote to something.

Weede went into the private toilet adjoining his office. We picked up the paper cups, moved the chairs to their original positions and tidied up in general, reluctant to leave these small tasks to Mrs. Kling, who over the years had managed to become one of the most feared individuals in the company. On the way to my office I stopped by Hallie Lewin's desk and massaged her neck. She was typing a memo marked confidential. I could see that my name was not on the routing list.

"How was the meeting, David?"

"Ended in the usual fistfight. What do you want for Christmas, Hallie?"

"An abortion," she said.

"What's that you're typing?"

"Get away. You're not supposed to look at that."

"Is it about me?" I said, moving my hands down her back.

"You're the last person around here who has anything to worry about. Really. I've been hearing good things about you, David."

I followed Quincy Willet and Jones Perkins down the corridor, snapping my fingers lightly and bouncing on my toes. Quincy needed a haircut.

"Did you hear?" Jones said. "Merrill hired a Negro. Blaisdell met him yesterday. Said he seems like a nice clean-cut guy."

"Let's go look at him," Quincy said.

I went around to my office. Binky followed me in. She wasn't wearing a brassiere, I noticed. She skipped over to the sofa and bounced on it a few times before settling down. She always let out a bit on Friday. I sat behind the desk.

"What's new?" I said.

"Somebody named Wendy Judd called. She wants you to call back."

"What else?"

"Warren Beasley called. No message."

"What else?"

"Your father wants you to meet him at the Grand Prix at twelve-thirty."

"What else?"

75

"That's all," she said. "How was the meeting?"

"Ended in the usual fistfight. Phelps Lawrence didn't show up. I guess they gave him the news already."

"Have you heard the latest? It's really getting wild."

"What?" I said.

"Mars Tyler and Reeves Chubb."

"What about them?"

"The ax."

"Where'd you hear that?"

"I'm not supposed to tell," she said.

"Binky baby."

"Hallie Lewin told me about Reeves. Penny Holton told me about Mars."

"Who's Penny Holton?"

"Carter Hemmings' secretary."

"The one with stereophonic tits?"

"David. Don't be crappy now."

"Her breasts point to opposite ends of the room."

"Isn't it something though?" Binky said.

"That's not all," I said. "Carter Hemmings may be next. It's just a rumor right now so don't say anything."

"I won't."

"Also I noticed that Chandler Bates had his door closed when I went by his office just a minute ago. I mentioned it casually to Jody and she said it's been closed all morning."

"What do you think it means?"

"He's either firing somebody or getting fired himself."

"It can't be that Chandler's getting fired," she said. "He's buddy-buddy with Livingston. He's Livingston's fair-haired boy. Livingston's the one who hired him away from the CBC."

"I heard Livingston's being phased out."

"That's too much."

"Like an obsolete medium-range bomber," I said. "Keep it under your hat."

"You'd think they'd have some kind of Christmas spirit. What a lousy time for a purge."

"Enough chitchat. Get Carter Hemmings in here and tell him to step lively."

She went out and I called Sullivan. The phone rang eight times and she didn't answer. I let it ring some more.

("Dear God, I have to get out of here," I said into the mouthpiece.)

Finally I hung up. Carter Hemmings came in then. He made his way to the sofa, moving sideways and in a very tentative manner, hunched slightly, feudal and obsequious.

"Carter, I thought we agreed that you were going to see Weede this morning with some kind of progress report on the laser beam thing."

"The way I understood it, Dave, I was supposed to see you first thing in the morning. But when I came by your office, Binky said you weren't in yet. I came back ten minutes later and she said you had just gone to Weede's office for the meeting."

"Your name came up during the drone-fest, Carter. Weede said he's going to put your ass in a sling if you're not careful. What do you hear from B.G. Haines? She told me she had a rotten time that night. I haven't been hearing good things about you, Carter. Everybody has to pull his weight. You'll find that Weede can be ruthless when the occasion warrants. Your secretary is a fucking blabbermouth. I have work to do now."

He left. I tore up the notes I had taken during the meeting. I took a box of paper clips out of the middle drawer and began fitting one clip inside another, making a chain. In ten minutes or so I fastened about one hundred paper clips. Then I fitted together the two at each end. This gave me a circle, which I spread before me on the desk. I put nine pencils inside the circle, arranging them in three triangles of three pencils each. I put an eraser inside each triangle. Then I took the torn note paper, dropped it into an ashtray, lit a match and set the paper on fire. I placed the ashtray with the burning paper at a point roughly equidistant from the nearest corner of each triangle and at the approximate center of the circle. When the fire was about to go out I tore up more paper and tossed it into the ashtray. I kept doing this until Binky came in to get her coat, which she always hung behind my door.

"Lunchtime already?"

"What's that?" she said.

"Demonology."

She came around to my side of the desk for a closer look. I slumped in the chair, leaned over and put my hand on her calf, making slow figure eights with the tips of my fingers.

"It's weird, David."

"Works quite well, I think. Note the circular ashtray. Circles within circles. Like the pain in my head. The erasers don't do much for it though. Next time you're in the supply room see if they have any triangular erasers. This is serious stuff."

"What's it supposed to mean?"

"It's a calling forth of the powers of darkness. Is Hallie Lewin pregnant or was she just kidding?"

My hand was at the soft cove behind the knee which, when the leg is bent, has always seemed to me one of the very best places on a woman's body; then, as if obliging my bias, she shifted her weight to that leg, the left, so that her knee, answering the shift and in complete control of it, buckled slightly, creating that scooped-out and supremely tender indentation for the rent-free pleasure of my hand. Weede Denney was standing in the doorway.

"Come on in, Weede," I said. "Say, how's your wife these days?"

Binky edged away from me. I could see the doors opening in the dark room in my mind, three, four, five doors opening, and fresh light planking down across the floor. In the past I had always been able to control the doors but now they seemed to swing open freely, wind-driven, banging the walls. Control was still possible but I did not try to attain it. Light began to fill the room and I thought I might reach eight doors, a new record.

"Didn't mean to disturb you," Weede said, flushing somewhat. "Just wanted to see you for a moment or two; it can wait."

"Binky, I don't know if you've ever met Mrs. Denney. She's an absolutely intrepid woman. Weede, tell Binky about the time Mrs. Denney walked right up to a family of hippos during your camera safari in Kenya. She just had to have that picture and she didn't care a whit about her personal safety. Weede told us about it at lunch yesterday. I can't wait to see those slides, Weede. Binky, I think you should see them too. Weede has promised to invite us up for a showing some time soon. Binky's a photography buff, Weede. Weede has quite a collection of photos, Binky."

"I'd love to see them," Binky said. "Well, I've got a lunch date with Jody Moore and she hates to be kept waiting."

She left, putting on her coat as she walked out, and Weede moved clear of the doorway as she made her exit. One touch, he seemed to fear, would reduce them both to a state of nervous collapse. I tried to close the doors. They would not close. He walked up to the desk, put both hands flat on the far edge and leaned toward me.

"I want to ask you something," he said. "It concerns a matter of some delicacy. I understand you're tuned in to many of the undercurrents. What either of us says here mustn't go any further than this office. Is Reeves Chubb a homosexual? You don't have to answer if you don't want to."

"There have been rumors to that effect. Somebody wrote something to that effect on the wall in the thirty-seventh-floor men's room."

"I'd like to take a look at that."

"It's not there anymore," I said. "This was last week. It was written with a red crayon above the urinals. It looked like

Quincy Willet's handwriting. Those two don't exactly hit it off, you know."

"What precisely did it say? This may be important."

"I don't think I care to repeat it, Weede."

"Was it rough?"

"The roughest."

"We're two mature people, Dave. I'll tell you why I brought this up in the first place. I know I can trust you to keep any privileged material within the four walls of this room."

"Shall I close the door?" I said.

"By all means. I should have thought of that myself."

As I swung the door shut Quincy passed my office and gave me a questioning glance. Weede went over to the sofa and I returned to the chair behind the desk.

"As you know, Dave, we hire people on the basis of ability alone. This has always been the network's policy. Personally I have no interest in a man's private life. What a man does in his free time is no concern of mine, within reason."

"I can attest to that, Weede."

"But there's another issue at stake here. The State Department doesn't want any queers working on the China thing. Far be it from me to challenge the thinking of people whose most vital concern is our own national security. A meeting was held in a midtown hotel last week. For the most part it was inconclusive. Reeves is a married man, you know."

"Sometimes that happens," I said.

"Exactly, Dave. Those people at State are sharp. They tell some amazing stories. We spent a whole afternoon discussing it."

"It's a shadow world. It's a sickness. It can happen to anyone."

"Did you know that Reeves sleeps in his office two or three nights a week? Something like that makes you wonder. What does his wife think about something like that?"

"There's a rumor going around that Jones Perkins might be bisex. I don't necessarily mean he goes both ways. It's just

80

that some of his secondary sexual characteristics are thought to be a bit suspicious. He might actually *be* both ways if you get the distinction. But it's just a rumor at this point."

"I give no credence to stories like that."

"Only a fool would."

"Well, I just wanted to get your thinking on the subject, Dave. I hope it turns out to be nothing at all."

"Weede, one of the very best ways to arrive at some kind of conclusive determination in a situation like this with a man's whole future at stake is simply to think back on it. Think back on Reeves. Think of small incidents, anecdotes he's told, his reactions to certain words or phrases, the way he holds those little cigars of his, favorite expressions he uses, his sensibilities, his literary preferences, the amount of time he spends in the john, the kind of shoes he wears. It all has a bearing. Now then. Can I work on the Navaho thing on my own?"

"Quincy giving you trouble?"

"He has marital problems. His mind is preoccupied."

"I'll take it under advisement, Dave."

"Thanks much."

"Let you know more when I get back from the Coast," he said.

"Maybe we can break bread."

All the doors were open. I felt I was going insane. The entire conversation seemed to be taking place in a dream and I truly could not believe what we were saying to each other. The headache had become a ringing numbness, like that caused by a shot of Novocain. I had ceased to exercise the slightest control over my remarks and I didn't care anymore. It was neither a good nor a bad feeling. It was hardly a feeling at all. My head seemed to be a telephone delivering an endless busy signal.

"Are you sure you can't tell me what the red crayon said in the bathroom? It may be important."

"Reeves Chubb climbs palm trees to suck off sleeping apes."

I took the elevator down and walked the two blocks to the

Grand Prix. I didn't wear a coat. I never wore a coat when I went to lunch, no matter how cold it was. JFK.

The restaurant's decor was automotive. My father was already there, sitting at a corner table. His stocky figure, in fine British tweeds, seemed to dominate that part of the room. He was shouting friendly abuse to someone at a nearby table. I watched for a moment. He ran his hand over his head, over the thinning hair, then toyed with the cutlery. He had a new pair of glasses, I noticed, black-rimmed and intimidating. His face did not have the strength of sharp definition, being fairly anonymous, but there was a blunt authority in his eyes which could not be ignored. We did not look at all alike.

My father had just turned fifty-five, a fact which seemed to have transformed him, virtually overnight, into a role of elder statesman. Prior to our meeting in the restaurant I had seen him just once since his birthday. On that occasion, a drink after work, he had seemed very conscious of his elbows. When he spoke he would pivot on the barstool and lean toward me with both elbows flung out and up like delta wings. At other times, head hanging loosely over his drink, he would raise his right index finger and then use it to tap his left elbow, which lay bent on the bar. He did this only when making an important point and I wondered whether the significance of his remark might be fully uncovered only by opening up the elbow and picking with a delicate surgical instrument among its connective tissues. That evening he had made me think of John Foster Dulles and Casey Stengel, two elder statesmen who knew how to use their elbows.

"Sorry I'm late, dad. Merry Christmas."

"I hear Stennis is in trouble," he said. "I never liked that son of a bitch. How much does he make? Squatez-vous, kid. We can have only one drink. I've got a two o'clock client meeting."

"I didn't know you knew Stennis."

"We're agency-of-record for the mental illness series everybody's talking about. Stennis told us the ten-second spots

82

we've been running are in bad taste considering the subject matter of the program. He said the network has been getting complaints. You know what I'm talking about, the animated jingles. We'll have two dry martinis on the rocks, waiter. Then wait ten minutes and bring us the boeuf Bourguignon. We won't have time for dessert or coffee."

"What are your plans for Christmas day?" I said. "I thought I might drive up to the house."

"Fine, sport, do that. Bring a girl along. We'll have a few drinks and drive up to the Admiral Benbow for some turkey. Your mother used to make a swell turkey. I should sell that house but I can't. How's Merry these days? I miss that girl. Damn sweet kid."

"She's fine, dad."

"Listen, I don't deny I've done some screwing around in my time. Man's not worth much if he doesn't get the urge now and then. But how can I marry some big-hipped peroxide bitch after all those years living with your mother? I married your mother when I was twenty-two years old. We lived in a cold-water flat on upper Broadway. When Mary was born I went out and got drunk. Forget the nostalgia. Those were rotten days, pally. Now I've reached the age when a man feels he has to make some kind of summing up. But screw golf. It's sure death for someone like me. Everybody wants me to go out and play golf with them. The last seven, eight years, since your mother's death, all I hear is golf. I work all week-end, either home or in the office. Work is better than death. Look, I've got a little thing going with my secretary. What good does it do? Can I depend on something like her for the long haul? I said on the rocks, waiter."

"How old is she?" I said.

"I don't know, about twenty-four. When you get to be my age, they all look the same. If you want to go out with her, I'll fix it up."

"What's she like?"

"She goes down," he whispered.

"That's not what I mean."

"You're trying to find out if she's suitable for me. That's all right. I don't mind. I respect your views, kid. But I'm the last of the old school in this business. I've got six account men and nine assistant account men working for me. Harvard Business School. I wouldn't give them the sweat off my balls if they needed it to press their pants. And I'll tell you something else. They respect me. And I'll tell you why. They respect me because they know I can do their jobs better than they can. You need a little color in this business. All the account guys in our shop look like laboratory specimens soaking in formaldehyde. If you know your job you can afford to be yourself, up to a point. I learned that many years ago. They put four of those ugly gray padded chairs in my office. I threw them out the window into an alley. You know how word travels on the Avenue. Inside a week I had six new job offers. Client thinks I'm the greatest thing ever came down the pike. We have lunch every Tuesday at the Yale Club. Hell of a nice guy. Prince among men. Played football and lacrosse in college. I sent him to my tailor."

"Here we are," I said. "Drink up. Merry Christmas."

"Merry Christmas, Dave. God bless you."

My father collected reels of TV commercials. The basement of the house in Old Holly was full of these reels, carefully filed and cross-indexed as to length, type of product, audience recall, product identification and a number of other categories. The index cards filled two file cabinets and the reels themselves stood upright in hundreds of numbered slots in a series of floor-to-ceiling filmshelves which he had designed and built himself. The wine cellar, my mother used to call it. He had a screen and projector and he spent several nights a week viewing the commercials and making notes. He had been doing this for many years. He considered it part of his job. His purpose, he told the family, was to find the common threads and nuances of those commercials which had achieved high test ratings; to learn the relationship between certain

kinds of commercials and their impact in the marketplace, as
he called it. We spent many of our adolescent nights, Mary
and Jane and I, sitting in that dark basement watching television commercials. We looked forward to seeing every new
reel he brought home. While my mother wandered through
the large old house, the rest of us slouched in the flickering
basement and argued about which new commercial was best.
My father used to arbitrate our bitter disputes. It doesn't
matter how funny or pretty a commercial is, he used to say;
if it doesn't move the merchandise off the shelves, it's not
doing the job; it has to move the merch. And now, as the
waiter put our plates before us, I thought of him standing by
the projector as the first new reel of the evening thrust its
image through the dust-drizzling church-light toward the
screen, an alphabet boy eating freckled soup perhaps, a man
carving his Thanksgiving teeth, the tongues of seven naked
housewives lapping at a bowl of dog food. I wished he were
dead. It was the first honest thought which had entered my
mind all day. My freedom depended on his death.

"Why is it that all the advertising people I've ever known
want to get out?" I said. "They all want to build their own
schooners, plank by plank, and sail to the Tasman Sea. I know
a copywriter at Creighton Insko Dale. At lunch one day he
started to cry."

"I love the business," my father said. "It's dog eat dog. It's
a crap game in an alley for six million bucks. Where else can
a man like me make the kind of money I make? I have the
right brand image. You know that as well as I do. Wall Street
would kick me out on my ass. But at my age I don't worry
about money anymore. I've been reading Tolstoy. Every man
feels he has a novel in him. He feels he has a novel and a
Eurasian mistress. Tolstoy makes me want to write a novel.
Your mother was ill a good deal of the time but she had
something these bitches today couldn't touch. My secretary?
Maxine? She has soap under her fingernails. Seven out of
eight times I look at her fingernails I see little slivers of soap.

Compare that with your mother. At my age you come to realize that you did everything wrong. No matter who you are, everything you did was wrong. Maybe I'll turn Catholic."

"I didn't know you were thinking along those lines."

"There's something there," he said to his elbow. "I've been doing a lot of reading. I was never much for religion but there's something there. You know the Catholic church in Old Holly, Sacred Bones or whatever it's called? I called up the head priest one night, the pastor, and we had an interesting talk. Hell of a nice guy. He knew who I was. He told me all about the human soul. The soul has a transcendental connection to the body. It informs the body. The soul becomes aware of its own essence after it separates from the body. Once you're dead, your soul can be directly illuminated by God. I sent him a case of Johnnie Walker Red."

"What time is it?" I said.

"Yeah, I have to get going. Listen, sport, see what you can find out about Stennis. Find out how much he makes."

It was snowing again and people moved head-down, clutching their hats, shouldering into the wind. I walked across the wide gray lobby. In a far corner there was an exhibit of prize-winning war photographs. One of them was an immense color blow-up, about ten feet high and twenty feet wide. In the center of the picture was a woman holding a dead child in her arms, and behind her and on either side were eight other children; some of them looked at the woman while others were smiling and waving, apparently at the camera. A young man was down on one knee in the middle of the lobby, photographing the photograph. I stood behind him for a moment and the effect was unforgettable. Time and distance were annihilated and it seemed that the children were smiling and waving at him. Such is the prestige of the camera, its almost religious authority, its hypnotic power to command reverence from subject and bystander alike, that I stood absolutely motionless until the young man snapped the picture. It was as though I feared that any small movement on my part might distract one of those bandaged children and possibly ruin the photograph.

I continued across the lobby. Three network people, a few yards ahead of me, stamped their feet as they walked, trying to get the snow off their shoes. Just then Weede Denney emerged from an elevator bank and headed toward us, hat in one hand, suitcase in the other, wearing his Japanese smile. I moved up closer to the other three men and also stamped my feet.

"Gentlemen."

"Weede."

"Weede."

"Weede."

"Weede."

There were nine or ten people on the elevator. Nobody said anything. There was a Christmas carol coming over the Muzak. When we reached the twentieth floor I took the emergency telephone out of its small tinplate compartment. But I couldn't think of anything funny to say and so I put it back. Binky wasn't at her desk. I went into the office and dialed Tana Elkbridge's extension. She was a secretary in the news division, married seven years. Our affair was a month old. It had begun at a party when she asked me if I would care to read some of her short pieces. I had no idea what she was talking about. Her short pieces turned out to be prose poems, the kind of thing student nurses write before they see their first amputation. Tana was dark and magnificently shaped and wore her hair in braids. Her boss answered the phone and I hung up immediately. I had done this at least a dozen times since joining the network. It is a debasing experience but when you are having an affair with a married woman, or when you yourself are married, it is better not to take chances. Her boss was a lean nervous man and I could imagine his irritation, the ungovernable mutiny of his starved features, as that inimical click went off in his ear. It gave me no pleasure. Quincy came in, closed the door behind him, walked slowly across

87

the room and put one ample haunch on the corner of my desk, the upper part of his thigh flattening and spreading, and I thought of a science-fiction organism pulsating menacingly in some neglected corner of a laboratory.

"Was that Weede in here just before lunch?"

"No."

"That was Weede," he said. "Listen, how come he's going to the Coast? People don't usually go on business trips just before Christmas. It must be something important. Did he say anything about it?"

"Quincy, I'd tell you if I could. But it's privileged material."

"Come on, Dave. How long have I known you? We've come up through this thing together. You've seen my wife naked how many times?"

"I can't say a word."

"Well, is he taking Kitty along with him at least? I can't believe he'd let his wife stay behind over Christmas. It can't be that important."

"They're having marital problems," I said.

"A lot of things are happening around here. Just before lunch I picked up my phone and I could hear voices. The wires must have got crossed. It was Walter Faye talking to somebody I didn't recognize. Walter was giving him the salaries of everybody in Weede's unit. Reeves Chubb makes more than we do."

The door of Quincy's office was orange and his sofa was dark gray. Some of us in Weede's group had doors of the same color but sofas of a different color. Some had identical sofas but different doors. Weede himself was the only one who had a red sofa. Weede and Ted Warburton were the only ones with black doors. Warburton's sofa was dark green and so was Mars Tyler's door. But Mars Tyler's sofa was ecru, a shade lighter than Grove Palmer's door. I had all this down on paper. On slow afternoons I used to study it, trying to find a pattern. I thought there might be a subtle color scheme designed by management and based on a man's salary, ability, and prospects for advancement or decline. Why did no two people have identical sofas and doors? Why was Ted Warburton allowed to have a black door when the only other black door belonged to Weede Denney? Why was Reeves Chubb the only one with a primrose sofa? Why was Paul Joyner's perfectly good maroon sofa replaced by a royal blue one? Why was my sofa the same color as Weede's door? There were others who felt as I did. When Paul Joyner walked in to find a new sofa in his office he immediately started a rumor that he was being fired. But this sofa incident had taken place two years prior to the current rumor, the origins of which were never disclosed. He had not been fired; it was not that easy to find the connection. The connection was tenuous but I was sure it was there. At least a dozen times I had taken that piece of paper out of my files and tried to correlate a man's standing with the color of his door and sofa. There had to be a key. If only I could find it. What I would do when and if I found it was a question that did not disturb me. I would do something. I would change something. I would have protection. I would know the riddle.

"I had Mexican food for lunch," Quincy said. "I have to go to a meeting in Livingston-that-son-of-a-bitch's office in five minutes. Smell my breath, will you?"

He leaned over and exhaled.

"It's fine," I said. "Rose petals."

"Tacos are hard to get off your breath. I brushed my teeth twice."

"Okay," I said. "Now you smell my breath."

He leaned over again.

"No problem," he said. "Not the slightest little inkling."

We were both lying. Half an hour later Binky came in, hung her coat behind the door and went right out again. I dialed her extension.

"Miss Lister."

"Welcome back to the animal farm," I said. "Are you mad at me? Wait'll you see what I'm getting you for Christmas.

You're the best secretary I've ever had. Cross my heart and piss in a ditch."

"What was that all about?" she said. "I didn't understand what you were trying to do. I went out and got stoned on bloody marys."

"I'm sorry, Bink. I've been tense and neuralgic. I really have. I've been here seven years. It gets to you. Come in for a minute."

"No."

"You're the only friend I have in this place."

"I told Jody what happened. She thinks you're cracking up."

"My coat and yours, Binky. Hanging together behind the door. Thunderin' jasus, a grand feeling it is to know our respective bearskins are huddling back there in the darkness. Darlin', will you be coming in now for just a pop of the cork? I've been reading the Irish playwrights. C'mon, Bink."

"No."

"Bejasus, Binky. Your truly winning calf. That tiny secret grotto behind your knee."

"Drop dead, David."

I wanted to go home and sleep but it was too dangerous to leave this early. Although Weede had gone, Mrs. Kling had not, and it was her practice to make spot checks whenever he was out of the office. I closed the door. I got out the bottle of Cutty Sark I kept hidden in the cabinet, poured out half a glass and drank it neat in four swallows. Then I crumpled a piece of paper into a tight little ball and tossed it toward the wastebasket. Two points. I retrieved the ball and started practicing my hook shot. I moved slowly over the rug in a minstrel shuffle and as my right hand made dribbling motions I expelled air from my nose, synchronizing breath with dribble; and then, my back to the basket, I lifted the right leg, raised the left arm slightly for balance, and swung the right arm over my head and let loose a fifteen-footer.

"Swish," I said.

I changed to foul shots for a while, then to left-hand hooks and finally to the breathtakingly intricate pattern of my double headfake turn-around jump shot. In that cloistered office I played my silent game. I experienced no sense of boyish self-amusement. No, I played quite seriously, my tie bellying out at each jump shot, sweat blossoming under my arms. No one, not even Binky, knew about these basketball games. I had been my team's leading scorer in prep school; first in scoring, last in assists. Since then the game had followed me, the high amber shine of the gymnasium floor, the squeak of rubber sneakers, the crowd, the crowd, and at parties years later I would turn a cocktail peanut between my fingers and gaze at a distant fishbowl. Basketball has always seemed to me the most American of sports, a smalltown thing, two kids in a driveway and a daddy-built backboard. And now I jumped, released and missed. I picked up the paper ball, stepped back ten feet for an easy one-hander, and missed again. Six times I missed from that distance. The phone rang and I shot again and missed again. I knew I wouldn't answer the phone until I had made that simple shot. I was perspiring heavily as I fired twice more and missed both times. Cursing, I picked up the ball again. The ringing stopped and I figured that Binky had answered on her phone. I went back to precisely the same spot. This time I hit. I stood there for a moment, trembling, then went to the sofa and dropped. The door opened and Binky came in.

"That was Warren Beasley again," she said. "Why didn't you answer your phone? You look rotten."

"Smell my breath."

"It stinks."

"I knew it," I said. "That bastard Quincy."

"Mr. Beasley said to tell you he didn't call."

"What do you mean?"

"That was his message. He didn't call. But he'll call back."

"I think I'll have another drink," I said. "Join me?"

"What do you have?"

"Scotch."

"On top of bloody marys?" she said.

"Don't be fastidious. These are urgent pleasure-grabbing times, or don't you know there's a war on."

I got another glass from the cabinet and blew out the dust, a shoulder-holstered Sterling Hayden holed up in a rooming house. I poured the two drinks.

"I don't think I could take it straight, David."

"I think there's some froggy water left in that carafe."

"I'd better close the door," she said.

We drank in silence. It was very warm in the office and sleet struck the window at intervals. I expected Mrs. Kling to walk in at any minute. I imagined her sitting now in Weede's office, watching television, a cigarette planted in the center of her mouth, knees angled out, hands coupled on abdomen. During an office party several years before I had gone into Walter Faye's office, pursuing a rumor of striptease and frolic, and there had stood Mrs. Kling, alone and unaware of me, standing rigid, shoeless and blouseless, brassiered like a bank vault almost neck to navel, her left foot forward, two clenched fists raised before her, left guarding the face, right lower, the classic Queensberry stance of the pier brawlers. It had been one of those moments for which an explanation evades the mind forever, an underwater moment tilted and warped by a rapture of the deep. Much later, shod and bloused again, she returned to the party. And then, as if to demonstrate the excellent craftsmanship of her digestive tract, its grinding and juicing abilities, she heaved all over a cluttered desk, thus creating, simultaneously, both a legend and a monument to that legend, the Thelma Kling Memorial Desk.

Binky curled up on the sofa and went to sleep, a rippling child-snore rolling off her lips. I finished my drink and saw that the bottle was empty. For a second, seriously, I thought of taking off my clothes and then undressing her as well. Instead I lifted her coat from its hanger and covered her with it, aware that the room was well heated but feeling an overwhelming need to display some tenderness, if only in this trite way. The phone rang.

"Hello, Tab. I was in Hollywood recently. I drove my car into a palm tree and twelve guys fell out. They all looked exactly like you. Norman Rockwell soda jerks."

"Hello, Warren."

"When I called before, your secretary said you were in the office committing suicide. I called back hoping I'd be the last person to speak to you alive. Warren Beasley, the controversial radio personality, was probably the last person to talk to the popular young television executive. Mr. Beasley said that Bell, twenty-eight, had been despondent over the loss of his old fielder's glove. The deceased bore a strong facial resemblance to a number of Hollywood stars known for their interchangeability. His body will be sent airmail express to the West Coast for possible casting in a new movie spectacular based on the siege of Leningrad."

"You sound as morbidly chipper as ever," I said.

"I'm calling to invite you to my wedding. If all precedents hold, the honeymoon promises to be a veritable jubilee of ejaculatio praecox."

Warren Beasley had his own radio program on a local station. It was called "Death Is Just Around the Corner," and it was broadcast from two to five in the morning. I had listened to the program, or at least parts of it, close to a hundred times, and not once on all those occasions had I heard Warren repeat himself to any extensive degree. He invited no guests, played no records and gave no news bulletins, except of his own making. The show had ten or twelve steady sponsors and many irregulars—hair restorers, makers of artificial limbs, ear-piercing shops, a metaphysician in Long Island City, an illuminator of manuscripts and scrolls, several dog kennels. Most of the sponsors wrote their own commercials and they were usually read by Warren in what can only be called a mounting orgasmic frenzy. Warren also delivered commercials for nonexistent products. He talked for three solid hours every morning but Monday, sometimes with style, humor and intelligence, sometimes with scatological glee, sometimes in the bitter self-pitying tone of a genuinely desperate man. Warren had a brilliant mind, I thought, but he was completely irresponsible and it wasn't easy to characterize his audience. "Death" had more than its share of freak-appeal and it probably attracted most of the area's neo-Nazis, transsexuals, interplanetary travelers, coprophiles, whip and chain collectors, astral seers, blood-drinkers and morgue attendants—all the caffeine dregs of a century of national insomnia. His frequent use of obscenity, both primitive and surreal, had drawn no comment from the FCC, either because they were not listening or because the time had finally come for the electrical transmission of wordsex into America's silent bedrooms. Naturally Warren was considered a prophet by some, a menace by others. He encouraged neither view; nor did he encourage that sentiment of unity and common purpose, that sense of underground comradeship, which his listeners undoubtedly shared. Too much like the Masons, he said. Warren had started in broadcasting many years before as a weatherman on a Los Angeles TV station. He had managed to acquire a kinescope of what turned out to be his last program and he showed it to me one evening in a screening room at the network. What I recall most vividly are his eyes, relentlessly drilling, trying to pierce the prohibitive limbo so familiar to those who have stood before a camera in a small studio. He was able to speak for almost a full minute before somebody woke up and cut him off. He began by saying that there was no weather in Los Angeles and there never had been. The true weather was in ourselves; the true weather report had been concealed from the public all these years. Storm warnings up and down the subconscious. Ten-foot drifts along the outlying areas of the soul. Winds of gale force should reach the suburban psyche by midnight. There will be no flights in or out of the major idports. Then he had done a tapdance and sung a lyric that went "hey jig-a-jig go fuck a rubber pig." He

94

had come a long way since then. His total earnings were close to a hundred thousand a year. Several national magazines had done stories on him. He accepted invitations to appear on many television talk shows. He had written a nonbook. Educated by Jesuits for eight years, Warren was able to regard his money, his notoriety, his four ex-wives with a combination of dispassionate wit, profound distress and a monumental Thomistic sense of the divine logic behind it all.

"Not again," I said.

"It's the real thing this time, Tab. She's got big pink Renoir tits and she can cook. But I fear her crotch is haunted by the ghost of Joan of Arc, that prissy little suffragette. We're going to Dublin on our honeymoon, which may sound self-defeating, but I've always wanted to do something like that."

"When's the wedding? I wouldn't think of missing it."

"It's on her lunch hour," he said. "Tuesday, noon, Supreme Court Building. She's a dental hygienist. She cleans your teeth before Dr. Dachau takes over with all his dangling pain-utensils. She has to be back in the office by one-thirty but he's giving her a week off beginning the next day so I can fly her to old Dub and pretend she's Molly Bloom, the only woman I've ever really wanted to scissor with. The fantasies are taking over my life."

"Warren, isn't this the third dental hygienist you've married?"

"Second," he said. "The one you're thinking of was a radiologist. Tried to zap my gonads once or twice. Tuesday then."

I read two pages of a script about the melting of the polar ice caps and then called my father. His secretary said he would be with me in a minute. I tried to picture the soap beneath her fingernails.

"Hiya, pally. What's new?"

"Stennis makes forty-five," I said.

"That's all? You're sure?"

"Unimpeachable source."

"God bless you, sport."

A few minutes later the phone rang. As I lifted the receiver Binky shifted positions and the coat slipped onto the floor and her skirt moved up her leg, making that fine hushing sound, and twisted nicely around her thighs. The telephone was quacking and I plugged it into my head.

"Dave Bell's my name; TV's my game."

"David, why didn't you call me back? You are coming this evening, aren't you?"

"What do you want for Christmas, Wendy?"

"I won't say it over the phone. But if you were here, darling."

"You're just lonely," I said.

"Remember college, David? Wasn't it wild? You're one of my oldest and dearest friends. Please come to my dinner party tonight. You can leave early if you want to. Do you still have your T-Bird and those super poems you used to write? You have no idea how upset I was when you showed up with a wife that last year. Listen, I have to tell you this one final thing. Are you listening? I got a card from my ex today. You wouldn't believe where he's spending the holidays."

There were thirty-six small holes in the mouthpiece of my telephone. They were arranged in three circles of six, twelve, and eighteen holes each. There were only six holes in the earpiece. This disparity seemed significant but I didn't know exactly why. My eyes were on the sleeping girl on my sofa while my mouth and ear were engaged with the mouth and ear of Wendy Judd. I felt I was being sucked into the telephone. Only my eyes seemed to resist the whistling tunnel pressure of those forty-two holes. Wendy's mouth, enormous and frenzied, was burning at my ear; as I listened, my hand moved to that part of my thigh which corresponded to the area below the hem of Binky's skirt which my eyes had selected a moment before. My senses, it seemed, were scattering, eyes and hand allied, mouth and ears receding into the phone, drawn by the urgent voice, by the image I could not envision; and then, fiercely and strangely excited, I moved my hand across my lap and did a mad kind of loin dance, not moving from the chair, not taking my eyes from that land and sea arrangement of dress and leg, not resisting the tunneling lure of the telephone, the place where Wendy dwelt, unimaginably desirable, a victory of mouth and ear. It was my secretary who gave flesh to the disassembled words, who modeled for me the image on the other end of the wire, the picture I couldn't see without her help. I closed my eyes, feeling it was all too much, too involving, and cut across Wendy in midsentence, an incivility I knew she would not mind.

"I'll be there," I said.

I hung up and immediately called Sullivan. She answered after the seventh ring. I felt a sudden chill, the vast white silence of my mother's deathbed, candlewax and linen, her enormous eyes, the breathing shallow and bad. Beneath the blanket her body was little more than ash, crumbs of bone; her hands were dry kindling. Death became her well, so horribly well, and when I heard the bells of an ice cream truck I had almost laughed. American sky-chariot come to take mother to the mansion with the familiar orange roof and the twenty-eight flavors. I had almost, but not quite, laughed; and then the chill had entered and she died.

"I have to get out of here, Sully."

"David?"

"I no longer control the doors. Words blow in and out. I can hear them perfectly, with really astounding clarity, but I can't believe they're coming from my mouth. I think it's time to leave."

"Nothing will be solved out there, you know. It's just telephone poles stringing together the cities. Those distances out there will only confuse you."

"I had lunch with a friend recently. He cried. He wanted to build a boat and sail to Tasmania. I laughed at him. A week later he had a cerebral hemorrhage. We learn nothing from the stereotypes around us, not even that we're all the same."

"I know what your problem is. You don't have any Jewish friends. Why don't you come on over tonight? I'm working on something new. I'd like you to take a look at it."

"I'll be there," I said.

I put down the phone. The door opened slightly, revealing the condensed figure of Mrs. Kling, six inches wide, armless and hipless. With the door open just a crack I didn't know whether she could see Binky on the sofa.

"Somebody took my stapler," she said. "It was on my desk when I went into Mr. Denney's office. Now it's gone. I've had it for nine years. My name is Scotch-taped to the bottom of it. I'm telling everybody that if it's not back on my desk by nine sharp on Monday morning there'll be trouble. That gives all of you the whole weekend to make up your mind."

"Reeves Chubb took it. I saw him."

"You're lying. Don't think I don't know how much lying goes on around here. What's she doing on your sofa with her legs like that?"

"She gets these mild attacks," I said. "It's some kind of minor diabetes thing. No cause for concern, Mrs. K."

"I can see bare flesh above her stockings. Why are your hands under the desk?"

"I was just picking some loose skin off my fingers. You know the way the skin gets loose around the fingernails. I was kidding before about Reeves taking your stapler. Walter Faye took it. Say, I like your shoes, Mrs. K. I didn't know Dr. Scholl's had merged with Walt Disney Productions."

After she left I dialed Ted Warburton's extension.

"Warburton here."

"Hello, Ted. It's Dave Bell. I just wanted to say that I enjoyed that remark you made about Chip Moerdler. It's most gratifying to be supported by a man of your stature. What was it you called him—an ignominious baboon?"

"A thundering ignoramus."

"Superb," I said.

"I was sorry to hear your show is being cancelled. It had

its faults but it was one of the few programs I made it a point to watch. Don't be disappointed, Dave. You're young and able. One of the turks. I've been hearing good things about you."

"Coming from you, Ted, those are encouraging words indeed."

"I shouldn't have thought you'd need any encouragement, particularly from an old buzzard like me."

"How long have you been living here, Ted? I've been meaning to ask."

"Since 1951," he said. "I had always hoped to retire to England one day. But in a few months I'll probably be dead. My wife is American, you know."

"No, I didn't."

"You'll have to come over for dinner some night. We weren't able to have children."

"Ted, there's one other thing I'd like to ask you. Did you read the Mad Memo-Writer's latest effort? The St. Augustine quote? Actually I don't usually refer to him as the Mad Memo-Writer. I call him Trotsky. It seems appropriate somehow."

"Trotsky," he said. "Quite good. I like that."

"What I wanted to ask you was whether you could clear up the meaning of that particular quotation for me. You're really the only one around here who might conceivably shed some light."

"I don't think I know precisely what you're talking about."

"The St. Augustine thing. *And never can a man be more disastrously in death than when death itself shall be deathless.* I've committed it to memory. It overwhelms me. I'm not sure why but it just hits me. It knocks me out."

"It is a somewhat killing remark, isn't it? But I don't see why you think I can unravel it for you. I'm the kind of man who likes to rest his wits with anagrams. Theology is a bit out of my line."

"The endless leagues of China," I said.

"I don't understand."

99

"You recited that passage from Kafka to confuse them. I was watching your face. You were playing a game with them."

"Weede is an overbearing jabberwock and Reeves Chubb is beyond all hope of redemption; nevertheless, one is my superior and the other a fellow human being entitled to cherish the illusion of his dignity, if nothing more. I abhor deceit and trickery in others and I try to the best of my waning ability to exclude these particularly shabby vices from my own repertoire. No, young man, I was playing no game. I'm afraid you misinterpreted whatever it was you saw on my face."

"In that case I apologize, Ted. I guess I tied the two things together. The memo and your remarks about China. I thought there was a connection."

"You were mistaken. I'm not who you think I am. I'm a man trying to do a job of work and having a bloody difficult time of it if you want to know the truth. These tiresome phone calls don't help any. People ring me up automatically when they need an answer to some infantile question or a question for some ungodly answer. I am not the research department. I am not dial-a-prayer. And I most assuredly am not the Bishop of Hippo."

"I'm sorry, Ted. I really am. Please forgive me."

"We are endlessly dying," Warburton said. "We begin dying when we are born. A short time later we die. By universal consent, more or less, this is known as death. In time the so-called resurrection of the body takes place. Soul and body become joined in what we have already defined as the state of death. But although we are in the state of death we are not dead because body and soul are intact once again and there is no recourse but to resume the process of dying. Or, if you will, the process of living—the words are interchangeable really. And since this process of dying goes on for all eternity we cannot be said to be waiting for death. Nor are we looking back on death, for the simple reason that we cannot look back on something which is not there but here. In this paradoxical, redundant and somewhat comical passage, what

Augustine is getting at beyond all the gibberish is that death never dies and that man shall remain forever in the state of death. There is always the chance, of course, that I have misunderstood every word. I managed to obtain a key to the multilith room. I run off the copies after midnight and then distribute them. If I'm not able to get it all done before daybreak, I distribute the remaining copies during lunchtime, as was the case yesterday. I work quickly and stealthily. Naturally I am above suspicion."

He hung up. I kept the phone at my ear for a long moment, almost expecting his voice to return, drumming and bagpiping, overwhelming the animistic buzz of the telephone. Then I returned the receiver to its cradle and went for a walk. All the office doors were closed and I opened them one by one as I progressed through the corridors. Jones Perkins was down on one knee, golf club in hand, lining up a seven-foot putt; a tipped-over paper container served as cup. Walter Faye was reading the *Kama Sutra* to his secretary. Mars Tyler was at his desk, running a strand of dental floss between his teeth. Reeves Chubb was in the process of changing his shirt. Richter Janes and Grove Palmer were pitching quarters to the wall. Quincy Willet was having his shoes shined by the freelance bootblack. Paul Joyner sat on his royal blue sofa, barefoot, in the lotus position. I was like a movie camera catching documentary glimpses of everyday life in a prison, on an aircraft carrier, in a home for the criminally insane. Phelps Lawrence had gone but his secretary, Ellen Quint, was in his office, his ex-office, pacing, eyes red, hair ribbon undone. Carter Hemmings was strumming his guitar. Nobody was in Chandler Bates' office and I did not open Ted Warburton's door.

Then I saw Jennifer Fine turning a corner and I went into the men's room. Later I went back to my office, woke up Binky and told her to go home. As she put on her coat she nearly fell, stone zombie drunk, and I had to help her to the elevator. On the way back I stopped at Jody Moore's desk and we talked about her upcoming trip to Indonesia. Then I got my coat and went down to the Gut Bucket. The bartender Leon, who was studying to be an actor, ignored me for five minutes while he talked to a girl wearing an eyepatch and a zoot suit. Finally he sauntered over, set both hands flat on the bar and gave me his ironical Marlonesque cowboy grin.

"The usual," I said.

"Now what would that be?"

"I thought you were Monty. Monty usually works this end of the bar. Cutty Sark on the rocks. It's so goddamn dark in here."

"One Cutty it is."

I was on my second drink when five or six network people came in, laughing and stomping, all gloved, scarved and rosy. They joined me at the bar. The men shook hands with me and the women kissed me. We were there for about two hours, in our coats and rubber boots, standing in snow puddles. I bought the last three rounds and then they left, complaining about trains and taxis, cursing the husbands who would be waiting for dinner to be cooked, the wives and Volkswagens meeting the trains, the children demanding their gifts, the boyfriends who would be jealous, the pets who would claw the furniture, the relatives who would be arriving, the time, the season, the epoch, the age. I told them to have a nice weekend. Then I had another drink, drew a smile from the girl in the eyepatch and departed without leaving a tip.

Wendy Judd lived in the east eighties, an area which always made me think of a drugstore stretching to infinity. Her building was called Modigliani Terrace Apts. The lobby was bleached in fluorescent lighting and decorated with gold-fringed mirrors and balding tapestries. There was a pool, full of cigarette butts, with a graceful stone naiad standing in the middle, rusty water trickling from her navel. Murals depicted Montmartre, Fort Lauderdale and Mount Fujiyama. The doorman asked my name and then called Wendy on the intercom and announced me. In the elevator was a printed notice pointing out that for the safety and convenience of the tenants there were hidden TV cameras in all the elevators as well as in the laundry room and in both the Giacometti and Lipchitz sculpture gardens. I walked down a long corridor. There was a Christmas wreath on Wendy's door with a note pinned to it that read: *Dis is de place.* She ushered me in, missing my mouth with a pigeon kiss. Then I had to stand at the entrance to the living room while she called off the names of the other guests, adding coy biographical notes. They nodded when introduced, one of the ladies raising her hand with kindergarten brightness, the men lifting their rumps from sofa and chairs like pianos that do not wish to be hoisted. Wendy took my coat.

"And this is David Bell, one of my ex-lovers," she said. "Isn't he something, girls? Pow."

Her apartment was decorated with revolutionary wall posters in Chinese script. There were smooth brown Buddhas sitting on the bookshelves along with several shiny volumes of Oriental art reproductions and a number of miniature samurai swords that seemed to be part of an ashtray arrangement. In addition to Wendy and myself, there were four men and four women in the room. None of them appeared to be beautiful, handsome or talented. I sensed tremendous hostility.

I sat on the sofa next to a girl whose left leg was in a cast.

"What do you do?" she said.

"I do things with McAndrew at Amherst."

"Have I heard of him?"

"No," I said.

"If you're wondering about the leg, I broke it skiing."

"I was about to ask."

"Are you a good lover?" she said.

"Even a hawk is an eagle among crows."

"You're real quick. I won't mess with you anymore. You're too quick for me. I was trying to get you off balance and you come up with a terrific line probably from some great old Randolph Scott movie in that green Technicolor. Where do you drink? We all drink at the Bow-Wow on Second Avenue.

The bartender's name is Roone. He's real quick too. Some of the things he says. Too much. But I don't like him visually. We're all sharing a house at Fire Island this summer. There's a half a share left. If you're interested, tell Barry or Spike. A half a share costs a hundred and sixty. Then you chip in for food, liquor and incidentals. Bring a blanket because it gets cold at night. The house we're getting this year is just one house down from the dunes. Are you a Scorpio by any chance?"

Then Wendy walked in, dragged a chair to the middle of the room and straddled it in the manner of a Berlin nightclub singer in the disillusioned twenties.

"I'm so delighted David could come tonight. David Bell is the only one who can save me. We were lovers in college. David had this white Thunderbird and we used to drive into the desert and take our clothes off. Pow. Where can you do that in New York? I went up to one of the sundecks in my blue bikini last August and they wouldn't even let me take off the top. In Panama City I had a lover who had David's eyes. It was fantastically uncanny. But he was a freak in every-thing else. I couldn't believe this man. He was some kind of banana agent and he had this thing about tarantulas. We were in a restaurant once and he said what if a big furry tarantula suddenly crawls out of your food; what will you do; you have to be ready for something like that in this part of the world. I've had some freaky lovers. Antony Ambrose wanted to put me to work in a SoHo striptease joint because of my breasts. I couldn't believe that man. When we split up he told me thanks for the mammaries."

I went into the bathroom. There were books, woodcuts, a magazine rack, two scatter rugs, a small bronze gong. I sat on the rim of the tub and flipped through a magazine article about the war. Each page of the article was adorned with color photographs. Opposite a picture of several decapitated villagers was a full-page advertisement for a new kind of panty-girdle. The model was extraordinarily lovely, a tall dove-colored girl holding a camel whip. The copy said this high-fashiony girdle clings to your bodyskin and comes in three huggy colors. I turned to a brandy ad. A woman in a white evening dress was walking a leashed panther across the lawn of a Newport estate. The war article covered about fifteen pages, the text set in very small type. I realized the bathtub was full of water bugs. I went into the kitchen and Wendy turned and then we were all over each other, heavy and ravenous, jammed into a corner, and what I saw in my mind was Binky asleep on my sofa.

Dinner was chicken and rice. We sat around the living room, plates on knees, and searched each other's raincloud faces for some clue to our dilemma. I counted the greeting cards which Wendy had placed on exhibit throughout the room. There were sixty-four of them.

"There are water bugs in your bathtub," I said.

"That's impossible," Wendy said, her mouth puffed with rice, and I was sure that all ten of us shared a skittering image of quick black creatures nesting in every scoop of rice in every bowl.

"I tried to count them but there were too many."

"This is a new building. It has a sanitary code you wouldn't believe. David is just being macabre, everyone. It's his own special brand of humor. Just go on eating and don't worry about a thing. Once a week they clean and scrub every inch of this building from top to bottom with the most modern equipment available."

"There were at least twenty," I said. "You have to be ready for something like that in this part of the world. I'm sure they've been scanned on the radar by this time. One of them was having babies."

Dessert was a nervous affair. The women did not remain seated and even avoided standing in one spot for more than a few minutes at a time. I said I had to catch a big silver bird to the Coast early the next morning and Wendy saw me to the door. She reprimanded me for being naughty and then, tongue to my ear, promised me a night of canal-zone pleasures if only I would remain. The elevator was not working and I had to walk down sixteen flights. It was snowing heavily. On Second Avenue dozens of off-duty cabs went by. Finally one of them pulled up. I got in and the driver batted down the flag and started off toward lower Manhattan at high speed in the total snow.

Sullivan lived in a top-floor loft on Greene Street. Her reputation was growing locally and I felt it wouldn't be long before the critics and art marketeers and all those natty little gallery men with vicious shoes and dagger sideburns recognized that she belonged in the top rank of American sculptors. She worked in mahogany, epoxy and automobile paint. In her own words, everything she did pursued a curve. The smoothness of her shapes and the dull blunt colors she used seemed to suggest a horrible softness, that of slugs or worms, boneless things curling at the edge of one's sleep. Several people had told her they were afraid to touch her pieces of wood and this pleased her but only to a point; she said her highest ambition was to give people the feeling that they were eating small live wet amphibians. The Whitney owned two of Sullivan's works and private collectors accounted for about ten more. At least thirty had been bought by various corporations. A chemical firm in Muncie had recently purchased three of her smaller things and placed them in the lobby. This had surprised and delighted me. Like all those who loiter around talent I tended to overpraise Sullivan and to consider her work one of the essential measures in the salvation of the republic, and it did not seem impossible to me that Indiana might rise to new spiritual heights thanks to Sullivan's three pieces of carefully handcrafted afterbirth. She told me not to get too excited. The chemical firm was merely trying to improve its image; they had even sent a number of their executives to a mountain retreat where they walked around in sandals and togas; and it was all a tax gimmick anyway. I had met Sullivan when our unit at the network did a half-hour filmed report on something we called the phenomenon of power-art, meaning art produced by electric tools. Two minutes were devoted to Sullivan and her fantastic studio. It took almost a whole day to film this segment and she and I spent a good part of it in conversation. She said she liked me because I was so beautiful and sad, so squarely in the American tradition. Only Sullivan, I believed, could save me.

The front door was off its hinges. It stood in the tiled hallway with the word DOOR painted white across the glass pane which composed its upper half. I walked up the first flight. The two doors were marked GOOD and EVIL. I kept climbing. The tiled steps were rounded and black at the edges. I passed four more doors. One was labeled BREAST and the others were marked JUSTICE, MARTYRDOM and RIVER. Climbing the final flight to Sullivan's loft, I smelled something terrible blowing through the building, some presence that carried with it a sudden vivid evocation of open wounds, swamp, panic and disease, the stench of a retreating army, and it was so strange and pervasive that I knew I must make a joke of it, as I did, ultimately, with all those things I did not understand, and so I assembled an opening remark to toss at Sullivan. The remark would be both clever and graphic and I was still working on the exact phrasing when I opened the unmarked door and walked into the room.

She was not there. Seven coiled shapes, hulking and purgatorial, stood around the loft. They were much larger than anything she had done before and far more complex, wheels inside wheels, scythes rising from the rounded edge of a ludicrous shield, men or burial urns, industrial menace of cogs and inner clocks, a massive butter churn, all fearful, indefinable in the end, looming and never still, her long soul in wood. To shape, bond and coat. She said it was the blessing of God, the final grace, to have given us opposable thumbs. I could never enter Sullivan's studio without feeling that I had just stepped, unwillingly, into an alien country, one visited in the past but with a landscape that remained no more than the barest of memories. There were first the shapes circling in and out of their own smooth contours. There were the two spotlights placed on pedestals at opposite ends of the room. There was the wood-dust covering everything and then the hungry tools with teeth and claws, the radial-arm saw and saber saw, the orbital sander, the huge band saw and stationary sander, all their wires looped in the dust. There was, finally, most alien, the membranous chemical material which covered the walls and ceiling. Similar to the kind of wrapping used to keep sandwiches fresh, but somewhat more dull and opaque, this material was not wallpapered on in sections; it was a single tentlike unit, clinging, billowing slightly at times, bubbled with air pockets between itself and the walls. One rectangular section corresponding to the length and width of the door had been cut away so that people could enter and leave. The thing had been placed in the loft by the previous tenant, a Swiss inventor and collagist who was totally, rampagingly mad as only the Swiss can be. He referred to this, his lifework, as the Cocoon, and to himself as the Cocoonist. It had been his hope to fashion an environment that would be a work of life as opposed to one of art, an organism insulated from the hostile outer topography, a clump of palpitating caterpillars, a micro world, a man beyond the man who made it. The material, after all, was made of chemical substances and therefore could be said to possess some basic life-force different in degree but not in essence from that shared by all things which crawled or walked. This is what he told Sullivan and this is what Sullivan told me. The Cocoon had been just the beginning of his work but soon after it was floated into the loft he ran out of money, got into trouble with the landlord for setting fire to an alley cat as part of a formal satanic ritual and finally borrowed enough money to book passage on a freighter bound for North Africa, departing in a pair of Sullivan's flyless dungarees and the Lady Hathaway shirt I had given her as a birthday present.

The membrane had microscopic pores which enabled air to enter. Natural light could barely penetrate but the spotlights were an adequate substitute. Sullivan preferred them actually, claiming that sunlight was overrated. I put my fingers to one of the pieces of sculpture; the paint was dry, a deep gray; the others were browns of varying flat tones, a black and bone-white, a glacial silver. The three windows in the loft, pale and wavering behind the skin of the sandwich wrap, were shut tight, and yet the wrapping undulated as if grazed by a sea breeze. Some of the smaller power tools lay on a workbench. I went from figure to figure, thumbing each one, running the back of my hand over the bending surfaces. The building was quiet. I wondered why this one door had not been marked; to give a door the name River was an act of odd joy, or poetry, or childhood. I thought of the river in Old Holly then, and then of leaves, palms up, turning in a gentle current above the long, still, suspended fish with silver-dollar eyes, and then the woman ironing clothes in the shingled house, standing in her slip, the blinds not quite shut, and the September music of that warm night, elms and leisures of a dark street when the lawns smell of sweet wet grass and you are a boy, the hopelessness of lust, her bare arms and the shine of silk moving as her slow body moved, twice my age at least, ironing with the smooth movements of a lioness caressing her cubs, and I held to a tree and watched for an hour or more, twice my age, her light brown hair, lazy eyes, the softness of her face, never seen before and never since. All I wanted now was sleep.

A stained chunk of foam rubber, the remains of a mattress, lay under the workbench. I dragged it out and rolled my body into a ball and went immediately to sleep inside the plastic envelope of that room. Sins and rivers passed through my dreams, underwater faces fish-staring in my mind. I woke up to silence and chill, the accusations of the klieg lights. The city was full of people searching for the man or woman who might save them. My body stank of cold sweat, liquor and fear. The loft seemed endless, a scene lifted from the sandy bottom of a dream. A shape in the shape of my mother was forming in the doorway.

5

I was wearing green military-advisor sunglasses, a pair of wolf-hide moccasins, black chinos, a tight T-shirt and a khaki fatigue cap cocked low over my eyes. Pike was sprawled in the back seat and Sullivan was at my side watching New England un-bury itself from the last snow of winter bleeding now into the earth. The radio was announcing a sale on ground round steak and then some old-time rock came on, lush and mystical, cockney voices wailing through a prayer wheel of electric sitars, and we roared past Boston in a low cloud of crematory smoke. The windows were closed and the heater on and I moaned and chanted in the wrap-around fallopian coziness of my red Mustang, an infinitely more religious vehicle than the T-Bird I had owned in college. All America was on the verge of spring and the countryside was coming to glory, what we could see of the countryside through the smoke and billboards. There is nothing more thrilling than the first days of a long journey on wheels into the slavering mouth of an incredible and restless country. I shouted as I drove, exceeded speed limits, quoted poetry and folksong. Proper old Boston was behind us, its churches and gang killings, and ahead was

Maine where surf blew over the rocks, where ruddy lobstermen in yellow hats and hip boots crackled with tales of the
deep. We stopped in Salem for lunch and then visited the
House of the Seven Gables, where the pretty little guide
would not accompany us up the secret staircase, fearing quick
cougar paws in the dark, and in late afternoon we reached the
coast of Maine and saw a black apocalyptic storm clenched
over the ocean, the air cool and tense, about to break, and
when it came I thought the car might bust wide open and
Pike woke up thinking we were all about to die and then told
us about the great elliptical migrations of the cranes of Europe.
I spurred the frisky Mustang past hundreds of bungalows,
guest cottages and motels, twenty-five hundred miles from
Marlboro country, and neon lobster phantasms swam across
the wet road. It was evening when we got to Millsgate, a small
white town on Penobscot Bay. The rain had stopped and we
had dinner in a fishnet restaurant and then set out on foot to
search for Bobby Brand's ascetic garage, Brand in exile, Brand
junkless, Brand writing the novel that would detonate in the
gut of America like a fiery bacterial bombshell. We went up
a small hill, walking in the middle of the street. There were
no cars, no sounds at all, and the air was so sharp it seemed
to scratch the lungs. Four dogs came toward us and Pike
barked at them but they just trotted by. The moon was full,
obscured every few seconds by long swift clouds, and the
whole sky seemed to be breathing. At the top of the hill I
found the street we were looking for and we turned left and
walked past the village green. A row of white houses flanked
one side of the green; opposite the houses was a white clapboard church with a steeple. The high school was set back at
the far end of the lawn, facing the street. Several porchlights
were on and we could see the cannon and the black pocked
balls stacked on the grass beside it. Up ahead there was a gap
in the trees and I looked down to the water which was streaked
silver from the moon and from the white lights of the houses

set in the woods above the small coves on either side of the bay.

"New England is the most sexless place in the hemisphere," Sullivan said. "It has the sex appeal of Hyde Park in London on a warm afternoon when they all take off their shirts and collapse on the grass and then you understand why they had to go to Africa to get their kicks."

We reached the garage.

"To be human is to go through stages," Brand said. "I've been through them all. But that's over now. I eat, sleep and write. I'm all through shooting smack. I'm all through dropping acid. I'm working all that New York insanity and violence out of my system. I go over to the high school and play basketball with the kids. It's beautiful here and this is where I am. I'm purifying myself. You can help me, Davy. My brain needs cleaning out. I think the way I talk. The way I'm trying not to talk anymore. You can help me get rid of the slang. You have my permission to correct me whenever I fall back into the old drug argot or military talk. One of the things I've figured out for myself up here in exile is that there's too much slang in my head. It's insidious. It leads to violence. You can help, Davy. I want to be colorless."

We were sitting around a small table in his camper, inside the garage, drinking instant Maxwell House. The main part of the camper was plastic, designed to fit over the cab and back of a Ford F-250 pickup truck. The truck itself was black, the rest of the unit a dark gray with black trim around the windows and door. Inside were three bunks, a table, a hotplate and a typewriter; this was where Brand lived. I had met him years before when Merry and I went out to East Hampton one weekend. He seemed to be a one-man dispensary of meth, acid, hashish and various amphetamines. I was drawn to Brand. He represented the danger that was lacking in my life, real danger, not the plastic stuff available in great quantities at the network or the celluloid peril of those movie roles with which I challenged the premise of my marriage. All the bright young men of Madison Avenue searched for some facsimile of danger, some black root which might crack the foundation of their basic Episcopalianism, and we looked to the milder psychedelics, the study of karate, the weekend skydiving club, the sports-car rally. That weekend Brand gave me a tab to slip under my tongue, a ticket to unapproachable regions, and what I remember is the sight of myself at the age of sixty, mangled larvae clinging to the bleak flesh, the pit, the hellish comedy of my face; and that was the last occasion, save one, on which I tried to cross the swamp all alone. Brand had gone from Yale straight into the Air Force, where he flew an F-4 fighter-bomber over the elephant grass of a disappearing province. After his discharge (which may have been medical) he lived in a rooming house in the West Nineties shooting heroin and cocaine, then drifted into peace movements of the sing-along type and finally discovered acid, political activism and writing. Brand was roughly my age. He was tall, had sandy hair, wore glasses, was likable and frightening, lived off his family most of the time, seemed to change his personality every few weeks and sometimes minutes, could easily be visualized lying on a bed in a college dorm wearing a sweatshirt, denims, loafers and white socks, reading an economics textbook, dreaming of spoons and blue flame. He had a pair of copulating dogs tattooed on his right forearm.

"My aunt Mildred owns this garage. She lives right down the street but she's in Bangor now finishing up some legal business. Too bad you can't meet her. She plays the clarinet."

"When do we leave?" I said.

"Tomorrow's fine with me. I've leaving my manuscript behind. It needs a rest. Did you bring your camera?"

"It's in the car. I've also got a battery-operated tape recorder. And Sullivan brought along her fantastic NordMende fifteen-band portable radio. It gets the whole world."

"That's great."

"Do we sleep here tonight?" Sullivan said.

"We may as well get used to it," I said.

"We don't have to. Mildred left me the keys to her house. We'll be less crowded there. She's always asking me to move in with her but I tell her the garage is magical. It's full of emanations. I can't write anywhere but here. When do you have to be in Arizona?"

"Three weeks from yesterday. If all goes well, the crew will have everything set up by the time I get there. I hope you'll all decide to hang around while we're shooting. I don't know whether I'll be able to drive back with you. Most likely I'll have to fly. Pike, you and Sully can pick up my car here and take it back for me."

"My license expired eighteen years ago," Pike said.

We got our bags from the car and walked over to Brand's aunt's house. It was a fine old house, the place where everyone's grandmother lives in television commercials, full of other people's memories and yet warmed by a mood of love and simplicity that was universal. Starched lean men and little girls with straight blond hair looked darkly from photographs hung in the hallway. The living room was all chintz and needlepoint and bible kindness, wallpapered with faded yellow roses and soaked in an odor of old bodies rocking toward sleep. Brand took Sullivan and Pike upstairs and I wandered through the kitchen and pantry, feeling I had come to the heart of something, to the secret of the terror of small towns on Sunday, the eucharistic silence of coffee and buns after the long walk back from church. How long had it been since I had stood in a pantry at midnight, the dark shelves lined with cookie jars, jam and spices? Taste and smell can safecrack memory in the shadow of an instant, and in that pantry, nibbling dry cookies with the compulsive fervor of a penitent seeking the message of his past, I returned to a tight hot room in another town, the idle perfume of a summer.

I turned off the lights and went upstairs. Brand and Pike were sharing one of the bedrooms. They sat on their beds, the career soldier and the recruit, untying shoelaces, yawning, yanking T-shirts over their heads. Brand told me the other bedroom was at the far end of the hall and as I left them I heard Pike begin his account of the wanton slaughter of the buffalo in the eighteen sixties and seventies, herds three miles long and two miles wide decimated by Sunday huntsmen firing from trains. Sullivan was already in bed, reading her Yeats. The room obviously had not been used for a while and it was bare except for the lamp, the small table on which it stood, one chair, Sullivan's bed, and the cot where I would be sleeping. The roof sloped down over this part of the house and my cot was at the shallow end of the room. Sullivan turned off the light and I undressed, standing naked for a few seconds next to the cot, wondering whether she could see me. It felt wonderful to be sleeping in the same room as Sullivan. I slipped between the cold sheets. The ceiling angled down right over me and I raised my arm and touched it with my fingertips. All children, I thought, should be permitted to sleep in such a room; the child loves nooks and odd angles and is frightened into nightmare by equidistance, by parallel planes which conceal nothing.

"Pike is telling about the bison."

"His saddest tale," she said.

"We'll be out there soon."

"David on the way to Oz."

"I wonder if there are any Arapahoes still left. Or Chiricahuas. My favorite tribe. The Chiricahua Apaches. Burt Lancaster with that paisley headband."

"Will you get your blizzard?"

"I guess not. It'll be April soon."

"Desert flowers will be blooming."

"Did you ever notice? Darkness seems to make people speak in short sentences."

"Yes," she said. "And when the lights come on, we open up and ramble and say absolutely nothing. But in bed in the dark we're urged on by the monkey waiting in our sleep."

"What monkey?"

"We become documentary. We become newsreels telling what we think is the truth. Our listener is really no more than a fragment of the dark. The true audience is darkness itself. We unwrap our lives to it, trying to appease the monkey."

"What monkey?" I said.

"The Viennese monkey. But what we say really adds up to little more than empty daytime chatter. It's nothing compared to the revelation yet to come."

"Which is?"

"The single unending sentence."

"Sleep and dream."

"Yes."

"Tell me a story," I said.

"What kind?"

"About the great golden West and the Indians and the big outdoor soul of America."

"Do I have to speak in short sentences?"

"No."

"I have just the thing," she said. "It's about a wise old holy man of the Oglala Sioux and what he said to me once on a moonlit night."

"Is this for real or are you going to make it up as you go along?"

"This is for real," Sullivan said.

"Tell me then."

"He was a hundred years old and he looked like the stump of an oak tree. As a boy he had fought at the Little Bighorn with Crazy Horse. Even then he had disliked bloodshed and he spent most of the years of his adulthood fasting and praying. Some time ago, through the good offices of an anthropologist who had once been a friend of my father, I was permitted to visit Black Knife in his shack in the hills of South Dakota. I asked him a few polite questions which he chose to ignore, displaying at the very outset a splendid contempt for the amenities. He puffed on an ugly old corncob pipe. I think it must have been filled with mud and wet leaves. Then I asked him if things had changed much since he was a boy. He said that was the most intelligent question anyone had ever asked him. Things had changed hardly at all. Only materials had changed, technologies; we were still the same nation of ascetics, efficiency experts, haters of waste. We have been redesigning our landscape all these years to cut out unneeded objects such as trees, mountains and all those buildings which do not make practical use of every inch of space. The ascetic hates waste. We plan the destruction of everything which does not serve the cause of efficiency. Hard to believe, he said, that we are ascetics. But we are, more than all the fake saints across the sea."

"He said this to you, this old Sioux mystic?"

"He kept well abreast of things with newspapers and periodicals."

"Go on."

"What we really want to do, he said, deep in the secret recesses of our heart, all of us, is to destroy the forests, white saltbox houses, covered bridges, brownstones, azalea gardens, big red barns, colonial inns, riverboats, whaling villages, cider mills, waterwheels, antebellum mansions, log cabins, lovely old churches and snug little railroad depots. All of us secretly favor this destruction, even conservationists, even those embattled individuals who make a career out of picketing graceful and historic old buildings to protest their demolition. It's what we are. Straight lines and right angles. We feel a private thrill, admit it, at the sight of beauty in flames. We wish to blast all the fine old things to oblivion and replace them with tasteless identical structures. Boxes of cancer cells. Neat gray chambers for meditation and the reading of advertisements. Imagine the fantastic prairie motels we could build if only we would give in completely to the demons of our true nature; imagine the automobiles that might take us from motel to motel; imagine the monolithic fifty-story machines for disposing of the victims of automobile accidents without the bother of funerals and the waste of tombstones or sepulchres. Let the police run wild. Let the mad leaders of our nation destroy whomever they choose. That's what we really want, Black Knife told me. We want to be totally engulfed by all the so-called worst elements of our national life and character. We want to wallow in the terrible gleaming mudcunt of Mother America. (That's what he said.) We want to come to terms with the false anger we so often display at the increasing signs of sterility and violence in our culture. Kill the old brownstones and ornate railroad terminals. Kill the rotten stinking smalltown courthouses. Blow up the Brooklyn Bridge. Blow up Nantucket. Blow up the Blue Ridge Parkway. We must realize we are living in Megamerica. Neon, fiber glass, Plexiglass, polyurethane, Mylar, Acrylite."

"Was his shack located on a windy mountaintop? And had you gone there to find out the true meaning of life?"

"San Francisco would be completely leveled," Sullivan said. "Georgetown would be razed. In their place we would construct motels and houses that were identical in every detail. The new San Francisco would have no hills. The coast of Maine would be indistinguishable from Des Moines, Iowa. In the new gray Washington all the senators would spend eight hours a day in their identical offices, chained to radiators, being flogged by French tarts. This is known as the philosophy lesson, wisdom of the old world, the culture we so badly lack. Nobody would ever sweat. Sweating is wastefulness. If you were caught sweating you would be shot on sight. The air conditioners in every room in the country would be permanently set at fifty degrees fahrenheit. There would be no way to turn them off."

"What else did he say?"

"He said that all the new universities would consist of only one small room. It would work this way. At the beginning of each semester the entire student body—which would have to number at least five hundred thousand in order to give the computers enough to do—would assemble in a large open space in front of a TV camera. They would be televised and put on videotape. In a separate operation the instructors would also be videotaped, individually. Then two TV sets would be placed in the single room which represented the university. The room would be in a small blockhouse at the edge of a thirty-six-lane freeway; this proximity would help facilitate transmission of electronic equipment. Oh, there might be some banners on the wall and maybe a plaque or two, but aside from these the only things in the room would be the TV sets. At nine o'clock in the morning of the first day of classes, a computer would turn on the two television sets, which would be facing each other. The videotape of the students would then watch the videotape of the instructors. Eventually the system could be refined so that there would be only one university in the whole country."

"Frankly I think Black Knife is a little bit out of date."

"The biggest surprise was yet to come. Black Knife went on to say, with a full moon above us, that this massive surrender to our deepest dreams and impulses would be the best thing that could happen. After all, it was the true expression of ourselves in the most profound darkness of our beings. We would attain complete self-realization. We would set forth on the world's longest march of vulgarity, evil and decadence. We would establish the greatest superstate of them all. The world would be on its knees before our crazed power—if it isn't already. And then, having set one foot into the mud, one foot and three toes, we would stop for a moment, take a look around, and decide whether to sink further and eventually die or whether to return to firm land and begin again, living off roots and berries but no symbols, shedding the ascetic curse, letting the buffalo run free, knowing everything a nation can know about itself and proceeding with the benefit of this knowledge and the awareness that we have chosen not to die. It's worth the risk, he said, for if we took the latter course we would become, finally, the America that fulfills all of its possibilities. The America that belongs to the world. The America

120

we thought we lived in when we were children. Small children. Very small children indeed."

"And he told you all this. This broken-down swatch of buffalo hide."

"It was a cold night," she said. "And the moon was full."

In the morning it rained. I was the last one down. It felt good to sit in the kitchen, yawning, and smell coffee and bacon and hear rain slanting through the trees. I watched the others move from stove to refrigerator and back, bumping into each other, barely awake and walking through webs.

"What do you do for a living?" Brand said.

"That's a mute point," Pike said.

"Why don't you tell him?" I said.

"I'm a humanist of animals."

"Tell him," Sullivan said.

"I'm the proprietor of an electrical appliance repair shop on Fourteenth Street."

"Tell him what you specialize in."

"Toasters with doors and prewar radios. I have problems with pop-up things and things that are combinations of things like clock-radios or radio-phonographs. You have to read to keep up-to-date. I haven't read a book in twenty years. I don't have a head for numbers. I don't like voltage. My shop is small and I do what I can to encourage people to keep out."

"I have a head for numbers," I said. "Numbers fascinate me. Numbers have power. The whole country runs on numbers. I love to count things. I love to add and subtract. Everybody has numbers. Everybody is a number. Is that so terrible? Maybe it is. I frankly don't know."

"Listen up now," Pike said.

"Everybody start eating," Sullivan said. "I plan to fry myself an absolutely perfect egg. An astonishing egg. Perfect whites and yellows. Tone, texture, integrity."

"I want everybody to listen up now because this is important. In a fair fight who would emerge victorious, a tiger or a polar bear? Now the tiger is a fast powerful sinewy animal that has everything it takes to make a good hunter and killer. The tiger is classic. But you'll be making a big mistake if you underrate the polar bear. Polar bear can take off your arm with one lazy swipe of the paw. Polar bear has amazing speed for his size and he can camouflage himself in the snow. Natural selection is the name we give to this phenomenon. Tiger or polar bear."

"Where are they fighting?" Brand said.

"What do you mean?"

"If they're fighting in the arctic circle you have to favor the polar bear. In the jungle the tiger is the big stud. Nobody messes with the tiger on his own turf. He's the main man, the big bopper."

"Look, Jack, they're just fighting. It could be anywhere. Who can beat who is the thing we're concerned with."

"Let me posit something here," Brand said. "If a middle-weight from Akron goes to defend his title in Panama City against a local boy, the bookmakers take cognizance of that fact. Odds are laid accordingly. Now perhaps my analogy limps. Perhaps it limps. Nevertheless you station a tiger on an ice floe against some big white mother and he'll keep slipping around on his hindquarters while the polar bear tears him apart. Vice versa in the jungle. Bear would collapse from heat prostration. You can't have them fighting in a vacuum. And you can't pick a neutral site either, like the desert or the mountains, because then both of them will be out of their natural elements and the fight won't be a true test of their abilities. The contest is much too hypothetical to be given serious consideration."

Pike ate his breakfast in silence. His eyes schemed like dice. An entire philosophy had been questioned, its precepts put in grave doubt, and some serious thinking had to be done, some material reassembled, before he could meet his antagonist in open debate. Sullivan filled the moody silence by announcing that my digression on numbers was somewhat less than Euclidean in its sweep and purity; that one of my main faults was a tendency to get blinded by the neon of an idea, never reaching truly inside it; that to follow a number to infinity was not necessarily to arrive at God. With her fork she bisected a crisp slice of bacon, a piece so brittle the fork barely had to touch it; she then halved the two fragments, then the smaller four, then the resulting eight, and so on, working with the quietly fanatical precision of all those people whose job it is to divide small things into smaller things, who live on the rim of insanity; finally there was nothing left of the slice but a hundred decimal points. Did the bacon represent the insignificance of numbers; the futile quest for infinity; the indivisible nature of God as opposed to the fractional promiscuity of numbers? Was it all a lesson in prime matter and substantial form: Were the bits of bacon supposed to be numbers and the fried egg God? Brand looked on in fascination. I finished eating and went upstairs. I found a telephone and called Binky, collect, at the office.

"What's new?"

"Too much," she said.

"What?"

"Reeves Chubb, Carter Hemmings, Mars Tyler, Quincy Willet, Paul Joyner, Chandler Bates and Walter Faye."

"Axed?" I said.

"Sandbagged, throttled and axed. Drawn and quartered. It's official."

"Jumping mother balls. A mass execution. The magnificent seven gunned down at the OK Corral. Some sweaty little infighting among the survivors, what?"

"I think you're getting promoted," Binky said. "It's just a rumor at this point but Jody thinks it's on the level."

"Protect my interests, Bink, and I'll take you to the top with me. We'll be like Cary Grant and Roz Russell. Sipping martinis in my penthouse office. Has Weede begun hiring new people yet?"

"Just one so far."

"What's his name?"

"Harris Hodge."

"How old is he?" I said.

"I don't know, David. He won't be starting until next week. I haven't even seen him yet."

"Find out how old he is. I'll call you in a few days. Do you miss me?"

"I have to hang up now," she said.

I went into the bathroom, took off my shirt and began shaving my chest with an electric razor. It was a ritual cleansing of the body, a prelude to the sacred journey. The rain had stopped. I was happy. Through the bathroom window, as I shaved, I could see most of the town of Millsgate, white houses massed in a jest of innocence, fresh sunlight on the steeple. A girl went along the street skipping rope, head back, eyes seeking the break in the clouds; two white sloops, heeling severely, played at the mouth of the bay. I tried to imagine, to remember really, what it was like to live without the terminal fears of the city, for I had loved a town once without knowing it, and the love would not release me. There was a vein of murder snaking across the continent beneath highways, smokestacks, oilrigs and gasworks, a casual savagery fed by the mute cities, and I wondered what impossible distance must be traveled to get from there to here, what language crossed, how many levels of being. My hair went willingly into the fish-mouth of the razor.

A woman came down the steps of an old house. She wore a blue dress and carried pruning shears. I stopped shaving to watch her. She was close to forty, I guessed, fair-skinned, wearing flat heels, appealing in the almost abstract way a waitress is appealing in her plain white dress and the easy cadence of her body as she walks away from your table. The woman began to trim the hedge, handling the large shears with uncommon ease, and then, perhaps feeling the intensity of my stare, she looked up and saw me. I did not move and soon she went back to work, humming softly, proceeding along the hedge, her arms beating, somewhat like a bird discovering flight. I watched her for a least half an hour. She would never know it, of course, but she had given me the strangest, darkest, most horrifying idea of my life. It was an idea for a film I might make somewhere out there among the lost towns of America.

They were waiting for me. Brand locked the house and we carried our suitcases to the garage and put them in the camper. Then I trotted down to my car and drove it to the garage. I transferred my movie camera and tape recorder to the camper. Brand backed the F-250 out as we stood on the sidewalk counting the dents and bruises. Then he came out to give it one final look, circling slowly with a thoughtful expression on his face. He adjusted his glasses, blinking rapidly into the sun.

"She's ready, Davy," he said. "The old plastic bitch is ready to roll. You're the captain. Which way are we going?"

"West," I said. "Aim her more or less to the west."

I put my car in the garage and Brand locked up. We flipped coins and it was determined that I would ride up front with him for the first fifty miles. We assumed our respective posts. The school bell began to ring. Brand put the camper into gear.

PART TWO

6

Men on small islands would do well to avoid the pursuit of philosophy. The island illusion, that solitude and wisdom invented each other, is a very convincing one. Day by day I seem to grow more profound. Often I feel I am on the verge of some great philosophical discovery. Man. War. Truth. Time. Fortunately I always return to myself. I look beyond the white lace of the surf to my own unassembled past and I decide to let others stitch together the systems. I enjoy the triteness of the situation, man and island, exile in the ultimate suburb. The surf is massing and rolling, uneven now, page after page of terrible wild words. All the colors borrow, sea from beach from sky, and after a while I follow my own footprints back to the house.

(The film is projected.)

There were many visions in the land, all fragments of the exploded dream, and some of the darkest of these visions were those processed in triplicate by our generals and industrialists—the manganese empires, the super-sophisticated gunnery, the consortiums and privileges. Something else was left over for the rest of us, or some of the rest of us, and it was the dream of the good life, innocent enough, simple enough on the surface, beginning for me as soon as I could read and continuing through the era of the early astronauts, the red carpet welcome on the aircraft carrier as the band played on. It encompassed all those things which all people are said to want, materials and objects and the shadows they cast, and yet the dream had its complexities, its edges of illusion and self-deception, an implication of serio-comic death. To achieve an existence almost totally symbolic is less simple than mining the buried metals of other countries or sending the pilots of your squadron to hang their bombs over some illiterate village. And so purity of intention, simplicity and all its harvests, these were with the mightiest of the visionaries, those strong enough to confront the larger madness. For the rest of us, the true sons of the dream, there was only complexity. The dream made no allowance for the truth beneath the symbols, for the interlinear notes, the presence of something black (and somehow very funny) at the mirror rim of one's awareness. This was difficult at times. But as a boy, and even later, quite a bit later, I believed all of it, the institutional messages, the psalms and placards, the pictures, the words. Better living through chemistry. The Sears, Roebuck catalog. Aunt Jemima. All the impulses of all the media were fed into the circuitry of my dreams. One thinks of echoes. One thinks of an image made in the image and likeness of images. It was that complex.

Old Holly was a suburb of New York only in the strict geographical sense; unlike the surrounding communities it was not an extension of the city's monoxide spirit, a point of mere arrival and departure. The town did not have the sheen of a manicurist's artistry about it. The houses were very old, most of them, and agreeably shabby, two or three stories with small shuttered windows, high ceilings, gabled roofs, porches which in some cases went entirely around the houses, repeating the eccentric angles sketched by the roof-edges. Through all the houses drifted some thin plasm of identity, stirring the senses of the casual visitor. One enters here and tastes clove or mellow tobacco in the air; the next house smells faintly of mint, varnish somewhere, the soft thick snuff of an old rug; one hears music elsewhere, no more than intimations from the keys of a lidded piano, no more than cutlery and voices, the indolent sermon of a saw on wood, no more than silence or the stagnant inner sound which silence contains in all old rooms deep in sunlight. In certain rooms in some of the houses, the floors were slightly tilted, moldings loose, ceiling beams off-center, and when you got out of bed at night for a glass of water and there was wind and rain the sensation was not unlike that of being at sea in a storm. If you were a boy it was a simple matter to pretend your house was a ship, for the stairs creaked and there were small dark corners where you could put your hand to the wall and feel the house sigh in the wild currents of the wind. The dim persuasions of sameness, the low clean lines which imply neither victory nor defeat but only stalemate, equation, the century's dry science, were nowhere present among these houses. Only two pieces of property included swimming pools. The country club was on the verge of bankruptcy.

Physically, then, Old Holly might have been set in the middle of Connecticut or in some Pennsylvania valley which owed the fact of its livelihood to no large city. In spirit, the town was even less suburban. It had not been built with the automobile in mind; the streets were somewhat less than broad and people could be seen walking at all hours of the day and evening to the stores on Ridge Street. There were no parking lots in the middle of town, no need for them, and no shopping center or aluminum custard stand flanked by a miniature golf course and a driving range. There were many small hills, nagging little curves instead of neat intersections, and the sight of headlights picking out trees through low fog was, to a boy, something beautiful and rare, for the car was alien to this environment, its passage difficult and bizarre. Most of the people who lived in Old Holly worked there as well, tradesmen, factory hands, professional men, and the train depot was never crowded at the regular commuter hours. We were a town then, American in our outlook, plain and meat-eating, relatively unhurried, willing to die for our country, or for photographs of our country.

Harkavy Clinton Bell, my father's father, spent the last seven years of his life in Old Holly. Before retiring he had been one of advertising's early legends, the second man to use a coupon in a newspaper ad. It was he who left the house to my father. I was six when we moved from West End Avenue; Jane was nine and Mary ten. I was happy there as a child. It was a house of dubious architectural parentage, a bastard house, a stray, to be loved as mongrels are. Harkavy's portrait was over the mantelpiece, misty hills behind his head, and he looked like Mona Lisa's corrupt uncle. I filled my room with fishing rods, college pennants, baseballs and model planes.

Winter of my twelfth year.

The boys vanished in the heavy snow. I ran inside and took off my boots, coat and hat. I was always running then and I was always leaving on my hat till last. I stood by the window and watched the snow pile up. It was the first snowfall of the year, filling the evening with silence and falling heaviest inside the light of the streetlamps. A parked car was covered, humped in white, and nothing moved but soft light across sleeves of snow on the branches of every tree. It was warm inside the house and I could hear my mother and older sister preparing dinner. Soon my father came home and I ran to greet him. He stood in the hallway, big and pink, shaking off snow, clapping his gloves together, breathing smoke. After dinner I went back to the window and chewed on homemade cookies. Mary washed the dishes; Jane drew a picture of my mother with chalk on a slate; my father turned the pages of a magazine; the radiator whistled. All these sounds in the warm house, of water running and steam, of shrill chalk and the rustling of paper, of voices known and of time moving down the grandfather clock, all these, inflections of the house itself, all-comforting and essential, told me that I was safe.

And then the first sound of men with shovels was heard.

I could not see them but I knew they were out there, bulky men folded behind their shovels. The shovels chipped at ice, scraped on concrete, and my father began to get interested. He stirred and put down the magazine. My mother quoted something she had read the day before, grim statistics about shoveling snow and heart attacks, about pneumonia, sprained backs, broken hips. My father said he had a long way to go before he started worrying about such things and in a little while he got up and put on his coat. There is no denying a man who wants to shovel snow.

Outside a car went by, slowly, wipers working, and then my father emerged from the basement with the shovel. I could see three streetlamps from the window and each beam of light brimmed with snow. Soon it would be Christmas and there would be visitors and gifts and too much food. And if we were lucky enough to have snow then it was that much better because there was nothing ahead but school and the bleak dark months before the first true day of spring. But it was too early to look forward to spring because there was still Christmas ahead. The worst stretch was after Christmas. It was a long time to spring and there was nothing but school. My mother began to cry.

I went outside and stood by the gate. My father was shoveling snow and didn't see me and all up and down the street other men were shoveling and not talking and they were all breathing smoke and in the quiet and unfaltering tenor of the snow they looked like ancient men engaged in timeless professions, shepherds in a field or patient fishermen whose lines sprawl in the water of a winter lake. The night air was keen and thin. No cars passed and it was too cold now for walking your dog or for boys testing the snow for its snowball qualities. I wanted to do some shoveling myself but there was only one shovel and it was something I knew my father enjoyed so I let it go. I thought of all the people in town I liked and all those I didn't like. I imagined myself crawling through the woods, a commando, with a knife between my teeth. It was hot and the jungle birds were screaming. I moved up to the house on my belly through the trees. It was the doctor's house, Weber's, and I climbed through the window. He came downstairs and I stood behind the kitchen door. He walked in and reached for the light-switch and then quickly, hand over mouth, knife to throat, softly, softly, whispering my vengeance to his warm ear, I killed him.

In the snow now the joyous men shoveled. I went up the stairs and felt something hit me in the back. I turned and saw my father shaking the snow from his hands and smiling. I waited until he returned the shovel to the basement. Then we went into the house together.

My best friend was Tommy Valerio. Whenever I went to his house, his mother would squeeze my cheeks and rub her knuckles on my head. It used to embarrass me and soon I found excuses to stay away. When Tommy was sixteen his father died of a heart attack and Tommy took possession of the family car, a '46 Chevy. We kept a bayonet under the front seat. We didn't have licenses and Tommy used to sit on a pillow when he was driving so that he would look taller and therefore older. One day he told me that the police chief's youngest daughter, Kathy, was available for experiments of all kinds. We drove her over to the yacht club and took turns in the back seat. She chewed gum throughout. The police chief's name was Brandon Lovell. He and my father used to shoot skeet together. I was going to prep school in New Hampshire but I was home about six weekends that winter and there would always be one afternoon in the yacht club parking lot. One Saturday I borrowed the car and drove over to the drugstore on Ridge Street. Kathy was there and I took her to the lot. She told me that her father used to walk around the house naked. That was why her two older sisters had left home. Once he wore his gunbelt and holster and nothing else and fired six bullets into the sofa. I asked her who she liked better and she said Tommy. I took the bayonet out from under the seat and asked her again. I didn't know whether I was kidding or not. She said Tommy. I hit her in the jaw with the blunt end of the bayonet and threw her out of the car.

That summer, with my father's consent, I got a junior driver's license. He owned an MG at the time and we went driving almost every weekend. One night he agreed to lend me the car even though I wasn't supposed to drive after dark. I told him that a friend of mine from Larchmont, a classmate, had just died of amnesia, and this was the last night of the wake. I had spent a long time working out the minor details of the lie but he gave me the keys without asking questions. There was a movie I had to see.

I sat through it twice. During the intermission an usher came around with a tin can for the heart fund. It was even better the second time. There was an immensity to Burt which transcended plot, action, characterization. In my mind he would be forever caught in that peculiar gray silveriness of the movie screen, his body radiating a slight visual static. I saw him in person once at Yankee Stadium and even then, before he left in the fourth inning because the autograph hunters would not leave him alone, even then, in civvies and dark shades, Burt was the supreme topkick, inseparable from the noisy destinies of 1941. I was glad I had not asked anyone to come to the movies with me. This was religion and it needed privacy. I drove home slowly. My father followed me up to my room. I was sitting on the bed, one shoe just off, still in my hand, when he entered.

"How could anybody die of amnesia?" he said.

"Amnesia? I thought I said anemia."

"You said amnesia, sport. I didn't realize it till you left. But even granting you meant anemia, the question still goes. Who dies of anemia today? Didn't this friend of yours get enough to eat?"

"It's a blood thing, dad. It has nothing to do with malnutrition. The red corpuscles don't get enough hemoglobin. Something like that."

"You were out with that little piece of tail, weren't you? Lovell's daughter. If you don't get the clap off her, you'll never get it. That's dynamite you're fooling around with, pally. Lovell's a friend of mine but he's got some kind of maniac inside him. Some big mean redneck waving a shotgun. If he finds out you're fooling around with his daughter, he'll blow your head off. What I'm giving you is sound advice based on a pragmatic interpretation of the facts as I see them. I'm not moralizing, Dave. That's your mother's department. Listen to your old man. Have I ever given you a bum steer?"

"I went to the movies," I said.

"Yeah."

"It's the truth this time."

"Let's forget it."

"Can I drink beer at the dinner table from now on?"

"Can you drink beer?" he said. "I don't give a rat's ass if you drink double bourbons. Do you good. But that's also your mother's department. Maybe if you sipped it from a sherry glass she'd give you the okay."

I laughed and took off the other shoe.

"Is she still making preparations for the big party?"

"She's moving into second gear. A full month in advance. She's a honey all right, your mother is. Nobody like her."

"Will you let Arondella come to the party?"

"Don't mention his name in this house," my father said.

At the table my mother usually talked about food. When she was riding in a car, her conversation centered around cars and driving. Knitting, she talked about clothes; sweeping, about the virtues of cleanliness; watching television, about watching television.

When she was feeling well, we became absorbed in her,

grateful for every simple moment. But she was rarely well. There was no pattern to her illness, none that we could discern anyway. Each break in the bad weather gave us hope and my father would put off until another time the necessary task of seeking professional help. He understood nothing and therefore did nothing. She was not a photograph that could be retouched. The maimed child could not be cropped out of the picture. She was not an advertising campaign and so he did not know what to do about her. When she was well, he lived within latitudes defined by her intelligence and grace, as we all did, lovingly. The rest of the time we did our best to pretend she was not there.

She was blond, blessed with smooth lovely skin, with almost musical hands. She was quite small. In her simplest actions was a delicacy so theatrical and self-aware that one often felt witness to some lonely child's performance. Virginia born, the only daughter of a minister and a minister's daughter, she met my father when he was visiting relatives in Alexandria. Two months later they were married. It embarrassed me to hear stories of their courtship, such as it was, and the early years of their marriage. She was seventeen when they were married and I was born five years later. She told me the story of those years dozens of times. She seemed to consider my birth the culmination of a series of preparatory events almost ceremonial in meaning and scope.

The Episcopal church in Old Holly was called Calvary. My mother spent a lot of time there. The church had organized a permanent fund-raising drive for the orphans of Asia. My mother was in charge of Burma and South Korea. Although she was genuinely devout, I think she was uneasy about the whole idea of the passion of Christ. Perhaps he sweated too much for her taste. I say that without facetiousness. She used to tell me charming little fables about Jesus. It wasn't until much later that I realized she made them up. In her fables Jesus was a blond energetic lad who helped his mother around the house and occasionally performed a nifty miracle. "And after Jesus cured the blind man," she would say, "he went home to the farm and helped his daddy milk the cows."

As a child I was devoted to her. But we had our differences. Most of our arguments were pedantic flurries and whoever lost would usually try to even things up with a senseless display of spitefulness. I was playing baseball one day, or hardball as we called it, standing out in center field, when I saw her coming across the grass toward me.

"Good little boys do not pick their nose," she said.

"Do not pick their noses. Boys is plural so noses has to be plural."

"Boys *are* plural," she said. "I was quite a brilliant little grammarian as a girl. I also played the harpsichord."

She turned and left before I could say anything. The game resumed and when the inning was over I trotted in and sat on the grass behind the first-base line. Tommy came over and sat next to me. He asked me what she had wanted. I told him.

"If that was my mother," he said, "I'd have told her to go take a flying fuck at the moon."

Her bedroom was full of childhood things. Several cloth dolls sat on the dresser, slumped over in their dull colors, limbs woefully bent. There was a set of toy dinnerware in the closet as well as a small dollhouse, a teddy bear and bunny, six or seven coloring books. Jane and Mary were not allowed to play with any of these things. Music boxes were everywhere.

At times her presence in the house seemed accidental. She was one of those people who turn up now and then only to fade into some parenthesis of the middle distance; one catches glimpses of such people in parks and museums. Walking down the hallway I would see her move from room to room, a quick white daze of cloth, hair, bare arms; turning the bend in the staircase I would see first her feet, then knees, hands, face, a tired light in the eyes. She liked to sit on the top step. There was an apparitional quality about my mother. She seemed almost translucent and no expectation of eye or mind could ever fully prepare me for the sudden glimmers of her comings and goings.

When we were alone in the house I sometimes sat on the steps with her. That's where she first told me about Dr. Weber. It was a summer afternoon. The house was full of sunlight. A bear's great warm slumber was spread over everything. The girls were playing tennis.

"The minister and the doctor are the heart of every community," she said. "Your great-grandfather on my mother's side, Philip Thatcher, was a fine country doctor. We've had doctors and ministers in our family practically all the way back to Jamestown. I've always had the greatest respect for doctors. In my family the doctor was second only to the minister. It was the tradition. And that's why Dr. Weber surprised me so. Dr. Weber is part of no tradition I know of, and if he's second to anyone it's probably a field hand. If I'm going to tell this story—and I am because one day you'll realize that true education is made up of shocks and rude surprises, so I am going to tell it—but first I have to tell you what an internal examination is. It's an examination of a woman's most intimate parts. Don't ask me why, but these things are necessary from time to time. Dr. Weber told me to take off my clothing and put on a white gown. It was like the gown you wore when you had your tonsils taken out. Then he asked me to recline on a big funny table and he put my legs in a pair of stirrups. Then he put a pillow on my stomach so I couldn't see what he was doing down there. I can tell you there wasn't much dignity to any of this. Then he began to do things. He asked me if I liked it. Naturally I said no. He said of course you do, everybody does, it's only natural, and what a pretty young thing you are to have three children; what a pretty young woman and already three times a mother; so young and pretty, he kept saying, and do you like it and of course you do and you're the prettiest woman I've ever seen, Ann, and no one will ever know. He called me by my first name."

Whenever I saw my mother go through the house with the can of air-freshener I knew the Reverend Potter was expected. They had informal discussions every few weeks. She had known him since she was a girl in Alexandria. She talked of him often. She would run through the litany of his credits as if he were a make of automobile that had competed successfully in the various economy runs and endurance trials. The Boston Latin School. Harvard. The Protestant Episcopal Theological Seminary in Alexandria. Holy Trinity Church in Philadelphia. St. Bartholomew's in New York. Rector of Calvary Church in Old Holly. Added to the resonance of the man was his full name, William Stockbridge Potter; that Stockbridge was perfect, implying great girth and distinction, and it did not disappoint, for he was big, hearty and companionable. So I would see her spraying all the rooms with lavender sachet and I would find an inconspicuous chair in the living room and duck my head behind a copy of *Treasure Island* or the favorite sports stories of Bill Stern.

"Ann, this tea is delightful. You know how carefully I choose my words and I say this tea is delightful."

"What about the Judeo-Christian ethic?" she said.

"What about it, Ann?"

"I came across it in a magazine. I said to Clinton I must ask William Potter about this."

"Correct."

"Well, what about it?"

"I suppose it refers to certain common elements in our heritage and theirs. I suppose it distinguishes these elements from those of the Moslem ethic, if there is such a thing."

Reverend Potter sat in titanic splendor, slouched elegantly in the armchair, legs high and crossed at the knees, hands joined just beneath his lower lip, fingers barely touching. I was fascinated by the length of his fingers and by the small gray hair-fields above and below the joints of each finger. I had never seen such long fingers, nor fingers with so much hair growing on them. His black shoes gleamed. His hair was long and gray. He had harsh blue eyes and his voice seemed like steel struck on rock in a deep cave. The sight and sound of him filled me with fright and pleasure. To me, he could not have been more striking if he were an Abyssinian chieftain. But despite the beauty of his voice, there was something odd about the way he spoke. He often inserted long pauses between sentences and even words. Sometimes he would not respond to my mother's simplest question without a full minute's pause. Listening to him had its own measure of suspense. I used to imagine words tangled up in his throat and I would silently encourage them to spring out. There were times, the longest pauses, the slow hinging and unhinging of his jaw, the tentative sound echoing up his larynx, when he appeared to be on the verge of a torrential belch. It was part of his fascination. When he did speak finally, there seemed to be a curious disparity between the sounds he made and the movement of his lips; somehow they did not quite mesh. Perhaps the long pauses, the expectation, created an illusion of imbalance, but it seemed real enough then. It wasn't until years later, when I joined the network, that I found a term which perfectly described the way his words issued from an unrelated mouth. William Stockbridge Potter was out of sync.

"What about death?" she said.

"Ah."

"I don't think I could bear it. What can people do who are afraid to die? I saw my father die. It was slow and agonizing."

"This is one of the basic questions of our time," he said. "If we knew how to make a good job of death, it wouldn't be so frightful, would it? The famous prizefighter Joe Louis has been quoted as saying that everybody wants to go to heaven but nobody wants to die. I've used that in many of my sermons. Laughter, ah, is a great catalyst. It eases tension and helps clear the atmosphere. I'm a great believer in the power of laughter. People think High Church is drab and humorless. This is nonsense."

"But what are we to do?" she said.

"We must draw up a blueprint for dying."

"I think it's all so stupid, this high-low business."

"Will I see you at evensong? And the boy?"

"By all means."

"I must be going."

"Next time I want to hear about the Oxford Tracts."

"I have plenty of ammunition on that subject. I've just been reading up on the great Alonzo Potter; no relation incidentally, although I admit to you in confidence that I cherish the happy coincidence of our names, the serpent of vanity notwithstanding."

"You haven't touched your cookies."

"I really must be going."

"And I want to hear more about death."

"I'll be ready," he said. "Now then, shall we stroll out through the garden?"

"There is no garden."

"Ah."

"Say goodbye, David."

"Your mother is a smart little gal, young man. She was one of the great young beauties of Virginia. And her generosity to the church knows no bounds. You're a very fortunate boy to be so tall and straight. He has your eyes, Ann. What do you want to be when you grow up?"

"A soldier," I said.

"He speaks out directly. I like that. Not a hint of equivocation in his voice. He's a fine-looking boy."

"We share each other's secrets," she said.

"Well done."

"Goodbye," I said.

"A soldier," he said. "I like that. No nonsense about this boy. If I had not become a minister of Christ, I would have become a soldier myself. They're not so very different, you know."

At Leighton Gage College I wanted to be known as Kinch. This is Stephen Dedalus' nickname in *Ulysses*, which I was reading at the time. But I soon learned that nobody at Leighton Gage had a nickname, except of the most disparaging kind. There were no athletic teams there either. There were no grades or formal examinations. There were no traditions. The faculty was good but somewhat lazy and I suppose the reverse could be said of the students.

At the beginning I became friendly with a boy named Leonard Zajac, who was known to the wits in the poetry society as Young Man Carbuncular. We had several classes together and I was impressed by his nervous high-speed humor, his iconoclasm, the way he turned familiar ideas around and gave fresh meaning to them without necessarily believing his own version more than the original. Leonard was a fat and lonely boy with furious purple inflammations all over the back of his neck. People spoke to him only when necessary and even the faculty tried to ignore him. His obesity, his poor complexion, his heavy ghetto clothing seemed tragically out of place in the sleek setting of southern California. Leonard spent a good deal of time in the library. He and I got along well. With his help I felt I could develop my mind into a fine cutting instrument. Kinch. The knife-blade. Leonard was generous with his time and ideas. It wasn't long before I began to imagine him as a brilliant satirist and social critic, a personage of Swiftian eminence, a post-Renaissance phenomenon, a bonfire around which we would all huddle for lessons and warmth. To me, at eighteen, there was a certain attraction to Leonard's kind of life. Chronic boils and obesity eliminate all possible illusions; snuggle up to loneliness and make the library your womb-home and chapel. Then it all crumbled. Leonard told me he was in love with Page Talbot. She was a Kansas girl with long blond hair, the kind of woman who looks absolutely stunning at a distance of ten feet; within closer range, however, Page's green eyes seemed washed out, her skin sallow, and the lack of expression on her face suggested lifelong bereavement over the death of a pet rabbit. But coming toward you or moving along in front with a barely manageable sway, in salt-bleached blue jeans and faded blue farmgirl shirt, Page could make you feel she was worth following, on foot, all the way back to Kansas City. In the library one day Leonard told me about his fantasies. He imagined making love to her underwater, on horseback, on top of professors' desks, inside phone booths. Then he said he wanted to be like me; he would give anything, he said, to be like me, trim, good-looking, popular. His confession forced some strange shift in the sheer balances of my mind. That night I visited Page Talbot in her room. I wore tan chinos, the closest I could come to the fresh creased suntans of the United States Army. I stood in the doorway and thought of Burt Lancaster standing in the rain waiting for Deborah Kerr to open the door. My career as an intellectual was over.

In junior year I met Ken Wild. I left my room one morning, late for class, and was going down the stairs, past the second floor, when I heard music, the deep bounce of a tenor saxophone. I stood there a moment, listening, then went down the corridor. The sound was coming from a record player turned up to what seemed full volume. A husky young man was sitting on the edge of the bed, forearms on knees, head faintly nodding. He was wearing red and black boxer's trunks, an Everlast trademark across the elastic band. He looked up briefly, cracking open a big grin, and waved me to a chair. About ten minutes later the record ended and the tone arm swung back.

"Coltrane," he said.

Wild was from Chicago, an ex-marine. We spent the rest of the morning listening to his records. I felt this music had been in me all along, the smoky blue smell of it, mornings in

Paris and cat intestines spilled on Lenox Avenue. I pleased myself by thinking, as white men will do, that some Afro-instinct burned in an early part of my being.

Wild and I were friends from the beginning. We argued, kidded, sparred with open hands, and committed the usual collegiate blasphemies of word and deed, using as our text the gleeful God-baiting of Buck Mulligan in the first few pages of *Ulysses*. That was our sacred scroll and we regretted that there had been no gray Jesuits to darken our childhoods and none now to swoop down on us with deathmask and Summa.

Both of us wrote poetry. I enjoyed strangling the words and trying to get them on paper still living but when I failed to finish what I had planned to do, or even to begin it, I was less than seriously troubled. After all I had my camera. But Wild went at it with total commitment, all or nothing, sending no envoys out to treaty with failure. We joined the school's poetry society so that we could stay away from their meetings and have our memberships revoked and then found a rival society. But we never bothered.

We used to go through anthologies, loving and hating all fierce gigantic talent. It was the loose image we picked out and petted, little boys in a lion kennel. Wild would go into a fine frenzy at these sessions, turning pages, jumping from book to book, shouting out the beatific phrases, and we would spin off into storms of laughter at the joy and wonder and misery of those lines. We tried to write with jazz and wine. But I guess I would have been better off in bed with Wendy Judd.

People dream of money and love. It was Wendy's ambition to be hired as an extra in a big-budget Technicolor movie. She had no illusions of stardom. Fragmentation, the settling of a myth into the realism of its component parts, had come to the West quite early, and Wendy was a native Californian. She would have been satisfied to get the back of her head in a movie, her revolutionary fist raised in a Bastille crowd scene. She spent a lot of time with Simmons St. Jean, who taught film theory and criticism at Leighton Gage. Simmons was only thirty or so but he tried to come on like the post-accident Montgomery Clift, a hollow echoing man. He worked on his pallor the way the rest of us teased our suntans. At the same time he tried to let his male students know that for an old man he was doing all right with the girlies. Since I majored in film and since Simmons considered me the man to beat for stud honors, we had a certain wary interest in each other. Our discussions were full of small-arms fire. Wendy Judd and I had coffee with him one day.

"I'm just fascinated by you kids," Simmons said. "I was with one of my students the other night, the other evening I should say, girl named Pamela something, and I was virtually in awe of her unselfconsciousness and total lack of provincialism. Her quiet command of her own feelings. You kids are so wonderfully free and open. You have none of the hangups I had in college. It's a beautiful thing to see."

"How come you look so tired and beat-up all the time?" Wendy said. "Not that it's not attractive."

"I'd just as soon not talk about myself. I've exhausted all hope of defining who or what I am. Perhaps some time, Wendy, if Dave permits, I'll tell you the story of my life. But for the time being I'd much rather listen to you two talk about yourselves. One of the many pleasures of teaching at a place like this is the uninhibited exchange between students and faculty. There's really nothing like it anywhere in the country. Dave, what kind of thesis are you planning this year?"

"I'm shooting it in the desert, Simmons. It'll be almost pure imagery. A small shade of meaning for those who crave it."

"I thrive on imagery. It seems to have a laxative effect."

"David showed me the thing he made last year," Wendy said. "Wasn't it wild, Simmons—all those reflections and shadows?"

"He didn't like it," I said.

"I wouldn't say that, Dave. It had its moments."

"He said it was meekly derivative. He mentioned, I believe, the early Kurosawa."

"The prenatal Kurosawa would have been more like it," Simmons said. "I'd dearly love to pursue this further but I've got a class in ten minutes. My freshmen tend to get anxious if I don't show up on time. Father figure and all that."

"I'm going that way," Wendy said.

"I thought you and I might drive over to the lake," I said. "Why don't you come along, Simmons? We never see you at the lake. We look for you, Wendy and I, but we never see you."

"I've got a class to get to. Which way are you heading, Wendy?"

"We're going to the lake," I said. "If you don't have a bathing suit, Simmons, you can borrow one of mine."

"I'm sure you have enough swimwear for a brigade of life-guards, Dave, but I'm afraid I'll have to take a rain check on that."

"It's not raining."

"You can use some sun," Wendy said.

"You have to get out there and cop those rays, Simmons. You're spending too much time in the dark."

"I console myself with the thought that nothing very interesting happens in well-lighted places."

"Pow," Wendy said.

Having secured the more essential of victories, I did not dispute the loser's right to get in the last word. Everybody knows how much solace the older generation takes in saving face.

Although there were no athletic teams at Leighton Gage, we were probably more serious about sports than the average student body. But we played games of a different kind—non-team, swift, dangerous. One of the important things money buys is speed. Speed and a glimpse of death. We drove sports cars and motorcycles in informal competition, rode beach buggies over the desert, raced motorboats on the artificial lake near the campus. Several students owned planes and if you were friendly with one of them you could go up to L.A. for party weekends and on the return flight test your desire for an early poetic death. The force behind these activities was essentially spiritual. There were many injuries, several fatalities, and we reacted to these with professional dispassion. That's something money can't buy. But either you learn it or you go back to baseball.

Page Talbot's father bought her a fiberglass runabout for her birthday and had it sent out to the anti-lake about a mile north of the campus. She painted it lilac and yellow and planned to install a bedroom canopy until somebody talked her out of it. The first time she asked me to go sailing, as she called it, the outboard fell off and while we waited for someone to tow us in we sat there drinking beer, drifting in small circles, relatively content, pretending we were on an Arab dhow lazing through the papyrus slogs of the Sudanese Nile.

"I made it with Ken Wild last night," she said.

"I didn't know you knew each other."

"We didn't."

"Well I don't want to hear about it."

"He's nice really."

"Did I tell you I'm thinking of getting married? I met this girl back home last summer and we've been corresponding. She's in London now touring the epitaphs. I've been thinking of popping the old question."

"Frankly I don't know why anybody our age would want to get married," Page said. "Frankly it sounds to me like the end of the road."

"Don't you have an urge to play house?"

"If it's a triplex on Montego Bay."

"Tell me about Wild," I said. "Is he good in bed? Is he better than I am? I don't have to know any details. Just say yes or no. It's important."

The Young Man Carbuncular vanished from the campus

three months before graduation. Nobody knew where he went. I thought his disappearance might arouse some guilt in those who had ignored and ridiculed him. Instead it became a joke. People said he had gone to Tibet to find a holy man who might cure his boils; or was wandering in the desert, delirious, singing hit songs of the late forties; or had barricaded himself in the men's room of the library with a submachine gun, several hundred rounds of ammo and a can of spray-on deodorant. I went to Leonard's room one night hoping to find some indication of his whereabouts, a passage underlined in a book, a road map, a letter from his parents. All I found was a piece of paper on which was written:

> Something tells me
> that I shall dream tonight of newspapers
> wrapped in fish

Leonard Zajac had been four years with us, a man for all his waddling pity, and the mystery of his flight, perhaps in overwhelming dread, was met with nothing more than mild relief. He returned the day after commencement. Some of us were still on campus, loading up cars, completing plans for vacations in the Andes, on the Balearic Islands, aboard schooners bound for the East Indies. In three months we would all have to start earning a living and there was a pitch of hysteria to the dialogue of that last day. Merry and I, who would be starting east in an hour or so, were talking with some friends on the quadrangle when Leonard touched me on the shoulder to whisper hello and goodbye. He said he had come to pick up his books. He had been living with the Havasupai Indians in Arizona, he said, and he planned to return immediately and to remain forever. When he asked me what my own plans were, I could only shrug. His inflammations were gone. He appeared to have lost about forty pounds. I did not introduce him to the others because, for the moment, I had forgotten his name.

Everything begins in California. It is like the hip lexicon of the ghetto; as soon as Madison Avenue breaks the code, Harlem devises a new one. So with California and New York. When surfing and nudity moved east, California got all decked out in flowing madras and went indoors to discover the commune. I liked it out there and might have stayed. But my father was back east, living alone in the music-box house, insistent on remaining. We all have something we are trying to forget. If we're smart we take off for parts unknown. But my father could not leave the house and I didn't have enough sense to remain at the shallow end of the continent. So I began to swim.

Big Bob Davidson first showed up in Old Holly when I was eighteen; that would make Jane twenty-one. Bob was working in New York at the time and he came out one weekend to meet the family. I was home for the summer, working on my golf and tennis, doing a bit of sailing. Jane suggested I might spend a few hours with Bob. Play some tennis and have a few beers. Make him feel welcome. So he and I drove over to the club, trying not to be too polite with each other, sparring easily, probing for sensibilities. Bob seemed a nice enough guy. He was tall and heavy. His face was an odd wet pink color, as if a dog had been licking it, and his blond hair was very straight. He wore his sport shirt outside his pants, a faded checked shirt with a pencil clipped to the breast pocket. As it turned out, Bob always had a pencil clipped to the breast pocket of his shirt or suit jacket and whenever I saw him I had the feeling he was going to take out an invoice pad and start writing an order for three dozen lawn mowers.

We changed and began playing. My game was better than ever and I thought I'd take it easy at the outset and see what kind of pace Bob had in mind. It soon became clear that he was out to destroy me. He ranged all over the court, grim and dusty, playing in a low cloud of clay, tersely announcing the score before every serve. The harder he tried, the worse he got. His serve was erratic and he had no backhand to speak of. I was just beginning to get bored when I saw my father sitting on one of the benches that lined the courts. After the first set he called me over.

"I just got here," he said. "Who's winning?"

"I took the first set."

"What to what?"

"I think it was six–one. Bob's keeping score. Tell you the truth, I'm not very involved in this particular match."

"Well, get involved," he said. "I want you to whip his ass. I want you to beat him in straight sets. I want to walk into that house later and tell them it was no contest. Straight sets. That's what I want to say. The kid beat him in straight sets."

"Don't you like him, dad?"

"It's not a question of whether or not I like him. I don't even know the guy. It's a family thing. It's a question of him coming into our house and Christ only knows what goes on between him and Jane. Jesus, look at him. He's so goddamn big. He could hurt her or something. For all I know he's the sweetest guy in the world. But that's not the point. It's a family thing, kid. Now go get him. Go run his ass ragged."

"Right," I said.

I beat him in straight sets, easily, embarrassing him, taunting him with soft raindrop shots which sent him from one end of the net to the other, then drilling a hummer past his ear. When it was over my father clapped me on the back, rubbed my neck, congratulated me on what he called a truly historic blitz, a glorious rout. All at the expense of the interloper, it was one of those strange bursts of bloodlove which are both puzzling and overpowering in the dimensions of their joy. I told my father I had barely worked up a sweat and he laughed at that as if it were quite the funniest thing he had ever heard. Then we walked to the locker room with our arms around each other's shoulders. Big Bob preceded us like a snowplow.

*   *   *

My father drank Irish stout. He bought most of his suits in England. He liked Dutch cigars and drove Italian and British automobiles. Most of the books in his library were about London before the Great Fire and the American West before the Little Bighorn. His shoes were handcrafted in London by a firm which had cast impressions of his feet the day after they first stepped on British soil. Although he didn't ride much he had several Western saddles in his den as well as a small collection of Winchester 73s and one Sharps .50 caliber rifle which he liked to call his buffalo gun. He favored German cameras and smoked Danish pipes that cost almost two hundred dollars each.

He used to have lunch at the Playboy Club about twice a week. Later he began accompanying friends or clients to their clubs for lunch—the Harvard or Princeton Club, the New York A.C., the Yale, the New York Yacht Club. My father was a graduate of Long Island University. He used a brand of men's cologne that was aged in oak casks and blended with over three hundred ingredients. The cars he owned at one time or another included an MG, a Jaguar, a Ferrari, an Aston-Martin and a Maserati. I don't know whether or not all that horsepower was supposed to take the curse off LIU.

"A man works hard to get two hundred thousand dollars," he said to me once as we drove through the outskirts of town in the Mark IX Jag. "You save, you finagle, you invest. You work yourself up to x-amount of dollars and if you plan well and get lucky in the market you can begin to build something for your family. That's what makes a democracy worth all the sweat and corruption. Security for your wife and children after you're gone. What if something happens to me? Your mother hates to hear me talk like that but you have to prepare for such contingencies. That's your job as head of a family in a free republic. I've got about nine different kinds of policies that'll provide for you and your mother and your sisters if anything should happen to me. It could happen any time, you know. Right now a dog could walk across the road, I swerve the car, and bang. Understand what I'm talking about? The turning point was the money my father left me. That put us over the top. But if you're not careful, all you get is stomach trouble. I'll tell you a true story right out of one of the country's most distinguished scientific journals. They pulled an experiment on these two monkeys. They gave them electric shocks every sixty seconds. Now the first monkey had a button and all he had to do was press it and he wouldn't get any shock. The second monkey also had a button but it was completely useless. Eventually monkey-A caught on to the gimmick and started pressing the button like mad to avoid that juice. Whereas monkey-B realized his button wasn't worth shit and he just squatted in the corner, scratching himself and getting jolted every minute. So what happens? The first monkey gets stomach ulcers and kicks off in two weeks. The second monkey, who had resigned himself to the shocks, lives happily ever after. That little experiment is a moral for our time. It shows the price you have to pay for working yourself up to a decision-making post. I'll have to show you around the office sometime. You'll see sixty–five executive monkeys weeping into their telephones and pissing blood. That's the kind of business your old man is in. But don't worry about me, kid. I've got cast iron in my gut and I'm an odds-on favorite to pull through. In my heart I'm deeply conservative. I come from a long line of secret Presbyterian drinkers. My grandfather was a blacksmith in Sag Harbor. What was the point I was trying to make?"

One summer evening my father came home from work and told the family what had happened on the 6:17 out of Grand Central. There was blood all over his suit and shirt.

"We were all reading our newspapers. All up and down the car you saw nothing but newspapers. The conductor came around and started punching tickets. At this point we were still underground and I remember I was just finishing up the stock page when the train boomed out of the tunnel and started going through Harlem. That's when the first rock hit. It hit a window across the aisle from me and glass went flying in every direction. Strange thing is nobody said a word. The next rock hit on my side of the train and the window two windows in front of me shattered and then I realized we were being bombarded by more than one or two wise guys and I looked out my window and then out the window across the aisle and there they were, standing up above us behind the fence, Puerto Rican kids, and they were flinging rocks like crazy, dozens of kids, a whole row of them on each side of the train, laughing and heaving rocks at us. Nobody was reading newspapers now. We were all scrambling under the seats and again it was strange but nobody said anything. It was as though we knew it was coming sooner or later. And today was the day. Rocks were bouncing off the side of the train and smashing through the windows. Little kids. Twelve, thirteen years old. Anyway it stopped then. It stopped for about ten seconds and we started coming up when the next barrage hit. These were Negro kids and they really busted up that train. Negro kids on rooftops. More windows went and there was somebody moaning at the back of the car, some guy either hit by a rock or who cut himself on the glass that was all over the floor. We thought it was over when we got out of Harlem and we started pushing the glass off our seats and a few guys even came out with some funny remarks that had us all laughing even though they weren't really funny. It was shock-laughter if you know what I mean. But the rocks started flying again in the south Bronx. All through the Bronx we got hit in flurries. It wasn't as concentrated there for some reason. But that's where some little spic sharpshooter hit my window and a piece of glass caught me on the hand. It finally stopped up around Woodlawn. The inside of that train looked like a tornado hit it. Glass, rocks, newspapers were all over the place. Nobody seemed outraged or bitter. Just mildly upset. And when I got off the train there were three or four other men getting off with me and we walked to our cars and nobody even mentioned that we had nearly been killed back there. Those little bastards. What did we ever do to them?"

"You moved to the suburbs," my sister Mary said. "Have a nice day at the office tomorrow, daddy. And if you decide to work late and stay in the city overnight, we'll all understand."

St. Dymphna's was located in southwestern New Hampshire and it was a nice place to be educated. It was quiet and picturesque. The leaves turned color in autumn and there was plenty of snow in winter. Everybody dressed neatly. Here and there a building was showing signs of falling apart but this didn't bother anybody; it was one of the traditions of the well-bred Northeast. The staff, wholly Episcopalian clergy at one time, now included many laymen, a few Unitarian ministers, a Duck River Baptist, and a lovable Irish janitor named Petey who was always challenging freshmen to identify the Four Horsemen of Notre Dame. The student body was composed almost wholly of cynical little anti-religious boys. My guidance counselor was a layman and on Reciprocity Day he introduced himself to my mother and father.

"My name is Thomas Fearing. My clubs are the Millbrook Golf and Tennis, the Rhinebeck Tennis and Saddle, the Players of New York, the Nassau of Princeton, the Princeton of New York, and the Church Street Social of Millbrook."

"Most impressive," my father said.

During my third year a controversy developed. There was a boy on the basketball team named Brad Dennis who used to make the sign of the cross before taking foul shots. Brad's mother was a very militant Roman Catholic and apparently she had not only ordered him to bless himself before taking foul shots but had also told him that St. Dymphna was an exclusively Catholic saint and that the Episcopalians, as nice and neat as they were, had no claim to her patronage and absolutely no right to use her name in connection with one of their prep schools, as fine and proper as that school might

155

be. Brad spread the word and for his trouble got himself black-belted on the ass by the dean of discipline. This only aroused him to greater fervor and to an early-Christian lust for martyrdom. I began to get interested. Brad was like an anarchist running loose in the Pentagon. He distributed literature published by the Knights of Columbus and he offered to debate anyone his age on the relative merits of the world's great religions. Some of us would meet illegally in his room after lights-out to hear him discourse on the transubstantiation and papal infallibility. It was evident that some of his zeal was being transmitted to the small circle of disciples which had gathered about him. The student body began to take sides and the subjects of free speech and the right to proselytize soon became the main topics of conversation. Since the faculty knew little or nothing of Brad's post-flogging activities, there was an exciting underground feeling to those days. Many sided with Brad simply because of his run-in with the dean of discipline, who was known as the Son of Dracula and was universally feared and despised. Others seemed genuinely interested in the doctrines he promulgated. Those who were against him called him a papist, a crossback, an anti-intellectual and a pissyhole. I decided it was time for me to get to the root of the controversy and that was St. Dymphna herself. I asked Brad for one of his leaflets. It was put out by the Franciscan Missions and it had these words on the front page:

ST. DYMPHNA
(pronounced dimf-nah)

PATRONESS OF THOSE AFFLICTED
WITH NERVOUS DISORDERS
AND MENTAL ILLNESS

"The Nervous Breakdown Saint"

It turned out that St. Dymphna had been born in Ireland, the only child of the pagan king of Oriel. When her mother died, Dymphna's father decided to seek a second wife. Ultimately he concluded there was only one female worthy enough—his own daughter. Dymphna, who had been baptized by a priest of the church, was fourteen years old. With all the persuasiveness he could muster, the king outlined his scheme to his trembling daughter. Dymphna sought safety in flight, settling finally in Belgium along with her confessor. Spies, however, traced the exiles' route and it all ended when the king drew his sword and struck off the head of his only child. In time, many people with mental problems were cured due to the intercession of St. Dymphna, whose fame as the nervous breakdown saint gradually spread from Belgium to Ireland and thence to almost every corner of the globe.

The story fascinated me. I felt much the same way I would months later when Jane would read her YWCA notes on the primitive religions of the world. All those magnificently demented people made me feel small and well-dressed. I even liked St. Dymphna's father. I pictured him with a red beard, drinking mead from a ram's horn and secretly worrying about his masculinity. I went to Brad Dennis' room to return the leaflet and hopefully to engage in a fiery conversation about science, religion and eternity. Miles Warren was in there with Brad. Miles, fresh from two weeks of atheism, was the most brilliant student at St. Dymphna's. When I gave Brad the leaflet and told him how much I had liked the story of St. Dymphna, he said he had given me the wrong material. This is a childish piece of whimsy, he said. With that, he handed me a booklet titled *Some Preliminary Concepts of Metaphysical Psychology.*

"The Little Sisters of the Poor are the only people who believe that kid stuff about virgin saints," he said. "The modern Catholic is a hard-nosed kind of guy who asks piercing questions. The whole thing can be brought down to a question of metaphysics and first principles. Whatever is, is."

"What about the Inquisition?" Miles said.

"The modern Catholic isn't afraid of that question anymore."

"What about all those popes who had wives and mistresses?" Miles said.

"Speaking retroactively, we can say they weren't truly part of the mystical body of Christ in the doctrinal sense. It's like the lying and cheating General Motors does. You still need cars."

"If a tree falls in the forest," Miles said, "and there's no one around to hear it fall, does that tree in fact make a sound when it hits earth or is the phenomenon of sound contingent on the presence of someone or something which possesses the faculty of hearing? Is the absolute dependent on an agent who can interpret it? Or is the absolute what the word itself implies? The question is as old as Plato."

"Whatever is, is," Brad said.

The best part of prep school was suiting up for a baseball or basketball game. I loved that phrase—*suiting up*. We would sit around the locker room mentally preparing ourselves for the game. We had all read about pro football players who become so tense prior to kickoff that they get sick to the stomach. There was a kid on our basketball team named Rich Higgins who would always go into the small toilet just off the locker room and try to throw up. He never got any further than the dry heaves but it made us feel good to know that one of our teammates was so affected by the impending contest that he was in the toilet with his finger down his throat. As soon as Rich Higgins returned, drained of emotion if nothing else, Coach Emery would say: "This is it! Let's suit up!" And we would all suit up. It was more fun to suit up for baseball games because there was more to wear. Brad Dennis was the shortstop on the baseball team. He never blessed himself, as he did in basketball, but with his bat he used to make the sign of the cross in the dirt just outside the batter's box before he stepped in to hit. He batted eighth in the order, which brought about a mild complaint from his mother.

America, then as later, was a sanitarium for every kind of statistic. We took care of them. We tried to understand them. We did what we could to make them well. Numbers were important because whatever fears we might have had concerning the shattering of our minds were largely dispelled by the satisfaction of knowing precisely how we were being driven mad, at what decibel rating, what mach-ratio, what force of aerodynamic drag. So there was a transferred madness, a doubling, between the numbers themselves and those who made them and cared for them. We needed them badly; there is no arguing that point. With numbers we were able to conceal doubt. Numbers rendered the present day endurable, heralded the impressive excesses of the future and stocked with a fine deceptive configuration our memories, such as they were, of the past. We were all natural scientists. War or peace, we thrived on the body-count.

Numbers matter less now that the adding machines, the super-calculators, the numerical systems and sub-systems have been uninvented. However, thinking back, I recall how important it was for me, personally, to define a situation, or a period of time, with as many numbers as I could assemble. They seemed the very valets of clarity. If I were on my death-bed today, and did not know the date, my cells would probably refuse to surrender. Without a calendar, a stopwatch, a measuring cup on the night table, I couldn't possibly know how to die.

It was in the winter of my fifteenth year that Mary met Arondella. This means that Mary was nineteen at the time. It also means that Jane was eighteen, that my best friend Tommy was sixteen, that Kathy Lovell was fourteen, that my father was forty-two and my mother thirty-seven. That was the winter in which Tommy and I first took Kathy to the yacht club and it was the winter before the summer in which, age sixteen, I sat through two showings of *From Here to Eternity* starring Burt Lancaster. That same summer was the summer of the party.

Excepting Mary, no one in the family ever referred to Arondella by anything but his last name, and that only rarely. The second time they saw each other was on Christmas Eve. After she'd left to meet him somewhere, the rest of us sat in the living room looking at the tree.

"I wonder how old he is," Jane said. "She won't tell me a thing so I wouldn't be surprised if he's a lot older than she is."

"It's not his age I'm worried about as much as what he does for a living," my father said.

"Mary says he's in the rackets," I said.

"Yeah, well, you never know when Mary's telling the truth and when she's playing games. If he is in the rackets, all hell is going to break loose around here. No daughter of mine is going to be seen dead with any two-bit racky. I'll break both his arms for him. Wait and see if I don't."

"Clinton, your bark has always been worse than your bite. Now tell the truth, dear, hasn't it? You're forever threatening to dismember someone. But when the time comes I look around and where's Clinton? Oh, he's in the den, mother, polishing his saddles. Jane, I swear to you if fire ever breaks out in this house, you just head straight for the den and there will be your daddy, polishing his saddles. Fire, plague or famine, there you'll be, Clinton, far from the madding crowd."

"Let's unwrap the presents and get it over with," Jane said.

"I think we should wait for Mary to come home. That's always been the tradition in this house and I don't see why we should alter it now simply because she's taken leave of her senses temporarily. We'll wait for Mary."

"What if he comes back with her?" I said.

"Your father will suggest that he leave. There are diplomatic ways of handling such things. I see no reason to hurt the man's feelings."

"What if he won't go? If he's in the rackets, he's probably

not used to getting pushed around. Did you see *Cry of the City*, Jane? Victor Mature and Richard Conte. Richard Conte plays a gangster and Victor Mature is his old buddy from the same neighborhood who became a detective instead."

"Is that what you do up in New Hampshire?" my father said. "Go to the movies every night? It's costing me a small fortune to send you to that school."

Mary was not a pretty girl. But there was an animation to her face, an intelligence, which nullified her plainness. She read her favorite authors in curiously appropriate ways—Proust supinely, Faulkner with bourbon, O'Casey wearing my father's turtleneck. She was a fine swimmer and tennis player, although at times there seemed a touch of condescension in her attitude toward sport; it was all so easy, so predictable in outcome. She treated the family almost the same way she might treat her tennis racket, with rough affection and a charming lighthearted contempt. The latter did not extend to me, however. Her kid brother. I think she loved me very much. Almost everything my father said was received by Mary in a spirit of high delight. "Daddy," she used to say, "you're almost as funny as Eisenhower." But he was not delighted by her as much as bewildered. I think she made my father question the structure of his own nature, for to him it was surely apparent that only the rebel mischief of his seed could have produced this stray comedienne.

Mary and I were playing checkers in the attic. A cold rain was falling. She was drinking rum, neat, from a beer glass, and smoking a cigarette like Lauren Bacall, the cool appeal of those sleepy rhythms. Although it was late afternoon she was still in pajamas.

"How did you meet him?" I said.

"Thereby hangs a tale, brother. But I may as well let you in on it, if only to forestall another trouncing by the checker king of Westchester. After I made my controversial decision to leave school, one little thing kept nagging at me. What would I do next? I didn't want to come back here, as we all know by now, but I wasn't very anxious to get an apartment in the city and pursue a career in stenography either. The thought alone made my knees buckle. All I knew was that I had to get out of college. Massachusetts is no place to get educated, despite all the raving about intellectual ferment. My most vivid memory is of earnest young men banging their pipes into ashtrays, a sight that depresses me more than I can say. I was sick of the whole thing. I was sick of hearing the same expressions over and over. Just constantly. The same phrases, sentences, paragraphs. I'm hypersensitive, I know, but I was under the impression that up there, if nowhere else, my petty talent for finding fault might be allowed to dwindle and die. It was a false impression. The whole place was too inbred for me. The whole educational complex and the particular lollipop factory I was privileged to attend. The passion for ritual was overpowering. And of course nobody learned anything. One nice and bitchy memory I'll keep. Our democratic little sorority had a sort of informal initiation process. About one-fifth of us were in on it. The others thought it much too unladylike. It was simple. Whenever a new girl sat down to her first dinner in the house, one of us would say to another: Pass the motherfucking carrots, please. Or words to that effect. The response would be in a similar vein and we'd usually keep it up all through the meal, tossing off the worst obscenities imaginable and doing it with a certain politesse, as if we were discussing sisal-growing in the Bahamas. By the time dessert arrived, the newcomer was in an advanced state of shock. I'm getting way off the mark, aren't I?"

"Arondella," I said.

"Want a sip of rum?"

"Okay."

"I finally packed it in," Mary said. "I took a cab to town and got on the first bus to Boston. Then I took another cab to the railroad station. I paid the driver, stepped onto the sidewalk and there he was. Sitting in that blue whale of his. Combing his hair. It was forty degrees but he had the top down. He was wearing a light windbreaker with the sleeves rolled all the way up. He was sitting on the passenger's side of the front seat. He put the comb away and placed his right arm out over the top of the door. The arm was flexed and his bicep was pressing against the door so that it would look enormous. I was trying to carry two heavy suitcases, an overnight bag and a purse. And I knew he was watching me. He said hey. I stopped and looked at him—he obviously thought he was God's gift to the virgins of Boston—and he said I'll take you wherever you want to go. Anywhere in the continental United States. I said New York. He said hey, that was the one place I really meant. And we both smiled. Leslie Howard and Ingrid Bergman. Later I found out he had been sent to Boston to kill a man."

"Did he do it?"

"The man had been arrested the night before. Some kind of narcotics charge. Eventually he was killed in prison."

"Last week daddy said if Arondella's in the rackets you won't be allowed to see him anymore."

"David, I won't be living here much longer."

"Are you going away with him?"

"Yes."

"When?"

"I don't know," she said. "He's got a wife and three children. It's a delicate situation to say the least. All sorts of relatives are applying all sorts of pressures."

"What exactly does he do in the rackets?"

"He goes places. He's in Syracuse now. He makes business trips. That's what he calls them. His territory seems to be upstate and New England."

"Does he kill people?"

"I imagine so. He as much as told me. I don't think the Boston trip was an isolated instance. But there are different kinds of death, David. And I prefer that kind, his kind, to the death I've been fighting all my life."

"Give me some more rum," I said.

"Don't you love it when it rains like this? So gray and dark. I love dark chill days. We're doing just the right thing for a day like this. Sitting in the attic drinking rum. It's nice up here, isn't it? Those skinny gray trees outside and the sound of the rain. We should have some music. Organ music would be perfect."

"I'll go get the radio."

"Leave this house," she said. "As soon as you can, get out of here. Run like hell, David. This place is haunted and everybody in it is haunted. Mother is terribly ill. And if she goes, if she slides all the way out, she'll try to take you with her. I know her, David. I'm the only one who knows her."

Meredith and I were married between my junior and senior years at Leighton Gage. A week before the event, I got a letter from Ken Wild.

I'm writing because I want somebody to tell me whether I am alive or dead. I have been asked that question recently and I couldn't think of an answer. So if you get this letter, write back as soon as you can. This way I'll know I'm alive. Are you really going to marry Miss Dairy Products USA?

I'm in the Michigan woods photosynthesizing. My big problem this summer, aside from life and death, is that I don't have any classes to stay away from. A man should never be left without a class to cut. I flew up here in my father's company's plane, which was full of territorial managers on their way to hunting lodge for business meeting and ribald chortling. Two thousand pounds of condemned pork. Just before we were due to land, an engine flamed out. First thing I did was put out my cigarette. I believe this is called coolness under fire. But a second later I found myself on the edge of panic. Nobody else seemed even slightly upset. Were they really a planeload of Zen masters? Then we were landing, no trouble at all, and I was filled with disappointment. Because it had not been enough. I wanted to land in flames with crash-wagons screaming down the runway. Perhaps you understand this sort of pathos.

Dostoyevsky sat next to me
barbering his humorous fingernails

I fish, I hunt, I write my wounded lines. My father wants me to join the firm after graduation. For the moment all I have to do is assure him I'll think about it seriously. Everybody craves assurance. It's the coin they insert in reality. It doesn't matter whether anything comes out of the machine as long as they get their money back. What a pity it is that you're reading this with such lack of compassion. Saying poor dumb Wild he's like everybody else, pissing all over his own toes. I am writing a mock-epic poem—you won't believe this—I am writing a mock-epic poem about a boy who grows up among wolves somewhere in Siberia. Several distinguished publishers have indicated a wary interest.

Write to me with news of the archduke. Jesus I hate this kind of letter. If only I were less sane. I could write poems the size of cathedrals!

I had taken Wild's letter, along with paper and pen and three cans of beer, to my favorite spot in Old Holly. This was the slope behind the firehouse, a green and treeless place, always private, facing west so that the grass turned slowly golden green as the sun circled toward the far hills. The slope dropped a hundred feet or so to a sort of lesser valley, a barren area of boulders, stunted trees and the scratched earth of a dried-out creekbed. Across the valley was a small hill, and on top of it, at the eastern limit of a large estate, was a pasture; and from the slope you could see the horses moving slowly, heads down, the lovely mild curves of their necks, grazing, moving against the more distant hills; or standing, where the hills dropped away as if to graze also on some low meadow, standing against the sky and the rich citrus setting of the sun.

Wild, of course, had yet to meet Meredith. Miss Dairy Products USA was a name of my own making and Wild was merely repeating my own bad joke. I had known, as junior year drew to a close, that I would ask her to marry me. I also knew, pending her acceptance, that we would return together to Leighton Gage for my final year. My classmates in their evolving worldliness would consider Merry too pure, too naive, too inexperienced to be let loose outside of Disneyland. So I tried to prepare them—a joke here, an anecdote there, an occasional nervous quip. And as I said these things I would often think of her, in a London park or square, on a bench beneath some granite admiral, and she'd be so pretty, nodding as the pigeons nodded, pouting at the pouting children in their prams, so pretty and white, those thrifty breasts, salvation of Western man, furling a yellow umbrella. Some good-bad nights I spent, loving my self-hatred. I was trying to prepare them, that's all; take the glint off their eager scalpels. I punished myself by going for long underwater swims in the artificial lake, coming up gasping, the sky regarding me through misty spectacles, quite curiously. And still I tried to prepare them. These are the things men do when they have orchestrated their lives to the rumble of public opinion. Merry arrived with me on campus the following autumn. They all said she was a nice girl and seven of us took a mass touchless shower.

Writing to Wild on the slope I did not mention her. I made no reference to the flaming engine and his soul's need for crisis. I said nothing of his mock-epic poem, which was obviously just another scenic dream. In fact I wrote just one line: *I didn't get your letter*. Then I sipped beer for an hour. I thought of adding something about his desire for less sanity. Wild truly believed that he would never be a great poet because he was not sufficiently insane. I tended to agree with him but I didn't bother getting into it. I was on the third can of beer by this time and it tasted warm and flat. The sun had set and it was time to be getting home.

Even from this long way off, in the magnet-grip of an impending century, it is painful to write about her. It has taken me this long just to organize my thoughts. And although I think I have come to terms with everything, it will be interesting to see whether I can put it on paper clearly and openly. Or whether I must blow some smoke into this or that passage—some smoke to hide the fire.

One summer she bought two dolls, one for Jane and one for Mary. Jane put both dolls on her dresser. But my mother objected and so Mary's doll was put into Mary's abandoned room. Jane was always trying to discuss these things with me. In her confusion she was comforted by the sound of voices. It was an article of her faith that tragedy could be averted, or at least detained in the sweep of its tidal and incomprehensible darkness, by two reasoning people sitting in a familiar room and discussing the matter. I didn't want to talk about it. I feared silence less than the involvement of words. Distance, silence, darkness. In the vastness of these things I hoped to evade all need to understand and to cancel all possibility of explaining. Jane came into my room with a pot of tea and closed the door behind her.

"What are we going to do?" she said.

"About what?"

"You know what."

"There's nothing to do," I said. "We should see about a doctor. Some shrink on Park Avenue. But that's up to daddy, isn't it? I'd like to finish this book and get it back to the library before they close."

"What are we going to do about the dolls?"

"Leave them where they are and forget it."

"What do you think it means, David?"

"How the hell do I know? Now let me finish this book in peace."

"You can finish the book tomorrow."

"It'll be overdue."

"It must have something to do with our childhoods," Jane said. "She must be trying to make up for something."

"Sure. Childhood. Absolutely."

"I'm trying to remember whether I had any dolls like this

167

when I was little. Maybe we wanted this particular kind of doll and she didn't buy them because they were very expensive. They look expensive. I wish Mary was here."

"Look, she bought a couple of dolls. I don't understand what all the fuss is about. All I can say is I'm hurt that she didn't get anything for me. I wanted a fire engine. No fire gingin for Dabid. Dabid want big wed fire gingin. Dabid want to play with Jane and Mary. But mommy no buy him pwetty toys. Jane go way now so Dabid can wead his wittle book. Go way, Jane. Bye-bye. Jane go way. See Jane go. Jane is mad. See how mad Jane is. Jane slam Dabid's door. What a bad wittle girl. Jane all gone. Bye-bye, Jane."

The following April, at school, I was summoned to the telephone. It was my father. I remember what I was wearing. I was wearing white Top-Siders, white sweatsocks, a pair of olive chinos, and an old basketball jersey, white with blue trim and lettering, bearing the number nine. While we spoke I studied these articles of clothing intensely, as if keeping a mescaline vigil, my eyes seeking those immense explosions of beauty which are known to occur in the swirl of a grain of cloth.

"Bad news," he said.

"What is it?"

"Your mother's come down with something bad."

"She's sick? What is it?"

"I think she's dying, kid. They found it too late."

"What?" I said.

"What?"

"What did they find?"

"It looks like cancer. She doesn't want to go to the hospital."

"Cancer where? What part?"

"Take the first plane you can get. Wire and I'll meet you at the airport. You need money, I'll send it right out. But, look, hurry it up if you can. I should have called you weeks ago but I couldn't get myself to believe it. Everything's caving in. How the hell am I going to get in touch with Mary?"

"Where's the cancer?" I said.

"It's inside. It's in the female region. Look, can't we talk about it later? The doctor can tell you these things better than I can."

"Who's the doctor?"

"I got Weber."

"Get him the fuck out of there," I said. "I don't want Weber in there with her. Get another doctor. Anybody. Just get Weber out."

"It's all my fault," he said. "I've done everything wrong. I should have had her examined years ago. I should have had her examined for the other thing. Now there's this thing and it's too late. It's funny, kid, but she said the same thing you did. She said to get Weber out."

The plane, smelling vaguely of a child's vomit, ranged through stormclouds over the mountains and then broke clear into a calm blue afternoon. When I came out of the toilet a man stopped me to introduce himself. He said his wife would like to have my autograph. He said she had recognized me and he wondered if I would say hello to her on the way back to my seat. I told him she had mistaken me for someone else. He said it didn't matter; sign any name. And I did, I signed Buster Keaton, and when I stopped at her seat she took my hand and told me how very nice it was to meet me, how kind I was to interrupt my busy flying schedule in order to say hello to an admirer. An hour before we landed, the man came to my seat and offered me a twenty-dollar bill. Throughout the flight I kept getting mental pictures, against my will, of a growth inside my mother's womb.

The vase held seven wizened zinnias. My father whispered to me as she slept. It was the cervix. It had been discovered at an advanced stage. The doctor had wanted to take everything out. She had refused. She told my father that she had known about it for a long time. There had been unexplained bleeding and she told him she had felt the thing spreading, a radial plague, spreading like medieval death. Only her col-

169

lapse had told him that something was wrong. And she had refused to let them take anything out. God has been defeated, she said. And nothing anybody could do with their knives and clamps could ever change the fact of this defeat. He was in my body and I let Him out. He was the light of my body and I blew Him out. I believe in the Middle Ages. Fire for witches and plague for the sins of the world. I believe in ancient Egypt. These things were read to me in a garden full of sunlight by a beautiful and shining woman.

I opened the window. All the sweet reek of April filled the room and when I sighed it was almost possible to believe that something out there returned the sigh, something raving in the wind as it stirred those groping trees, something terrible on the grass, an instant in which nature gave in to rape, birdshaped and muddied in blood.

Jane touched me on the shoulder. The Reverend Potter was standing in the doorway like a ship in an upright bottle. My father leaned over to tie his shoe. I heard the bells of the ice-cream truck.

And in the morning I cut myself shaving. The bleeding stopped seven minutes later and I knew it was safe to go out.

"She was a different breed of cat," my father said. "She knew things nobody else knew. There was something magic about that woman. I don't believe in devils or saints or evil spirits. If you can't see it, is my theory, then it isn't there. But when your mother talked about these things it wasn't so easy to be a skeptic. Her mother drowned when she was a little girl. Maybe it did something to her. She remembered things that happened to her when she was only two years old. Maybe she just dreamed them but if they were just dreams she could make them sound deadly real. When she was carrying Mary, the minute she knew she was carrying Mary, she said it was a girl. She said it was the kite-soul of her mother. The kite-soul. It sounds Oriental, doesn't it? Something Buddhists or Hindus might believe in. Something to do with

170

reincarnation. I've never come across that phrase before or since. But to get back to Mary. Mary when she was born resembled me more than anyone. And when Jane was born it seemed a sure bet that the blond side of the family had been lost somewhere, your mother's side, and her mother's side. Ann felt desolate. I think she felt a whole race had faded away in some genetic catastrophe. Then you were born. She looked at you and said there he is, up out of the Irish seas like Lycidas. I loved her like I'll never love anything in this world again. When you were born she was happy and I didn't care what she said or how little I understood. She was happy and that was all that mattered. I have that much to thank you for anyway."

As she edged closer to death, he said, he began drinking heavily. Then one day he stopped drinking. He cut it out completely. He stopped drinking and got into his Maserati and took the first of a series of strange drives over the dark narrow roads around town. He would go out shortly after midnight and begin driving. He would take it up to 110, corner at 75, slam it way out to the fringe, the delicate pressure of his foot on the accelerator becoming part of a game of tender balances, and his hands on the wheel daring him closer to the bright splashing eyes in the adjacent lane. In the rain one night he went into a spin and ended up in a ditch. He got out of the car, bleeding around the head, and walked back to town. He went about a mile out of his way to pass through the Negro section of Old Holly, past the bars and old frame houses. He was waiting for a man with a knife to come out of a doorway at him. All this time, he told me, he had been trying to steal death from her body. By confronting it himself, he would keep it away from her. And on that last night a man leaned out of a bar and began following him. My father turned a corner, clenched his fists and waited. It was still raining and he could taste the rain mixed with blood running into his mouth. The man came around the corner and walked up to him and began to tapdance. My father stood there and the man danced around him, shuffling slowly and mumbling some old scat lyric. When he started to walk away, the man followed at a distance of several yards, gliding and tapping with the loose elegance of the indomitably drunk. My father walked backwards for almost half a block, watching the man come closer. Then he turned quickly and began to run, and he could hear the feet still tapping behind him, diminishing now, and the voice growing dimmer, a weary moan from swamps or cotton, words of an unknown language.

For several years I had thought of my father as the witness. Now, at her death, he became more than that. Our bond tightened and he closed in on me. We stood on the grass with scores of people. The splendor of her coffin was a comfort to everyone. I watched them and knew they were proud of her. To be buried in such luxury. Surely her life must have been something of a grand episode. For a moment I thought of those fabled khans and their nymphomaniacs who are always crashing into trees somewhere between Paris and Nice. There is substance to most clichés and we admire these men and women for having the wit to die as they have lived. The thought passed quickly and then down went mother in her silver Ferrari, a single rose clinging to the lid.

"She's watching us," my father said. "You think she's down there but she's not. Not her. She's watching us. She's watching to see what we're going to do to each other."

When Meredith returned from England she got a secretarial job in Manhattan. I went into the city one day to buy some shoes and we met later for lunch.

"How's the job coming along?"

"I love it," she said.

"Back in the swing of things yet? I guess it takes a while. That was quite a vacation."

"New York is the most exciting place in the world to work. London is fun to walk around in and New York is fun to work in."

"I missed you," I said. "I guess you could tell that from my letters."

"They were nice letters. They were very creative. I can't tell you how sorry I was to hear about your mother."

"I'm asking you to marry me."

"I'm not the one you need," she said.

"Two daiquiris on the rocks."

"You need someone who's much more mature than I am."

"Will you marry me?"

"No."

"Will you at least think about it? I'd feel much better if you'd at least think about it. You can promise me that much. That you'll think about it for a week or so. Then we can discuss it again. I can drive over to your house and we'll go somewhere, some quiet place, and have a quiet dinner and talk about it. I know just the place. It's just outside Westport. It's a nice ride over there at this time of year. You'll like this place. The top of the bar is plated with ha'pennies. Real English ha'pennies. We'll have a quiet dinner and talk about it and then I'll take you right back home."

Mary was delighted by the fact that Arondella wore taps on his shoes.

The study of dead Englishmen flourished in the afternoon. We looked forward to them, sons of Bread Street and Aldwinkle Rectory. It was May of my senior year at Leighton Gage and on Tuesday and Thursday afternoons we sat in an air-conditioned hourglass and savored our own total incomprehension as an assistant professor charted the poems of Dryden, Lovelace, Fanshawe and Suckling. They were all so incomparably dead, the Penguin poets, and we loved them because their lines meant less to us than the dark side of the moon. It was the best kind of class to have in the afternoon, an exercise in almost pure language, demanding nothing more than fractional consciousness since there wasn't the slightest hope of understanding what those poems were all about, and we drowsed and smiled, happy in our own little angel-infancy, snug in our Thamesian punt, and when the sonic belch of experimental jets went ripping across the desert we came close to applauding the symbolism; but a trembling applause it would have been, for we knew that it signaled the death of our drowsy England and the beginning of a new mortality, just months away now, the start of job, mate, child, desk, drink, sit, squat, quiver, die. Afternoon was for political science or dead Englishmen. That's why Monday afternoons were so terrible. Monday meant Zen.

Hiroshi Oh was an alarmingly fragile man. In the lecture hall he would ease into his chair in careful stages, always on the verge of blowing away, and then he'd smile desolately at his children. Tall blond milwaukees—prepare for Zen! I always enjoyed that opening smile. It was the smile of the bored Orient, tired of truth, bound in inland stillness, indifferent to westernization. The lecturer's chair and desk were on a platform in front of the huge sanitized hall, which resembled a cafeteria in the second-best pavilion at some international exposition. There were enough seats for two hundred students but only thirty of us were enrolled with Dr. Oh. We were well spread out, a half dozen or so at the very back of the room, the rest scattered here and there, presenting a difficult target, some of us seeking camouflage in the depth of our suntans, which matched the burnt sienna of the desks. The walls were glass, as was the low ceiling; the floor was something that made me think of crushed beetles, a whole civilization of black beetles smashed, baked and tiled in the Kitchens of Sara Lee. It was a perfect place for Zen.

Sunlight and viscid insect juice were the colors of those Monday afternoons. Zen had little in common with dead Englishmen and no one dared to drowse. It was total sleep or total awareness. All chose sleep, yet it seemed to elude us; it seemed always seconds away, a magical sleep filled with the soft tempera of spring, with new green trees standing alert to the wind, with the odors of earth pulsing and the riddle of a petaled woman crossing a footbridge. It was the perfect sleep but it never quite descended. It filled the hall above us and waited at the frontier of every mind. We desired this sleep because we were twenty years old and already beginning to learn there was no such thing as invincibility. We wished to take what was left of our courage and hope, and retire it to a dream. Beauty was too difficult and truth in the West had died with Chief Crazy Horse; a lifetime of small defeats was waiting. We knew this, and we knew that sleep was the only industry in life that did not diminish one's possibilities. But the perfect sleep never came. The sun held at the window and we listened, on those long afternoons, to Hiroshi Oh speaking of the need to cleanse our mouths of the word Buddha; speaking of drawing water and gathering fuel, how marvelous, how miraculous; speaking of the stillness in movement, the need for becoming a bamboo; humming tirelessly of these delicate things, his voice a tiny motor propelling a butterfly, while we all turned toward the sun at the window and dreamed of the sleep that would shine like awakening. Oh sieged us with tons of sparrow feathers; it was indeed marvelous and miraculous, smelling so of the unattainable and the old that in some dark part of our souls we instinctively revolted. It was in Oh's class that a student named Humbro ate his copy of D. T. Suzuki's introduction to Zen. Humbro sat three seats away from me but there was nobody between us. One day I saw him tear a page out of the book and eat it. He seemed to enjoy it. At every class he'd eat a few more pages. By the beginning of May he had eaten the whole book. Humbro was revered as an existential hero. In the course of eating the book he made no attempt to conceal his actions from Dr. Oh but the professor didn't seem to mind; at least he never mentioned it and we all thought he secretly approved. One must become a book before one can know what is inside it.

We came into the last Monday of May, the last week of

that last year, with cries of career opportunity sounding through campus, flutter and caw of mortality, General Dynamics and IBM, rumors loose in the land, huge shingled wings beating above the dorms, true love and baseball, vernal equinox, the moon and the scoop of tides, a horn-rimmed diplomat from Boeing pointing to the sky. Only four of us showed up for Zen, four out of thirty. Dr. Oh treated us to a smile even more desolate than usual and led us outside to a remote grove where he would conduct class, medieval fashion, in the dubious shade of a palm tree. He sat at the base of the tree and we drew around him, sitting cross-legged in a final bid for his approval. Oh spoke of Emptiness. The mind is an empty box within an empty box. With his index finger he made a sign in the air, one motion, name-shape, the circle's single fulfilling line. I lay flat on my back and watched the sky move through the blue openings of the tree. Then I closed my eyes and thought of sleep. Emptiness is Fullness. Become the book. Become the bamboo. The darkness ran shallow green. Then it was black, welcoming as deep space, and I sighed audibly and advanced into a fresh galaxy. What did I understand of all this? Episcopalian with chapped lips. Oh hummed and chanted. Note the paradox. Empty box within empty box. He went into more paradox, more gentle conflict, more questions of interpretation in which ancient masters nodded their disagreement. It was Oh's practice to reveal some deep Zen principle, carefully planting evidence of its undeniable truth, and then to confront us with a totally different theory of equally undeniable truth. He seemed to enjoy trying to break our minds, crush us with centuries of confusion, as if to say: If the great teachers and enlightened ones of history cannot find a common interpretation, how will you ever know what to believe, you poor white gullible bastards? In the speckled dark, flat on my back, I listened to the water of his voice and tried to hear the silences he so expertly inserted between words. Remove your eyelids. Empty your minds. See the stone as other stones see it. Here, outside, on the warm female grass, the promise of an immortal sleep was never more strong. I felt myself leaving the universe. But the doctor's words, sounding centuries away, brought me back every time. I tried again and again and each time returned. Then I opened my eyes and sat up and they were all on their backs, my fellow students, eyes closed and bellies softly throbbing, trying to leave this plane of existence. Oh looked at me and motioned me down again, a whisper of his eyes, down, my child, this is your last chance, tomorrow the corporations come calling, never again will you come close to this moment, the chance to capture the sleep of awakening. I lay back and closed my eyes again. I wondered if any of the others had found it. Humbro was here, the eater of Zen, five feet away. Wild was not here. Wild was in the sun lounge, grinning, no doubt, tracing the history of third stream jazz for some little girl from a cold climate. The darkness spread wide open and ·I knew there was room for me way inside but I could not escape. Remember the Arizona. I opened my eyes and saw Dr. Oh get to his feet and then I heard him say: "Rise, little children."

And we rose. We gathered in the sun lounge and took a poll. No one had slept, not one of us. Wild told us to get ready. The corporations were indeed coming, with charts and natural shoulders. He stood and gave us a simple nondenominational blessing, not knowing the formal procedure for last rites.

"We spring from a humane tradition," my mother said. "One of my forebears interceded with President Lincoln himself on behalf of the poor misguided Indians of Minnesota."

"Ann, what's that got to do with the college we send him to?"

"The University of Virginia was good enough for my forebears."

"He wants to go to this place out West. Let him go where he wants."

"I've made up my mind," I said. "That's definitely where I want to go."

"Your father and I have been arguing over Princeton and Virginia for three years now. Suddenly you come waltzing into the house and announce that you plan to attend some unheard-of school in California. Mary is behind this, isn't she? She's told you to make tracks away from this house. Well, goddamn it, I won't allow you to be running loose three thousand miles from home."

"Ann, relax. We'll talk about it tomorrow."

"Shut up. All of you shut up. That little slut is behind this. That ugly little bitch. Whose is she? She's not mine. She doesn't resemble me. She doesn't think like me. He's mine. That boy. He is mine. To whom does Mary belong, Clinton? If not to me, then to whom? By simple process of elimination, we arrive at you, do we not? I was a brilliant little grammarian as a girl. I can tell you that. God. Dear God. Do whatever you like, David. In the end, who cares? Who cares what happens to anyone?"

Summer in a small town can be deadly, even worse in a way than slum summers or the deep wet summers of gulf ports. It isn't the deadliness of filth or despair and it doesn't afflict everyone. But there are days when a terrible message seems to be passing from sunlight to shadow at the edge of a striped afternoon in the returning fathoms of time. Summer unfolds slowly, a carpeted silence rolling out across expanding steel, and the days begin to rhyme, distance swelling with the bridges, heat bending the air, small breaks in the pavement, those days when nothing seems to live on the earth but butterflies, the tranquilized mantis, the spider scaling the length of the mudcaked broken rake inside the dark garage. A scream seems imminent at every window. The menace of the history of quiet lives is that when the moment comes, the slow opened motion of the mouth, the sound which erupts will shatter everything that moves for miles around. The threat is at its worst in summer, in the wide rows of sunlight, as old people cross the lawns, humming like insects, as they sit in the painted gray stillness of spare rooms, breezing themselves with magazines about Siam and bare-breasted Zanzibar, as they stand on porches trying to gather in the shade, as they eat ice cream in the drugstore, two spinsters revolving on their stools beneath the halted fans, and all will come apart when the moment arrives. It is not felt every day and only some people can feel it. It may not be as violent as slums, tar melting on rooftops and boys wailing their hate at white helmets, but in the very silence and craft of its rhyming days summer in a small town can invert one's emotions with the speed of insanity.

One feels it most of all on Sundays. The neat white churches stand in groves of sunlight. Grandfather cops, absurd gunbelts over their paunches, direct whatever traffic is coming out of the church parking lots after services. The worshippers come down the steps blinking and damp, moving slowly and with the extreme caution which a new and vaster environment always exacts, heading across lawns or toward the parking lots where their cars seem to be swimming in the bluesteel incandescence of the gravel. Metal hot to the touch and hellstench inside. On Sundays, in the wide rows of light, it's as though all the torpor of Christianity itself is spread over the land. In the blaze of those moments, men in tight collars and the neat white shoes of little girls on the steps of churches, one feels all the silence of Luther, of Baptist picnics, divinity students playing softball, popes on their chamber pots, scary Methodists driving jalopies over cliffs; of teen-age Jehovah girls handing out leaflets, of Greek archbishops, revivalists fondling snakes in the Great Smokies, Calvinists blowing bagpipes, Gideon bibles turning yellow all over Missouri. All these, in a river of silence, remember to rest on the seventh day.

My mother, Jane and I walked home from church. People nodded to each other, faces tight in the glare, and went toward their separate streets. A few cars moved past, lakebound, filled with rubber floats and children in swimsuits. We turned into our street and I began to run. I ran upstairs and changed into old clothes. Then my father came in with a white bag full of buns. This happened every Sunday. I opened the bag and took out the buns and small bits of sugar frosting stuck to my fingers. Soon coffee was ready. Jane didn't want bacon and eggs because it was already too hot to eat a real breakfast. My mother would not have air conditioning in the house. We all sat down and ate the buns. We ate in silence. Then my mother said something about breakfast being the most important meal of the day. In Virginia they used to have hot cereal, strawberries, eggs, ham, and real farm bread. They used to put butter and marmalade on the bread. Everyone drank fresh milk instead of coffee. After this we were all silent again. It was ten o'clock in the morning.

I went out on the porch. It was only ten o'clock but it was already as hot as three in the afternoon. Jane came out and remembered that when we were younger we used to sit on the porch together and try to guess what kind of automobile would pass the house next. She remembered that she had once guessed three Buicks in a row and had been right every time. But it was Mary who had guessed the three Buicks in a row. I didn't mention this to Jane.

I walked down to the lake. There were swings and sliding ponds beneath the trees. I sat at the edge of one of the sliding ponds and watched little kids splashing in the shallow water and older boys and girls pushing each other off the white raft. The boys had white lotion on their noses and two girls sat on the raft with their backs to the sun and the straps of their bathing suits untied and hanging over their breasts. I turned and saw a small girl standing on the top step of the sliding pond. I moved out of the way and she bounced down the metal ramp slowly and clumsily. I didn't feel like swimming or watching other people swim so I walked over to Ridge Street and bought a magazine in the drugstore. The store had a wooden floor and a soda fountain. I was in one of those lonely moods which come over sixteen-year-olds when it occurs to them that in other parts of the world young men are hunting condors on high white crags and making love to whispering women who were born in Singapore. In its lonely way this is the most romantic of moods. You go for long walks that are like episodes in French novels. You feel that some great encounter is about to take place, something that will change the course of your life. Some old gardener will take you into an attic room, play the violin as it has never been played before and tell you the secret of existence. A dark woman will draw alongside in a new convertible and then lean over, without a word, and open the door for you; she will drive you to Mexico and undress you very slowly. It was a baseball magazine. I went home to read it on the porch. Some people waved at me from a car. It was very hot and nothing moved now. My father came out.

"What time's the party?" I said.

"Starts at eight."

"Do you think I'll have to get dressed?"

"Definitely."

"I hope it cools off tonight."

He went back in. In a little while my mother came out.

"You'll have to get dressed," she said. "Make no mistake about that."

She went inside and I read another article in the magazine. Then I went inside. My mother was in the kitchen looking at a tray of French pastries. I sat in the living room. There was a feeling of density in the air. Tides of light came through the windows, pulsing with dust. I was sitting in my mother's chair, a big green rocker. At my feet was a sewing basket. Is this how people die, I thought. My right arm was extended along the armrest, on the tight floral fabric, hand curled over the ornamental woodwork, a rounded section of rich mahogany in the shape of a lion's paw. My left arm hung loosely over the side of the chair. My feet were crossed at the ankles. I was wearing brown loafers, white socks, dungarees and an old navy-blue sweatshirt with the sleeves cut off about four-fifths of the way up the arm. I was not rocking. My mood had changed from lonely wanderlust to an odd European species of nothingness. I felt I could sit there forever, suffering. It seemed a valuable thing to do. Sit still for years on end and eventually things will begin to revolve around you, ideas and people and wars, depending for their folly and brilliance on that source of light which is human inertia. If you stay in one spot long enough, generals and statesmen will come to you and ask for your opinion. Maybe it wasn't European as much as Asian or North African. But it seemed European too, Russian at any rate, sitting in exile through long wolf-lean winters as governments fell and men made fools of themselves. Then finally a knock on the door. Word has reached us that you have been sitting here doing nothing. You must be a very wise man. Come to the capital and help us sort things out.

I sat in my mother's chair thinking of these things, more or less, and testing myself by trying not to blink. Then I heard a sound and when it grew louder I could guess what it was, motorcycles, a low throttling growl from that distance but coming closer now, rumbling and cracking, and I knew there would be more than two or three. I went to the window and then they came down the street with a sound that seemed to rip and sunder beneath the tires themselves, cracking off into smaller sounds which were then snapped apart by the next set of wheels and the next, and I counted ten, now twelve bikes, the riders screaming something as they went, eighteen now, an even twenty, dressed in silver and black, the colors of their bikes, and they went past screaming into the sounds of their machines, shouting a curse or warning over the empty lawns. They were gone in seconds and it was as though a hurricane or plague had struck the town. We were all in one piece. But now, as silence began to fill in the holes left by those marauding bikes, I could almost feel every man and woman in town looking from windows down that street and experiencing a strange mixture of longing and terror. We were all in one piece. But we were not quite the same people we had been ten seconds before.

We had cold cuts for lunch. On the radio Mel Allen was describing a nip and tuck ball game, the first of two, and he was saying there's plenty of room out here, folks; you can see the remainder of this game and all of the next; so why don't you come on out and bring the family. Then Jane began to talk about a course she was taking in the primitive religions of the world. It was given two nights a week at the YWCA in a nearby community. The Algonquin Indians heard dead men chirp like crickets. Fijian priests used to stare endlessly at a whale's tooth and then have convulsions. In funeral services in Fiji, the major part of the ceremony was to strangle the dead man's wives, friends and slaves. Jane went upstairs then to get her notebook. We ate in silence. She returned a minute later. Eisenhower was on the radio now with a brief recorded announcement in which he urged people to support their local community chest. The Chinese make a hole in the roof to let out the soul at death. When a Watchandi warrior slew his first victim, the spirit of the dead man entered the warrior's body and became his woorie, or warning spirit; it resided near his liver and warned him of danger by scratching or tickling. It was the custom of the Aztecs to pour the blood of slaughtered victims into the mouths of idols. A Mandingo priest would hold a newborn child in his arms, whisper in its ear and spit three times in its face. The Ojibwas believed that hatchets and kettles have souls. A saying of the Zulus was that the stuffed body cannot see secret things. The Zulu doctor prepared himself for dialogue with the spirits by fasting, suffering and long quiet walks. The Yakuts of Siberia worshipped the bear, their beloved uncle. According to the Dayaks, the human soul enters the trunks of trees. Evil spirits had sexual congress with Samoan women at night, causing supernatural conceptions. The Nicaraguans offered human sacrifices to Popogatepec by tossing bodies into volcanic craters. The Ahts of Vancouver's Island considered the moon as husband and the sun as wife. The Mintira people feared a water-demon which had a dog's head and an alligator's mouth. It sucked blood from men's thumbs and big toes until they died. To the Assyrians, insanity was possession by demons. When a Kayan of Borneo died, his slaves were killed so that they could follow him to the next world and obey all his behests. First the female relatives of the deceased master wounded the slaves slightly with spears. Then the male relatives took up these same spears and killed the victims. The human soul weighs three to four ounces.

"All that cruelty and superstition," my mother said.

"Life was cheap in those days, Ann."

"Who were all those people?" she said. "Think of them all, living in caves and huts. Back to the dawn of time. Worshipping bears and monkeys. Millions of souls. How insignificant they seem."

"I know what you mean," my father said. "It's almost impossible to conceive of all those people killing each other and praying to the sun. It makes you think that what you do in your life doesn't make a whole lot of difference. Why should we be any more significant than those primitives?"

"But we are, Clinton."

"Those are good notes, Jane," I said.

"I take them down in shorthand and then copy them out later," she said. "It's the best way to do it."

"It's incredible," my father said. "The way they disregarded human life. But still they were men and women. We're sitting here on a Sunday afternoon eating lunch and listening to the ball game. Those people couldn't be more remote. And yet they were men and women. They believed in something."

"The more magical a race is," my mother said, "the less significant the individual is. Magic overwhelms everything. We in the West value human life almost desperately because we have no magic."

"God is magic," Jane said.

"No. God is the opposite of magic. I've talked to William Potter about this. The subject is foreign to him. We all have magic in us, some more than others, but everything we've been taught tends to bury the magic. Consider what we're eating, Clinton. The body of an animal. What could be more primitive?"

"But we don't worship the animal," I said.

"Only because God took human form. What if He had decided to visit earth in the guise of a lion? The primitives seem insignificant to us because they're so remote in time and creed, as your father says, but also because they were so insignificant to each other. That was magic. Magic made them less important than the animals or planets they worshipped. They were not so far from the mark really. I hold with magic. I'm not sure whether it's good or evil. But I know it's there."

"That's good, Ann," my father said. "That's extremely interesting."

There was nothing to do. All afternoon I sat on the porch, motionless, thinking of the wet bodies of women. It was getting hotter. The stillness was almost absolute. There was a taste of water in the air, warm salt biting the lips. I felt heavy. I wished it would rain. Is this how people die, watching along the street for some sign that will tell them the moment is here, at last, rise up and act, the time is upon us, quickly, into the streets, now, grenades and motorcycles, a warning word, salt on the wet bodies of women. Dr. Weber walked down the street. He was a short man with a mustache. The machete is a most effective weapon, doctor. You are surprised that I speak your language? Harvard. Class of '34. He was carrying his bag. He wore a dark suit. There was a gravy stain on his shirtfront. I waited for him to look toward the porch and give me that yellow smile which doctors and dentists employ so often, a clenched wry smile as the money changes hands, and when he did I turned away and yawned. Practitioner. Oath-taker. I rode out the afternoon on that yawn.

Later, from the window of my room, I watched them arrive

for the party. The Old Holly people came mostly on foot. Those from nearby suburbs or from the city, my father's crowd, arrived in cars or took the cab from the station. There was no particular reason for the party but in a way it was something of a debut for me. It was judged that I was old enough now to partake in adult games, presumably on the fringe of things, nursing a tall cool rum collins (or something to that effect) while everyone admired my preppy manners and told me how much I had grown. Between forty and fifty people would be coming. It had been arranged—this I learned from Jane—that a couple named Loomis would be bringing along their daughter Amy, who was my age. Jane herself had invited her current boyfriend, John Retley Tucker, who was Big Bob Davidson's immediate predecessor in virtually every sense of the word. I called him Sweatley Retley. Mary had not been told about the party because nobody knew where she was.

They arrived with the setting of the sun—the Smiths, Bradshaws, Morgans, Hills, Rayburns, Gossages, Peppers, Stevensons, Halidays, Torgesons, Bakers, Hunters, Taylors, Colliers, Barbers and Fishers. Andrew Alexander drove up in his claret-colored Packard, a vintage model which was said to have been owned at one time by Al Capone or F. Scott Fitzgerald, depending on who was telling the story. William Judge and his wife looked up and saw me. I returned their wave and snapped into a midshipman smile, properly wholesome and humble. August Riddle strolled across the lawn. He was the town's crusty old lawyer, reputed to know more about deeds and mortgages than any man in the county. He was a bachelor. His office was suitably cluttered and he was always drinking black coffee and smoking long thin cigars. Mary and I had decided some time ago that Lee J. Cobb or Paul Muni would star in his film biography. He poked his cigar in my direction. The evening was warm and still. I saw a hawk. No sign of rain.

I put on a suit, white shirt and tie. I went downstairs and

into the kitchen. The maid, Justina Simpson, who came in four days a week, had been joined for the party by her daughter Mae and her son-in-law Buford Long, who would be serving as bartender. I watched Buford set things up and I decided that tending bar might be a pretty good way to spend one's life. Spanking down big foaming steins of beer to be encircled by the huge skeet-shooting hands of virile novelists. Rattling the cocktail shaker and doing a little samba step for the amusement of the ladies. To be an expert at something. I asked Buford how he liked tending bar and he said the ice made his knuckles cold and sent weird shooting pains up to his head. My mother looked in then and urged me to make an appearance. I stayed for a moment longer and watched Mae carving turkey. She wore a white uniform. She wasn't wearing a slip and I could see the shadow of the inside of her thighs through the sheer white cotton. I went into the living room.

"Why, you're taller than Clyde," Mrs. Hunter said.

The Gossages felt me up, Henry and Lucy, and I spoke with Justin Hill about the Southeast Conference versus the Big Ten. My father had his arm around me for a few minutes. We were talking with Claire Collier, a tall good-looking woman. We were all talking simultaneously. I went over to the Rayburns and Taylors and said all the same things I had just said to Mrs. Collier. My mother usually referred to Mrs. Collier as "the Collier woman." This seemed to imply some distant scandal. I was aware that Amy Loomis and I, who had been at opposite ends of the room, were slowly approaching a confrontation. It was as though all the energies broadcast from the bodies of those forty adults were impelling us toward each other. Amy was tiny. She was talking with Andrew Alexander, who kept patting his own head. My mother had my elbow in her hand and then she was introducing me to Amy, pinching my elbow during the brief silences and letting up as soon as I said something. Amy and I were alone.

"Do you know Jim Gibson?" she said.

"No, I don't think so."

"He's got a green catamaran called Belleweather?"

"What's his name again?"

"Jim Gibson."

"I don't know him."

"That cat really flies."

"I'd like to get one myself. They really go."

"Do you know Marty Hammer?" she said.

"It sounds familiar."

"His father's got a yawl? He gave Marty carte blanche with the yawl for his sixteenth birthday? It's something like fifty-five feet?"

"No, that's not the one I'm thinking of. Does he have a brother named Frank?"

"No."

"Then that's not the one," I said.

"Do you know Tim Lerner?"

"Didn't he drown in Peconic Bay last summer?"

"That's the one."

"Do you know Billy Shaw?"

"I know two Billy Shaws," she said.

People were filling plates with sliced ham and turkey and trying to eat standing up. It was very warm in the room. The Gossages joined us. Henry rubbed my shoulder. Lucy Gossage held my hand as she talked to Amy. Mrs. Loomis came over with Tod Morgan and asked how we were doing. Lucy Gossage held my hand up near her breast and kept caressing it with her other hand. Ray Smith came over and went into the boxing routine he always used when we met. Head tucked down on his left shoulder, he threw some mock lefts and rights at my belly, snorting with each punch. Then there was a brief lull and we heard Mrs. Loomis telling Amy to smile once in a while. Then we all started talking. Jane stopped by and introduced her boyfriend to everyone. Tod Morgan handed me what he called a real drink. It was scotch and water. It made me very warm and I didn't like the taste much. But I seemed to be having a good time. They were nice people.

They had no scars or broken noses. They dressed more or less the same. They talked the same way and said the same things and I didn't know how dull they were or that they were more or less interchangeable. I was one of them, after all. I was not a stranger among them and I liked their hands on my body.

"Did anyone see those motorcycles today?" Tod Morgan said.

The Collier woman and I stood by the fireplace drinking. I assumed a clubby slouch. Then Lucy Gossage had her arm around me and her husband, Henry, was whispering a dirty joke in my ear. I had trouble picking up his words. Soon he started laughing and I knew the joke was over. We both stood there laughing. Henry looked right into my face, searching for genuine appreciation, wanting to be sure I understood the point of the story. I kept nodding and laughing. When he was satisfied he went away.

August Riddle had a teardrop of flesh on each sagging jowl. I watched him. Amy was talking to me about somebody named Bobby Springer's Austin Healey. Mr. Riddle was talking with the Stevensons. He lit his cigar and then waved out the match with a circular flourish. He dropped the match on the floor. Mae carried a platter of pineapple rings into the room. I tried to catch her eye so I could smile at her. Amy was talking into my chest. It was all settled as far as she was concerned. It was between Wellesley and Bryn Mawr. She had red hair and big green eyes. I imagined being in bed with her and her mother. Amy was drinking the champagne punch. Nobody seemed drunk yet. I asked her if she wanted to go out on the porch where it would be cooler and she said no. Just plain no. There was a terrible silence then which made me nervous and I found myself asking her if she knew by any chance how the Yankees had made out in the second game. My father came over and shook my hand for some reason. Then he was gone. Andrew Alexander was talking to Amy. You young people, he kept saying. You young people. He patted his own head. He couldn't have been trying to keep his hair in place, for it was cut short and it was thick and firm. Every time he patted, his eyeballs rolled up. He and Amy were discussing the color beige. I watched his eyeballs slide up and down. He asked if Amy and I were engaged. I excused myself then and went into the kitchen to watch Buford Long mix drinks. He had an unlit cigarette in his mouth. Pouring club soda with his right hand, he took a matchbook out of his breast pocket with the other hand, flipped up the cover with his thumb and, using his index finger and his thumb again, bent a match at its middle and struck it. I liked the way he did that. I had never seen anyone do that before. I also liked the fact that he was left-handed. Left-handed people seem to do things with more style. I've always envied them. Warren Spahn the stylish southpaw.

"Where do you normally work, Buford? Tend bar in some bar or something?"

"I'm a maintenance man. Mae and I, we live down Manhattan in the West Twenties. I maintain six buildings. I collect garbage from outside their doors and bring it downstairs. I fix things need fixing. I shine things up."

"What's it like? Hard work, I bet."

"It's not hard so much as menial. But at least it's got some intrinsics to it. It gives you clues to human nature. Garbage tells you more than living with a person."

"You don't mind it too much then."

"Oh, I love it," he said.

"Is the garbage different in different buildings?"

"Sure it's different. There's clues that tell you that. You don't even have to see the garbage. Anytime you see a cracked mirror in the hallway you know the garbage isn't going to be any good."

"I guess it's satisfying to help keep the city clean."

"It overjoys me," Buford said.

"They say pound for pound Sugar Ray Robinson is the best fighter ever."

My mother was in the doorway telling me that Amy was all alone. I went out there and stood next to her. John Retley Tucker came by. I asked him if he had ever met my other sister and he said Jane had never mentioned any sister. He stood there talking to us and the index finger of his right hand was stuck between his shirt collar and the back of his neck. This meant his elbow was up around ear level. I saw Amy staring at the patch of sweat under his arm. John Retley was about six-four and two-twenty and he looked like a cop directing traffic on a Sunday afternoon and not minding it at all. The Collier woman approached again and I disengaged myself to talk to her. She was wearing beige.

"I want to tell you something," she said. "You're a young man now and there's no reason why you shouldn't know this. You've grown to almost your full stature. You have a man's body and a man's appetites. This is what I want to say. Women love to be loved."

"Yes."

"Who is that man behind you?"

"John Retley Tucker. My sister Jane's boyfriend."

"There's something indecent about a man with thumbs that large."

I needed some air. I told Amy I was going out for a while. She said she'd come with me. I left her there on the porch for a moment and went back inside for two drinks and brought them out. I didn't turn on the porch light.

"Do you drink a lot?" she said.

"I drink quite a bit. I drink quite a bit, yes."

"Do you know a boy named David Bell? He drinks incredible amounts of liquor. He does it on a dare. He can really hold it."

"I'm David Bell," I said.

"I got confused. I meant Dick Davis."

"Freudian slip," I said. "They say if you use somebody's name like that by mistake it means you like that person very much."

"Don't get ideas, mister."

"I was only kidding."

"Your parents are very nice."

"So are yours. Do you think I'm handsome, Amy?"

"What a question."

"I know it's an ambivalent thing to ask but I heard you discussing colors with old Andy Alexander and you seem to have good taste and I was just wondering what you thought. I'm sure you wonder if people think you're pretty. Do you think I'm handsome?"

"Yes," she said.

"Do you want to know if I think you're pretty?"

"Okay."

"I think you just miss," I said. "What's your opinion of Burt Lancaster? I think he's the all-time greatest."

Henry Gossage came out on the porch. He took a deep breath and clubbed himself on the chest with both his baby fists. Then he saw us standing by the rail and pretended to be startled, drawing his body back and raising his arms in self-defense. "Two purple shadows in the snow," he sang. I hoped he wouldn't tell another joke.

"Our kids are away at camp," he said. "Oldest is a counselor. Middle waits on tables but he'll be a counselor next year. Youngest is only twelve so he's got a ways to go yet before he gets out of the camper category."

"How's Hank?" I said.

"He's the oldest. Henry Jr. He's fine. Appreciate your asking."

"Give him my best."

"Will do. Damn good of you, lad. Damn nice of you, Dave boy. Damn sweet thing to say. Where can I throw up?"

"In the hedge," I said.

"It's all right. I don't think I have to anymore."

Amy said she thought it would be a good idea to get back inside. Everybody stood talking and eating. At the far end of the room Tod Morgan and Peter Fisher's wife were talking.

I was watching his face when he laughed. His features stretched and quivered. He looked extraordinarily ugly. I imagined a small explosion in his head. He was laughing in an exaggerated manner, overdoing it, creating the laugh as if with ceramics, and I watched his head come apart in slow motion, different sections tumbling through the air, nose-part, ear-part, jaw with lower teeth. I went through the kitchen and out the back door.

The small porch out there was full of empty bottles. I walked along the edge of the woods past Harris, Torgeson and Weber. The Harris and Weber houses were lit. I cut across a lawn and walked the five blocks to Ridge Street. The drugstore was closed. There were four or five people in the ice cream parlor. I had a soda and waited for Kathy Lovell to turn up but she didn't. I almost went to the movie theater to look for her. Then I started walking toward her house. Finally I went back to the ice cream parlor and called her from there. Her father answered and I hung up. Ten minutes later I was on Green Street. It was dark and quiet. There was the beginning of a breeze. I stood beneath an elm and watched a woman in a shingled house ironing clothes. No one passed on the street. It was a Sunday night in early September and my body beat with sorrow at the beauty and mockery of all bodies.

There were only about fifteen people left when I returned to the house. They seemed to have too much room to move around in. Unfinished drinks were everywhere and the chairs and sofas were occupied now. On the floor was a white slice of turkey with a shoeprint on it. Most of the women were sitting together at one end of the room. The men were drifting in and out of the kitchen. They all seemed to be drinking beer now. I walked across the room smiling. I went upstairs and took off my jacket and tie. I could hear voices from Jane's room. I stood very still. Jane was apparently showing her boyfriend a family photo album.

"This is mother as a little girl," she said. "That's her father and that's her uncle Jess who wrote poems and killed himself.

193

This is me as a little girl. This was taken on West End Avenue, where we used to live. This was taken in Central Park. This is Old Holly and that's daddy. This is Aunt Grace in Alexandria. This is mother again. So's this. So's this. This is David when he was two years old. This is daddy in his office."

"Jane," he said. "Jane."

I went downstairs to the kitchen and got a beer out of the refrigerator. Harold Torgeson was standing in the corner. He was drinking a glass of milk. We were alone.

"I've always wanted to be a writer," he said. "Right out there in that room tonight there were forty or fifty good stories. I tried to write when I was a young man but I had no staying power. I'd get started in a burst of energy and goodwill and then I'd just fade out and die. Let's face it, I was born to be an insurance agent. But the thing gnaws at me even now, lad. Sometimes I have trouble sleeping and I get out of bed and light a cigarette and sit by the open window. And I get this bittersweet feeling about my life and what I've done and what I haven't done. You're too young to understand that. But there's something poetic about sitting by an open window at midnight smoking a cigarette. The cigarette is part of it. There are memories in the smoking of a cigarette. I just sit there thinking about my life. I killed three Japanese in the war that I know of. I'm telling you these things because they'll be useful to you someday."

Ray Smith had come in halfway through Torgeson's monologue. He went over and shook Torgeson's hand. Then he got a beer from the refrigerator.

"My own story begins in wartime London," he said. "There was a nurse named Celia Archer."

Three other men were standing in the kitchen entrance, listening. I slipped past them into the living room. The ladies didn't seem to have very much to say to each other. Through the window I saw my father out on the porch. William Judge and I were the only men in the room. Nobody said anything. My mother looked strange. Then Jane and her boyfriend came down the stairs. Someone asked what they had been doing up there and everyone laughed. The laughter was a signal. They had all been waiting for it. They got up now and began to leave. My father came inside and stood by the door, trying not to look delighted. My mother was standing in the middle of the room. Her hands whisked back and forth as if she were trying to sweep everyone out the door. People kept leaving and then returning seconds later for things they had forgotten. Finally they were gone for good. My father began turning out lights and locking doors. Jane was already upstairs. Soon I was alone in the living room. Someone had left almost a full glass of something on the buffet table. I took a sip, closed my eyes, concentrated, could not determine what it was, and slowly finished it off. I realized my father had not said good-night to anyone. I turned off the hall lamp and the house was dark except for the kitchen. I started in and then stopped at the doorway. My mother was in there. The refrigerator door was open. She was wearing just one shoe. The other was on the floor, a black shoe, upright, near the wall. She held a tray of ice cubes in her hands and she was spitting on the cubes. She disappeared behind the refrigerator door and I could hear her open the freezer compartment and slide the tray back in. I moved away as the freezer slammed shut. I went upstairs and into my room. I closed the door behind me as quietly as I could. I took off my shirt and my shoes and lay on the bed, knowing it was too hot to sleep. I thought of Harold Torgeson sitting by his open window smoking a cigarette. I wondered how many novels he had dictated to himself that way. After a long time I passed into a thin dreamless sleep, less a state of mind than a dislocation of the senses. Coming up out of it for only seconds at a time, I did not know where I was or whether it was morning or the middle of the night. It disturbed me not to know where I was and yet I was content to slip off again into the river, the not at all deep or treacherous river, the river which is language without thought, and in seconds, what seemed like seconds, I would come up again and wonder where I was but somehow never who; that much did not escape me. Then I was wide awake. My hand was on my belt buckle and I realized I hadn't taken off my pants. I lay there without moving, aware that sleep was impossible now. I listened for trains or cars but there was nothing. Trains are lovely things to hear when you are waiting for sleep. I imagined that the novel Torgeson was dictating to himself at that moment was the kind of novel in which young lovers hear a train in the distance or in which somewhere a dog is barking or in which laughter is always floating across the lawn. I felt tense and restless. It was my body that was awake but not my mind. I would think of something and then try to come back to it and it would be gone. I could not keep a thought going. Nothing connected. I got up and looked out the window. Then I went downstairs. The kitchen light was still on but she was in the pantry. I could barely see her. She was sitting on a stool against the bare wall that faced the door. On either side the high shelves were stocked with bottles, jars and cartons.

"It was only a matter of time," she said.

"I'd better turn on the light."

It was a low-watt bulb and the light seemed almost brown in that narrow room full of dark jars. She was standing now.

"There is nothing but time. Time is the only thing that happens of itself. We should learn to let it take us along. The Collier woman is a fool."

I did not move. I felt close to some overwhelming moment. In the dim light her shadow behind her consumed my own. I knew what was happening and I did not care to argue with the doctors of that knowledge. Let it be. Inside her was something splintered and bright, something that might have been left by the spiral passage of my own body. She was before me now, looking up, her hands on my shoulders. The sense of tightness I had felt in my room was beginning to yield to a promise of fantastic release. It was going to happen. Whatever would happen. The cage would open, the mad bird soar, and

196

I would cry in epic joy and pain at the freeing of a single moment, the beginning of time. Then I heard my father's bare feet on the stairs. That was all.

We sat in the Aston-Martin inside the garage. There were still some traces of snow on the windshield.

"My father's name was Harkavy Clinton Bell. They named me Clinton Harkavy Bell. He made his money late in life. Not that we weren't comfortable early on. But it was his reputation that came first, before he started earning top dollar. He told me the story dozens of times. He was on a Union Pacific train somewhere between Omaha and Cheyenne. He was sitting next to a man named McHenry who owned a pajama company named McHenry Woolens. McHenry took out a bottle and he and my father got good and soused. He told my father he was on the verge of bankruptcy. So old Harkavy tells him what he needs is a catchy advertising campaign. You've got a good American name and you're not using it to advantage. McHenry. Fort McHenry. Where Francis Scott Key wrote 'The Star-Spangled Banner.' And with that my father takes out a pencil and starts making a layout on the back of a big manila envelope. He draws a battle scene, get it, ships, rockets, a fort, hundreds of troops and a big flag flying on the battlements. Then he writes a single line at the bottom of the layout. *McHenry—the Star-Spangled Pajamas.* Then—this is the crusher—he tells McHenry that what he has to do to nail it down solid is to sew forty-eight stars on every pair of pajamas he manufactures. That did it. It was the greatest merchandising gimmick of the decade. It made McHenry rich and my father famous. That's how they wrote ads in the old days, kid—sloshed to the eyeballs on the Union Pacific Railroad. He told me that story dozens of times. I think it has a fine innocence to it. I mean the whole idea of getting plastered with a stranger. And the campaign itself. The star-spangled pajamas. It has a lovely innocence to it. You could afford to be innocent in the old days."

About a week after the party Tommy Valerio and I went over to a deserted ballfield on the edge of town. The field was surrounded by woods. Only the bare outlines of basepaths and a pitcher's mound remained, and what should have been the skin part of the infield was covered with weeds. Tommy had a long thin fungo bat and we took turns hitting fly balls to each other. It was a cool day for September, generously blue, football weather really, and I ranged across the outfield making casual basket catches, hunching my shoulder and pounding the glove twice like Willie Mays, and trying to adjust to the sudden change of season; not sorry to see summer go because autumn was all gold and wine in the New Hampshire fields and I would be going into senior year at St. Dymphna's, where I would amble along the gray lanes in my tweed sport-coat. And yet something was coming to an end, not just summer but something like the idea of what I was, the time I occupied like space, that private time in which one moves and thinks and knows the questions. Time had been warped and I looked back to the week before and could not find myself. It wasn't until years later, in the period of the affairs, that I began to struggle against this disappearance; to give nothing to Jennifer Fine for fear there would be nothing left for myself. I drifted back to the edge of the trees and caught a long high drive.

"Let's switch," Tommy shouted.

"Keep on hitting," I said. "I want to shag a few more."

I stayed out there for a long time. Tommy got tired of swinging the bat but I kept telling him to hit a few more, just a few more. I didn't want to stop. The ball would rise from the bat and then I would hear the light crack of contact and it would go up into the cloudless sky, almost vanishing, black at its apogee, coming down white and bruised, an old ball bruised green from the grass. I began to get serious. I would crouch as Tommy went into his swing, meat-hand on my right knee, glove-hand dangling straight down. Ball in the air, I would break quickly, watching just the first second of its flight, and then run head-down to the spot where I knew it would land, the spot dictated by the memory of that first second and a knowledge of the wind and Tommy's power and the sound of ball on bat. Ball caught, I would fire it back as hard and straight as I could, as if a runner had been tagging from third. Tommy would let my throw bounce into the sagging backstop. It went on like this. I was nobody. I was instinct and speed and a memory that extended back for no more than seconds. That was all. I could have gone on all day. But Tommy got exhausted and finally called it quits. I went home, oiled my glove and put it away for the winter.

That night I left my room and headed toward the stairs. I passed Mary's room and saw my mother in there, small and blue, a question mark curled on the bed. I went downstairs. I sat on the rocker for a while. Then my father called me and I descended the steps into the basement.

Jane sat on a folding chair eating an apple. My father stood by the projector. He nodded to me and I switched off the light and then sat next to Jane. The first commercial lasted twenty seconds. A house stood on a quiet suburban street at night. Inside, a man and a woman were having an argument. A teen-age girl leaned against the TV set listening to them. She was very homely. Then she disappeared, returning seconds later with a small bottle of something. The man and woman looked at the bottle, embraced and began to sing. The next commercial was one minute long. A boy wearing thick glasses was practicing the piano. A hockey stick was propped against the wall behind him. In the distance could be heard the shouts and laughter of children his own age. The boy got to his feet, picked up the hockey stick and raced toward the door. A woman emerged from the next room. She was holding a toothbrush. She ran after the boy, waving the toothbrush and screaming. The boy opened the door and tripped. He fell down the steps and lay on the stone path, motionless. His glasses had been broken. Blood was flowing from a severe gash at a point directly above the bridge of his nose. He appeared to be unconscious. It was a beautiful night, a cool and clear and almost autumn night. The wind rushed across the grass outside the high basement window. The sky was howling with stars. I thought of old men playing violins and of women in white convertibles driving me to Mexico.

PART THREE

7

Passing them on the roads as they journeyed toward their own interior limits, one might easily be inspired to twist the thumb of a famous first sentence. It was the worst of times, it was the worst of times. On foot they traveled, in old and new cars, in motorcycle packs, in trucks and buses and camp trailers, the young and the very young, leaving their medieval cities, tall stone citadels of corruption and plague, not hopeless in their flight, not yet manic in their search, the lost, the found, the nameless, the brilliant, the stoned, the dazed and the simply weary, shouting their honest love of country across the broken white line, faces lost in disbelief and hair, the drummer, the mystic, the fascist, an occasional female eye peering from a rear window, the noise at the back of her head a short song of peace.

We were nearing the end of the first week, determined not to stray even for a moment beyond the borders of our native land, carefully avoiding all those big footprint lakes and the specter of guiltless Canada. Sullivan slept up front, in the part of the camper that extended over the cab. Pike did most of the cooking. Brand did most of the driving. I yelled and read aloud from road maps.

With us all the way had been Sullivan's three-antenna marine-band hi-fi portable radio, a never-ending squall of disc jockey babytalk, commercials for death, upstate bluegrass Jesus, and as we drove through the cloverleaf bedlams and past the morbid gray towns I perceived that all was in harmony, the stunned land feeding the convulsive radio, every acre of the night bursting with a kinetic unity, the logic beyond delirium.

When it rained Sullivan put on her old buttonless trenchcoat even though we were inside the camper. What a mysterious and sacramental journey, I thought, not knowing most of the time where we were, depending on Pike to get us from place to place. Every time I saw a river I thought it was the Mississippi. Every gas station attendant we talked to was named Earl.

I taped many of our conversations.

"This big blue yawning country," Brand said early one evening over sandwiches. "I want to piss on all the trees, tumble down hills, chase jackrabbits, climb up rooftops, crucify myself on TV aerials. I want to say hi neighbor to everybody we meet. It's beautiful. It's too much. Baby, it's wild. It's the strangest, wildest, freakingest country in history. Davy, keep me bland."

"Tell us about your novel," Sullivan said.

"Writers never talk about work in progress," I said. "Isn't that right, Bobby? It destroys the necessary tension. If they talked about it, they wouldn't have to write it anymore. Essentially people write to break the tension. Right, Brand? If the creative tension is broken prematurely, the original motivation is lost. I'm surprised to hear you ask a question like that, Sully. You of all people."

"It's about a man who turns into a woman," Brand said. "He's the former president of the United States. He's completed his two terms but he's still very popular and he's always speaking at important banquets. At the same time he's turning into a woman. He's beginning to grow breasts and his genitals are shrinking. His voice is becoming high and faggy. He wears a garter belt for the secret thrill it gives him. He's a WASP, the ex-president. But de new president is black. He's patterned after Sonny Liston. He's very hip and magical. He turns on every night and he's making it with all the wives and daughters of the southern senators and even with some of the senators themselves. It'll be over a thousand pages long. It's called *Coitus Interruptus*. The theme is whatever you want it to be because appearance is all that matters, man. The whole country's going to puke blood when they read it."

"I want to talk about this idea I've got for a movie," I said.

"We're all ears," Pike said.

"I'm thinking of making a long messy autobiographical-type film, part of which I'd like to do out here in the Midwest, if that's where we are—a long unmanageable movie full of fragments of everything that's part of my life, maybe ultimately taking two or three or more full days to screen and only a minutely small part of which I'd like to do out here. Pick out some sleepy town and shoot some film."

"How long will that take?" Sullivan said. "You'll be filming Indians in a couple of weeks."

"We've got time. The part I want to do now will take only two or three days. Either three days or seventeen years. I'll use available light. I don't care how primitive it is technically. Besides, I won't be filming Indians personally. I won't actually be handling a camera. My job will be to supervise and be supervised. The movie I want to make will be a different kind of thing completely. I'm just starting to get it straightened out in my head. It's funny how it came to me. I saw a woman trimming a hedge. Almost immediately it became something else. And it's still changing."

"I wasn't finished talking about my novel," Brand said.

Pike was exploring his ear with a toothpick wrapped in tissue paper. When he was done he went up front to drive.

It was dusk now, bent rust powdering the western sky, neon-blooming motels, the dull sulfuric cast of roadlights, a jalopy abandoned in a field, hood raised like the peak of a baseball cap, a scene from the rural thirties. Sullivan hummed a medley of what appeared to be antiwar tunes. Brand was curled up with his British-made rolling machine and Zig-Zag cigarette paper. We seemed to be passing a resort area now. There were the white toy cottages with pink shutters from Hansel and Gretel and the filling stations of the back streets of small towns with a lone old pump and a dog asleep in grease. I remembered to turn off the tape recorder. Then I turned on the radio. Ali Akbar Khan was performing an evening raga, a sad liquid joy spilling from the strings of his sarod, and I thought of a blind Bengali walking a tightrope over nothing. I began in the dark and would no doubt end the same way. But somewhere between beginning and end there would have to be an attempt to explain the darkness, if only to myself, no matter how strange a form the explanation would take, and regardless of consequence. Maybe it was her hair. Maybe it was the way she moved as she cut the hedge, with the beautifully stylized bearing of a child who knows she is being watched. Sullivan kept on humming. A police helicopter appeared over the trees and went beating past us down the highway. Brand sucked smoke deep into his body.

"Where the fuck have all the flowers gone," he sang, hurrying the words to make them fit.

Pike turned onto a side road and eventually pulled into an A&P parking lot, fitting the camper between two station wagons waiting to be gorged. We entered by the great glass omniscient door, which knew we were coming and opened of itself. Brand and I peeled off from the others and followed a dark attractive woman down a side aisle to the peaches and plums. Her fingers skipped among the peaches, testing and prodding, and we moved alongside, our cart nudging her cart.

"Peaches," Brand said.

She gave us no sign.

"Look at the word come out of my mouth all moist and fuzzy. Peaches. It's the perfect word for the perfect thing. Now we're all standing here. If we all watch my lips, we'll all see it come out. Peaches. What do you think, miss, if that's your name. Should we pick up a pound or two? We're just a couple of good-looking guys from the East Coast, especially him. Listen, I've got some grass back at the plastic bitch."

She moved over to the plums and we followed. She was tall and her hips swung terrifically behind the shopping cart.

"Come on back to the truck with us and let loose for a while. We'll eat plums and smoke dope. I'm writing a novel using the direct interior monologue technique."

She looked around for a rescuer and I studied the plum in her fine Mediterranean hand. She was the kind of woman you imagine meeting in Port Said, older, wiser than you, pigmented of earth and made of many bloods, amused at your blond boyish Yankee ways, dispensing shattering truth in short sentences, and here she was, incredibly, among the plums of Middle America.

"Air is not invisible," Brand said.

She soon vanished. We put our cart into reverse. The shelves were long and brilliant, and I thought of my father. This was his spangled ark, cans of dessert-whip with squiggly pricklike tops, mythology and thunderbolts, the green giant's loins, buckets of power and white beyond white, trauma in the rectangles of evangelistic writ. (You have to move the merch off the shelves.) A baby sat in a grocery cart, crying; his mother gave him a stalk of celery to play with and he was content. "Who loves mommy," she said. "Say who loves her, stinky-pants. Baby loves mommy. Yes, baby loves mommy. Say it, stinky-pants. Baby loves mommy. Yes, yes, yes." Women put their heads into monstrous freezers and came out alive. Checkout girls moved their hips against the cash registers. An old lady fell down.

In time we came to a town called Fort Curtis. I was alone up front, driving slowly, wearing my green shades and a pair of old khaki trousers with huge back pockets that might have been designed to conceal rope, flashlights and barbwire cutters. It was late afternoon, an unseasonably warm day, bug juice all over the windshield, an idle insect hum coming from the tall grass by the river. The river might have been the Wabash or the Ohio or the Mississippi for all I knew. I drove slowly through the town's shady dead streets. Brick and frame houses stood under large elms. The porches had carved posts. There were lilac bushes in the gardens, moss at the base of telephone poles and a bandstand in the park at the edge of town. I drove around a little longer and then stopped in front of a three-story white frame hotel. We needed baths.

There were four elderly people sitting in the lobby, turning the pages of identical magazines. I got a room with a bath and then went back out to the camper. Brand and Sullivan were asleep on cots. Pike was sitting at the table in his World War I side-button shorts, drinking bourbon and smelling his armpits. I woke up Sullivan. She put some things into an overnight bag and went into the hotel. I waited ten minutes and went up to the room. As I reached for the doorknob I heard water running in the tub. The door was open. Some of her clothes were on the bed. I studied the plain brown robe, an item suitable for Lenten mortification. The room was painted a surly municipal green. Dust, paper clips and scraps of plaster had been swept into a corner. There was no TV set. The fabric on the armchair was thinning out. I heard Sullivan sink into the tub.

"Those dear old things in the lobby," she said. "What's the name of this place—the Menopause Hilton?"

"How did you know I was here?"

"My secret will die with me, Igor."

"Listen," I said. "When you wash your legs, do you lift one leg way up out of the water and sort of scrub it slowly and sensually like the models in TV commercials?"

"No."

"Can I come in and watch?"

"No, she said."

"Why not? We're adults."

"Exactly."

"If I promise to keep one hand over my eyes, can I come in and scrub your back?"

"Where are you sitting?"

"On the bed."

"See if you can find my cigarettes."

"They're not here," I said. "Want me to go down and get them?"

"Don't bother."

I tossed the cigarettes and matches under the bed.

"Sully, would you mind if we stayed around this town for a couple of days?"

"For your movie?"

"I'll look around this evening and then decide."

"What's so special about this place?"

"It seems old and simple and dull."

"I don't mind. Have you asked the others?"

"I think they'll go along with it. Everybody's pretty exhausted. We can use a few days of rest."

"Where are we anyway?" she said.

"It could be Indiana. But it could be Illinois or Kentucky. I'm not sure."

"I guess it doesn't matter. I don't know why I ask, but what's west of here?"

"Iowa, I think. Although maybe Iowa is further north. I'm trying to remember what's below Iowa."

"Never mind. It doesn't matter. I don't know why I asked."

I sat on the bed listening to the room tone, or general background noise, and filming in my mind a line of light and shade across the armchair. The room seemed beyond time, beyond present tense at any rate, in tone, in appearance, in the very quality of its light and air. I thought of it as the kind of room which, years before, or decades, had little purpose but to await the hardware salesman and his whisky flings.

Most likely the room had looked as shabby then as it did now. Maybe that was the dream in those days, a touch of cluttered lust, long gone now, for a new image had awakened our instincts, brides and bawds and gunmen of the West, an image to fit our ascetic scheme, the rise of the low motel, neat and clean at ground zero, electronic rabbit at the end of the bed. An arm and breast hung from the open door of the bathroom. I picked her robe off the bed and tossed it toward her wrist. The room's mood was dead. It was thirty years or more dead and gone.

That evening I got out my camera and went for a walk. It was a 16mm Canon Scoopic, modified to work as a sync rig with my tape recorder, a late-model Nagra. The camera didn't have an interchangeable lens but it was light, easy to handle and went to work in a hurry. Originally all I had wanted to do on the trip west was shoot some simple film, the white clapboard faces of Mennonite farmers, the spare Kansans in their churchgoing clothes. But now my plans were a bit more ambitious, scaring me somewhat, at least in their unedited form. I clutched the handgrip, rested the camera on my right shoulder and walked through the quiet streets. Soon a small crowd was following me.

Remarkably the bench wasn't green. It was light blue and it faced the yellow bandstand. The playground area, off to the side, was even more cheery in color, perhaps to counterbalance the stark forbidding nature of much of the apparatus. I sat on the bench and watched a small girl sail a book of matches in a puddle below the water fountain. I waited and slowly they approached, six welcomers in two loosely joined teams of three. First came an old man and two old ladies; then a teen-age boy leading two men who looked as though they might have shared a watch or two on a tin can off Guadal (in the Warner Brothers forties) and talked about the body-and-fender shop they would open when they got back to the States. Of course it was the camera they were interested in, that postlinear conversation piece, and they gathered around me in stages, introducing themselves, asking questions, being exceedingly friendly, secretly preparing their outrage for the moment of my incivility. But I remained well-mannered throughout, a guest in sacred places.

The old man was Mr. Hutchins, who said he liked to be called either Mr. H or Hutch, the latter name being favored by his Florida cronies. The women were his wife and his sister, Flora and Veejean, and they appeared to be in their mid-sixties, beautiful, smiling and silent, a pair of lace curtains fixed in sunlight. Hutch had once owned an Argus that he'd sent away for. He said the whole works only cost him one hundred fifty dollars—camera, projector, tripod screen, camera case, roll of film. His footage of the Everglades had been shown to a packed house in the basement of the Methodist Church.

The other men were Glenn Yost and Owney Pine and the boy was Glenn Yost Jr., who preferred to be called Bud. It turned out that each group knew the other only by sight, living in different ends of town, having been collected here, as it were, by the sight of the camera, the boy's curiosity equal to the old man's.

"How much the camera cost?" Bud said.

"Twelve hundred and change."

That was good for a whistle from Mr. H.

"I might get a super 8 this summer," the boy said. "I'm hoping the Bolex 155. We have a club at school. So far I haven't done much because the equipment they have is pretty limited. But if I can get a Bolex, I'd go right out of my mind. What kind of diopter range that thing give you?"

His father stood behind him, reflective and gloomy, left eye jumping, head tilted far to one side, almost resting on his shoulder, and I was reminded of the ancient relief pitcher Hoyt Wilhelm standing on the mound waiting for the sign to be given, fingers knuckling along the seams of the ball, men on first and third and none out, nobody caring anywhere in the world. There was a young man with a guitar sitting on the edge of the bandstand.

Mr. Hutchins described himself, in no particular context, as a stickler for accuracy. He and the ladies said goodnight then, time to catch Bob Hope on TV, and we watched them walk past a huge skeletal flywheel and out into the street. Bud and I tried to top each other and intimidate the two older men with all sorts of insane technical data. Owney Pine finally put one of his fat white arms around the boy's head, muffling him in jest and holding him that way for a minute or so, a quality of mutual affection informing the little scene as the man quietly jostled and bumped, barely aware of the struggling boy, who, at an overgrown fifteen or sixteen, could not have been easy to hold.

"Plan to be here awhile?" Glenn said.

"A few days maybe. My camera seems interested in this place."

"Are you one of those people from the mass media?" Owney said, still keeping Bud from wriggling out.

"I'm an independent filmmaker. I'm scouting locales at the moment. How'd you like to be in the movies?"

"Sheee."

"You think about it," I said.

Bud cut in then with another question and Owney released him. We talked a bit longer. The young man eased down off the bandstand and headed toward us. He carried the guitar over his shoulder and dragged a knapsack along the ground behind him. He seemed a skinny broken kid in decomposing clothes, enormously happy about something. The others backed off slightly at his approach—an ethnologic retreat really, one that I sensed rather than actually witnessed.

"Hey, what's that? That an 8 or 16?"

"It's a Scoopic 16. It's basically a news camera."

"I'm walking to California," he said.

He stood there, smiling, in ankle-high basketball sneakers. Glenn Yost said he and Bud had better be getting on home to have a look at the bloodworms. He said the boy dug up worms and sold them for bait. They were kept in large jars in the basement. He and Bud liked to look in on the worms every evening about sundown because that was the time the worms did most of their writhing and both father and son got a special kick out of seeing worms writhe, especially in masses. Glenn's left eye stuttered again. I couldn't be sure whether or not this was some local brand of double-reverse sophisti-cated humor. The boy's face was noncommittal and I thought they might be playing games with me, satirizing the outsider's conviction that smalltown life is a surrender to just such tiny deaths, worm-watching and Masonic handshakes. (Or were they trying to negate the serpent power of the longhair, dis-tract him with worms while the townspeople put their torches to his guitar?) Owney Pine said he would tag along with them. The park lights came on.

"I started walking about three months ago," the young man said. "I started out from Washington, D.C., so it'll be almost a coast-to-coast walk. I've been trying to do it in a straight line, D.C. to Frisco, but I've strayed a little south. There's plenty of time to adjust, I guess."

"About two thousand miles. I'm Dave Bell. What's your name?"

"Richard Spector. Sometimes I have trouble remembering it. It seems so long ago that it meant anything."

He sat next to me, feet up on the bench and knees high as he huddled against his own legs. He was very frail and his hair covered much of his face. He looked directly at me when he spoke but with no implication of challenge in his eyes, no sense of ideologies about to clash, and I felt he had whittled these things out of his way, settling down to a position defined only by the length of each footsore day.

"People have been taking good care of me," he said. "They feed me and sometimes give me places to sleep. At first I get a lot of strange what-is-it looks. But when I tell them I'm walking to California, they get all caught up in the craziness of the thing. People are real great if you can get them off details and onto something crazy. They've really been taking tremendous care of me. I brought along all the savings I had, about seven hundred dollars in cash and traveler's checks, and in three months I've had to spend only about a hundred and fifty dollars for food and for sleeping in hotels whenever it was too cold at night for outdoor-type sleeping and I couldn't find anywhere else to stay."

"I don't want to sound discouraging, Richard, but you look awfully tired and run-down."

"You should have seen me before I left."

We both laughed and then he asked if he could handle the camera. I removed the lens hood for him and he took the camera and stood up, putting his eye to the rubber eyecup and then slowly covering the park in a virtuoso 360-degree pan. I heard a car come to an abrupt stop and I turned and saw first a young woman's face at the window on the passenger side, and then the head and shoulders of a man about my age rising over the car's roof from the other side as he looked in our direction. Apparently satisfied that he had been right in stopping, he returned to the driver's seat, threw the car into reverse and quickly parked, tires marking the pavement. He got out, again looking our way, closing the door with a certain disdainful élan, and then came through the park entrance, looking now, it was clear, not at Richard or at me—a considerable relief—but at the camera in Richard's hands. The girl followed, quite slowly, a lissome blonde of twenty-five or so, in her quiet prime, pretty and tarrying and yet to be hurt, not at all in love. Richard extended the camera to me. The man's eyes followed it right into my hands.

"Does that thing put out a sync pulse?"

"That's right," I said.

"Sound," he said.

"That's right."

"I'm Austin Wakely. The lady is Carol Deming. I saw that thing from the car and I said let me get a closer look. What kind of action are you into?"

"Under the underground," I said.

"But with sound."

"Some sound. Here and there."

"I'm an actor," he said.

215

"He's studying to be an actor," Carol said.

I introduced myself, told them where I was from and asked them to join me on the bench. I realized Richard Spector was gone. Then I saw him sitting once more on the edge of the bandstand.

"I'm studying with Drotty," Austin said.

"Who's he?"

"He's originally from Minneapolis. He worked with Guthrie there. But he's a very freeform individual and it became more and more untenable for him to try and function in a structured environment. That's why he came over to McCompex. That's the new institute five miles east of here. You haven't heard of it back East yet but you will. The full name is the McDowd Communication Arts Complex. The regular session ends next month. I'm staying on for the summer session. Before I came out to McCompex I worked at a variety of odd jobs around the country. I'm originally from Washington, state of."

Carol was sitting between us.

"It's a question of who I am and what I want to be," Austin said. "I have to relate to something. Drotty is nonsocietal. I've learned a lot from him. He's a homosexual of course. They all are. He has his tensions and anxieties and he smokes a great deal. They all do. But Drotty has taught me something and it's this. Societal pressure is fierce but you've always got the option to repattern. Acting is love. What was it Nazimova said?"

I moved my leg slightly, the slimmest fraction of an inch, and Carol and I were touching. She sat absolutely still as Austin continued to speak. I moved again and we were touching now thigh to knee. The occasion was one of infinite subtlety. She may not have noticed the scant pressure of my leg; she may have noticed but thought nothing of it; or she may have known all along what I was doing. I edged my arm toward hers. Austin kept talking. Now our forearms were touching, the faintest inshore breeze of our bare flesh barely in contact, flesh resting on points of almost invisible silver hair. Still she was motionless, no sign either way. I waited several minutes. Then I moved my right hand across my lap and let it rest above my right knee. Carol was looking straight ahead. I was extremely nervous. The next few seconds would tell whether or not she knew and how she saw fit to respond to the knowledge. I did not want to be disappointed. It was important that she give me the right sign. I let my hand slide very slowly into the crease formed by our two legs. I let it rest there. We were both looking straight ahead. Then I felt a slight pressure from her thigh, a slight and pleasant heat on the tips of my fingers, the slightest suggestion of shifting weight, a muscle tensing, her body not moving and yet expressing movement, finding a new balance, shifting inside itself, shifting toward me. I returned the pressure and then moved several inches away. Austin kept talking and I began to relax. Carol and I looked straight ahead. It was my first ego-moment since New York.

Austin told me how to get in touch with him and said he would like to hear more about my plans. I realized for the first time how handsome he was. He had dark hair and eyes. His shoulders were broad. There was a splendid intensity about him. We all got up and Austin and I shook hands. Carol stood off to the side, her arms folded under her breasts, normally a housewife's backyard stance, trading gossip and detergent advice, but her hips were thrust forward somewhat, eyes interested and musing, and this more than redeemed the moment. I told Austin I liked his car, a green Barracuda, and in the course of the next few sentences I managed to point out that my red Mustang, now in Maine, had the same kind of high-back buckets, plus dual racing mirrors.

As they drove away, I nodded to Richard and he slipped off the bandstand and walked back to the camper with me. We talked with the others for a while. Later, over a dinner of corned beef and sangria, Sullivan announced that Richard Spector would henceforth be known as Kyrie Eleison. I reached for the tape recorder.

"I used to be a mailboy in the Justice Department in Washington," he said. "I felt I was becoming transparent. I had the feeling that after I ate dinner, people could see the food in my stomach. That's just one of the things that was happening to me. I began to fear that chunks of government buildings would dislodge and fall on top of me. But I think the worst thing of all was when I was walking on a crowded street. You know how people jockey back and forth, the fast walkers trying to overtake the slow walkers. There's always a lot of shoving and the fast walkers are always stepping on the slow ones and knocking their shoes off. I was a fast walker. I was always hurrying even when I was just going for an aimless stroll, and I used to get annoyed when slow walkers got in my way. One day I was trying to get around an old man who kept drifting toward the curb and blocking my path and suddenly I found myself shouting at him in my own head, shouting inwardly and silently: LOOK OUT! LOOK OUT! I never actually spoke the words. I just shouted them mentally. I began to do that all the time. LOOK OUT, I would say to people. MOVE! MOVE! And I could see the words in my head in big block letters like in a cartoon. Then one day a woman slowed down suddenly and I almost crashed into her. I found myself shouting a new word in my head: DIE! If I had said it aloud she probably would have died. It was really a hideous inner scream and I could see the word in my head in red letters with a big exclamation point. I began to realize I was abnormal. I was a person who walked along the street mentally shouting DIE at innocent people. After several months of this I tried to make a conscious effort to stop shouting the word. But it was too late. It just popped into my head automatically. DIE! DIE! I'll tell you the kind of person I was. I was the kind of person who's always falling in love with the wives of his best friends."

"Have you stopped shouting DIE?" Sullivan said.

"I stopped shouting it the day I quit my job and I haven't shouted it since. I haven't shouted anything since. I'll tell you what else I was. I was the kind of person who always reads those lists of the dead and missing that newspapers print after plane crashes. I read the lists compulsively. I don't know what I expected to find. The name of a friend? My own name? A long list of dead people's names is the most depressing thing you can read. Some of the names are incomplete and some have no hometowns next to them. Then they list the missing. How could anybody be missing from a plane crash? Where could they go? I'll tell you what else I used to do. I had a strange kind of embarrassment about saying people's names, especially the names of good friends and relatives. For some reason I could never address them by their right names. It was some goofy form of embarrassment. I used to call people Max, Charlie, Guido or Steve. Those were the four names I used most often. I didn't use one particular name for one particular person. The names and people were interchangeable. I might address somebody as Max one day and as Guido the next. It could even change from sentence to sentence. Nobody seemed to mind. I guess it's like being referred to as buddy or pal or friend. I don't know why I picked Max, Charlie, Guido and Steve. I had no trouble with women. I always called women by their right names. Why couldn't I call men by their right names?"

"Has that changed too?" I said.

"Everything's changed," he said. "I no longer have any anxiety about not being able to speak French. It used to worry me. My father speaks French very well. He was always inviting people to dinner and speaking French with them. It was his way of maintaining power over me. But now I don't care about that stuff anymore. I'm no longer frightened. There's a whole bunch of people like me who have broken out. We're not interested in the power that older people grasp for. They try to keep us down by speaking French and knowing how to mix whisky sours and wearing suits where the buttons on the coatsleeves really unbutton. But a lot of us have broken out. We don't care if we don't know how to pronounce the names of French wines. What's wrong with California wine anyway? What the heck, this is America. Bad as it is, we have to learn to live with it."

Kyrie slept in the hotel room that night. The rest of us settled down on our cots inside the camper. Just before I went to sleep, I imagined myself fighting with Brand. We hit each other dozens of times. Then something else moved across my mind, possessions, things in my home, shapes of objects unfondled of late, the Olivetti Lettera 32, the Nikon F, and then girls in purple stockings rolling across a paper plain, and James Joyce and Antonioni and Samuel Beckett sitting in my living room, six legs crossed at the ankles, Tana Elkbridge naked on Riverside Drive while her husband read *Business Week* at thirty thousand feet, and Jennifer naked in the West Eighties, something touching about her hipbones, and Meredith naked in Gramercy Park, and Sullivan naked in the bath. Then we were fighting again. I backed away from a long right and came back with a left to the cheekbone and a short straight right square on the point of the chin. Brand went to his knees and hung there, breathing blood. I kicked him in the stomach and went to sleep.

We had breakfast in a diner the next morning. Men in short-sleeve shirts came and went. I formed my hand into a claw. Brand sat at the table laughing. Then Sullivan began to laugh. People at the counter turned to look at them. Brand was slumped over the table, arms folded, and his head rocked as he laughed. Sullivan sat rigidly, facing Brand, laughing out over his head. I formed both hands into claws and bobbed up and down in the chair. Lips parted slightly, curling down at the corners, I bared my lower set of teeth and dug them into my upper lip. I knew they were not laughing at me and yet I continued to make ghoulish faces and claw at the air. I did not like to be left out. I did not know why they were laughing and so I pretended they were laughing at me. Pike began to laugh. I turned toward the people at the counter and clawed at their backs. Kyrie was laughing now. The waitress came with our food and Brand looked up at her and nearly fell off the chair howling. My claws became hands again. Kyrie pointed at his scrambled eggs and this set them off on a fresh wave of laughter. The waitress smiled as she stood by the table writing out the check. Brand pointed at her pencil. She looked at it and began to laugh. Everything was funny. It was a clear day in spring and suddenly everything was funny. I went to the bathroom and looked at myself in the mirror.

They laughed all through breakfast. Somebody would point to something and they'd all laugh. The ketchup bottle was hilarious. Brand continually took off his glasses and wiped them with a napkin. His was the universal face of alumni bulletins. Assistant plant manager of the general foam division, Tenneco Chemicals, East Rutherford, N.J. Training and education officer, Air University's Warfare Systems School, Maxwell AFB, Ala. Brand the junior partner. The young Republican. He was about an inch taller than I was. He weighed 210 or so. His eyes were panes of muddy glass, gray and very distant. Now he stood and blessed the restaurant, his face deadpan again, his right hand making crosses over the heads of the assembled men and women. I finished breakfast and left a twenty-dollar bill on the table. Pike followed me out. We stood on the sidewalk in front of the hotel. It was called Ames House, I noticed.

"See if you can answer this," Pike said. "Think about it as long as you want before answering. Here it is. Open up the stomach of a killer whale and roughly how many seals and porpoises are you likely to find?"

"You'd better let me think about it."

"Two dozen," he said.

Checkout time was noon. I went up to the room, called downstairs and asked the voice to get the office in New York. When the switchboard girl at the network came on, I asked to speak with David Bell. It was an odd feeling. Binky answered.

"Miss me?" I said.

"Who's this?"

"The person you admire most in the whole world."

"Stop fooling around."

"Dave Bell's my name; cinematography's my game."

"David, how are you?"

"Miss me?"

"Yes, it's so boring around here."

"It's boring out here too."

"Where are you?" she said.

"Fifty-third and Lex."

"Guess what? There's a rumor going around that Grove Palmer is a fag. Jody told me Sid Slote ran into him accidentally in Bermuda and he was hanging around with some very swishy types."

"It figures. I always wondered about that guy."

"Guess what else?"

"Go ahead."

"I was waiting for you to guess. Harris Hodge? The first replacement Weede hired after the mass rape and execution? He showed up yesterday."

"What's he look like?"

"He's a very neat guy, David. A terrific sense of humor. And he's really cute-looking. Hallie thinks he looks like Paul Newman, only younger."

"How much younger? I want to know his exact age."

"I haven't been able to find out yet."

"If you got off your ass once in a while."

"Don't get angry."

"What else?" I said.

"Trotsky struck again."

"When?"

"Two days ago."

"Great, great. Whose name was signed to the memo? Wait, I want to guess."

"Like forget it," she said.

"I figure we were about due for a Giambattista Vico."

"Forget it, sweetie."

"I was thinking about Beckett last night. Was it Beckett?"

"You'll never guess so I may as well tell you. It's a three-name person. Otto Durer Obenwahr."

"Trotsky really pulled one out of the hat this time."

"I'll say. Everybody's trying to figure out who Otto Durer Obenwahr is. Ed Watchold sent his secretary to the library this morning. The place is in a minor uproar."

"What does it say? What's the quote?"

"I saved it for you. Ready? *Fools! Fools! To square the circle is child's play. It is the reverse which leads to the beatific vision.*"

"Interesting," I said.

"What do you think it means?"

"Very interesting."

"Thanks a lot."

"Listen, find out everything you can about this bastard Harris Hodge. But especially how old he is."

"Okay."

"Does Weede like him?"

"They're having lunch tomorrow."

"Find out if Weede likes him. I'll call you again somewhere between here and the Navahos."

"Okay. Have a good time."

"So long, Bink."

"David, I almost forgot."

"Yes?"

"Ted Warburton had to be rushed to the hospital."

"When was this?"

"Yesterday afternoon. He collapsed at his desk."

"Goodbye," I said.

All five of us sat in the camper all afternoon. Pike drank Old Crow from a paper cup and made occasional growling sounds. Ahead were the Rockies, dripping sweat, paws scraping the earth, set to pounce, his keeper the lion. Brand was lost behind his glasses, traveling back, I thought, to some timeless room at the center of his being, bungled memories of four walls and the gray medicine man. Kyrie bit the knuckle of his right thumb. Somebody parking a car hit our rear bumper lightly and we nodded. I was wearing my Comanche moccasins, a pair of green wide-wale cords with a garrison belt, and a black sport shirt.

"Sully, who's Otto Durer Obenwahr?"

"Expert on liquid oxygen and high altitude drogue chutes."

"Seriously, ever hear of him?"

She seemed to be trying to tear circles out of the newspaper she was reading. She tore circles and handed them to Kyrie. He was sitting on the floor. He handed the circles up to Brand.

"I'm going for a walk," I said.

"Bring back some Mars Bars," Brand said.

"You owe me change of twenty," I said. "I left a twenty on the table."

"Don't look at me, Davy. I didn't pay the check."

"I didn't pay it," Kyrie said. "Don't look at me."

"Somebody owes me change of twenty."

"I left when you left," Pike said.

"Somebody owes me change. I've been paying for everything around here."

"Bring back some jujubes," Kyrie said.

I walked down a street that had the sadness of all roads leading out of town, a blues-song street, oil spilled by huge trucks, a traffic light swinging high over an empty intersection. I crossed to a building with a neon beer-sign out front. I found the telephone, called the McDowd Communication Arts Complex and asked for Carol Deming. I was using a wall phone at the back of the room. Three auto mechanics were at the bar. I noticed a pinball machine, a bowling machine, a jukebox and a shuffleboard with three steel discs sitting in rosin. Then I heard Carol's voice.

"North Atlantic Treaty Organization."

"Hi, I didn't know if I'd find you there. It's David Bell— from the park."

"I'm sorry, you've reached the answering service for NATO Brussels. They're all out. Would you care to leave a message?"

"I'm in a bar on Howley Road."

"Buster's," she said. "It used to be a firehouse."

"Do you have a car?"

"I can take Austin's."

"He won't mind?"

"Of course he'll mind."

I sat at the bar and had a scotch. The ashtray in front of me was full of pared fingernails. I was on the third drink when she arrived. The way she walked made her skirt sway lightly across her legs and I felt lucky and full of improvisation, a nice loose music in my head, and I knew the auto mechanics were watching her but not with sludge and crankcase lust; rather with a small joy, I thought, a tiny leap of flesh, the light lucky feeling of seeing a pretty girl with bare legs walking across a room behind a smile that says she likes being a woman being watched. I tried not to look so pleased. She glanced at my drink and asked for the same.

"I wasn't sure you were living at McCompex too. I thought it might be just him. You didn't say anything about it yesterday. Was it yesterday we met?"

"There isn't much to say, David. It's just something to do while I wait for my husband to divorce me. I had some money saved and I've always wanted to study acting. So I came on down."

"From where?"

"Detroit," she said.

"That your hometown?"

"I was an army brat. I've lived in nine states."

"What did you do in Detroit?"

"We used to have a drink every Friday evening at the Zebra Lounge. That's what we did."

"You mean people from the office."

"You know how it is on Friday. Everybody wants to unwind

225

with a drink or two. They used to have canapés for the regular crowd. We were the regular crowd."

We talked and drank for a while. I was feeling good and loose, on the verge of inspired dialogue, drink number four, a pale flame rising. Carol took a pack of Gauloises out of her handbag. I lit one for her and a sweet evil smell lay flat on the hanging smoke.

"Did the regular crowd at the Zebra include one extrovert who was always joking with the waiter and who liked to order exotic drinks?"

"Fred Blasingame," she said.

"What were some of the drinks he ordered? This is important."

"I remember once he ordered an Americano. I remember another time he ordered a Black Russian."

"I think we're really getting somewhere. When you take a bath, Carol, do you like to lift one leg out of the water and wash it sort of slowly and sensually?"

"You're going too far."

"Carol, how do you feel about the war?"

"I can't seem to get involved, maybe because the whole thing is so halfhearted."

"People are dying."

"I know. Isn't it terrible?"

"Can you identify Otto Durer Obenwahr?" I said.

"Didn't he play lead guitar with Grand Funk Railroad?"

"Let me ask you this if I may. What is the most pressing need in America today?"

"Patriotism," she said. "Our sons must return to their mother. She is waiting with open legs. Killing the pig-eyed and the slope-headed must once again become a matter of national priority."

"Did the Zebra have piped-in music? Please answer at once."

"Yes," she said.

"Did the regular crowd ever have friendly arguments about the name of a certain tune?"

"That used to happen all the time. Carl Stoner, who was in premiums, was always having arguments with Martha Leggett. Martha Leggett was the funniest little girl you ever saw. She was less than five feet tall and Freddy B. used to let her take puffs on his cigar. We surrounded ourselves with smoke and loud noise. That's the way we chose to live. I'm prepared to defend it."

"Did the rumors about Carl Stoner and Fred Blasingame's wife have any basis in fact?"

"Come on now. There weren't any rumors like that. And anyway you haven't even asked me about the summerhouse."

I ordered two more scotches. I didn't know where we were headed and I was in no hurry to find out. It was obvious that the feints and jugglery of the moment did not confuse her one bit. Her answers were almost too easy in coming. Her voice changed, even the structure of her sentences, and as we went along I realized she was no mere student of theatercraft. She seemed perfectly relaxed, almost bored, content to let me find a pace and theme, breaking inflection from sentence to sentence and yet never relinquishing the bedrock irony, the closed fist of the Midwest. Her eyes emitted quick blue light. She was far from being the worst thing you could expect to find in an old firehouse in Iowa or Missouri or Illinois.

"Have you ever been to New York?" I said.

"We used to go over to the pier on Gansevoort Street and watch the sun go down. We used to eat soul food on Tenth Avenue."

"After several or more drinks, did any of the men in the regular crowd at the Zebra ever slip their hands under the table and try to caress either of your thighs?"

"I guess that sort of thing is unavoidable if you're going to have a few drinks in mixed company. But there was never any trouble about it. I mean all I did was sort of shift in my chair a little and they would get the idea and that would be the end of it."

"Did tiny Martha Leggett shift in her chair?"

"I have no way of knowing."

"I applaud your loyalty."

"She was a plucky little skylarking girl. She and Fred Blasingame were like a comedy team. George and Gracie. That's what we used to call them. My father's name was George."

"That brings us to the summerhouse," I said.

"Tall grass and lemonade. Those lazy afternoons at auntie Nell's. I was such a silly thing at fifteen. This is difficult."

"Please try."

"He came from the base to visit me, taller than the grass, so bright and shining in the sun. He was in uniform. Nell made lemonade. We sat out front beneath the big elm, just the three of us and John Morning. Daddy had brought me a book of poems, sonnets written by a southern lady whose lover was killed at Vicksburg. Nell went inside to start dinner. John Morning sang a spiritual and then went off to the stables. Daddy read the sonnets to me and I cried and called myself a silly thing and he laughed softly in that gentle way of his. We drank the lemonade and watched the sun go down over the big elm."

"Where was the Jamison boy?" I said.

"The Jamison boy had drowned in Loon Lake just three weeks before. Daddy knew about it, of course, but was gentle enough and wise enough to make no mention of the tragedy. After dinner we walked through the tall grass beneath the moon. We listened to the crickets and daddy held my hand. Then we went back to the house. Nell made some lemonade and John Morning told us the yearling was coming along just fine. Daddy went out to the stables to look at the yearling. I went to my room and he came up later and spoke softly in the darkness of war and death, touching me softly in soft places. He made no mention of the tragedy of the Jamison boy and he said nothing about the summerhouse."

"At what hour were you awakened by the strange sound?"

"It was almost dawn when I was awakened by a strange sound. I got out of bed and put on my riding pants and the green sweater with the button missing. I still have that sweater. It was the sweater I was wearing the last time I saw the Jamison boy, two nights before he drowned. We were on the back porch drinking lemonade. John Morning was singing a spiritual. The Jamison boy asked me whether I'd be spending the whole summer this time or just a few weeks as in the past. I said it was up to mother. He said he was tired of all the mystery about mother. He wanted to know the truth."

"So you told him about the summerhouse."

"Yes, I told him," she said. "He was the only one who knew the horrible secret. And two nights later he drowned. I still have that sweater locked away somewhere in a trunk. Do you have any idea how difficult this is?"

"Carol, when did you first realize that his death was not an accident?"

"When I was awakened by the strange sound. I knew what the sound was and I realized the Jamison boy had been shot to death prior to being drowned. I put on my red satin dress with the plunging neckline, the dress I wore to mother's second funeral. Needless to say, the sound was coming from the summerhouse. I walked through the tall grass, which was wet with dew. The sun was coming up over the big elm. I opened the door of the summerhouse."

"What did you see?"

"It was daddy. He was naked except for his uniform."

"What was he doing?"

"Really I can't go on."

"What was he doing, Carol?"

"He was firing bullets into John Morning's drowned body."

"What did you see in John Morning's hand?"

"The locket. Mother's silver locket."

"Did any of the men in the regular crowd habitually break his swizzle stick with a loud plastic snap?"

"Bob Kirkpatrick."

"Perfect," I said. "What can you tell us about him?"

"He looked like a redwood tree."

"Can you identify the governor of California?"

"There is no such place."

"Excellent. If a redwood tree falls in a deserted forest, does it make a sound? Or is sound dependent on a sentient being?"

"It makes a sound."

"What kind of sound?" I said.

"One hand clapping."

"You're going too far, Carol. But I'll try to stay with you. You mentioned your husband earlier in the evening. Was your husband part of the regular crowd?"

"My husband is part of no crowd, regular, irregular or otherwise. He's black. Blackest black."

"You're telling me he's a Negro."

"What used to be called an American Negro."

I was getting drunk. The bartender put two more drinks in front of us. I lit another cigarette for her and she turned away when she exhaled and then swung her head slowly back and looked at me with a grieving smile. The three mechanics were at the pinball machine. Four young men drank beer at the other end of the bar.

"What are you doing here?" she said.

"I wanted to escape from the regular crowd. It reached the point where I was seeing ghosts. I was asleep in a loft one night. I was tired and drunk and I fell asleep. I dreamed about the town where I grew up. When I opened my eyes I thought I saw my mother's ghost in the room. But it was just an apparition I dragged up out of the dream. What I saw was the woman who owned the loft. Whose studio it was. She had come in and was standing in the doorway when I opened my eyes. What, if anything, do you make of all this?"

"David, I'm out on my feet. I'm really tired. It's been a long day. If you don't mind I think I'll be getting on back."

"I want you in my film," I said.

They were having dinner when I got back to the camper. Afterward, for Kyrie's benefit, Brand tensed and untensed his forearm in rhythm so that the tattooed dogs seemed to be moving. I kept waiting for someone to complain about our stay here. Kyrie went to sleep under the table. I took Sullivan's radio to bed with me. I turned it on, low volume, and listened in the dark. Every time Pike snored I punched the side of the camper and he would stop for a while. Unable to sleep, I listened to the radio half the night, changing stations, countries, hemispheres, switching to shortwave and ships at sea, the whole nightworld scratching out there, entangled languages, voices in storms of passion and static, commercials, prayers, newscasts, poems, soccer riots, threats of death and war and revolution, laughter from the mountains and appeals to reason from the broad plains, demonstration in La Paz, landslide in Zurich, assassination in Dakar, fire in Melbourne, confusion in Toyko, tragedy in Athens. Then I heard a familiar voice.

"At the sound of the gong it will be exactly three o'clock in the morning. Three o'killing clock. This is Beastly here and we've still got two hours to go. But these next crucial minutes will tell all. Time to pluck the lint from your omphalos. Time to gnaw at the legs of chairs. I know you're out there in mamaland, tens of thousands of you, humped up on the floor whimpering, licking the cold steel of the barrel of your shotgun. The agon begins. Time to scream into the pillow. Time to brainpaper the walls. But if we make the next ten minutes we make the night. Three in the morning and werewolves slink in the parlor. American Mean Time. You came home from work to find your wife in bed with your sister. Curiously refreshing. You stayed to watch. Sure, I know what it's like out there. One big succulent eyeball bouncing on your tongue. Eye of goat. Black gleaming eye of master fucker of all the

231

baby sheep you counted in your wetty bed. I know what it's like. I, Beastly, have foresuffered almost all. Forced by my priestly capillaries to go all the way to Dublin to attain suitable erection and staying power. Mollycuddling my bloomless bride. Mother of twin anxieties. Indeed I know your secrets. For the past three days you've been followed all over town by a gigantic bald Malayan wearing a mackintosh. You've placed an ad in the L.A. *Free Press*. Studs, butches and house-broken pets interested in self-stimulation. Adding no freaks please in small type. Using a box number corresponding to the day, month and year of your first holy communion. You are drowning in porn and prury. You are unmasked and emasculated. We interrupt this program for a news bulletin. The president rose at noon, breakfasted with cabinet members, lashed out at his critics, shook hands with a Negro, had a steambath, and lunched with Nguyen Cao Dung, the former head of an undisclosed country ostensibly run by the CIA as a nonprofit organization. This is Warren Beasley at the White House in Washington saying this is Warren Beasley at the White House in Washington. We return you now to our studios. I feel silence out there tonight. Nothing stirs but a faint gray figure limping through the bus terminals and train stations. Lonely onanist in his chilly calculations. Where is the charitable ear for my intemperate prattle? I keep my caricatures to keep me company. Lord Greystoke, the British adventurer, plans to sail a Chinese junk singlehandedly between Malta and Crete in order to prove that the Mediterranean was once a lake in Sinkiang Province. I know you're out there somewhere, all you prankish gunmen, pacing your scurvy rooms, making lists of likely targets with your Scriptomatic ballpoints, thinking incredibly in your wistfulness of the grandeur of state funerals. Photos on the wall of grouped adolphs. That hot thunder in your head, every drum since Goliath. This is Simon called Peter speaking on behalf of the Bumble-bee tuna packers of America and wishing all of you a safe and sane ascent into heaven. You're in good hands with God the

Father. The kid I wouldn't be so sure. A real maven. But tough in the clutch. Three after three, les misérables. The enemy grows bold. Just enough time for some random news items. Europe has apparently vanished. Its whereabouts are completely unknown. However, seamen aboard a Liberian tanker off Greenland have reportedly sighted oil slicks and all sorts of Louis Quatorze debris. Time to dig at the issues behind the news. Time to sit at the gurgling Wurlitzer beneath the streets and like that unloved phantom of the lower depths to let a single tear flow down your brutish but sensitive face. But first a word from our alternate testicle. Women, here's a remarkable new way to give junior and sis the kind of nutrition they need for those growing-up years. Kill your husband and feed him to the kids. You'd love that, wouldn't you? All that melting butterflesh. All the animosities in your soul washed away by his flavor-rich enzymes. What subtle gravies you could conjure with those executive haunches. Enough and more again for all the saucepans of Bloomingdale's. Sweet waves of acidic backwash. Alfresco would be nice. Save the uglies for junior. To make him brave. Garnish with parsley. But I go too far, even for this audience of one-celled organisms. It is my own fake flesh I mean to cook. Delirium. There is but one truly serious philosophical problem and that is the station break. The clock crows. It's all numbers. Numbers and Deuteronomy. I'm losing my edge but stay with me. It's your only hope. Four minutes to death. No time to waste so you'd better listen fast. The bird is beginning to grimace inside the cuckoo clock. Quick—pray. Bow down to the god of your choice and pray for the end of yourself. Pray for new eyes and ears. Pray for shapes to change. Pray for fresh juice to take with you into your imminent climacteric. Pray for short and hunless winters. Pray for the Upper East Side, all those white tile buildings full of lonely girls quoting phony Persians to boys in love with jockstraps. Pray for adriaticated Venice. Pray for desirelessness and the dice-play of cunning. Pray for the insides of things, men and batteries, that they be shaved

233

to coolest precision. Pray for the walls of things, that they secure the things they secure against the anti-wall. Pray for the scrotum sacs of industrialists. Pray for poets who summer at Nantucket. Pray for 1958 two-toned Oldsmobiles. Pray for Umbriago, the mayor of New York and of Chicago. Pray seriously for the Austrialians because if they ever get the bomb it'll be a muddy rugger for us all. Pray for the bald eagle and his meddling beak. Pray that we stop replaying our lives into the sucking tapeworm. Pray that we not disappear O Lord into thy vastly impractical nightmind (from whence we came) without first preparing for the abrupt change of pace. Pray for expressiveness, that we cast away these welder's masks we wear to hide our grief and joy. Vulva! Vulva! Vulva! Seep inward and test what's left against the night. Be persistent as Java man was not. Water your mousterian cranium. Return to the primeval fertile crescent. Dar es Salaam! Abu Simbel! Chou-Kou-Tien! But the truth, I fear, is that I fear the dark days of the Arabian nights. I've got the Stephen Dedalus Blues and it's a long way to Leopoldville. Black panic in the filter of my kingsize Kent. We have awakened from the nightmare of history. Put your logical fork to the mushroom omelette. An unpleasant interruption in the assuring continuity. No precedents for the legal apparatus to pick at. No scrolls for men to jot their histories on, their art, their powerings of flag-draped armies. No sequels for the moviegoers in the think tanks. Riddled genes of Japan, we watch the dripping of your questions into the earth. Exeunt all and remember. King Kong died for your sins. Time for a final prayer as the cuckoo door swings open. The Queen James version. Strategic Air Command, which art in heaven, swallowed be thy planes. Thy kingdom come, thy will be done, on earth as it is in Omaha, Nebraska. Give us this day our daily dread and forgive us our strontium as we forgive those who strontium against us. And lead us not into annihilation but deliver us from rubble, for thine is the power and the power and the power, forever and never, oh man."

I had some frightening dreams that night and in the morning one image in particular stayed with me, a blue bus moving down a highway in the desert, and the picture was so clear in my mind that I might still have been asleep and dreaming, that flash of bright blue metal across the lionskin desert. For the first time in my life I could be certain that I dreamed in color. I don't know why but this cheered me tremendously.

After breakfast Kyrie said it was time for him to be moving on. We drove him the three or four blocks to Howley Road and parked in front of Buster's. We had a last cup of coffee in the back of the camper.

"I'm dedicating this walk to my buddy Art Levy," Kyrie said. "We were mailboys together in the Justice Department. A bunch of lawyers there started a motorcycle club. Eventually they let clerical workers and even mailboys join up. Art bought a stripped-down Harley secondhand and got into the club. They all wore real weird outfits—bandannas, army tunics, safari jackets, combat boots, leggings, football jerseys, cowhide vests. Lawyers and others. The Justice Department. I came into the office one morning and one of them came over to me and said Art got snuffed. I didn't know what he meant. He said he got snuffed by a fire engine. He ran into a fire engine and got a fractured skull and all kinds of massive internal injuries. He died the same night. So I tell everybody that helps me that I'm dedicating this walk to the memory of my buddy Art Levy, who gave up his life in an unequal encounter with tremendous contemporary forces."

"What will you do when you get to California?" Sullivan said.

"Learn how to play this guitar."

We got out of the camper and stood together on Howley Road. It was a black morning, cool and blowing and smelling of storm. Dirt blew up from the untended lots of the three or four houses on the road and the traffic light swung on its lanyard. Kyrie smiled and kissed each of us goodbye. Then he walked down the road, guitar and knapsack, a distinctly

235

neo-Chaplinesque finale, and the wind filled his shirt and nearly knocked him over. We tried to find a good reason for not leaving the camper exactly where it was; nobody could come up with anything and we got back inside. Pike lifted a bottle out of his seaman's bag. It started to rain then, a steady plastic murmur above our heads. Pike told us about the cougar, its speed, cunning and resourcefulness, how it could broad-jump thirty-five to forty feet, thus comparing favorably with the impala although the latter got all the publicity, and he told us about the animal's great energy, quoting a recorded case in which a single mountain lion had killed 192 sheep in one night. Later that day I trotted halfway across town in the rain in order to do some work at the library. At night I sat alone in the front of the camper, listening to the insects. I felt an urge to leave that place, to go roaring onto a long straight expressway into the West; to forget the film and what it was beginning to mean to me; to face mountains and deserts; to smash my likeness, prism of all my images, and become finally a man who lives by his own power and smell. In Venice I had met an elderly gentleman at the American Express office. We were standing in line to cash traveler's checks. I commented on what a fine sunny day it was.

"Know what we call this weather back in Pima County, Arizona?" he said.

"What's that?"

"Rain," he said. "We call it rain."

He winked at me and proceeded to the counter. The black cats of Venice slumbered in the alleys. Of Italy, its wet sun and white tablecloths, coconut slices being sprinkled in the markets, sinister knife-blade priests everywhere. I went to Florence then and Meredith pointed at the stones and shouted how stupendous. Then, alone, down to rusty dead Roma, German tourists saluting each other, everyone waiting for Fellini to come skipping along the Via Veneto in clownface and opera cape, trailed by virgins, camels, nubians, publicity men. Through it all an idea had haunted me, a vision of mesas and buttes, the cut of the dry winds, long cool shadows and horses' faces hung on fences, Navahos tending their sheep, the stitched earth of Arizona. We call it rain. But I made the mistake of staying on Howley Road.

I woke in the middle of the night and smelled chocolate pudding, a thick rich gripping smell. Then I thought of my mother's blue apron, the old chipped stove, so terribly real, the blue apron with the flowers, the way she stood there stirring the pudding, her hand a small limp triumph of continuity and grace, an assertion of order in the universe. In the morning I loaded the camera.

9

The illusion of motion was barely relevant. Perhaps it wasn't a movie I was creating so much as a scroll, a delicate bit of papyrus that feared discovery. Veterans of the film industry would swear the whole thing pre-dated Edison's kinetoscope. My answer to them is simple. It takes centuries to invent the primitive.

Glenn Yost opened the door. His long tired head leaned to the left and the crazed eye flared. I imagined that in some green diamond-shaped pasture of his mind the bases were loaded and a big eager rookie was striding to the plate, man-mountain with heavy lumber, a golden eater of cereal. Glenn lived in a two-story white frame house on a street of very old houses, almost all white, several needing paint. He led me downstairs to the basement, where his son was sprawled in a corner watching a Kirk Douglas western on TV.

"The wife is using the big set," Glenn said. "I thought we'd be quieter down here but I see the creature beat us to it."

"The All-Seeing Eye," Bud said.

"It's fine with me. I wanted to talk to Bud anyway."

"Let's sit down."

"What do you do for a living, Glenn?"

"I'm partners in a lumber yard."

"How's business?"

"Retirement's not exactly looming on the horizon."

"That's really neither here not there. My question I mean. I was just being polite, leading into the real subject of my visit. Which is: would you be at all interested in appearing in the thing I plan to shoot in this area in the next week or so? It wouldn't take more than a couple of hours of your time. All you have to do is read some lines before the camera. Actually read from a script, a piece of paper. No memory work, no preparation. Just showing up and reading. I know it doesn't sound like the most intriguing thing in the world, especially since I can't pay you a dime, but you wouldn't be losing more than a couple of hours' time and maybe you'd have some fun. I know one thing. You'd be doing me a tremendous, a really great favor. Bud, how old are you?"

"Be sixteen in three months."

"You too," I said. "A couple of hours."

"I don't know anything about reading lines," Glenn said.

"Everything out of your mouth is a line," Bud said. "You never mean anything. He never means anything. He tells people he was in the submarine paratroopers during the war. They used to bail out of submarines. They'd drop up instead of down."

"All right, wise ass."

"How old are you, Glenn, if you don't mind my asking?"

"I guess I'm forty-seven."

"Aside from jumping out of submarines, did you actually serve in World War II?"

"He was in the Bataan death march," Bud said.

Glenn went upstairs for some beer and then we watched the movie until it ended about an hour later. I loved the landscapes, the sense of near equation called forth by man and space, the cowboy facing silent hills; there it was, the true subject of film, space itself, how to arrange it and people it, time hung in a desert window, how to win out over sand and bone. (It's just a cowboy picture, I reminded myself.) Owney Pine came down the stairs then, short and slightly bowlegged, ample in his width, roundhead, crewcut, ferrying across the floor now and docking with a bump, belly opening and automobiles pouring out.

In the morning I took my camera over to the hotel and told the desk clerk I wanted the same room, indefinitely this time. Traces of a sneeze lingered in his mustache. He looked at my camera, wondered whether or not to comment, and then simply pushed the key across the desk.

Upstairs I set the camera on the bed and sat in a chair looking at it. I blew on the tips of my fingers. I unbuttoned each shirtcuff and rolled the sleeves tightly to a point one inch below my elbows. I moved my shoulders back and forth, trying to loosen the muscles. I took out my keychain and cleaned my fingernails with the mailbox key. I blew on the knuckle of the index finger of my right hand. With the other hand I juggled my testicles until they were comfortable. Then I expelled air three times through my nose.

Austin Wakely showed up precisely on time. He was wearing, as directed, a pair of brown shoes, army-issue and spit-shined, and fresh clean summer khakis. Pants and shirt had come from the wardrobe room at McCompex; the shoes were borrowed. Austin asked ten or twelve questions, only two of which I answered—that there was no plot to this thing, that I'd be shooting in black and white all the way. The answers upset him only slightly less than the non-answers had.

"Granted I don't know much about it," he said, "but there doesn't seem to be enough light in here."

"I want it natural. I brought along some high-watt bulbs. We'll use those and pray we don't blow a fuse. I think we'll make that floor lamp the key light. This whole thing is what is known in some circles as inspired amateurism. Today's little task is pretty simple, a sort of signature that could be used as both beginning and end. When we start using sound I'll give you the words as far in advance as possible. That means twenty-four hours at most. I hope you'll be able to read my handwriting."

"I'll read it."

"Now listen," I said.

I gave him final instructions, changed the light bulbs and then set the film rating and f.p.s. dial. I adjusted the eyepiece. Austin cleared his throat although he had no lines to speak. He was standing with his back to a full-length mirror, facing directly into the camera. I moved him slightly to one side. I used a single camera position and shot straight on from the foot of the bed for about twenty seconds, a popular commercial length.

When we were done it became clear that Austin's mood had changed. He talked enthusiastically of the film and his unknown role in it. His image had been placed in the time bank and this was sufficient cause for elation. For the first time since I'd met him, I felt myself gaining the edge. There would have to be no subtle bloodshed, no long campaign to dominate another individual. I had the camera and that was enough.

After he'd gone I took a shower and then asked the voice at the switchboard to get me the network.

"I'm naked," I said.

"How exciting. Who's with you?"

"The Mormon Tabernacle Choir."

"Lucky them," Binky said. "I didn't think you'd call again so soon."

"How old is Harris Hodge?"

"David, he's twenty-six. Don't get mad. He looks older."

"Okay, how's Ted Warburton?"

"He collapsed at his desk and had to be rushed to the hospital."

"You already told me that, goddamn it, and I think you used exactly those words. When did you become a recorded announcement? I want to know if there's been any word from the hospital."

"I don't know. I'll ask around."

"Hasn't Weede tried to get in touch with Mrs. Warburton?"

"I don't know," she said.

"Well, find out. Next time you're in bed with Weede, ask him if he's tried to get in touch with Mrs. Warburton. Use exactly those words. Do you think you can do that for me, Binky?"

"Yes."

"I'm sorry," I said.

"So am I, David. I feel terrible about Ted Warburton. I really do. If you want, I can find out what hospital he's in and you can call him."

"No, don't do that. If Ted's really bad I'd just as soon not talk to him. I can't stand talking to people who are really bad. Just find out how he is and I'll call you next week."

"Okay."

"I'm sorry about what I said about Weede."

"It's okay. Everybody knows anyway. When you said you were with the Mormon Tabernacle Choir, did that mean you're in Utah?"

"Yes."

"Utah's right above Arizona."

"Is it?" I said.

"So you'll be on location any day now."

"Precisely."

"Everybody's very excited about the project."

"Don't talk that way."

"Are you really naked?"

"Starkers."

"I'm sorry about Harris Hodge."

I thought of asking Binky to switch my call to Tana Elkbridge's phone. But then she would suspect that Tana and I were having an affair and since Tana was married this was not a good idea. Of course I could have given her Tana's extension, not telling her who the number belonged to, but she would have been able to find out simply by going through the network directory. It was better not to take chances. When Binky and I were finished talking I hung up and then had the voice call the network all over again. I asked for Tana Elkbridge. Her boss answered. I hung up immediately. Then I called Meredith at her office.

"Where are you?" she said.

"Out here in the Midwest. How's everything in Gramercy Park? Bombs, strikes, riots, plague?"

"Everything's fine here but I've had some upsetting news from Turkey. Mother is in a hospital in Ankara. She's been drinking again. I guess it got really bad. She fell down some steps."

"I wish I could be with you."

"So do I, David."

"I miss you."

"Yes."

"I think we've both matured," I said.

"Has the trip been good for you?"

"Whole new perspective."

"Before I forget, David, I saw my cousin Edwina a few days ago. You've heard me talk about her. She's the cousin I stayed with when I was in London that time. Her husband is here on business and they just spent three days in New York. They're in Boston now and they're going to Toronto next and then to Chicago. They're spending just two days in Chicago and I thought if you were close by you could go and see them. Edwina doesn't know a soul there and Charles will be going to meetings all day long."

I wrote down the details and then commiserated with her some more about her mother's health. I asked if there were any exciting new men in her life. She was noncommittal.

"Listen," I said. "Guess what? I dream in color."

"Are you sure?"

"I had a dream the other night about a big blue bus on a desert highway. When I woke up I was absolutely sure the bus was blue. It was the first time I knew for sure that I dream in color."

"David, that's great."

"Yeah."

"Take care of yourself now. Have a good time. Good luck with the Indians. And do try to get to Chicago."

"It was nice talking to you, Merry."

"It was sweet of you to call, David."

My father's secretary said he was in a meeting. I told her I was calling long-distance and that it was a matter of some urgency. She said she'd get him.

"What's up, sport?"

"How are you, dad? Working hard?"

"We just picked up some P and G business. A whole new line of toiletries they've come out with. This country is toilet-oriented. You know that as well as I do. We spend all our time in the toilet. We do everything in there but shit and piss. Maxine, go type that call report. The toilet is holy soil. Understand what I'm talking about?"

"Sounds like it might be a good account."

"What's on your mind, Dave? Where the hell are you anyway?"

"I'm out here in the Midwest."

"You need any money I'll have Maxine wire it right out."

"No, no, I just called to ask you something."

"Shoot."

"You never talked much about your experiences in the war. All I ever knew was that you served in the Pacific and got wounded a few times and received several decorations for valor. I was just wondering if you could tell me a little more about it."

"I don't talk about that," he said.

"That's what everybody says. But they all talk about it in the end."

"Not me, pally."

"Why not?"

"There's nothing to say. It's all over. You want to know what it was like, there are plenty of books on the subject."

"I want to know what it was like for you, not for other people. It's for something I'm writing."

"I buried a man alive," he said.

"Where was this, dad?"

"Some cruddy island. And don't sound so mournful."

"I won't ask you about it anymore. I'm sorry. It was for something I'm writing. Any word from Jane?"

"The kid's better. And Jane's knocked up again."

"I wonder if Mary has any children."

"Don't talk about Mary. There is no Mary."

"Remember what you told me about the kite-soul? The thing mother said when she was pregnant with Mary? That it was the kite-soul of her mother? You thought there was something Oriental about the phrase. In a way you were right. It comes from one of the children's books that mother used to keep in the bedroom. The book was so old it was falling apart. I just happened to be leafing through it one day and there was the phrase. It was a translation of a book for Japanese children. Beautifully illustrated."

"You like to hold on to small pieces of information, don't you? What else do you know that I don't? I'll tell you something, kid—I know more than you think. A lot more."

"Yes," I said.

"You better believe it. What's this thing you're writing?"

"Filmscript."

"Back on that kick again, are you?"

"I guess so."

"I'm growing a beard," he said. "It's coming right along. I'm not doing any trimming yet. I'll let it grow out to a big white flowing mane. There's a lot of white in it but it looks good. Wait'll you get back. It'll be all over my face by then."

"What are you growing a beard for?"

"Every man wants to grow a beard before he dies. It's one way of saying fuck you to everybody. Look, I'm nearing the finish line. I want a beard. It cheers me up just to look at it in the mirror. I'm not doing any trimming for at least another two weeks. If at all. If at all."

"I can't picture you with a beard."

"What do you sound so upset about?"

"I don't know, dad. It just seems strange. It changes things. I can't explain it."

"Look, I have to get my ass into that meeting. Give me a blast on the horn when you get back to the city. We'll have lunch."

"Right, dad. Don't work too hard."

"Thanks for the advice," he said.

I got my address book out of my wallet and tried to find some kind of listing for Ken Wild. I found his parents' phone number and address, which was that of a Chicago suburb. I got his father and told him I was an old college friend who wanted to get in touch. He said Ken was living in Chicago and he gave me both his home and office numbers. He said it was nice to hear from any friend of Ken's. He said any time I was in River Forest to drop over and use the swimming pool. I called Wild at the office.

"You are cordially invited to a black mass at your local martello tower. Roman collar. R.S.V.P."

"Oh Jesus," he said. "It can't be."

"It is."

"Where are you?"

"Nearby I think. At least relatively. I've been looking for your name, Wild. The Pulitzer committee has been strangely silent."

"My muse turned out to be a dike."

"Too bad," I said. "What are you doing?"

246

"I'm a project manager for my father's industrial systems outfit."

"I just talked to your father. He said I could use the swimming pool."

"Guilt," Wild said. "How long's it been? Six or seven years, hasn't it?"

"Seven," I said. "You married?"

"Divorced."

"So you're a project manager."

"Secret glee in your voice. What are you doing?"

"Making films," I said. "I've made a few documentaries. Sort of working my way up to a feature. I'm doing it all on an independent basis. Tek-Howard's been distributing my stuff. I'm on location now and I may have to get up there in a few days to pick up some equipment. That's what made me think of calling. Maybe we can get together."

"Great," he said. "Look forward to it. I really do."

I felt better than I had in quite some time. Once again I got the network. I asked for Weede Denney. I reached over, got a handkerchief out of my pants pocket and put it over the mouthpiece. Then I heard Mrs. Kling's eternally reproving voice, a model for impeachment proceedings.

"Mr. Denney's office. He's nowhere in sight."

"This is SDS. There's an invisible liquid device in your water cooler and it's programmed to explode the very second you put your phone back on the cradle."

I hung up, checked the address book again and found a number for Leighton Gage College. I asked to be connected with Simmons St. Jean.

"Still there, Simmons? This is David Bell. Remember me?"

"Certainly. What do you want?"

"I'm making films these days. Shooting in 16. Sort of working my way up to 35."

"Can you talk fast? I'm leaving for Marrakech in a matter of minutes."

"How are you, Simmons? Still saving every copy of *Cahiers*

du Cinéma? Listen, have you seen the new Bergman? More depressing than ever. I saw it just before I left New York. I'm out here in the Midwest working on my film. It's a very personal statement."

"Bergman is a prime example of the filmmaker as mortician. His films suffer from rigor mortis. I haven't looked at anything of his since the first mention of the spider-god. The new Paramount comedy-western is worth any number of Bergman's exegetical nightmares."

"Same old Simmons. Great to talk to you, Simmons. Remember Wendy Judd? She's living in New York these days. Absolute wildcat in bed. Now here's why I called. Remember the snowfall scene in *Ikiru?* The old man has cancer. He goes to a playground and sits on a swing. It begins to snow. I think it's the most beautiful scene ever put on film. Now this is what I want to find out. One: did Kurosawa shoot up at the old man? Two: did he shoot the whole scene without cutting? Three: did the old man swing on the swing or did he remain stationary? I've seen *Ikiru* three times but the last time was almost five years ago. And the scene I'm talking about is so beautiful that I always forget to study it, to see how he did it. I thought if anyone would know, you would."

"I've never seen *Ikiru*," he said.

"That's impossible."

"As for Wendy Judd, I tended to think of her as a sort of wild mouse rather than cat. I mean she loved to nibble, didn't she?"

"Simmons, you're lying. You're a lying sack of shit, Simmons. What do you plan to do in Marrakech—attend an Arab cartoon festival?"

I hung up and took a nap. When I came to, it was after five. I called downstairs and gave them Jennifer Fine's number.

"Jennifer, it's David. David Bell."

"Of course," she said finally.

"I wasn't sure you were still living at the same place but I figured what the hell, what could it cost me. I'm out here in the Midwest. In case I'm not coming through too well, that's why."

"I can hear you."

"I hope I'm not interrupting anything. Maybe I shouldn't have called. I just wanted to say hello. Nothing special. I'm naked and I've been calling people all over the country. I just wanted to say that I know how badly I treated you when we were seeing each other. You called me a fascist. Remember? That was a funny night in a way. At least it seems funny now, although at the time it was anything but. I think I've matured a lot since then, Jennifer. But I didn't mean to bring that up. I didn't have any special reason for calling. Just to talk. Sometimes on the phone the words just come out."

"My cat died," she said.

"I guess I didn't know you had a cat. That's too bad. I know how people sometimes get attached to animals. I'm really sorry to hear that. I'm out here making a film."

"She must have died this afternoon. The cleaning woman was in this morning and she didn't call me at the office so she must have died this afternoon. I came home from work and she was dead."

"That really is a shame."

"She's still on the floor. I can't bear to touch her."

"Jennifer, I think the best thing for me to do would be to hang up so you can call somebody to come over there and give you a hand. I'm sorry about everything. I'll get in touch with you when I get back to the city. We'll have lunch. I'm going to hang up now. Goodbye."

I put down the phone and then looked up Weede Denney's home number. I put the handkerchief over the mouthpiece again. Weede answered.

"This is Ted Warburton," I said. "I just want you to know that you're an overbearing jabberwock. You're a bloody fucking baldheaded sod."

I hung up, told the voice to get me Westchester information

249

and asked for Valerio, Old Holly. The operator said there were two Valerios listed, Annette and Joseph. Annette, I recalled, was the name of Tommy's mother. I wrote down the number. A man answered the phone.

"Is this where Tommy Valerio used to live?" I said. "I'm trying to get in touch with Tommy. We're old friends."

"Get in touch with Tommy?"

"Can you tell me where he is?"

"Tommy's been dead three years."

"What happened?"

"He got killed in the war."

"What happened?" I said. "I mean how did it happen?"

"What can I tell you? K.I.A. He got killed in action. He was a second lieutenant. He had all these men under him. Annette, how many men Tommy had under him? Anyway the President sent a letter. The President himself sent a letter to Tommy's mother."

"How's Mrs. Valerio?"

"She's fine. We're in the middle of dinner here."

"You must be Tommy's uncle. I think we met once or twice. My name is Dave Bell. Tommy and I were buddies."

"I don't recall him mentioning any Dave Bell. We're in the middle of dinner but maybe you want to talk to his mother. She's right here. It's somebody named Dave Bell."

"What?" I said.

"I'm talking to her. Friend of Tommy, he says. She's right here. Hold on."

"Don't bother. Tell her not to bother. I'm interrupting your dinner."

"She's right here."

"I have to go now. Tell her I'm sorry."

"He said he's sorry."

"Goodbye."

"She wants to know for what."

I called Wendy Judd at her apartment.

"It's David. I'm going to ask you something. I want a

straightforward factual answer. Did you ever go to bed with Simmons St. Jean back in the old days at Leighton Gage?"

"Who was he?"

"Film theory and criticism."

"Pale attractive guy with spooky eyes?"

"I guess that's a fair description."

"It's really none of your business, is it, David?"

I hung up and called Carol Deming at McCompex. It was several minutes before she came to the phone.

"How about a drink and then dinner?" I said. "We can meet at Buster's. I don't know where we can get something half-decent to eat in this town but maybe you can suggest a place. What's the story on seafood out here? I'm about dying for some fried shrimp."

"I just saw Austin. He seems enthused about whatever it is you two did earlier today. When's my turn?"

"We can talk about it."

"David, that's what I get all day in this place. Theater *is* talk. Motivations, sentiments, speeches, interpretations."

"The broken neck of the alphabet."

"Exactly," she said.

"I'm still working things out in terms of what I need you for. Let's have dinner and discuss it."

"David, I don't want to talk. Really I don't. Not to anyone. Just give me something to play. An idea, a role, a masquerade. Something the camera will understand even if no one else does. I'm trying to be direct."

"Look, a couple of drinks, that's all. One drink. I'm at Ames House in the center of town. I can walk to Buster's in fifteen minutes."

I had four drinks and she didn't show up. Finally I went across the street to the camper. Brand was alone in there, reclining on one of the cots, hands behind his head.

"It's happening," he said. "I can feel it in my skull. The old violence. I thought it was gone but I can feel it coming back. Correctly or not I associate blandness with nonviolence. That's why I want to be bland. To use bland words. Do bland things. I've been trying not to arouse the old instincts. You can arouse them with words, mainly slang words. The theory may seem stupid. Unproven at best. But it's true for me. And the thing is back. The old urge. Better keep your eye on me."

"You keep appearing and disappearing and reappearing," I said. "You've always been like that. I've never known exactly who you were. I've always liked you, Bobby. At least I've liked most of the different forms you take. But then you go away and come back different and I have to adjust. Which one do I keep my eye on?"

"Blandness would seem to be the easiest thing in the world to achieve. Physically I'm there. I've made it. I look like a million other people. Ten million. But inside my head the action is constant. I went to hard stuff to slow it down. I smoke grass to slow it down. But I can't slow it anymore. The old action. Zap those hostiles. Davy, you don't know what it's like to lay down some 20 mike-mike on a village. See it fall apart. Come down low and strafe a hootch or two. Your cans of nape. Your 500-pounders. Your rockets. I jumped a guy on a bike once. He was pedaling along outside a village. It was known to be hostile. I dropped down behind him, way behind him, and followed him up the road a bit, flying real low. When I was about a hundred meters behind him, I laid my fire all around him. He busted like a teacup. You see, there's a primal joy to hitting a thing in motion. It's one of the oldest pleasures there is. Something moves, *boom*, you wing it. Beast, bird or human, the thing to do is knock it down. It's primal, Davy. It's basic to the origin of the species. I'm learning to live with it."

Spared the nervous motorized genius of his father's eye, Bud Yost seemed typical in every way, the beneficiary of a morally solid upbringing, temperate weather and a balanced diet. He was somewhat large for his age and there was a slight quake to his movements, as if he were standing on a rocking chair. He came walking out of a passageway onto the empty floor of the high school gym, wearing his basketball uniform, white with gold trim and lettering. I had asked him to wear number nine if possible, my old number in prep school, but nine belonged to a kid six feet six and 235, so Bud wore his own uniform, eleven, *Ft. Curtis High* in gold script across the front. I took some readings and told him to do whatever he wanted out on the court and to pay no attention to the camera or to me. I shot first from above, from the row of seats high over the court. Alone on the slick and burnt-yellow floor of the gymnasium, weaving slowly downcourt, feinting, changing speed, he tossed in an easy lay-up. Then he went to jump shots, first from in close, then a few feet farther out, then farther, the ball sounding strange as it hit the floor or rim or backboard or slapped through the net, echoes melting into duplicates of original sounds. After a while I went down to court-level and got on one knee beneath the backboard and shot straight out at him. He pumped in four in a row from the top of the key, missed two, hit two more from the corner. He was good. He had a good eye and he was much less awkward running or shooting than he was just plain walking. Crouched low, left elbow hooked out, he dribbled around the key and hit from twenty feet. I stopped filming and took off my shoes and shirt. We had a one-on-one drill, taking turns on offense, and it went on for what seemed an hour, not a word passing between us. He was too fast for me and my shooting was way off. I was nearly in tears when I finally called a halt, bending over, trying to catch my breath, washed up at twenty-eight and resigned to a future of crumpled pieces of paper and khaki wastebaskets in the rooms of marooned hotels. I sat on the floor and began lacing my shoes.

"I hope you got what you want," he said.

"It should be okay. This camera was designed for sports, nature, news, that kind of thing. I may need you one more time."

"Can I ask a question?"

"That's all for today, gentlemen."

He laughed at that and then reached out a hand to help me to my feet.

Pike slept in the back of the camper. Brand and I were up front, waiting for Sullivan in the parking lot of a supermarket. I saw a group of women standing by a station wagon. There were seven of them, pushing cartons and shopping bags over the open tailgate into the rear of the car. Celery stalks and boxes of Gleem stuck out of the bags. I took the camera from my lap, raised it to my eye, leaned out the window a bit, and trained it on the ladies as if I were shooting. One of them saw me and immediately nudged her companion but without taking her eyes off the camera. They waved. One by one the others reacted. They all smiled and waved. They seemed supremely happy. Maybe they sensed that they were waving at themselves, waving in the hope that someday if evidence is demanded of their passage through time, demanded by their own doubts, a moment might be recalled when they stood in a dazzling plaza in the sun and were registered on the transparent plastic ribbon; and thirty years away, on that day when proof is needed, it could be hoped that their film is being projected on a screen somewhere, and there they stand, verified, in chemical reincarnation, waving at their own old age, smiling their reassurance to the decades, a race of eternal pilgrims in a marketplace in the dusty sunlight, seven arms extended in a fabulous salute to the forgetfulness of being. What better proof (if proof is ever needed) that they have truly been alive? Their happiness, I think, was made of this, the anticipation of incontestable evidence, and had nothing to do with the present moment, which would pass with all the others into whatever is the opposite of eternity. I pretended to keep shooting, gathering their wasted light, letting their smiles enter the lens and wander the camera-body seeking the magic spool, the gelatin which captures the image, the film which threads through the waiting gate. Sullivan came out of the supermarket and I lowered the camera. I could not help feeling that what I was discovering here was power of a sort.

In the evening we sat in the camper on Howley Road and listened to the radio. A war summary came on. I did not listen to the news, merely to the words themselves, the familiar oppressive phrases. It was like the graytalk of the network—not what something meant and often not its opposite.

"Who wants to be in my novel?" Brand said. "It'll cost you fifty dollars and I'm in a position to guarantee immortality."

"I want to be made a brain surgeon," Pike said.

"Eighty dollars even."

"A lover," I said. "Make me a great lover."

"A hundred and fifty dollars gets you into bed with the female character of your choice."

"Are you in the book?" I said to Sullivan.

"You're all in it," Brand said. "Everybody's in it."

"Put me down for the one-fifty then."

"You'll be wanting change," Sullivan said.

"I don't think so."

"Because I had an affair in someone else's novel many years ago. My partner found it less than satisfactory. He was a naval officer with heaps of experience. Of course I was just a girl then."

"Make me a brain surgeon with unsteady hands," Pike said. "You can build suspense around a theme like that."

"Suspense is no longer relevant," I said.

"Bullthrow," Pike shouted. "That's bullthrow."

"Easy," Sullivan said.

"Pike's pique reaches mountainous proportions," I said, very pleased with myself.

"Bullthrow."

The words issued smoothly from an intelligent face (no

doubt), running on past some reverse point of tolerance, and soon they seemed to generate an existence of their own, to demand an independence, to live in a silhouette of meaning more subtle, more cunning than the intelligence which bred them might ever know. We listened quietly for a while. The announcer said he had accidentally read the previous day's dispatch.

"I have fantasies about falling in love with a Vietnamese girl," Brand said. "But then she dies of a funny disease and I spend the rest of my life in pain."

The northern monsoon clouds were lifting. The killer teams were sweeping the villages. At night you could see the tracers streaking across the free-fire zones. There are twenty rounds to a magazine.

"America can be saved only by what it's trying to destroy," Sullivan said.

I spent much of the next two days in the library, doing research, thinking, worrying, writing monologues and dialogues. I walked over to the camper late in the afternoon of the second day and found Pike alone. I reported my plans to visit Chicago. Then I talked him into driving me up and down one of the quiet old streets in town while I shot some footage out the front window. I instructed him to drive at a walking speed or even less. I didn't have clamps with which to fasten the camera to the door frame and I wanted as little movement as possible. Also I liked the idea of drawing out the rows of houses, extending them in time, understanding them as more important in their appearances than in the voices and sorrows they contained. It was an interview in the new language. And with no people in sight I was able to shoot at higher than normal speeds, reducing vibration and prolonging the scene even more. By inches we moved along the street, each silent and lovely home a slow memorial to some shrill inner moment unquieted by time.

*   *   *

There is a motel in the heart of every man. Where the highway begins to dominate the landscape, beyond the limits of a large and reduplicating city, near a major point of arrival and departure: this is most likely where it stands. Postcards of itself at the desk. One hundred hermetic rooms. The four seasons of the year in aerosol cans inside the medicine chest. Repeated endlessly on the way to your room, you can easily forget who you are here; you can sit on your bed and become *man sitting on bed*, an abstraction to compete with infinity itself; out of such places and moments does modern chaos raise itself to the level of pure mathematics. Despite its great size, the motel seems temporary. This feeling may rise simply from the knowledge that no one lives here for more than one or two days at a time. Then, too, it may be explained by the motel's location, that windy hint of mystery encircling a lone building fixed in what was once a swamp; a cold gale blows from the lake or bay, sunlight cracks on the wingtips of distant planes, ducks tack upwind, and nowhere is there a sign of a human on foot. The motel seems to have been built solely of bathroom tile. The bedsheets are chilly and faintly damp. There are too many hangers in the closet, as if management were trying to compensate for a secret insufficiency too grievous to be imagined. From small gratings in the wall comes a steady and almost unendurable whisper of ventilation. But for all its spiritual impoverishments, this isn't the worst of places. It embodies a repetition so insistent and irresistible that, if not freedom, then liberation is possible, deliverance; possessed by chaos, you move into thinner realms, achieve refinements, mathematical integrity, and become, if you choose, the man on the bed in the next room. The forest lodge, the suite of mauve rooms, the fleabag above the hockshop, the borrowed apartment—all too personal, the unrecurring moment. Men hold this motel firmly in their hearts; here flows the dream of the confluence of travel and sex.

Edwina Meers was staying at such a motel near O'Hare Airport, roughly seventeen miles from the center of Chicago. Meredith had given me the name of the place and I had called Edwina and Charles and told them to expect me. Then I had borrowed Glenn Yost's car, a gray spastic Pontiac, and headed north in the night. It was good to be on the road again, daring the logic of the white line. Many trailer trucks went by, bearing the license plates of a dozen states, and the car rocked in their wind. I was part of the commerce, the romance of long-haul freight, the epic striding song of the Triple A travel guides.

It was nine in the morning and Edwina came to the door in a flowered zip-front skirt and tight undershirt top.

"You lucky man, I'm all alone. Do come in. Charles has already dashed off to a meeting. Our luggage is strewn about everywhere so you'll just have to sit on the bed. Do you mind if I leave the telly on? The broadcasts in this country are not to be believed."

"Why aren't you staying in town?"

"Charles balked at the notion. The dear man has an absolute obsession for punctuality and so he decided we had best park our hot little bodies as close to the airport as possible, since our shed-ule seems to be predicated on a split-second readiness that might do justice to a miss-isle system. Positively dreads being late for takeoffs. It's all very sexual, I suppose."

"We can drive in for lunch if you like. I've been to Chicago on business trips and I think I can find my way around fairly well."

"That's awfully nice of you, David. Really I'm so glad you could come. Meredith has told me so much about you. She's such a super girl, don't you think? So sort of fresh and homogenized."

Edwina had a round plain face, freckled slightly, like a pancake. She was probably in her mid-thirties and seemed delighted about the whole thing; the tensions of an unpretty youth now safely behind her, perhaps she was finding over-thirty to be her personal prime, the golden age of her passion and wit. There was a commercial on the television set. A woman in a bathtub was washing her legs with a bar of beauty soap. One knee out of the water, she slowly guided the soap along her calf, then up over her knee and down her thigh as the picture drifted into a slow dissolve. Now she was standing on the tile floor, a long soft-focus shot, head back, hands moving slowly over the towel across her belly and thighs. Edwina leaned against a chest of drawers.

"I'm confused," I said. "Somehow or other I had the impression you were American."

"I am, David."

"How long have you been living in England?"

"Funnily enough it's almost ten years to the day. Charles and I were married in Philadelphia and then off we went. I had a South American lover before I married Charles and all he wanted to do was produce babies. He was so sort of primitive and awful. Charles had a homosexual affair before he met me. His lover was best man at our wedding."

"Have you been to Chicago before?"

"No, and neither has Charles. We landed yesterday afternoon and rented a car. Then we settled in here and drove into town. We had been invited to a sort of fat businessmen's party given by a chap called either Lawrence Thomas or Thomas Lawrence. He's the man Charles is seeing on business. It was awfully sweet of him actually, going to all that trouble for the sole purpose of getting Charles acquainted with some of the local moneybags. But I must say it was far from being the most witty dinner party I've ever attended. The men talked about steel alloys and dyestuffs and the wives were even more boring if that's possible. Do you know there's a company called American Metal Climax Inc.? God, the man who thought that one up. Anyway, David, they served coq au vin for dinner and it was ten parts vin to one part coq. Then they kept handing me tall fruity rum drinks called Dormant Volcanoes. Needless to say, I soon got pissed as a newt.

Then this Thomas or Lawrence chap took our pale little bodies to another party in a smashing eleven-room flat belonging to a man who apparently *owns* Venezuela. You wouldn't believe what was hanging on the walls. Braque, Chagall, Mondrian, Renoir—I can't begin to list them. I've no doubt the poor man was duped into buying absolute fakes but I must confess it was a gorgeous sight, all those walls reeking of money. This man, who's apparently called Arno Tumbler, was off on his private island in the Caribbean where he's learning to be a French impressionist. The party itself was vile. First this Lawrence Thomas man practically raped me while we were dancing. Then a whole bunch of sort of speckled mad people arrived, all with painted faces and wearing the most bloody awful things really. A bunch of palsied twits if you ask me. One of them exposed his privates to me. All I did was remark to Charles that I didn't think a team of the Queen's own surgeons would be able to determine the sex of some of these creatures and the next thing I saw was this horrible little man looking me straight in the eye and smiling, with his george dangling amidships. Really, David, am I expected to find this sort of thing amusing? There were masses of these people jumping about in their robes and feathers. One felt oneself to be the center of attraction by mere dint of one's being so extraordinarily commonplace."

I had to keep reminding myself that she was American. Like a convert to a new religion, she was more dedicated than those who have been singing the psalms for two thousand years. I wondered what her English husband thought of this rainy patter.

"You're leaving when?"

"Tomorrow afternoon," she said. "We fly to Omaha, Denver, Little Rock and Atlanta. God, how dreary. Just before we left London, masses of postcards began arriving from virtually everyone we know, all on their hols in the most super places. Gwyllam is in Sardinia photographing bandits and smugglers. Dilys is apparently on the verge of being forcibly ejected from Portugal for sheer blatant hedonism. And dear old Harry and Nigel are in Madagascar again, writing their joint memoirs and buggering each other to death. Not that I'm complaining about the likes of Little Rock, mind you. It's great fun to be back in one's native land. But, really, David, the spectacular filth. I mean one reads about the Middle West and one expects to see all sorts of Shakers and Mennonites dashing about the countryside with brooms and paintbrushes. The weather is killing though, don't you think? I should like it to be like this in London. And I understand the steaks out here are absolutely top hole."

Several minutes later we were in bed. An open suitcase slid to the floor. She kept talking about her husband. I hit her and she was quiet. Naked she was even more plain, and the hunger I had expected from her did not show itself. Into her neutrality and silence I directed something like desperation. It was the old fascism. War, sadism, self-abasement, it was all that. She took it—but not to keep and not for herself. I thought she would want to feast on my body. I had been inserted into the televised dream of motel, the pleasure of being other and none. I had been hung in that dream, a thing out of modern fiction, beautiful boy plundered by the crumbling duchess. I had expected to enjoy it greatly, her greed and tongue and the dredgings of her fantasy. But she had climbed into bed like an old shoemaker and I found myself overburdened with parts—hers, mine, the dream's—and she did not seem to distinguish between what was authentic and what was ugly and brutal. It may have been that the final partition had fallen.

"Goodness, I wonder what Meredith would think of us. Do you suppose we've committed some medieval form of incest? Three times removed or something? It's all so wonderfully sordid, don't you think? But you must think I'm easy meat, darling. And you detest the way I speak. That's all right, David, you're not the first. I've had a long series of lovers, all of whom despised the earth I walk on and all of whom begged me to take them back when inevitably I sent them away out of sheer boredom. You see, my men think I bore them when in point of fact just the reverse is true. It never dawns on them, poor lambs, until their banishment is a fait accompli. They need me, you see. They need an empty room in which to unwrap their secret goodies. Do you believe in an afterlife?"

"For whom?" I said.

"For whom indeed. Quite a good answer. Perhaps the saintly people and the tedious people are all sort of jumbled up and sent indiscriminately to heaven or hell while the rest of us go absolutely nowhere. I shouldn't mind that actually. Sublime nothingness. I'm studying the Hindus. Cycles and cycles of existence. Vicky Glinn and I are taking lessons from a swami who lives in abject poverty in a tiny flat in Battersea. This man is very impressive, the genuine article I should think, but he communicates the most awful smell. Right now I think I'd like nothing better than two hours of precious sleep. I suggest you leave, David. This way I'll get my rest and you'll be free to analyze the entire episode. You're the type, aren't you? You see, I'm not a totally stupid woman. I have my moments of insight. Pick up that suitcase, will you please? And, David, when you get around to your session of deep analysis, do try to be kind to both of us."

In the car I could taste her on the back of my hand. I stopped for gas and called Ken Wild at his office. Then I drove into town and found a camera supply store. I bought some Kodak Tri-X reversal film, a wind filter and a light metal tripod with a pan-and-tilt head. An hour later Wild walked into a restaurant about three blocks from the Drake Hotel. He had gained some weight and his forehead had risen about half an inch. We stood at the bar and ordered drinks.

"Making films," he said. "That's great. Tell me about it. I hate my life. I'm at the point where I want to hear about other people's lives. It's like switching from fiction to biography. The beginning of the end."

"What I'm doing is kind of hard to talk about. It's a sort of first-person thing but without me in it in any physical sense, except fleetingly, not exactly in the Hitchcock manner but a brief personal appearance nonetheless, my mirror image at any rate. Also my voice when I start using sound. It's a reaching back for certain things. But not just that. It's also an attempt to explain, to consolidate. Jesus, I don't know. It'll be part dream, part fiction, part movies. An attempt to explore parts of my consciousness. Not quite autobiographical in the Jonas Mekas sense. I've said part movies. By that I mean certain juxtapositions of movies with reality, certain images that have stayed with me, certain influences too. I mean you can start with nothing but your own minor reality and end with an approximation of art. Ghosts and shadows everywhere in terms of technique. Bresson. Miklós Jancsó. Ozu. Shirley Clarke. The interview technique. The monologue. The anti-movie. The single camera position. The expressionless actor. The shot extended to its ultimate limit in time. I just got laid incidentally."

"You're really going strong," Wild said. "I haven't the slightest idea what the hell you're talking about but it sounds great, it sounds really heavy, it sounds committed."

"I feel I've got to do it. I'm also doing a documentary on the Navahos for television. That'll be done out in Arizona and around there. Where the reservation is."

"But you're not working for anybody."

"Independent basis," I said. "I don't want anybody making decisions for me. I'm not getting rich, mind you, but I'm holding my own. When all this is over I may do something for Svensk Filmindustri. Just outside Sweden there. I mean Stockholm. Bergman's turf. So you're divorced. I'm sorry to hear that."

"She was a bitch. I was a bastard. Good riddance to both of us. I hate my life. I really hate my life. What about you—married?"

"Actually I'm living with a Vietnamese girl," I said. "Marriage is a lost art. Maybe if we decide to have kids. If not, things are fine just the way they are."

"Their women are beautiful," Wild said.

We finished our drinks and got a table. Wild was obviously well known in here. He joked with the waiter, ordering an angst on pumpernickel. Then he asked for two more drinks.

"But you're making money, aren't you?"

"I'm making money," he said.

"I bet you've got a great apartment with all sorts of stunning creatures to choose from."

"This is bunnyland," he said. "Both ears and the tail for the sloppiest of kills."

We had a bottle of wine with lunch and two brandies at the table afterward. Then we went to the bar and ordered stingers. Wild was in no hurry to get back to the office. It was about three o'clock. I had been driving a good part of the previous night and I felt dazed and weary. We drank quietly for half an hour.

"We're consultants to government and industry," Wild said finally. "Want to know about production flow systems? Materials handling? Centralized processing and distribution? Automation you know isn't necessarily the answer. First you study the operation. Then you analyze the system in terms of costs and functional elements. Maybe automation isn't the answer at all. Maybe it's selective automation you want. One or two small changes can turn the trick. Relocate a conveyor line. Design a special component. Too many people think automation is the answer to everything. This is a fallacy. I work with good men. They do their job and they like what they're doing and they don't ever squawk. Once I dated one of their daughters for a period of several some odd months. She was all jugs. I liked her. But she kept using a word I couldn't stand. She was always using it. I tromped over to the museum. I went tromping through the park. I tromped down

Rush Street. Automation is no panacea. We understand that in my father's outfit. Systems planning is the true American artform. More than jazz for godsake. We excel at maintenance. We understand interrelationships. We make it all work, from parcel entry to in-plant distribution to truck routing and scheduling. We know exactly where to put the nail that holds the broom. A lot of countries can't do that. They don't know how. Practically nobody in Europe knows where to put the nail. You know that Frenchman who wrote that book, what he said? There are three great economic powers in the world. America. Russia. And America in Europe. We have to show them where to put the nail. But the Russians still lag. They lag in industrial research, in computerization, in automated systems. They lag. We know how to plan things, like overall corporate policy, like inventory management, like distribution, like site suitability. We're experts in containerization, unit loads, electronic data processing, feasibility studies. We know how to zero in. What's so terrible about that?"

About fifteen minutes later he said:

"Talent is everything. If you've got talent, nothing else matters. You can screw up your personal life something terrible. So what. If you've got talent, it's there in reserve. Anybody who has talent they know they have it and that's it. It's what makes you what you are. It tells you you're you. Talent is everything; sanity is nothing. I'm convinced of it. I think I had something once. I showed promise, didn't I, Dave? I mean I had something, didn't I? But I was too sane. I couldn't make the leap out of my own soul into the soul of the universe. That's the leap they all made. From Blake to Rimbaud. I don't write anything but checks. I read science fiction. I go on business trips to South Bend and Rochester. The one in Minnesota. Not Rochester, New York. Rochester, Minnesota. I couldn't make the leap."

The sun was going down when I opened my eyes. I was on a boat. I could see the towers of Marina City. I was on a sightseeing boat on the Chicago River, that silly little river which modern engineering has coaxed into flowing backwards. The ribs on my left side ached badly. It was sunset and somehow I had lost several hours. Then we docked and I started walking toward the Drake, trying to remember where the car was parked. I stopped in a drugstore and called Wild at his apartment.

"What happened? I just woke up. I was on a sightseeing boat."

"You son of a bitch," he said.

"We were at the bar. That's all I remember. I woke up ten minutes ago. What happened in between?"

"My goddamn neck."

"My ribs," I said.

"I shouldn't even talk to you."

"We were at the bar. We were drinking stingers."

"You got in an argument with Chin Po."

"Who's that?"

"Chin Po's the guy who was sitting next to you. I was sitting on one side and he was on the other."

"Right," I said. "Then what?"

"We started drinking toasts. You and I and Chin. We drank a number of toasts to Chiang Kai-shek."

"Wonderful. Really great."

"Then you started the argument. You and Chin."

"What were we arguing about?"

"An afterlife," he said. "Whether or not there's an afterlife."

"That's incredible. I don't even have any convictions on the subject. Which side was I taking—pro or con?"

"I don't know. That part is hazy. I just remember you and Chin arguing violently about an afterlife."

"Then what?"

"Then you took a swing at Chin."

"God."

"Luckily you just grazed him and before he had a chance to swing back I stepped in between and tried to calm you down."

"What happened then?"

"You got me in the headlock."

"Jesus, Ken."

"You got me in the headlock and I couldn't break it. You had my head twisted up under your armpit and I could hardly breathe."

"I'm really sorry. I just didn't know what I was doing."

"Then I blacked out," he said. "I couldn't break the hold and I just blacked out. When I came to, the bartender was punching you in the ribs to get you to let go of me and old Chin was back on his barstool calmly lighting a cigarette."

"That's incredible."

"The bartender, Frank, kept smashing you in the ribs until you finally let go. I headed straight for the john, bounced off some chairs, got in there, flashed once or twice, threw cold water on my face and then just sat on the floor. When I came out about five minutes later, you were gone. I'm not sure but I think you came in the john for a second and shook my hand. But I'm not sure."

"Ken, I don't know what to say. I'm really sorry."

"You'd be a lot sorrier if Chin Po had ever got his hands on you."

"Why?"

"Frank told me he's a black belt in karate."

"God."

"He'd have broken your windpipe just like that."

"God, I know."

"Fat old Chin. He'd have maimed you for life."

"And I still don't know what happened to the last two or three hours. Jesus God, it's frightening. I'm really sorry, Ken. I'll make it up to you somehow."

But I wasn't sorry. I was, if anything, exhilarated. Wild

was husky and compact; he brimmed with strength. And yet he hadn't been able to break the headlock I had put on him.

"Let's forget it," he said. "Look, I've been working hard and drinking kind of heavy and I think I need a vacation. Maybe I'll go dry out somewhere. You said you were going to Arizona or someplace to do a documentary. Maybe I can meet you out there. When are you due on location?"

"Tomorrow," I said, and that was the truth.

10

I hurried toward the hotel, my pockets full of scraps of paper, index cards, neatly creased sheets, Scotch-taped fragments, throwaways uncrumpled and hand-pressed, what detritus and joy, a grainy day, child of Godard and Coca-Cola.

I asked the desk clerk, an old man this time whose face was purplish with broken blood vessels, if he could turn up a portable TV set somewhere in the building. I needed it for an hour and I was willing to slip a discreetly folded five-dollar bill into the breast pocket of his sturdy mail-order shirt. He came up later carrying the thing, a bulky Motorola, as if it were a wounded man he could not wait to deposit somewhere. I plugged it in, turned the sound down to nothing, then set the Canon Scoopic on the tripod.

Soon Glenn Yost arrived. I thanked him for giving up his lunch break, explaining we had to film in the early afternoon in order to get the right kind of TV show and commercials, and then I asked him to go over the pages I had prepared for him. We would read and record on tape my questions and his answers; he would not appear on camera in this segment. I talked fast so he wouldn't have time for second thoughts.

A game show was on TV, young married contestants and a suavely gliding master of ceremonies; there were frequent commercials, the usual daytime spasms on behalf of detergents and oral hygiene. This is what I filmed for roughly eight minutes, the TV set, having to break twice for reloading, as Glenn and I, off camera, read from the wrinkled scattered script. Glenn spoke in a monotone throughout.

"We're going to talk about test patterns and shadows. Certain forms of darkness. A small corner of the twentieth century."

"I have all the answers."

"And I have the questions," I said. "We begin, simply enough, with a man watching television. Quite possibly he is being driven mad, slowly, in stages, program by program, interruption by interruption. Still, he watches. What is there in that box? Why is he watching?"

"The TV set is a package and it's full of products. Inside are detergents, automobiles, cameras, breakfast cereal, other television sets. Programs are not interrupted by commercials; exactly the reverse is true. A television set is an electronic form of packaging. It's as simple as that. Without the products there's nothing. Educational television's a joke. Who in America would want to watch TV without commercials?"

"How does a successful television commercial affect the viewer?"

"It makes him want to change the way he lives."

"In what way?" I said.

"It moves him from first person consciousness to third person. In this country there is a universal third person, the man we all want to be. Advertising has discovered this man. It uses him to express the possibilities open to the consumer. To consume in America is not to buy; it is to dream. Advertising is the suggestion that the dream of entering the third person singular might possibly be fulfilled."

"How then does a TV commercial differ from a movie? Movies are full of people we want to be."

"Advertising is never bigger than life. It tries not to edge too far over the fantasy line; in fact it often mocks different fantasy themes associated with the movies. Look, there's no reason why you can't fly Eastern to Acapulco and share two solid weeks of sex and adventure with a vacationing typist from Iowa City. But advertising never claims you can do it with Ava Gardner. Only Richard Burton can accomplish that. You can change your image but you can't change the image of the woman you take to bed. Advertising has merchandised this distinction. We have exploited the limitation of dreams. It's our greatest achievement."

"What makes a good advertising man?"

"He knows how to move the merch off the shelves. It's as simple as that. If the advertising business shut down tomorrow, I'd go over to Macy's and get a job selling men's underwear."

"Let's get back to images. Do the people who create commercials take into account this third person consciousness you've talked about with such persuasiveness and verve?"

"They just make their twenty-second art films. The third person was invented by the consumer, the great armchair dreamer. Advertising discovered the value of the third person but the consumer invented him. The country itself invented him. He came over on the *Mayflower*. I'm waiting for you to ask me about the anti-image."

"What's that?"

"It's the guerrilla warfare being fought behind the lines of the image. It's a picture of devastating spiritual atrocities. The perfect example of the anti-image in advertising is the slice-of-life commercial. A recognizable scene in a suburban home anywhere in the USA. Some dialogue between dad and junior or between Madge and the members of the bridge club. Problem: Madge is suffering from irregularity. Solution: Drink this stuff and the muses will squat. The rationale behind this kind of advertising is that the consumer will identify with Madge. This is a mistake. The consumer never identifies with the anti-image. He identifies only with the image. The Marlboro man. Frank Gifford and Bobby Hull in their Jantzen bathing suits. Slice-of-life commercials usually deal with the more depressing areas of life—odors, sores, old age, ugliness, pain. Fortunately the image is big enough to absorb the anti-image. Not that I object to the anti-image in principle. It has its possibilities; the time may not be far off when we tire of the dream. But the anti-image is being presented much too literally. The old themes. The stereotyped dialogue. It needs a touch of horror, some mad laughter from the graveyard. One of these days some smart copywriter will perceive the true inner mystery of America and develop an offshoot to the slice-of-life. The slice-of-death."

"Have you spent the major part of your adult life in the advertising business?"

"All but four years."

"Where were they spent?" I said.

"I served a hitch in the army during the war."

"Where?"

"The Pacific."

"Where in the Pacific?"

"The Philippines."

"Where in the Philippines?"

"Bataan: they made two movies about it."

"Do you ever feel uneasy about your place in the constantly unfolding incorporeal scheme of things?"

"Only when I try to pre-empt the truth."

"What does that mean?"

"One of the clients I service is the Nix Olympica Corporation. They make a whole line of products for the human body. Depilatories, salves, foot powder, styptic pencils, mouthwash, cotton swabs for the ears, deodorants for the armpit, deodorants for the male and female crotch, acne cream medication, sinus remedies, denture cleansers, laxatives, corn plasters. We were preparing a campaign for their Dentex Division; that's mouthwash primarily. Okay, so we zero in on one of the essential ingredients, quasi-cinnamaldehyde-plus. QCP. We take the hard-sell route. Dentex with QCP kills mouth poisons and odor-causing impurities thirty-two percent faster. Be specific. Be factual. Make a promise. Okay, so some little creep says to me in a meeting: thirty-two percent faster than what? Obvious, I tell him: thirty-two percent faster than if Dentex didn't have QCP. The fact that all mouthwashes have this cinnamaldehyde stuff is beside the point; we were the only ones talking about it. This is known as pre-empting the truth. The creative people do a storyboard. Open on Formula One racing car, number six, Watkins Glen. Action, noise, crowd, throttling, crack-ups, explosions. Number six comes in first. Beauty queen rushes up to car, leans over to kiss driver, then turns away with grimace. Bad breath. She doesn't want to kiss him. Cut to medical lab, guy with white smock. This is a dramatization—charts, diagrams, supers, QCP thirty-two percent faster. Back to original guy, number six, different race. Checkered flag drops, he wins, wreath around the neck, beauty queen kisses him, dissolve to victory party as they dance, kiss, whisper, dance, kiss. We took the idea to Dentex. They loved it. We took it upstairs to Nix Olympica. They loved it. They were delighted. They gave us the okay to shoot. We get cars and drivers and extras. We go up to Watkins Glen. We use helicopters, we use tracking shots, we use slow-motion, we use stop-action, we zoom, we wide-angle, we set up two small crashes and one monster explosion with a car turning over that nearly kills half the crew. I called a special meeting of the agency's planning board and ran the final print for them. They loved it. When I told them it cost as much, pro-rated, as the movie *Cleopatra*, they were delighted. They would have something to tell their wives that evening. The next day we showed the commercial to Dentex. They loved it. They were delighted. We took it upstairs to Nix Olympica. They turned it down flat. The money didn't bother them; they were impressed with the money; they would have something to tell their wives. But they turned it down flat. They ordered us to re-shoot both sequences in the winner's circle."

"Why?"

"Because of the Oriental. Because of the old man standing at the edge of the group of extras who were crowding around the winner's circle both times, first when the beauty queen refused to kiss number six and then when she did kiss him. Both times he was there, this small shrunken old man, this Oriental. Who was he? Who hired him? How did he get into the crowd? Nobody knew. But he was there all right and Nix Olympica spotted him. All the other extras were young healthy gleaming men and women. It's a commercial for mouthwash; you want health, happiness, freshness, mouth-appeal. And this sick-looking old man is hovering there, this really depressing downbeat Oriental. Look, I love the business. I thrive on it. But I can't help wondering if I've wasted my life simply because of the old man who ruined the mouthwash commercial. On a spring evening some years ago, during the time when my wife was very ill, when she was nearing the very end, I walked up a street in the upper Thirties and turned right onto Park Avenue and there was the Pan Am Building, a mile high and half-a-mile wide, every light blazing, an impossible slab of squared-off rock hulking above me and crowding everything else out of the way, even the sky. It looked like God. I had never seen the Pan Am Building from that particular spot and I wasn't prepared for the colossal surprise of it, the way it crowded out the sky, that overwhelming tier of lights. I swear to you it looked like God the Father. What was the point I was trying to make?"

"I don't know."

"Neither do I. I guess that's what comes of trying to pre-empt the truth."

"What is the role of commercial television in the twentieth century and beyond?"

"In my blackest moods I feel it spells chaos for all of us."

"How do you get over these moods?" I said.

274

"I take a mild and gentle Palmolive bath, brush my teeth with Crest, swallow two Sominex tablets, and try desperately to fall asleep on my Simmons Beautyrest mattress."

"Thank you."

I took a shower and then called the network and asked for myself, wondering what would happen if I answered.

"Mr. Bell's office," Binky said.

"This is Charles of the Ritz. Our lipstick of the month is salmon purée."

"David, where the hell are you?"

"Give me ten seconds. It'll come to me."

"Come on now, don't fool around, Mr. Denney is furious. There's a whole crew standing by at the reservation and they can't do a thing until you get there. Now where are you?"

"About fifteen hundred miles from where I'm supposed to be."

"I don't believe it. You're crazy. You'll get fired."

"Tell Weede to send Harris Hodge out there. He's young and willing. He can handle it. I've been hearing good things about him."

"It's your project, David. You've got to be there."

"I'm not going to Arizona, Binky. At least not right now. I'd rather be there than here. But I've got to do this thing I'm doing."

"What thing?"

"The only reason I called was to let you know I'm all right. I thought you might worry if you didn't hear anything."

"I am worried, David. What thing?"

"I'm crossing the swamp. Listen, how's Warburton?"

"He died," she said.

"I guess I've known it for the last couple of days. I hope he'll be buried in England. Did Freddy Fuck-Nuts write a memo?"

"Who's that?"

"Weede," I said. "Did he write a memo about Ted Warburton?"

"You shouldn't call him crappy names. Up to now he's been very good about your not showing up in Arizona. He's been backing you all the way. He told Livingston there must have been some unavoidable delay. An accident or something. David, I'll have to tell him you called and that you're not planning to go out there."

"What did the memo say? Did it say that Ted was a trusted friend and longtime associate and that no man is an island?"

"Something like that, I guess."

"Warburton was Trotsky," I said.

"David, no."

"Don't tell anyone. Let them figure it out for themselves, the bastards. No more memos. That was the only thing that made that place worthwhile anyway."

"Do you need any money?"

"I have enough traveler's checks for ten days or so. I won't be here any longer than that."

"Will you be coming back to New York?"

"I don't know, Bink."

"What will you do for money?"

"I don't know. I haven't thought about it."

"What about your apartment?"

"I haven't thought about it."

"Aren't you going to let me know where you are and what you're doing? I promise I won't tell anyone."

"It's okay, Binky. Everything's fine. I'll miss you. You and Trotsky's memos. The only things that made that place worthwhile."

"Thanks a whole hell of a lot," she said.

The old man came for the TV set. Then Carol Deming arrived wearing black pants, a black sweater and no makeup. I gave her a business kiss on the cheek, a gesture she acknowledged by smiling blankly at the camera. She sat in the armchair, her legs tucked up under her, and took another look at the script. Adjusting the tripod, I spoke to her from a directorial crouch. She bit her bent thumb, starlet in the enchanted light. The camera and tape recorder were cabled and ready to sync.

"Now the first part of this has to be simple, direct, wide open. In the second part you begin to draw back. I want to feel as though I'm listening to a stranger in a fog. The two women are very different. Maybe you've seen *Persona*. There are two women, a nurse and a patient, very different, who slowly begin to merge, to almost drift through each other's personalities and reappear with something added or subtracted, I'm not sure which, but a great movie, unparalleled, about the nature of diminishing existence. I'm getting off the point."

"How do you want me to sit, David?"

"Just the way you're sitting. I want the whole chair. Look directly at the camera. Very little voice. Keep the acting invisible. Then we'll cut and do part two."

"I'm scared."

"We all are."

"But I think I know what you want."

"Begin," I said.

"He had to borrow from his father at the beginning but after a while we were really on our own. It was a fun-type marriage. We had lots of friends and we were always calling them up on the spur of the moment and inviting them over. Whenever we ran out of things to say to each other we just picked up the telephone and called friends. If they couldn't come over we went to the movies. We went to the movies three or four times a week. We saw *Breathless* whenever it came back, at least half a dozen times. He loved it. I don't remember anything else we saw. We used to shop together for clothes and sometimes I'd buy things for him and sometimes he'd buy things for me. We liked to be seen together. We were invited everywhere and we always went. On weekends we discovered the city together. It was fabulous. Then came the period when he began to do strange things. He hit me once. He asked me to watch him do that thing that boys do. Out at the Hamptons he disappeared for twelve hours. When he came back he said he had been on a trip through the ages of man, meeting himself along the way. We called up our friends a lot during this period. We called up more and more friends and invited them over. I bought a lot of hats. I wanted a baby. I saw him in Rockefeller Center with a girl with a green raincoat. They were watching the skaters. She must have been freezing."

Carol went to the window and checked over the script. Without a word she tossed the pages to the floor, lit a cigarette and returned to the armchair, sitting this time with bare feet up on the chair, knees high and angled wide and with her back slumped, face framed by the knees, exhaling smoke out of that body-hut into the waiting eye of the camera. I began to shoot. Carol paused, most intelligently, for ten full seconds, contained in smoke, before beginning.

"His sense of insult was overwhelming. If someone used an obscene word in my presence, he demanded an immediate apology. He always got it, of course, his reputation being what it was. He was prepared to kill, quite literally to kill, in order to avenge the honor of someone he loved. He was always swearing on his mother's grave. In his company of men, there was no greater promise or proof of honor than to swear on your mother's grave. You could borrow any amount of money, get any favor, if you swore on your mother's grave to repay the debt. He told me about a friend of his called Mother Cabrini. Cabrini got a lot of mileage out of his mother's grave until it was learned that his mother was not dead. Telling this, he managed to be both outraged and amused. They were all children, of course, but not in the same way the rest of us are children. We have learned not to be afraid of the dark but we've forgotten that darkness means death. They haven't forgotten this. They are still in the hills of Sicily or Corsica or wherever they came from. They obey their mothers. They don't go into a dark cellar without expecting to be strangled by a zombie. They bless themselves constantly. And us, what do we do? We watch television and play Scrabble. So there it is, children of light and darkness. There are only several ways to die and I've just named two. I could no longer bear the way I was dying and so I decided to take my chances with him. We made love for the first time in the back seat of his Cadillac in somebody's driveway at ten o'clock in the evening somewhere between Boston and New York. I was not quite a virgin at the time and this upset him. He couldn't understand how a nineteen-year-old girl from a good family and so forth. We lived together, on and off. He'd go away on one of his business trips and I'd wonder how much the nature of his job meant to our relationship. I couldn't help suspecting I had manufactured the whole thing, my need for him, simply to avoid what I considered to be the alternatives. This is one of my very annoying traits. I can't sit back and let something grow of its own momentum and eventually reveal its truth or horror. I must probe from the outset. But there it is, take it or leave it, and I'd be alone in bed wondering whether I needed him at all, whether anyone would have done, anyone who spent his nights close to violent death. There must be a limit to the need to defeat boredom. In defeating it, I may have gone beyond the limit. I needed death in order to believe I was living, an atmosphere of death much more real and personal than anything the newspapers can offer. I didn't want him to get out of the business. I think I would have left him if he had. There we were then, the child of darkness and the child fleeing the light, him with his Sicilian knife shining in a cave and me with my hand between my legs at four in the morning, anticipating his bloody return. How many nights did I pass in dwelling over the beauty of his death? Gunned down in Utica, the hired assassin. Spinning in a blood-stunned barber chair. The prospect put me in something like heat. I used to imagine my quiet splendid sorrow. His would have been the most beautiful of deaths, filling me with life. He was tall and very handsome, very much a leading man of the nineteen thirties. He moved the way a proud, an almost over-bearingly proud animal might move, an animal that is all sex and death. He was afraid of the dark. He lifted weights to keep in shape, he said, but really for the vanity of his body. Often he came to the dinner table in his underwear. He blessed himself when he passed a church. He believed in ghosts and devils. He tried never to use bad language in my presence and he was shocked and delighted when I used it. He went to the racetrack often and lost heavily. He bought me a mink coat and took me to the Copa. He was everything to me, a man no more than a philosophy, and it's strange, isn't it, that someone like me, with my upbringing and edu-cation and presumably well-trained intellect, would have such a very significant thing in common with this man. It was his instinct that death is without meaning unless it is met vio-lently."

Sullivan tapped a few ashes from her cigarette into the salad she was tossing.

"We used to sit around our quarters after a strike," Brand said. "There'd be Thaw, Hoppy, Bookchester and this kid Eldred Peck who went to some obscure college down South where he wrote his master's thesis on the swastika in history. You know, tracing it way back to the early Buddhists, way back almost to the dawn of man. That was his favorite phrase. The dawn of man. And Eldred invented this game we'd play sitting around our quarters after a strike. Except it wasn't a game really. It was really a peculiar form of conversation, almost a religious chant. It even had a name. It was called Godsave. Eldred always started it off. He was younger than any of us and he had hair that was more white than blond, so white it was almost pink, a thin skinny kid who almost dis-appeared every time he put on his G-suit. Godsave the 94 women and children I vaporized this morning, he'd say. And we'd all follow in turn. Godsave the blind monk I incinerated with nape, Hoppy'd say. Godsave the nursery school I reduced to fine ash. Godsave the old folks' home I expunged with a 750-pounder. Godsave the 328 librarians I strafed into Swiss cheese. Godsave the team of neutral observers I burned to a crisp. Godsave the interdenominational missionary group on their 17-day excursion who never knew what hit them. After about a month Eldred refined the chanting. He made it more orthodox, more rigid; he purified it. He made us recite the same words every time. Each man had his own chant and it was the only one he was allowed to use and we'd go through the group in order, Eldred first, then Bookchester, Thaw, Hoppy and me, repeating the godsaves sometimes for two hours or more, the same five lines, one for each of us. Godsave the testaments of the increasingly real world. Godsave the poor bastards on our own side who get ubiquitized into all-pervasive spiritual flotsam by our well-intentioned bombs. Godsave our loved ones at home and may their vaginas expand and flourish. Godsave the dawn of man, which is once again imminent in the cyclic time-reversal mode. Godsave God. That was my chant. Godsave God. It was like a religious ceremony but full of ironies you don't find in most religions. And sometimes we laughed all through the chanting. Eldred was a strange kid. He was something like the way I am now. But he was way ahead of his time. He anticipated the comeback of the real world. Things become more real in proportion to the unreality of individual lives. The world has never been more real than it is now. I didn't learn that at Yale. I learned it from Eldred. The sky devoured him. He was the first to get it. But that wasn't the end of the godsaves. All we did was drop his chant and change Thaw's. Godsave Eldred Peck and his little pink pecker. Then Bookchester and Thaw got it on the same day. Hostile aircraft. Bad guys. Godsave God, I chanted that night. But Hoppy just slopped down his beer."

"Would you like me to roll one?" Sullivan said.

"Thank you, lady. But I think maybe later."

We ate lunch and then Sullivan and Brand decided to walk into town and find a place where they might buy a chess set. I was slightly annoyed at this because I didn't know the game at all. After they left I watched Pike tilt back his head and swallow, face cracking as the whisky burned its way down.

"We can leave for Colorado in a week or so if you like."

"What for?" he said.

"You want to confront a cougar before you die, don't you? No iron bars in the way. We'll go up into the Rockies."

"Pass me that ashtray."

"You want to go, don't you? That's why you came along in the first place, isn't it?"

"In Baltymore once I saw all manner of beast and fowl without leaving my room. I was blast-ass drunk for two, three weeks. Who needs the Rocky Mountains? This life isn't so big that it won't fit inside a bottle."

"Sully told me once that you saved her life. Did she mean that literally?"

"She means everything literally. Don't kid yourself about that lady. She means everything literally."

"How did you save her life?" I said.

"She had a fly eating her brain. This tiny fly had got stuck in her ear and then somehow crawled into her head. The buzzing was driving her nuts. Then it started eating her brain. She could hear the chewing in there. So we went up to her studio and I performed delicate brain surgery despite my unsteady hands. That fly was just a baby fly when it got in there but by the time I opened up her head and got it out after all the eating it did it was about the size of a good-size snail."

"Who pays for all the liquor you drink? I can't believe you've made that much money in your whole life."

"Take off, Jack."

"Name's Dave."

"Jack. Jackoff. Jackass. Jackdaw. Jackal. Jackal feeding on

dead cougar. Jackal B. DeMille. What do you know about making movies?"

"I've spent twenty-eight years in the movies," I said.

Austin Wakely was a fledgling actor and there was no mission he would not undertake to please the ego of the camera. He had been given only four hours to learn his lines but he professed to be never readier. I played with the tape recorder's giant dials.

"You know, this interview technique isn't anything new."

"I'm inventing the primitive," I said. "The others, in their anxiety, were merely stumbling upon certain pseudo-archaic forms. I myself did something of the sort for a TV show of my own devising. But that was TV."

"Can you pan with that tripod?"

"Not tonight."

"Don't you have a lavalier mike I can wear?"

"Nope."

"You know, they have things called diffusion filters that you can use to soften the actor's face in tight shots."

"Austin, let's dispense with terminology and see if we can weave a spell over this April evening. There won't be any tight shots. I want you standing against that bare stretch of wall. Is Carol married, by the way?"

"News to me if she is."

"Interesting girl," I said.

"Drotty thinks she's too intense. He wants her to exteriorize."

"Okay, we're ready. Try to avoid theatrical pauses. And keep inflection to a minimum."

I sighted on Austin against the wall and then started shooting, my voice a cheerful machine designed for the interrogation of the confused and the dislocated.

"Marital status."

"Divorced."

"Children."

"None."

"Appendix."

"Excised."

"What do you think of the war?" I said.

"I've seen it on television. It's sponsored by instant coffee among other things. The commercials are very tasteful in keeping with the serious theme of the program's content. Some of the commercials are racially integrated. Since I worked for seven years as an employee of the network responsible for the warcasts, I am in a position to point out that the network and the agency joined forces in order to convince the sponsor that integrated commercials were desirable. Their argument was that the war itself is integrated. Balanced programming has always been one of the network's chief aims."

"Draft status."

"I took my physical right after college. Trick knee. Terminal dandruff. They were more discriminating in those days."

"How long were you married?"

"About three years."

"Can you tell the camera why you didn't have children?"

"We wanted to have fun first. We decided that children could wait until after the fun was over, after Europe, after we became established."

"Did you go to Europe?"

"Not until we were divorced. We met in Florence and drank orangeade. I was staying in a fourteenth-century palazzo. In the dining room one evening I began a conversation with a very unattractive girl who turned out to be both German and lame. We spent part of the night in her—not my—room and in the morning I met my ex-wife on the Ponte Vecchio and we walked through the city for hours. By early evening she had developed a slight limp and I discovered I did not want to be with her anymore."

"What caused the divorce?"

"My image began to blur. This became a problem for both

of us. However, we have continued to be very fond of each other. Divorce is a wonderful invention, much better than protracted separation or murder. It destroys tension. It liberates many wholesome emotions which had been tyrannized by the various mental cruelties. Divorce is the most educating route to a deep understanding between two people. It's the second and most important step in arriving at a truly radiant form of self-donative love. Marriage, of course, is the first step."

"Parents."

"Mother deceased."

"Father."

"He's buried alive but still breathing. I don't really look forward to his death. But I admit it would bring relief."

"Why?" I said.

"I remember the sound of his bare feet on the stairs. He never wore slippers, my father. People were always giving him slippers for Christmas. But there is a certain kind of American masculinity which precludes the wearing of articles of clothing which might possibly dull the effect of the brutal truth of one's immediate environment."

"The camera dislikes evasiveness. As Mr. Hitchcock says, one must not use flashback to deceive. What are you proud of, if anything?"

"I've made many short movies of one kind or another. Weekend films. Orgy-porgies. Nonplot things with friends. More than a hobby but not much more. Until this point, of course. And I used to be proud of one of the things I did. It was done in Central Park during a ceremony following one of the assassinations. There was an old Negro couple standing at the back of the crowd. The man was tall and lean with a face like a rock pointing out to sea. He wore a black suit and a white shirt with a high starched collar, rounded at the edges, and a black tie knotted about an inch below the top button of his shirt. He held a black hat in his hand. The woman was almost as tall as he was and her face in its own way was just as strong, but softer somehow, not rock but earth. The word dignity is unavoidable. And I felt for some reason that they were not husband and wife but brother and sister. Whatever they were, they looked like pillars of the black Baptist Church. They stood listening to the speeches and music, standing absolutely straight, absolutely motionless, and I raised my camera and began to shoot. From time to time I'd go into the crowd or train the camera on one of the platform speakers. But I'd always come back to the old Negro couple. I must have looked at that scrap of film fifty times. It meant a lot to me. I was proud of it. It wasn't just a day in the park or something you see on the seven o'clock news. Those two faces seemed more enduring than the republic itself. The film began with them and ended with them. They framed a sense of confusion. At least that's what I thought. It took me a long time to see how wrong I was. The camera implies meaning where no meaning exists. I had not celebrated that brother and sister. I had mocked them. I had exploited their sorrow. I had tried to make them part of a hopeful message on the state of the Union. To be black is to be the actor. To be white is to be the critic."

"Is there anything else you'd like to tell the camera?"

"Simply hello. Hello to myself in the remote future, watching this in fear and darkness. Hello to that America, whatever it may be doing or undoing. I hope you've finally become part of your time, David. You were always a bit behind, held back by obsolete sensibilities."

"Do you have any particular ambition in life?"

"To get out of it alive."

"Thank you," I said.

I shut down all systems, tape and film, and we talked for a while on subjects of no interest to either of us. Then Austin left and I took a blank piece of paper, crumpled it into a tight sphere and began tossing jump shots at the wastebasket. I pretended to be Oscar Robertson against Jerry West. An hour later I banked in a long left-hand hook and went to bed. It was the eighth anniversary of my mother's death.

I bought a hat, the first I had owned since childhood, a gray plaid bop cap which I wore with a magical child's belief in the infinities of common things. During the drive from New York to Maine I had worn at times a khaki fatigue cap, borrowed from Pike, but he had taken it back and buried it in his sea bag; no war games allowed with his private battle gear. On the hotel bed I rested, cap over my eyes. A full morning brushed through the shuddering blinds. Fellini, master of hats and noses, understands the philosophical nature of costume. My twenty-eight years in the movies. Making of a life so easily made that a hat on the head could become the man. The hat wore me. Arrivato Zampanó: the trailer and the road, her flawed boy's body announcing the strongman, and he in chains, bellowing. My teeth clicking in the dark at the Bleecker Street Cinema as they dance across the sky, a necklace of chessmen, hands locked in the northern dawn. Eyes closed, I inhaled some industrial gloom from the hat's soft lining, L. S. Stratford Ltd., bit of Finney falling down the stairs. I looked between the cracks inside the dark. Burt Lancaster toweling his chest: (and we live there, grubbing, in the pores). Bell looking at the poster of Belmondo looking at the poster of purposeful Bogart. Old man on the swing, Watanabe, singing to his unseen infancy. I took a walk around the bed, missing those stale chambers on the West Side, nicely epicene in their way, a touch of seedy glamour drifting in off Needle Park, pale tapering men who live for the films of the thirties. Shane rides toward the immaculate mountains.

I walked out to Howley Road, a cool night frozen over with stars. The light was on inside the camper and as I approached there worked up through my stomach the boy's delightful feeling of being a scout moving into enemy territory, moving through the darkness toward an outpost where the unsuspecting enemy sits smoking, just seconds from silent expert death.

"Today's my birthday," Brand said. "We're trying to think of ways to celebrate."

"How old are you?"

"Thirty."

"You're two years older than I am. What's it like to be thirty? A friend of mine told me three things happened when he reached thirty. He gained weight around the middle. He stopped reading novels. And he had a recurring year-long dream about a tapeworm in his stomach that gets so big it begins literally to outgrow him. It feeds on his vital organs, getting bigger as he gets smaller and weaker, until finally when it works its way out of his mouth, eating his gums and teeth in the process, it weighs about one hundred and eighty pounds, most of it him, and he's down to thirty pounds of bone and translucent skin and he falls on the floor and sees the huge slimy jaws of the tapeworm fitting themselves around his head as he wakes up. Warren Beasley told me that story, the radio personality."

"What do you mean he stopped reading novels?" Brand said.

"That's what he told me. I don't know what he meant by it."

"I'm taking all the slang out of my book. I'm inventing new slang."

"Sully, have you seen *Ikiru* by any chance?"

"Wait a minute, Davy, we're talking about novels. I plan to take out the slang and replace it with new forms, new modes. Maybe I'll eliminate language itself. It may be possible to find a completely new mode. I've been thinking about this lately. I'd like your opinion."

"In my little home movie, the thing I'm doing, I haven't reduced the value of language at all. I've reinforced it, in fact. What I've reduced is movement, the kind of movement that tells a story or creates a harmony. I want language to evolve from static forms. The film is a sort of sub-species of the underground. What I'm shooting now is just a small segment of what will eventually include more general matter—funerals, traffic jams, furniture, real events, women, doors, windows. Auto-fiction. Actors, people playing themselves, lines of poetry. When I'm done I'd like to put the whole thing in a freezer and then run it uncut thirty years from now."

"I'll be sixty then," Brand said.

"I'll be dirt," Pike said.

"Sully, I wonder if you'd be willing to appear in the movie. It won't take long. We can do it tomorrow. A brief scene. I know I haven't been spending much time around here lately but it's only because I've been so busy. I'm very grateful that nobody's complained about the number of days we've been spending here. So will you do it? A brief scene. Speak to me, sad-eyed lady of the lowlands."

"Of course, David. Anything for you."

Brand wanted to arm-wrestle. We locked hands and exchanged iron glares. I didn't know whether or not he was serious. He began to exert pressure and I put my head down and concentrated, trying to keep my elbows square on the table. For several minutes we strained, giving and taking little. My forearm was tense, muscles humming, and I put everything I had into one pivotal offensive, all my strength, a vein leaping in my wrist, his arm starting to give, elbow losing traction; then he stiffened suddenly and we were stalemated again and Sullivan was standing over us holding a strange painted wood-and-wire doll.

"It's your birthday present," she said. "I made it for you this afternoon. It's a doll-god of India. A menacing bitchy hermaphroditic divinity."

"I think I'm afraid of it," Brand said.

The grass was wet and the steel supports of the swings behind the bandstand in the park were dull silver in the clear morning. This from the twelfth year, boys on sleds seen through gauze in slow motion, their round steaming faces fading in the snow, the great love I had for my heavy boots and their rusty interlocking buckles; entering winter, pure and empty, sea-creature (brain) pulsing in the cookie jar, art and science of the shovelers of snow, the rocking chair's steady knocks thundering through the house, her hands clenching the edges of the armrests, knuckles white, and I wondered how that worked, whether blood stayed dammed in the veins of the hand or moved up the arm waiting for the hand to go soft, rocking in her darkness, snow softly dropping. But there was no snow now and I would have to shoot by daylight. Sullivan stood behind one of the swings, no questions asked or explanations offered, a woman, a figure in a landscape although snow was impossible and disease did not blast her cells, an actor, a woman nonetheless whose generating force took from the camera some of its power, weakening thankfully what was for me an all too overarching moment. Birds rested on the chimneys of several homes, starlings or wrens, neo-pterodactyls for all I knew, Iowa for all I knew, Alexandria, Kamakura, and through the eyepiece I saw pass behind her a blue panel truck with the single word *Smith* in white across the side. Nearer Iowa then and more than small comfort. Eight o'clock in the morning. Turned-up bowl of the bandstand. Trees and wet grass. Sand impacted in the sandbox by last night's late rain. Gulley of an outflung leg. Four-finger handprint. Pail's perfect circle. I adjusted the wind filter and she sat on the swing now, a nautical creak working down the links of the chains, tips of her fingers lightly touching them. She began to rise toward me, nothing in her eyes.

"I see myself in a big stone house on the Oregon coast," Brand said. "I'm exactly sixty years old. I built the house myself, rock by rock. I see myself as one of those unique old writers who's still respected for his daring ideas and style. Young disciples make pilgrimages to visit me. They come hiking up to my house carrying knapsacks and copies of my books. There are no roads in the area. It's like Big Sur, only more lonely and remote. The house is right above the ocean and I can see seals basking on the rocks and big lean seabirds skimming over the waves and even an occasional shark, the fin of a big beautiful shark bright in the sunlight. The shark is my personal symbol. At the back of all my books there's an imprint of a shark just like the wolfhound on Alfred A. Knopf books. The surf thunders on the rocky beach. The wind comes off the water and blows past the house and goes whistling through the woods out back. I see myself as lean and craggy. The young disciples come from every corner of the world. Sometimes they come in groups, a bunch of young Frenchmen and their girlfriends bringing greetings from famous old French philosophers and writers, guys I shared symposiums with and signed petitions with, famous old French intellectuals who haven't given up their revolutionary ideas and who still exert a profound influence on French foreign policy. The young disciples usually stay a week or so. We have quiet talks and go walking on the beach. They ask me about my life and thought. Sometimes I get a stray, a young female disciple who comes all alone from Sweden at great personal expense and hardship. She is young and blond and lovely. The Swedish experiment has not worked, she says. We go to bed together. We can hear the wind and the gulls. There's nothing in the room except the four stone walls and the bed. Afterward she tells me I am like a man half my age. We speak only rarely. She cooks simple Swedish meals for me. We walk on the beach. I read her the first chapter of my work in progress and she tells me it is the best and truest I have done. She asks me about my wife. I had been married years before to a beautiful Vietnamese girl who died of a rare lung disease. I say nothing to the Swede. I merely take her hand and lead her to the bed. Two weeks later I tell her that she must go. My work demands the tension of loneliness. She understands. I go back to work. It is all hard and clean. The surf crashes on the rocks. A month later a tall lovely Australian girl with titian hair comes walking up the steep rocky path. She is carrying a knapsack and my lone book of verse."

In the afternoon I went to the library. Then I walked back out to Howley Road, almost not noticing the brightness and calm of the day, the trees in their easy bending eagerness smelling of higher terrain. Suddenly I regretted the calmness of lowlands, of sea level, and thought if this were mountain country all my earnest plans might be shoveled easily into the wind. In the pitiless insanity of nature above the timber-line no other resolution is needed than that of a river changing color as it flows down the continent toward its own promise and past. Pike was alone in the camper, barking softly in his sleep, and there was nobody in the bar across the road.

I spent sixteen straight hours slopping white paint on the dull green walls of my hotel room and then, using a much smaller brush, printing the two thousand words of the next part of the script in black paint over the white.

I finished early in the morning. I went out to the camper, where I spent most of the day either sleeping or watching Sullivan and Brand play chess. In the evening I went back to the hotel. Glenn Yost came up to the room and looked at the walls. I told him it had cost me two sizable bribes and a promise to pay for the repainting when I checked out. His crazed eye was very active. I told him that during filming he would stand by the armchair and read the words and sentences as they progressed around the room. He'd be on camera in-termittently; from time to time I'd pan one of the walls, per-haps in accord with the line he was reading, perhaps against the line, camera and man reading in opposite directions. I'd anticipate the script at times. I'd also shoot passages he had already recited. Somewhere along the way we'd cut, reload, re-position, and proceed again. I gave him time to read through the whole thing, showing him exactly where certain passages picked up after being interrupted by windows or door frames. The left eye jumped. I told him to be cool, that none of this mattered in the least.

"I stand here frankly amazed."

"The eye's really hopping," I said.

"I don't know but what I'd rather be at home fixing the screen door."

"Fellini says the right eye is for reality and the left eye is the fantasy eye. Whenever you're ready, Glenn."

"What the hell, let's go."

I stood over the tripod and gave him a hand-sign.

"Our luck was lean that year. There were about ten thousand of us. The rest were indigenous. We were spread all over the southern part of the peninsula, surrendering to anybody who happened to come around, all told about seventy thousand troops, American and Filipino, and the Japanese had to get us out of there so their own people could move in and prepare for a big assault on Corregidor. We were just in the way which was a new feeling for somebody who considered himself a pretty fair rifleman and his country the only invincible power on earth. The first thing they wanted to do was get us all assembled at a place called Balanga. We were to get there on our own from whatever company or platoon or command post had been shot away around us or starved or bored or diseased into submission. There were nine of us who started walking across a precleared firing area toward Balanga. It was only twelve or fifteen miles from where we were. They didn't give us any food but that was nothing new. We had been employing maximum stress procedure for some time and following the example of the indigenous personnel, eating dogs and monkeys and lizards. Once I saw one of them, a Filipino, eating the meat of a python. I never ate python and I never ate monkey after the first time. Lizard you can keep down but monkey-meat is like eating something that came jumping and swinging out of hell itself and I was willing to go just so far with the max stress routine. The other thing was malaria, which everybody had. But it really wasn't too bad. We got some sugar cane from the fields and ate that and there were streams to drink from. We had a colonel with us and he had a pass that some gink officer had given him when we surrendered. He showed this pass to anybody we ran into on the road and they didn't give us too much trouble. They searched us and took rings and watches and anything else they could find, like my Zippo lighter, which twenty years later I began to regret because it would have made a good ad in the campaign they were running, full-page black-and-white-bleed authentic owner testimonials. THIS ZIPPO SURVIVED THE BA-TAAN DEATH MARCH. We got to Balanga that night. We had covered the distance in one day with no strain at all. Then we heard the enemy had executed about four hundred indigenous military personnel, officers and noncoms. The Filipinos were on their way to Balanga like the rest of us when they were stopped by some ginks who were part of an aftermath reaction force. They let everybody go except the officers and noncoms, who were lined up in several columns and then tied together at the wrists with telephone wire. Then they took out their swords and bayonets and killed them. We heard they beheaded most of them. They didn't use any guns and it took about two hours to kill all four hundred. Must have been something to see. We heard it was revenge for something the indigenous personnel had done, but nobody knew what. To tell you the truth I don't think anybody cared. In the situation we were in, which was one of total, complete and utter heat and boredom and wondering what manner of crawling scabby insect you were going to dine on next, the fact of four hundred headless Filipinos was a topic for pleasant clubhouse gossip, something to discuss briefly in mild awe and almost admiration for the ginks for at least having a sense of spectacle and to be grateful for in a way because it took our minds off our own problems. Balanga was unforgettable. Thousands of men were pouring into the town. They put some of us in pastures. Others they kept in small yards behind barbed wire. We were all jammed together and it was impossible to sit down and the whole town smelled of defecation. The whole town. We were told to use a ditch but it was full of dead bodies and the smell of the dead and dying kept most of us away. Men with dysentery couldn't control themselves and had to defecate where they stood. Others just fell down and died. All this time in Balanga standing in the pasture and later burying some of the dead I tried to think of my wife and two small daughters, sanity, a home and a bed, her breasts and mouth and lovely hands, but she kept drifting away and I was too numb or unfeeling to care really whether I could bring her back, the sight of her standing naked in a dim room, and on the ground next to me a man I had thought to be dead was jacking off, flat on his back, beating it in a quiet frenzy. The ginks presented us with copies of the humane atrocity clause of the Cape Town Accords. Then they gave us rice to eat and sent us north. There were guards this time. We were walking to a place called Orani. We saw a lot of corpses on the road. Some indigenous noncombatants gave us food and we drank polluted water from streams or puddles. We weren't supposed to break ranks but we did anyway. We had to have water. It was worth the chance, no two ways about it. A lot of men were shot or bayoneted getting water. One of the guards was singing a song, walking along beside us in the hot sun smiling and singing a song. A sergeant named Ritchie, a demo expert with one of the anti-transit security outfits, broke ranks then and jumped the guard from behind and knocked his weapon into a ditch. Then he straddled the guard and started tearing at his throat. I don't think he particularly wanted to kill the guard. He just wanted to get inside him, open him up for inspection. Then two other ginks came trotting up the line and shot Ritchie in the back. We got to Orani and it stank even worse than Balanga. Just outside the town though, about a mile outside, I saw something so strange I thought it might be a vision, something brought on by the hunger and malaria. Under some trees at the edge of an empty field was a swing, an obviously homemade swing, just a board and two ropes fastened to a treelimb. Sitting on the swing was a gink officer and maybe it was the glare of the sun or maybe just the distance but he seemed to be a very old man, he seemed almost ancient, but at the same time I was sure he was wearing the uniform of a gink officer. He was looking at us, gliding very slowly on the swing a few inches forward, a few inches back, his small legs well off the ground, looking at us and singing a song. At first I hadn't realized he was singing but now I could hear it coming across the field, a slow and what seemed a very sorrowful song. Maybe it was my imagination and maybe just my ignorance of the language but it seemed to be the same song the guard was singing before Ritchie jumped him. And he just sat there, moving a few inches either way, singing that beautiful slow song and then making a gesture with his hand as if to bless us, but in a circle, a strange blessing. If it was a vision, then it was a mass vision because all of us looked that way as we went along the road. But nobody said anything. We just looked at him and listened to the song. A little ways further on we passed one of the village depacification centers set up by Tech II and Psy Ops before the enemy terminated the whole concept. We were in Orani about a day. Then we walked to another town, where they stuffed us in a warehouse. There must have been thousands of us in there, crushed and elbowing and going out of our minds. Nobody could sleep. I was dying for some mouthwash. Barrels of it for everybody, green and foamy. We were all locked together and the stink was worse than ever because we were indoors. From here we walked to a rail center where they had trains waiting for us. Some of us were given food here and some weren't. We all looked forward to the trains, some dim and still functioning part of our minds thinking of god knows what childhood times we had spent on trains, the Twin Cities Zephyr if you were from the Midwest, or the San Francisco Chief or Afternoon Hiawatha; some dim vision of going across the Great Plains on a Union Pacific train and everything is vast and wild and mysterious because you're ten years old and America is as wide as all the world and twice as invincible. We looked forward to the trains but we should have known better by this time. They put us in boxcars. Whatever position you found yourself in when you were pushed into the boxcar, that was it for the whole trip. There were no windows and the doors were closed. It was the warehouse again, this time on wheels. A few minutes after the train started, somebody began to moo. That set us off. Soon we all began mooing and snorting, making noises like sheep, cows, horses, pigs. The Psy Ops people never told us about this kind of environmental reaction. Nobody laughed. We weren't fooling around. This was no comic celebration of the indomitable human spirit. No protest against inhumanity. We were cattle now and we knew it. We were merely telling ourselves that we were cattle and we shouted moo and baa in absolute seriousness and total overwhelming self-hatred. We were livestock. How could anyone deny it? What else could we be but livestock, locked up as we were in boxcars and stepping in puddles of our own sick liquid shit. We didn't hate the ginks. They hadn't gotten us into this. We had, or our generals had, or our country which treasured the sacrifice of its sons, making slogans out of their death and selling war bonds with it or soap for all we knew. The ride seemed to take years. It seemed a trek across Asia. When we were all off the train we walked to the POW camp, where they processed us with one of our own incremental mode simulators. The march was over and I tried to get back to the small white beauty of her breasts and the two girls so beautifully flabby my fingers wanted to melt when I touched them. And the third child about to be born. But I couldn't return. West End Avenue. It seemed that everybody who lived there was taking music lessons. Harkavy the country squire drinking Jack Daniel's on the rocks in his star-spangled pajamas. And my mother (what was her name) dusting the old house like a pharaoh's widow come to clean the tomb every Thursday morning. Alexandria. Our wedding on the

297

lawn. It was all in a dark part of my mind and I had to get back there because it was in Balanga that they forced us to bury the dead. It was in Balanga that they forced us to bury the dead. It was in Balanga that they forced us to bury the dead and I was throwing dirt onto the body of a Filipino when he suddenly moved. Poor little blood-faced indigenous Filipino soldierboy. When he started to rise from the ditch. Dozens of dead men around him covered already with maggots, completely covered so that the ground, the earth, seemed to be moving, rotting bodies everywhere and the whole saddle trench about to erupt. When he lifted himself on his elbow. I dropped my shovel and leaned way over the edge of the trench, all those billions of ugly things swarming into the mouths of my dead buddies and their dead buddies and their buddies' buddies and the tough-little brown-little indigenous military personnel. When he tried to extend a hand to me. I leaned way down and then felt something jab me in the ribs. It was a guard jabbing me with his bayonet in a light, casual, condescending and almost upper-class manner like a bloody British officer of the 11th Light Dragoons poking an Indian stable boy with his riding crop. When he tried to rise. I pointed to him, trying to rise, and then the guard did some pointing of his own. He pointed his bayonet at the shovel on the ground and then at the boy in the ditch. It was rather a deft piece of understatement, I thought. He wanted me to bury the little wog anyway."

"What are you stopping for?" I said.

"That's all there is," Glenn said.

After he left I looked up Owney Pine's number in the local directory. He said he'd try anything once and we made a date for the next day.

If I could index all the hovering memories which announce themselves so insistently to me, sitting amid the distractions of yet another introspective evening (ship models, books, the last of the brandy), I would compile my index not in terms of good or bad memories, childhood or adult, innocent or guilty, but rather in two very broad and simple categories. Cooperative and uncooperative. Some memories seem content to be isolated units; they slip neatly into the proper slot and give no indication of continuum. Others, the uncooperative, insist on evasion, on camouflage, on dissolving into uninvited images. When I command snow to fall once again on the streets of Old Holly, my father's hands curled about a shovel, I can't be sure I'll get the precise moment I want. A second too soon and there is mother sitting in the rocker; too late and the memory subdivides, one part straying into fantasy: dull knife clamped in my teeth, I dog-crawl through the jungle, belly dragging, toward Dr. Weber's house. We are what we remember. The past is here, inside this black clock, more devious than night or fog, determining how we see and what we touch at this irreplaceable instant in time.

"How long have you been practicing medicine, doctor?"

"Let's see, I make it twenty-four years. Does that jibe with your figures?"

"It's not important," I said. "Where did you intern?"

"Interned first at Brooklyn Eye, Ear, Nose and Throat. Then at Pelham Senile, the New York City Mortuary, Jewish Discount, and Blessed Veronica Midwife. Followed by a brief stint on the coast at Pasadena Neuroland and Roy Rogers Lying-In. Mind if I smoke?"

"Not at all, doctor. And after your internship?"

"Private practice in Westchester. I was beloved out there. You can check that out with anybody in town. I was beloved by my parishioners. I mean my patients."

"Let's discuss the disease that's on everyone's mind today."

"The Big C. Love to."

"Would you tell the camera the different ways in which it might manifest itself."

"Look out for lumps of any kind. Look out for irregular bleeding from any orifice of the body. Look out for changes in color of moles or warts. Look out for persistent coughing, pain in your bones, indigestion, loss of weight. Look out for diarrhea. Look out for constipation. Look out for that tired worn-out feeling. Look out for painful urination and beware when you cough up blood or mucus. Look out for sores on the lips. Look out for aches in your lower back. Beware of swelling. If you develop a sudden distaste for meat, you're in big trouble. Look out for bloody stool, urinary retention, lumps in the throat, sputum flecked with blood, discharges from the nipple, lumps in the armpit. Beware of wens, canker, polyps, expanding birthmarks. We all have it to some extent. Oh yes. Cells expanding, running wild. Bandit cells. Oh yes. Massage the prostate. Whirl the poor bastard's urine at high speeds. Bombard the victim with sound waves—eight hundred thousand cycles per second. Sound kills bandit cells, drives victim crazy. Oh yes, oh yes. But by the grace of Aesculapius, god of medicine, we'll lick the Big C and make America safe for babies and other growing things. Radiation and/or surgery. Cut and burn, cut and burn. Toss me that pack of cigarettes."

"Did any of your patients despise the very earth you walked on?"

"You must be kidding. I was beloved by my patients. Making my rounds of a spring morning I would nod to them on the street and they would nod back. Many's the time they nodded first."

"Cervix, doctor."

"Neck of the womb. Scrape surface of vagina for fluid. Or get it out of there with a tube. Run a smear test, one of my favorites. Dry fluid on a glass slide. Stain it. Hand it over to a pathologist. Say the physician's prayer. Give me strength and leisure and zeal to enlarge my knowledge. Our work is great and the mind of man presses forward forever. Thou hast chosen me in Thy grace to watch over the life and death of Thy creatures. I am about to fulfill my duties. Guide me in this immense work so that it may benefit mankind, for without

Thy help not even the least thing will succeed. I like that part about leisure."

"Internal examination, doctor."

"Probe and investigate. Seek and find. Make soundings. Great earth and sea smell comes blowing out. Changing tides. Sandalwood and spices. Harvest time in Flanders. I like to dilly and dally just a bit. It relaxes them."

"Death, doctor."

"Never say die is what I say. Pump glycerol into the circulatory system. Put the body on ice in a plastic bag. Place in vacuum capsule full of liquid nitrogen. Cool to three hundred twenty degrees below. Once we figure out how to thaw the sons of bitches, we'll have mass resurrections from coast to coast."

"We've run out of time," I said.

"That'll be one hundred and fifty dollars."

Any description of the main street of Fort Curtis can begin and end inside this very sentence. Beyond that I find only redundancy. The same six words identify the thing to be described and serve to describe it. The main street of Fort Curtis.

It was there that I wandered about with my strolling players, Austin Wakely and Carol Deming, each of us filled with the crosscurrents of love that pass between collaborators in secret acts, creators, interpreters, artisans, mapmakers, weavers of the speed of light. People in the street passed us, distantly, unadvised of our commitment, fairly large numbers on that warm evening, moviegoing, shopping for seasonal items—paint, window screens, lightweight shoes. The breeze smelled of commerce, of leather goods and exhaust fumes, very pleasant in a way, the Greek figs of one's childhood. That street was a thoroughly American place, monument of collective nostalgia, and we read the store signs aloud and looked at the glossy stills behind paneled glass outside the movie theater. Nobody knew who we were and we didn't know each other.

They were fascinated by the walls of my room. I put up a bedsheet to block out the words in the area where they'd be sitting. Soon we were ready. Austin was in his jockey shorts, sitting in a chair in front of the bedsheet. Carol wore black underwear of the bikini type. She sat next to Austin in an identical straightback chair. I was getting very intricate here, not just tampering with the past, changing its color a bit, but mixing pasts together and ending at least in part with a film of a film. Terribly intricate. But the actors did not ask questions. Underwear is humorous and only the undemocratic mind interrogates humor.

Boy. Let's talk about the near future.

Girl. You start.

Boy. I think we should get married. We can go out to the Coast together for my senior year. It'll be a lot of fun. There's all kinds of water sports out there.

Girl. I'd like to learn how to water-ski. But marriage is such a big step.

Boy. Do you love me?

Girl. I don't know. I think so. I guess I do.

Boy. I'll have my car out there. We can drive into the desert. Maybe you can be in my movie. I'll be doing a movie. We can do pretty much what we want out there. We can take off our clothes and try to be free. When you think of all the people in the world who dress freely and who when they want to take off their clothes don't have to discuss it for hours on end, it's amazing.

Girl. This is my favorite set of underthings.

Boy. This is mine too.

Girl. How free is it out there? How many girls have you done things with?

Boy. One doesn't keep books.

Girl. That's very British and amusing.

Boy. Experience is important.

302

Girl. Experience is something I'd like to have without going through all the trouble of getting it.

Boy. As I see it, there's no reason why we shouldn't get married. We like each other a lot. We have mutual respect for each other's taste in clothes. We like to do a lot of the same things. And everybody says we're an attractive couple.

Girl. Aren't there other things to consider?

Boy. One doesn't keep books.

Girl. That really is an amusing remark.

Boy. I promise you one thing. If we get married I'll definitely put you in my film. We're supposed to use students as actors but I'm sure they'll make an exception in this case. It'll even have a soundtrack.

Girl. Can I wear what I'm wearing?

Boy. You can wear whatever you want. And you can say whatever you want.

Girl. It'll be wild. It'll be super. It'll be too much.

When Austin was dressed I asked him to leave and he said he'd wait outside in his car. Carol put on one of my shirts and read quietly through the next scene. I tried not to sneak looks at her as I played with the tape recorder. I felt it was important to keep things on a strictly professional level and I wanted to make a casual remark, something technical about sound or lighting, but nothing very scientific arrived at the tip of my tongue. Then Brand showed up, surprisingly, on time. Carol went into the bathroom and Brand stripped down to his shorts, long white things with green alarm clocks on them. She came out wearing a thigh-length nightgown and walked toward the bed without looking at either of us. Glances carefully prepared to indicate nothing more than mild interest were exchanged between Brand and me as we noted the soft commanding bounce of her breasts. Carol stood on the bed, hands on hips, looking about her as if to make sure the set had been cleared of all but essential personnel, and then lowered herself to a pillow, where she sat wrapped in her own limbs, an entrance and a place-taking of totally serious humor, one level of personality already in role and trying to demand obedience of the other, which perhaps was beginning to hate the camera. Brand sat on the other pillow. I told him to take off his glasses. Then we discussed what was to follow. Although Brand assured me that he had memorized his lines, I insisted on an improvised scene, first because I didn't trust him, second because I didn't like what I had written. I told them to retain the spirit of the thing and forget the details. Carol stared at the inkblue dogs on Brand's arm, the fornicating dogs. He blinked several times and reached for his glasses but I moved them out of reach. I set up camera and tripod at the foot of the bed.

Man. There was a red moon.

Woman. Schenectady is famous for its moons.

Man. Right away you start in. It's better you don't know anyway. I'm not supposed to tell you anything but you always get me to tell you.

Woman. You tell me where but that's all.

Man. That's enough. That's too much. Sometimes I wonder about you. Always asking. Isn't it better you don't know? You're too interested. You shouldn't be that interested.

Woman. You're my sweetheart. I want to know what you do on your business trips.

Man. It's not right that you should want to know. There's something wrong with it. Sometimes I wonder about you.

Woman. What's fascinating about people like you is your blazing sense of morality. Your devotion to the concept of a place for everything and everything in its place. When you get right down to it, that's what morality means to a moralist. It means shoot to kill but not in a hospital zone. You might wake the patients.

Man. What are you talking about? What's she talking about?

Woman. I'm talking about your underwear. Did you buy those shorts in Schenectady? Was it before or after you fulfilled the contract? I've never seen them before. They're marvelous. They go beyond the outlandish into some private area of metaphysics. All the clocks say nine forty-five. Do you suppose that's morning or evening? Somehow it seems terribly important. You must give me the name of the store so I can call them and ask. In the meantime I want you to tell me very specifically whether you were wearing those shorts when you fulfilled the contract.

Man. Let's get back to what we were saying.

Woman. You don't even remember what we were saying. Now answer my question. Were you wearing those shorts when you carried out the terms set down in the small print?

Man. Okay, I was wearing these shorts.

Woman. Now tell me exactly what time it was when you killed him.

Man. You know I don't talk about that. It's bad enough I tell you where. Details cause trouble. You learn that in this business. Details cause trouble.

Woman. Tell me what time it was. What harm could that possibly do?

Man. It was ten after one.

Woman. Repeat that.

Man. It was about ten after one in the morning.

Woman. I thought so. I knew it.

Man. How did you know?

Woman. It's written all over you. It's literally written all over you. Those clocks on your shorts are a dead giveaway.

Man. The clocks say nine forty-five.

Woman. Exactly. That's exactly the point. You've got to burn them as soon as possible. We can drive down to Nell's place and burn them there.

Man. Look, if you have to know exactly how I did it, I'll tell you.

Woman. I'm not interested.

Man. The last show was coming out. The ticket window was closed. The marquee was dark. Only about ten people came out. I got out of the car and walked up to him. I put out my hand as if I wanted to shake hands with him. It's your

305

natural reaction when a guy puts out his hand like I did that you take it. I knew who he was but he didn't know me like from Adam. He never saw me before. But he put out his hand anyway. That's the natural reaction. Anyone would have done the same thing. We stood there shaking hands and I had a big smile on my face and I called him by his name. He wanted to let go but I kept a tight grip on his hand. Then I put my left hand in my jacket, still holding him with the other hand, and I took out the .38 and fired three times right into the breast pocket of his shirt. There was a war movie playing.

Woman. What did it sound like?

Man. What's the difference what it sounded like?

Woman. Did it make a bang? Did it make a whimper? Did it crack, resound, boom, ping?

Man. It was like 20mm cannon fire. It was like hosing down an LZ with your 20 mike-mike. There's the slang again. There it is.

Woman. How did you feel later?

Man. How would you feel? It was a hospital zone.

Woman. You broke the cardinal rule.

Man. I broke the cardinal's back. He was riding his bike, this Buddhist cardinal, when I double-indemnitized him.

Woman. What were his politics, sweetheart?

Man. Slightly to the left of God.

Woman. That would make him a Taft Republican.

Man. Which Taft?

Woman. Which God?

Man. The one that made little green clocks.

Woman. And little white boys to wear them.

Man. Respect for your husband.

Woman. You're not my husband. My husband is black. Blacker. Blackest black.

Austin's car left the curb in a burst of hysterical rubber. I knew I wouldn't be able to sleep for a while so I walked out to Howley Road with Brand. We moved along, jogging part of the way, fighters doing roadwork, snapping out short lefts and rights as we dance-jogged, doing 360-degree turns without breaking stride, hog-grunting on the dark road. We slowed to a walk.

"I'm surprised you people have decided to stay on," I said. "I thought you'd get tired of this place. I didn't think this thing I'm doing would take this long."

"Nobody decided to stay on," he said. "We never discussed it. We've never discussed anything and nobody's made any decisions that I know of. We just stayed on."

"But aren't you tired of this place?"

"I never thought about it. Anyway where would we go without you? You're leading this expedition."

"I don't think that's in effect anymore. It's just that I didn't think it would take this long to do this thing I'm doing."

"Nobody's talked about moving on," he said.

"What about your book?"

"There is no book, Davy. There's eleven pages and seven of them don't have any words on them. And I'm not making any great claims for the other four."

"I thought you were writing all the time you were up in Maine. How long were you up there?"

"Almost a year," he said.

"What did you do all that time?"

"I don't know. I really don't remember much of it. I guess I was stoned most of the time. I think I blew a fuse or something. My head went dead. That's the only way to put it. Something in there burned out and blew away. Went dead."

"And you were in that garage for a whole year. And you weren't doing anything."

"I was doing something. I was killing my head."

"All right," I said. "Pike's barking in his sleep. He doesn't care where he is as long as he's got a bottle at his elbow. You don't have any novel in the works and you're in no hurry to get back to Maine or anywhere else. But what about Sully?"

"You'll have to ask her. I told you, nobody discusses anything in our family. We're a very tightlipped bunch."

"How long's your money going to hold out?"

"The lady's been picking up tabs the last ten days or so."

"I didn't know that," I said. "I wish I could lend you some money but I'm not fixed too well myself. I guess I'm out of a job by this time."

"I was wondering about that. I'd talk to the lady if I were you."

We jogged some more, drinking in the cool air, drinking it and snorting it out again, throwing punches at the wind. Then the four of us sat around the table in the camper making small sounds with our feet and elbows.

"I was wondering about that," Sullivan said. "I seemed to remember that you were due in the Southwest sometime last week but I wasn't sure. You didn't say anything."

"I've been busy."

"That was a good job, David."

"I was making twenty-four five. Look, I need you one more time for the thing."

"I'll be here," she said.

"He took my glasses away and tucked me in bed," Brand said. "It wasn't as much fun as I thought it might be. That Carol what's-her-name Deming. She got a little bit weird at the end. What's the point of the whole thing anyway?"

"Go play with your doll," I said.

Austin dressed as he had for the first sequence. I was wearing a lime nylon turtleneck and a pair of chinos with stovepipe stripes.

"Then the lame girl in Florence was real," he said.

"That's right. It took the edge off meeting my ex-wife. We'd been hinting to each other about a possible reconciliation. But the lame girl caused a strange kind of shift in my thinking.

Hard to explain. My ex-wife's parents were in Germany at the time. The lame girl was German. Then late in the day my ex-wife started limping. None of it meant anything. But it confused me somewhat. I tried to tie it all together. But it wouldn't quite tie. It was just enough to throw things off. The lame girl was homely and that didn't help matters."

"You tell me some things but not others. Why I'm in this uniform again for instance."

"Did Fred Zinnemann tell Burt Lancaster?"

"I'm used to doing what I'm told at McCompex," he said. "But there's no reason why you can't be a little less grudging."

"Up against the wall, motherfucker."

It was his final scene. I sighted on him standing against the printed black words. Then I narrated, making it up as I went along.

"The year is 1999. You are looking at a newsreel of an earlier time. A man is standing in a room in America. It is you, David, more or less. What can the two of you say to each other? How can you empty out the intervening decades? It's possible to put your hand to a movie screen and come away with a split second of light, say a taxicab turning a corner, and it's right there on your thumb, Forty-ninth Street and Madison Avenue. You can talk to the screen and it may answer. You barely remember the man you're looking at. Ask him anything. He knows all the answers. That's why he's silent. He has come through time to answer your questions. He is standing still but moving. He is silent with answers. You have twenty seconds to ask the questions." (I held on Austin Wakely, motionless against the wall, expressionless, and quietly I counted off the seconds—one through twenty.) "We come now to the end of the recorded silence."

Austin and I shared a bottle of warm Coke.

"Listen," I said. "Can you do something for me?"

"What's that?"

"Get me Drotty. I want Drotty for one hour."

"Why was he killed?"

"He made a clerical error. He messed up some sort of minor detail. Details cause trouble. He used to say that."

"How was he killed?"

"How are most businessmen killed? Their hearts fail and they fall down on the rug. He had heart failure with minor variations. No one can say his death was meaningless."

"What will you do now?"

"I'll go to Topeka, Kansas."

"Why there?"

"I've always wanted to sit in a laundromat in Topeka, Kansas. I think it has something to do with prenatal memories."

"Do you plan to get in touch with your family?"

"I prefer to let the bitterness linger. Any kind of contact at this point would only be confusing all around."

"Are you certain they're still bitter?"

"All but my brother. He never felt that way toward me."

"Will you get in touch with him, then?"

"No."

"Why not?"

"I'm afraid to see what has happened to him by this time."

"The camera appreciates your willingness to appear before it under such difficult circumstances."

I have tried up to now to avoid any grand revelations concerning the professionals in the cast. Carol and Austin were mixed things to me. I'm not sure exactly when I realized they could be valuable but I do know that the idea grew, in one form or another, out of first impressions. In Austin's case, appearance and age were vital; the fact that he was an actor meant nothing. Carol, both overflowing and annoyingly recessive, seemed, actress or not, to possess a talent for shading every moment, for moving across one's mental landscape like a teasing pattern of sunshine and cloud; it was a difficult talent, defying analysis and frustrating to witness until it displayed itself before the camera, a petty and even neurotic talent for concealing things not worth concealing, or for pretending to conceal, or pretending to disclose, or for dropping hints or sly eyelashes, a pain in the neck in other words, and perfect.

If these two people have seemed remote up to now, even indecipherable, mainly the girl, it should be understood that I did not want to understand them too well. They were mixed things to me, living people qualified (perhaps enlarged) by my own past, by my fantasies, mirror-seeking, honors, shames, and by those I loved or failed to love. Knowing them too well would have confused the issue, and the alter-issue, and the issue's bride, and the sister of the issue. And so I've tried to set them down as I knew them then, or failed to know them.

Now, in retrospect, and briefly, I think I can say that Carol was simply a lost girl trying to make the best of invisibility. Even her hair seemed questionably blond. It is worth pointing out that the moment she first appeared before my camera I ceased to care about her other roles, all those fluent ambiguities which at first had seemed so appealing and then so disturbing the night she talked me under the table at Buster's Bar & Grill. The camera chewed up these parts and spat them out. Carol was the best performer in the cast because she was the most consistently invisible.

With Austin Wakely it was easy for me to keep my interest to a minimum. I had no curiosity at all about Austin, either before or after he became one of my players. He had a good strong chin and gleaming teeth. If he had been born with a red, white and blue mole on his back, a mole in the shape of a flag, it still would have been his face that I put before the camera.

Carol sat in the armchair, eyes closed, working her way out of one thin atmosphere into another. The scene had been by far her easiest and yet she seemed exhausted. I went over to the window. A man put a coin in a parking meter and walked around the corner. It was just turning noon and the street was fairly crowded. The shoestore was having a sale. A car stalled at the light.

"I've just realized how few black faces I've seen since I got here."

"Even the bibles in this town are white," she said.

"The kind of town this is I'll bet they don't even know what's going on all over the goddamn country."

"They see it on the box. It's like watching the moon through a telescope."

"Everything's going on but it's still boring," I said.

Her eyes remained closed. I almost moved toward her. I remembered the bench in the park in town, the ego-moment of our bodies barely in contact. We sat that way, chair and windowsill, for a long time. Nothing that was good, even temporarily good, even for a slow second, could happen between us. I didn't know why I was so sure of that. Maybe she was just too far inside. It was at times the way I liked to think of myself and maybe I felt nothing could be stolen from her in return for what would have to be surrendered to get at that private awareness. Besides I didn't know what she thought of me. Not knowing that, I couldn't know what form we'd take together. Then there was the fact that her eyes were closed.

"You seem tired," I said.

"It's this weather, so full of life and sweet smells. It's a struggle to get through weather like this. I like to plot my existence on a fever chart in my head. In New York in the humid weather it used to rise and once in Montana at twenty below it nearly jumped off the chart and I thought I would die of too much life. I guess that sort of thing is mostly auto-suggestion though. I can talk myself into almost anything. When I die I'll talk myself into another womb and start all over. That's what they do in Tibet—people who couldn't even get into Princeton entering fresh wombs like crazy."

"Through a womb-door."

"That's right," she said. "And there are good wombs and bad wombs."

"I didn't know that."

"Absolutely."

"Are you hungry?" I said. "I'm hungry. Let's get something to eat."

"I have rehearsals to get to."

"Do you have to leave right away?"

"I'm afraid yes, David."

"We haven't had much of a chance to talk since the night of the summerhouse."

"There's less and less for people to talk to when they talk to me. I hope diminishing existence isn't contagious."

"Pandemic is more like it. I wish you'd open your eyes."

"Is there anything to see?"

"Maybe not."

"Even the bibles are white," she said. "We used to go over to the Gansevoort Street pier at sunset. Those humid evenings in that barren part of New York when I lived almost beyond living. And Roy said to me once now I know why New Jersey's where it is and not next to Alabama where it probably belongs. So the sun can go down over it."

Drotty wore black silk and pale green corduroy. He was a dagger of a man, a small jagged bad mood glinting in a corner. Yet he smoked his cigarette almost tenderly, every movement of his hand a soft and highly deliberate piece of orchestration. I hadn't expected him to be so young. In fact I hadn't expected him to show up at all. But he seemed perfectly willing to go along with what must have seemed to him an incomparably casual, if not barbaric, form of theater. This script was not bound; this hotel room was not soundproof; this director had little to say; this tape recorder was a sociological curse; this movie was doomed. Drotty mentioned none of these; he merely smoked and moved softly now about the room in black Spanish boots, a certain shrewish violence attaching to every step. His face, his small face, worked hard at being blank.

"I guess Austin and Carol have told you they've been part of this thing since the beginning."

"I don't mind if my people moonlight as long as it doesn't interfere with their work at the theater."

"I hope it hasn't."

"It hasn't," he said. "They seem intrigued by what you're doing. Perhaps I should be jealous."

"They seem a lot more intrigued by what you're doing. They talk about you all the time."

"They're getting bored. The regional theater bores everybody in the end. People come out of a sense of duty. We try to shock them but they've been in a state of shock for years. Do you know something? In five years the entire American theater including what's left of Broadway will be a government-subsidized semi-religious institution. Not unlike Yellowstone National Park. DO NOT LITTER signs will be everywhere."

"Cool boots," I said.

"These were given me by a lady professor of romance languages whose only copy of her seventh unproduced play was burned in my fireplace by an Afro-American who said his name was Abdul Murad Bey. I dreaded telling her about it but when the moment arrived she seemed relieved and it wasn't too many weeks later that she presented me with these boots. Recently I heard that Abdul Murad Bey was partly responsible for the burning of Philadelphia, an unproduced play in its own right."

He finished this anecdote by tightening his features and going even more blank than before. I didn't know whether I was supposed to laugh or not, so I merely sent some air down my nostrils, trying to make the sound a cheerful one. I realized that neither of us had yet called the other by name, first or last. This oversight haunted the beginning and end of every remark. Of course it wasn't just an oversight.

We discussed his lines. He placed the cigarette in an ashtray and walked slowly to the armchair and sat down. I had to put out the cigarette for him. Then we were ready to begin.

"Film must leave an emotional residue. The retentive aspect is the one true criterion. What do I take away from a film and of that what do I keep? Something more than underwear, I would hope. I think that what you've got to do at this point is stretch your aesthetic. My task is to help the more serious of my students develop some sort of cinematic lifestyle. I do admit to finding a marginal interest in your movie. It appeals to the child in me. I like silliness. I like silly ideas. Many great movies are basically silly and the movie hero is almost always a dope. Brando for example has portrayed dope after dope. So has Belmondo, so has O'Toole, so has Toshiro Mifune. It's all a question of levels. Preminger's vulgarity is postcollegiate; yours is still matriculating. Since this is our last meeting, I think total candor is in order. I dislike you very much. I've always disliked you. You have evinced little or no respect for me. Time and again, in the presence of female students, you have attempted to undermine my position as teacher and human being. You want very much to know about my relations with a certain young lady of our mutual acquaintance. You crave bad news, defeat, punishment. Defeat is always glorious on film. The loser is ennobled by suffering and death. No camera can resist the man going down to defeat. He commands every mechanism and the attention of every mind. Perhaps you see yourself as a wide-screen hero. I've totally forgotten what I'm supposed to say next."

Glenn Yost's wife was a large friendly woman who probably started wearing a housecoat when she was three. She was a toucher and kidder, obviously well loved by the two Glenns, the kind of woman who excels at picnics—laughing and telling jokes, slapping men's backs, pinching the kids, matching bosoms with the ladies, a vast warm-weather front moving across the plains. I didn't like having her around.

I introduced Sullivan to the family, and then Mrs. Yost, Laura, told us they had been waiting dessert until we got there, peach pie and vanilla ice cream, and we all sat down to talk and eat. The Yosts kept telling funny stories about each other. There was something extraordinary in their love, something laughable about it in the best sense; each seemed a legend to the others, a comic masterpiece of blunders, conceits and disastrous hobbies. Laura did most of the storytelling, moving from dining room to kitchen in her yellow housecoat, pouring coffee over the edges of our cups. I was there to finish an unreal job, to complete the worst part of the crossing, and the reality of all this unaffected warmth did me no good. Also my camera was not interested in oral tradition. I looked at Sullivan. She was bisecting crumbs of pie with her thumbnail.

"Can we get right at it, Glenn?"

"The pantry's in there," he said.

"Maybe Bud and Sully and I can go in right now and get it done. Take only a few minutes."

"Won't it be too dark?" Laura said.

The pantry was just off the kitchen. Glenn turned on the light for me and got out of the way. Moving fast, I put one of the kitchen chairs against the far wall of the pantry. I instructed Sullivan to sit there. I watched her for a moment. Then I realized that Bud was standing next to me holding the camera. Quickly I took it from him, focused on Sullivan in the chair and began shooting. When this was done, five or six seconds later, I asked her to stand against the wall and I moved Bud into the pantry facing her, his back to the camera. Then I was standing in the doorway again. Glenn and Laura were right behind me. I had to get them out of there. They were just so much honey sticking to my fingers and it was vinegar I needed to taste, vinegar and the pant of hot steel on my tongue, if I was ever to get this done. I asked them to leave. I told them to get completely out of the kitchen. Then, with Sullivan and the boy standing, I shot twenty seconds more, my very own commercial, a life in the life. Then I cut again and asked her to get closer to him and to put her hands on his shoulders. He turned and stared at me, either because he did not understand why I had sent his parents away or because this was very different from basketball in a high-school gym and he needed a look from me, a word, something. Then I saw it was mom and dad his eyes were balancing in their bitter light; there was that in his face, the knifed look hanging tight over a brother's small betrayal, not understanding what I had to do and yet not moving either, held there by the camera in my hands or by her, by her indeed, lean dank bird; of course; it would be impossible to slip one's shoulders out from the cool shellac of those hands, to turn one's back on such presence as this. The light in the pantry was bad. I was doing everything too quickly and I knew it would be nothing but blind luck if any of this found life at all, caught the silver crystal and began to grow. I could see it in foreflash, under-exposed, their bodies incomplete, her face a nest of scattered dusk, tangled gray light at the edges of the screen, and then I wondered if I would ever watch it, this or any part of it, and I wondered why this mute soliloquy of woman and boy should mean anything more, even to me, than what it so clearly was, face of one and head of the other, and I wondered of this commercial whether it would sell the product. I focused again, her hands on his shoulders, a strange, a very strange expression, something like the curiosity that follows a man out of a room, a totally uncharacteristic look in her eyes. I felt no power doing it this way. The light was worse than bad and I hadn't made the proper readings. I was going too quickly. I was not framing. I was ending the shots too soon. But I had to do it and be done with it and maybe this was the best way, to obliterate the memory by mocking it, no power at all, spilling seed into the uncaptured light. Then I began to shoot the last sequence and I found I could not stop. Through the

317

viewfinder I saw them, motionless, supremely patient, stead-fast, her long fingers knuckle to tip visible over his shoulders, her left eye looking past his ear and into the eye of the camera, and I kept shooting for two or three minutes, lost somewhere, bent back in twenty-five watts of brown light, listening for a sound behind me, and of all the things I wondered that evening the last was how much she knew.

Laura was not in the dining room. Glenn sat at the table without looking up. I thanked him for everything. I told him it was regrettable but necessary that sometimes certain things had to be done that seemed excessively rash. Sullivan was waiting for me at the door. I told him that people under pressure sometimes say or do things which appear necessary at the time but which later are seen to be foolish and unforgivable. Bud was in the kitchen doorway and I thanked him and apologized. Then I went to the table and offered my hand. Glenn looked up, took it, smiled, pressed, and softly cursed me. It was sweetly done, a nice bit of Hollywood there, the vintage years, and it won a smile in return. We released and I backed off. Then the capillaries flared in his wild eye, the thin whispering streaks, hints of cold deacon fury, the kind of cold that burns, the cold that sticks to hands, that furious cold light damning my soul, those arctic streaks, those veins in the cube of ice inside his eye.

She stood on the sidewalk looking at me come down off the porch. It was unlike her to wait. I had expected her to be halfway up the street and then I thought of the way she had stared at me all through the last sequence, those two or three minutes when I was not sure where I was. Something soft drifted off her now. The streetlights were on. I had the camera on my right shoulder.

"I'd like to take a bath," she said. "We've been taking sponge baths in the camper. When it's warm enough we go down to the river. At first it was only a nuisance. Now it's a nuisance that threatens to become a way of life."

"Have the others seen you without clothes?"

"We use great tact, David. I assure you. Elaborate schedules have been worked out. Pike is a master at that sort of thing. A quartermaster in fact. He's taken to posting all sorts of rosters, dockets and inventories. I assure you, it's all very discreetly done."

"Let's go to a motel," I said. "We can get a cab to take us."

"Is that necessary?"

"I don't think they care for men taking women up to their room at the hotel. They're pretty, you know, stodgy."

"We'll unstodge them."

Sullivan spent close to an hour in the bath. I sat looking at the partly open bathroom door, trying to think of nothing. Then I stood in the doorway. She lifted one leg out of the water, as I knew she would, and moved her hands along her calf and looked back at me over her shoulder. A word arrived then from the eye of the deacon Yost. Abomination. I went back to the bed and sat down. She had looked at me to see if I was pleased. I sat waiting. Then I turned on the lamp by the armchair and switched off the overhead light. She got out of the tub. I went in quickly and watched her dry off with a large white monogrammed towel. Then I moved closer and moved my hands over the towel over her body slowly. We said nothing. I was following her toward the bed, following a sense of unimaginable pleasure, knowing this was old Yankee guilt, salt and peter. The walls were black and white and she was at the bed. Abomination.

She was covered now, even her breasts, and lying rigid, a message that this was the end of a stanza, that now she would wait for the turn of my turn. How much she knew about that moment, and taught me, in her absurd concealment; that the true and best lewdness, that is to say the ugliest, is nothing more than modesty so fanatic it cannot bear to move for fear it might touch itself. I undressed standing by the bed as I had done that night in Maine, darkness then, wondering whether she could see me, lewd virgin Maine, a different kind of room.

She watched me standing above her and I tried to think of nothing. She was absolutely still, watching me, not a grass-blade of motion, opening new rooms by the systematic locking of doors. Knowing this, she did not reach out nor move toward nor away from me when I lay down on the bed. I stretched out on top of the sheets. I have always been proud of my body.

"Don't be afraid," she said. "Tell me what you want me to do."

"I don't know yet. Let's just stay like this for a moment. Do you remember the night we spent in Maine in that old house? You told me a bedtime story."

"Don't be afraid, David."

"I'm not."

"You were in terror back there."

"Yes," I said.

"You mustn't be afraid. I'll help you. I'll do anything you want me to do."

"First, before anything else, I want you to tell me a story. Like in Maine. Like the story you told that night before I went to sleep."

(So ready, so lewd and willing was Sullivan, so skilled the artist immersed in her craft that she did not even pause at this request, much less break into waves of saving laughter.)

"And a deep sleep it was," she said.

"A story. A bedtime story."

"I have just the thing. It's about an evil old uncle of mine and the incredible experience we shared in a small boat on a fog-shrouded day in Somes Sound."

"Are you going to make it up?"

"It's real," she said. "You made me think of it when you mentioned Maine."

"Tell me then."

"I had a hated and feared and bloody Ulsterman of an uncle," Sullivan said. "At the age of eighteen he left Dublin for Belfast, renouncing church, state, family and the adulterous shade of

Parnell. My father's brother he was, the blackest of ex-Catholics, a blasphemer of the militant and dour type, not at all merry and joshing and ribald like the likes of my dead dad. Years later he came to this country and settled eventually in Maine, in a small town not far from Bar Harbor. And I went to visit him once, seeking to redress an old family grievance. It was a quiet simple town, a fit and proper place for Uncle Malcolm. He came to the door and I had almost forgotten how wild and ominous a man he looked—bald, firm, compact, real as a keg of stout. His eyes were dark, two pilot lights burning, and he looked at me as though I were the Pope's most favored concubine. He hated Catholics. He hated my father like plague, like incense. Brothers they were, stem and stern, Shem and Shaun, tight Dublin and tighter Belfast. In my letter I had given no hint of the purpose of my visit. We sat on the porch. It was a moonlit night. Statues of patriots stood on the green. No barding lads or songsters rolled out of the pubs and not a dark hop of Guinness in sight. There were no pubs; there were statues. I sculpt, as you know, and those statues, David, chilled me. Such Christianity. Such Christlessness. They looked like buggered schoolmasters pretending it was only the corner of a desk behind them. There is some grace to war; certainly there was to our revolution. But it would take a blind man with very stubby fingers to think some grace into those stones. Nothing demonic, no swirl of tunic, no hunt, no bad dreams, no courage. Upright, upstanding and up the ass. (Lord forgive me.) Christianity anyway. The ages of Omdurman and Chillianwalla. Perversion of Christ. Infant of Prague on the plastic dashboard blessing the box of Kleenex over the back seat. Priests with stale breath clamoring after my soul in the stark black wilderness of a confessional, pursuing the curve of regenerative grace with their sleepy fingers. Uncle Malcolm and I were sitting on rockers. We were rocking in fact in step. He did not ask why I had come. He merely looked out at the statues in the dim light as if thinking that patriotic stone brings nothing to our grasp of history unless it rests beneath language; to be silent in the stone's silence is the beginning of a union with the past. But maybe he was thinking only of his boat. Because that's what he mentioned next. He owned a sloop, he said, a Hinckley sou-wester, and she was moored in a cove around the bend from Bar Harbor, which meant only twenty minutes by car from that very porch."

"This is getting boring," I said.

"You must permit me at least a fraction of the self-indulgence you reserve for your own tired ends. Not that I mean to sound harsh. But I've cooperated with you up to now and I'm willing to continue to whatever point you choose to take us. And you've asked for a bedtime story."

"I'm sorry. Please go on."

"Large issues will begin to manifest themselves out of the dull set of pieties I've been constructing here. This is not easy work for me."

"Have you rehearsed any of this?" I said.

"In bed at night I often converse with the great English-speaking figures of history. I think I can admit that to you. I develop philosophies, legends, autobiographical notes, small bits of feminine wisdom, anecdotes and lies. I present these to someone like Swift or Blake; then, as Swift or Blake, I comment and criticize. It may be only an illusion but my mind seems to be at its best just before sleep. I've had some brilliant dialogues with myself, I think; or, more to the point, with the great figures of the past. So your instinct is quite correct. In a sense I've rehearsed this story. In fact I've told it many times, refining, editing, polishing, getting nearer and nearer the awesome truth. But I have never yet revealed that truth. I have never told the whole story, not to Coleridge, not to Melville, not to Conrad. I've never revealed the mystery of the final hours of that fog-shrouded day in a thirty-five-foot sloop in Somes Sound—not to a soul living or dead."

"One second, please," I said. "I want to turn out the light."

"The rocking chairs went to and fro in perfect military formation. Uncle looked out on that dead historic vista, that Yorktown, Shiloh, that headless glimpse of Khartoum. Then he said he planned to go sailing the next morning and he asked if I would care to join him. A jolt between the eyes. But of course I accepted. There was all the moment of a biblical confrontation. To turn down such an offer would be to damn those issues which had sent Uncle hightailing it to Belfast and the likes of my dear dad down to the local for a pint of the bitterest. We spent most of the rest of the night in silence. He cooked us some stew which he served in two unmatching bowls, proclaiming even to such a disinterested party as a blood relative the depth and tenacity of his confirmed bachelorhood. We slept at opposite ends of the house. My room was a touch of the madness of Captain Ahab—bare, frigid, tilted like an afterdeck; not a sign of love for one's chosen element, not a sliver of scrimshawed ivory, not a mug, coastal rock, schooner print, even tombstone rubbing—bare, chilled, northern, damp as a foggy star. Cold cracking dawn it was when he hammered on my door. I went downstairs for a breakfast that was all molasses and agglutinating protein, some old seaman's notion of the need to cement one's bones for fear the wind will take them. In half an hour we were walking down the dock toward his dinghy and we rowed out through fog opened by the faintest lines of light and then his boat appeared, high on the water, green and white, heaving in easy slaps of tide, and even in that dimness I could see she had nothing of himself about her. We climbed aboard and he told me briefly where things were and what they did and how to crank this and ease off on that. The boat was called *Marston Moor* and she was the trimmest thing I'd ever seen. She was light and looked fast. Every inch of brightwork gleamed. She was a lovely thing, David, and brutally named, which was only to be expected. Uncle hoisted the jib. I cast us off the mooring and then raised the mainsail and we moved into a morning thick with unanswered questions, and unasked. Running lights picking out a red nun. Bells clanging. Gulls on the buoys. Lobster boats mooning about in the fog, their horns lowing and a bundled figure or two peering at us from the decks, so silent, so strategically silent, the cursed eye of the sailor who dreams his bones at fifty fathoms and resents the intruder because the intruder has not earned that particular plot of sea. What large fools those lobstermen must have thought us to be prowling through that gruel. Uncle glanced over the small wheel into the binnacle directly before him. Compass, wheel and mainsheet were his. I handled the jib. We said next to nothing to each other. In two hours the fog began to lift and we could see the pine forests of Mount Desert Island and then in time the foothills and then the broad brown summits of Cadillac and Pemetic mountains. It was a sight. Mist still curdling over bald spots on the slopes. The low green pines and carriage roads. Surf etching into juts and shank of rock. Frenchman's Bay. The bringing of the writ of royal Europe. By noon it was a different day, warmer, windier, all blue, crisp and squinting, sunlight beginning to butter us in godliness. For it was God's world, David, and no thought might enter the mind which did not acknowledge this. It was a sight. The blue of that water was an angel's blue. White lighthouses stood on jetties of land. We saw herring gulls and cormorants. Porpoises came bucking out of the sea and the black bells tolled. There was a sense of the firmament, an unencompassed word above us brushed by the tatters of a single cloud. The sunlight was a sword on that water. There was nothing out there that had been changed by anything but itself. God. The God-made and the untouched-by-hands. Even our boat, lovely leaning thing that she was, heeling in the wind across that great yoke of light, even *Marston Moor* was a mild virus, reducing our rag of sea to the status of a pretty photograph. Uncle pointed out Isle au Haut, that beautiful island which seemed to stand, as other islands sit or drowse, as the last high thing, the last of trees and soil, before the sweep of the Atlantic. I don't think we were ever out of sight of land. Some of the islands were large, banked with spruce and pine, and there were small villages set above the perimeter of rocks. Others were small and uninhabited, some not much more than sheer masses of granite. We were heeled way over now and I looked at Uncle. He still wore his foul-weather gear, right hand at the wheel, left trimming the main. He was riding that boat, not sailing it; he was riding a dolphin or a woman, a young bucking thing that might never be breached. I was starved and as soon as the wind dropped I went down to the cabin and cooked some lunch for us on the kerosene stove. He thanked me. Through the early part of the afternoon we were never quite becalmed but Uncle had to search out catspaws on the water to find some puff of wind. He never seemed to consider using the engine. I watched the islands through binoculars. I saw a woman carrying a laundry basket, and a boy running, and a man standing against the whitewashed curve of a lighthouse. They seemed incredible discoveries, pieces of rare blended mineral, land-sailors who had learned that straight lines kill. And the smaller islands. All blue and purest granite. Not a human soul. But not silent. No, they had the glory of a voice. Cry of sea birds and the endless spanning roar of surf. After a while I took the wheel and Uncle went below to consult his charts. The breeze freshened then and after a long tack into the sunset we lowered sail and motored into a cove formed by two tiny islands, mere smithereens of land, one almost solid rock, the other a bit larger and wooded. Uncle gave me the sounding lead and I tossed it in and called off the fathoms, trying to put a bit of nautical singsong in my hopeless voice. We dropped anchor then and sat on deck watching the sunset. Then we saw the windjammers, three of them, coming down at us out of that appallingly beautiful wound in the sky, square-rigged and running with the wind, blazing with the sky's iodine, completely unreal, passing now behind the smaller of our islands, one gone, two, and as the last of them vanished the first reappeared, spars crossing high over the granite, the dignity of those ships, their burnt passage from the red horizon to blue and now to darkness, the coming of the Magi. Uncle said they were packed to the bulkheads with tourists from Camden. Ah yes. After they'd gone we dined below on hash and eggs in the rocking bronze light. And I told him finally why I had come. The grievance was an old one, going even deeper than the fierce powder-burns between Orange and Green. Before his death—at St. Vincent's Hospital, New York—my father had told me that Uncle Malcolm, after leaving Dublin, had managed by unjust means to acquire title to a family plot of land on the west coast of Scotland above Lochcarron. Land willed to the family by some distant ancestor who, the story went, had blood connections to ancient clans. Land held for generations by chieftains, lairds, earls, assorted elite. And then finally—history turning like the chamber of a gun—by merchants, fools and migrant sons. All this new to me. Some inch of Scotland in my blood. The origins were lost, of course, and the mixture known possibly only by that man who first crossed down the Highlands and sailed the Northern Channel no doubt to Belfast, perhaps taking himself a bride who bore him sons who returned, perhaps, some of them, to the ancestral land, and some of them, perhaps, wandering son from father and settling in Eire to begin the new line which harvested my father's father, and himself, and his brother, my uncle Malcolm, soul of a cattle reiver. And telling this to me, more or less, my father by his eyes seemed to leave out bits and pieces. Get back the land. Be strong where I was docile. Settle all scores, avenge all injuries, please the memory of your dead mother who has also known the lows which that man has reached. Your poor dear mother. Poor lamb of an angel. Christ have mercy. I was to demand then what was my birthright. A speck of the Highlands. And there was the eye of it. All my rich hatreds and comfortable bigotries come to this. Scotch-Irish! American! (Ineluctable, Mr. Faulkner; coeval, Mr. Joyce.) Some sudden lurch in the runnings of my blood. Broadsword and pipers. Sagging dugs of the Ozarks. Centuries of the Scottish kirk. And that first part of it I told to Malcolm—the land above Lochcarron. He said it was his, acquired honorably, and would hear no more of it. What plans did he have for it then? He would live the last years of his life there, he said, and be buried in that soil. A will had been drawn up. Things had been properly administered. I had his word. He went up on deck and I followed him. All was calm. We observed an hour of silence, listening to a deranged bird shriek in the woods. Belfast and Maine. Dungeons of silence. Tons and eons of silence. To learn that history cannot inform our blood unless we listen for it. Secrets of the stone-cutters of New England. All those tight towns boasting their Bulfinch steeples and Paul Revere bells. Whose navies built on Belfast's silence. And aren't there eighteen Belfasts in America? And didn't Ulster stock the colonies? Men, potatoes and spinning wheels. Orange, not Green, dying in our revolution. But my hate could leap waterfalls with the insanity of salmon to find its pool of birth and truth. He sang me a song then, out there on deck in the darkness, barely voicing the words, a glimmer of Ireland and Scotland and even Shakespeare in his accent, and I don't think he even knew he was singing aloud.

> He came from the North, so his words were few
> But his voice was kind and his heart was true
> And I knew by his eyes that no guile had he
> So I lay with my man from the North Country

He repeated the verse several times, his voice a cradle-song, and then we went below. I slept in the cabin proper. Uncle settled down in the forepeak, coiled like heavy line. He talked in Gaelic in his sleep."

"Is that it?" I said.

"And in the morning we headed back in gray drizzle and far out upon the line of the ocean I watched the fog-bank building and rolling, a low brownish menace of a thing, and I waited in vain for Uncle to offer some note of reassurance. But he talked of everything but fog. He talked, yes, as if only some test, some hungry clap of danger, could blow away the mists in his soul. There were few boats out but those he saw inspired him to crisp elocutions of category and trait. Gaff-rigged. Or eating out to windward. Or beamy. Or port tack. Or watch her luff now. Or blue yawl from Darkharbor. Damned schoolmastering roundhead. We sailed all day through slow drizzle, a chill beginning to work deep into my bones and into the very rigging and floorboards of the sloop. And that shoulder of fog hunching toward us. And with it the yet unanswered questions, and unasked. This, David, as you will come to see, is basically a ghost story. Why had he asked me to join him on this pointless cruise? Did he know I had come to Maine with knowledge of the land? And my father. My pink soft pipe-smoking pint of a dad. What tiny delicacies had he neglected to serve from his final bed? Silence in the Tower of London. Silence on the village greens. Northern eye of wind. River of northern bloods devastating the starving dark south. In the name of the Christ of the dogs of war. Reiver fanning out to plunder lands and deities. Truly, England and the Church of God hath had a great favor from the Lord in this great victory given unto us; this is none other but the hand of God, and to Him alone belongs the glory. Matchlock and leather doublets. Pikemen in the center, musketeers on the flanks. And how ends it, this prayer from Marston Moor? Cromwell's axed head blinking on a pike at Tyburn gallows. And was Uncle then with his halloween tartan of Scot and Puritan and Ulster merely seeking to return to some sacred north? The land above Lochcarron. To wallow in the terrible gleaming mudhole of God and country. Black Knife, sitting wide as a stump on a moonlit night high in the Dakotas, had been the answering echo of my deepest hates. And the final question yet to be pondered as Mount Desert Island hove into view and Uncle ceased his chatter and made for the mouth of Somes Sound, an authentic fjord, a seven-mile gash in the high bluffs of the island. Had he thought to find refuge here, or greater danger for greater glory? The hills stood above us on both sides and we were about two miles into the sound when I turned and saw it coming, only yards away now, and then we were in it, and silence had met its darkness. Nordic fog it was, cold, wet and dark, the northernmost point, and he had come to the edge of the mystery, and sailed her deeper into the fjord, eyes leaking fog and fire, riding that boat like a man in a fury of religious heat riding the loins of a woman, and I was terrified, David, scared out of my Irish wits, terrified of the fog, of himself, of the final question which now, and not until now, began to answer itself. For they had met again, I recalled, father and uncle, long after the latter's renunciation of all held holy in the apostolic breast; had met shortly after my dad married my lovely frail lily of a mother; had come together in Derry, New Hampshire—where Uncle had then been living, a solid Ulster town—in a futile attempt to restore harmony. And some parts of this my mother had told me years before her death, that their simmerings and rages had nearly set the house ablaze, and something pale in her recollections, some loose end, could bring me now to my father's death-bed—are you with me?—and his own tactical omissions and could bring me also to Uncle's mention of a will and his word that the land, his own deathbed, would be rightly adminis-tered. And then a blade of silver struck across the darkness, viking sword on anvil, and we began to see faintly a trace of shoreline. Uncle's passion had been truly heaven-directed, or hell, and we appeared in no danger of running aground. Again I waited for a word from him. Suddenly the winds came and the boom began to lift and swing—winds from all directions it seemed, skirling about us in a noise like pipes of battle, truly fearsome, lifting the fog a bit but manhandling our small boat until I was sure we would capsize at any moment. Wind blowing down off the bluffs. Wind coming straight over the water from the mouth of the sound and the sea far beyond. Wind from all directions pitching us dangerously to starboard, then to port, mast straining, boom swinging, a batten flying out of the mainsail past my head as I tried to level the boom.

And even Uncle, even Uncle then began to lose his Christian calm. For these winds were biblical, thunderheads of a wrathful God he had not met in any kirk or clapboard meetinghouse. A sailing boat hates indecision and Uncle did not know what to do."

"Sully, I don't like this story."

"And the first angel sounded the trumpet. And the winds blew and the third part of those creatures died which had life in the sea, and the third part of the ships was destroyed. And through the silver and gray smoke there appeared a light on the shore at the last limits of the sound. And a figure held the light. And it was a stranger. And Uncle saw him and spoke. Jesus needs me. *Jesus needs me,* he said. And the light was a lantern and the face was like unto light itself. And in those days men shall seek death, and shall not find it; and they shall desire to die, and death shall fly from them. And Uncle had come to the end of the mystery, which is: that man receives his being as did Christ, in a gentle woman's womb, beyond the massed and silent armies, beyond eroded stone arranged across the lampless past; which is: that all energy runs down, all life expires, all except the force of all in all, or light lighting light; which is: the figure holding the lantern was a child. And from this knowledge he did turn and scorn and rant against his ship. For where was Christ the tiger in that pentecostal light? And then all mysteries were to find their unendingness, and all echoes to be answered only by their own voices. We were still in the violence of the winds and I begged him to lower sail and he looked at me and bellowed. *Damn your eyes, daughter.* And that was the answer to the final question. Radiant mother giving herself to that blackest of Orangemen. 'So I lay with my man from the North Country.' Eugene bloody O'Neill. And that in me then as well. Drums of Ulster. And he cried again. *Damn your eyes, daughter.* A few twigs snapped in my mind, I think. And then the winds stopped blowing and we came about pretty as a picture and began the voyage home. I turned around once but could see no lantern, nor child, nor bird of the forest. And I knew then that the war is not between North and South, black and white, young and old, rich and poor, crusader and heathen, warhawk and pacifist, God and the devil. The war is between Uncle Malcolm and Uncle Malcolm."

I woke in the middle of the night. Sullivan was gone. The wind blew a piece of paper across the bed and I got up and lowered the window. Then I smelled cookies baking.

11

Men like to be told of another man's defeat, failure, collapse, perdition; it makes them stronger. Women need such news of vanquished souls because it gives them hope of someone large and woeful wanting to be mothered. Sympathy resides in the glands; the breast is magic. Of course this doesn't even begin to explain what happened after Sullivan finished the bedtime story.

I turned on the light and slowly removed the sheet from her body. Once again I stood above her for a moment and she watched me. I kneeled on the bed and looked down at her. I took her hand and put it to my face and I bit and licked her fingers, which tasted of flavorless soap. I put both our right hands to her right breast. My hand guided hers to her own lips and down along her body and to the inside of my thigh and up to my chest and mouth. She was an artist and I wondered if she thought my body, which she had never truly seen until this night, to be beautiful. I placed her hand between her legs, which were together like lewd art. I lay prone across the bed and bit and licked her fingers, which tasted now of bath and light sweat. I looked into the opening.

I played with the soft flesh and spinning hair. I kissed her fingers, index and middle now bent around the tall hole, and then her middle finger was in my mouth and I sucked at the knuckle and swung my left arm near to her face and found her lips with my index finger and she sucked and licked at it. With my head, my ears, I forced her thighs apart and they gave slowly, grudgingly, with great art and lewdness, and then tongue to root I swam in my being toward defeat so satisying that no pleasure of mere sense could be noted or filed. I was on my knees again, high above her, and I dipped to her breasts and licked and smelled, playing with them, batting the nipples lightly with my finger. I asked her to stand against the wall facing the foot of the bed. She did this. I lay in the middle of the bed, my arms and legs spread wide. She looked at me. All I had to do was raise my head slightly and glance toward my middle. She advanced slowly, as all lewd advances must be made, and kneeled at the end of the bed and took my ankles in her hands and as her hands moved up my legs began to descend, with manifest deliberation, a mime of some creature that has been burrowing for centuries. Her hands were there now and they assembled a brief little pageant of phallus worship and then it was in her mouth and I began to twist and arch. Before very long I made myself ask her to stop and then I was on my knees again and she was on her back and looking up at me. Her head this time was at the foot of the bed and the simple fact of this opposition, this turning on an axis, seemed enormously lewd. I played some more with her breasts. I kissed her on the lips. Abomination. I curled my tongue between her legs again and kissed her once more on the lips in a dream of wheels in white rooms and into her then I went, evolving the basic topography, and entering her I was occupied by her, another turning on an axis, wrong way on the bed, the army occupied by the city. Abomination. I began to think her thoughts or what I imagined to be her thoughts. I became third person in my own mind. (Or her mind.) And in her as deep as I could go, hard and wild as I could strive, I listened to what she was thinking. Little mothers' sons. He wants to wake up alone. Michelangelo's David. Wasp of the Wild West. He is home at last.

I smelled the cookies baking. It lasted only seconds. Then I sank into the bed again and it was like a field on which a certain number of troops have pretended to be dead, trading their odors with the smell of the earth and feeling a deliciousness not known since the games of childhood. I went back to sleep then. When I came out of it, I was not even amazed at the ease with which I could put aside the previous night. It is so much simpler to bury reality than it is to dispose of dreams. I showered and shaved. With my curved scissor I clipped some hair from my nostrils. I looked not bad, things considered, the film-segment done and torn out of me (all blood and eyes), the black wish fulfilled (with all the accompanying panics of such a moment), very little money in my pocket and nowhere in particular to go.

1) New York was not waiting for me with microphones and fleets of ribboned limousines, sweet old Babylonian moviewhore of a city yawning like Mae West.

2) The network had by this time disposed of my corporate remains in some file cabinet marked *pending return of soul from limbo*.

3) To stay in Fort Curtis was out of the question; the town was now simply the sum of its unfilmed monotonies.

4) The camper itself seemed off-limits. What could Sullivan and I say to each other? (What had we ever said?)

But in the mirror, these things considered, I looked not bad. Indeed I remained David Bell. I brushed my teeth, dressed, and went to the armchair to pare my fingernails. Perhaps I could go to Montana and fall in love with a waitress in a white diner. Canada might be nice, the western part, for it was one of the very last of the non-guilty regions in the world. I could smoke hashish for a year squatting outside the Blue Mosque in Istanbul. A woman came in then, wearing an open robe over a pair of dungarees and a sweater. I had never seen her before. She changed the sheets, punching the bed repeatedly and then striking the pillow with the edge of her hand in karate fashion. She looked at me briefly in that analytical manner by which all hotel employees compute the biographies of lodgers. I continued to clip my nails, watching silver divots jump through the air. She finished with the bed and threw the used sheets into the hall. Then she reached past the door frame and dragged in a vacuum cleaner. Immediately I pulled in my legs. She activated the machine and began to vacuum, guiding it with one hand while with the other she tried to brush her hair out of her eyes. On her feet she wore heavy white socks and loafers. The robe was beltless and huge, possibly her husband's. The machine crawled past me, eating my fingernails, and I lifted my feet up onto the chair. She got on her knees and was about to clean under the bed when she turned and looked at me. I could go to Texas.

"There's some cigarettes under here and a book of matches. You want them or not?"

"No," I said.

She sucked them in. I had no idea what time it was. My fingernails in the machine. The hair of my belly and balls curled in the sheets in the hallway. She attached a small brush to the pipe and cleaned the blinds.

"That's a Vaculux, isn't it? My father used to handle that account. That was years ago. He's growing a beard now. Just the thought of it makes me uncomfortable."

"I just do my job," she said.

She left quietly then, one more irrelevant thing that would not go unremembered. My feet were still up on the chair. Inaction is the beginning of that kind of knowledge which has as its final end the realization that no action is necessary. It works forward to itself and then back again and there is nothing more relaxing and sweet. The chambermaid had left the door open and Sullivan was standing there in her gypsy trenchcoat. We smiled at each other. If I stayed in that chair long enough they would all come to me, chancellors, prefects, commissioners, dignitaries, wanting to know what I knew that could be of use.

"Come to view the body?" I said.

"May I sit down?"

"Please."

She sat at the head of the bed, on the pillow, imitating the characteristics of my own posture, knees high and tight, hands folded over them. Above her on the wall—a gap between the printed words—was a lithograph of an Indian paddling a canoe on a mountain lake. I have said much earlier that in describing Sullivan I would try to avoid analogy but at that moment she seemed herself an Indian, an avenging squaw who would descend the hill after battle to tear out the tongues of dead troopers so they would not be able to enjoy the buffalo meat of the spirit world. Daughter of Black Knife she seemed, a workmanlike piece of murder.

"I hope you didn't miss me this morning, David. I couldn't sleep so I walked back out to the camper. I didn't think you'd mind."

"What took place? What occurred or happened? It seems to have slipped my mind."

"It stopped raining and the fantasies came out to play. Your home movie had put you in a state of anguish. I tried to console you. You wanted to be drenched in sin and so I made it my business to help you along. Old friends have obligations to each other. David, I truly love you and hate you. I love you because you're a beautiful thing and a good boy. You're more innocent than a field mouse and I don't believe you have any evil in you, if that's possible. And I hate you because you're sick. Illness to a certain point inspires pity. Beyond that point it becomes hateful. It becomes very much like a personal insult. One wishes to destroy the sickness by destroying the patient. You're such a lovable cliché, my love, and I do hope you've found the center of your sin, although I must say that nothing we did last night struck me as being so terribly odd."

"Kiss my ass," I said.

336

"Do you need any money?"

"Brand tell you to ask me that?"

"He said you were running low. I have some. We're bound to bump into each other again. You can pay me back then."

"I can manage, Sully."

"Where are you going?"

"West, I guess."

"I hate to think of you all alone out there, David. Honest, I really do love you in my own spidery way. You'll have no one to talk to. And no one to play games with. And the distances are vast. We're parked right across the street. Come with us."

"Where?"

"Back to Maine. Then home."

"What about Brand? Will he stay in Maine?"

"He hasn't decided," she said. "It all depends on his auntie Mildred. If she comes across with some money he may try Mexico. Otherwise he goes back to the garage. His only real hope is to return to combat. I've suggested he re-enlist. I'm convinced it's the only way he'll survive. You've got to confront the demons here and now. Right, leftenant?"

"There aren't any demons bothering me," I said. "My problem is immense, as we both know, but it's strictly an ethnic one. I don't have any Jewish friends. How do you know so much about Brand?"

"He tells me things."

"Has he told you about his novel? The Great American Sheaf of Blank Paper."

"He whispered the sad details."

"When was this?" I said.

"That very first night in Maine."

"I don't seem to remember you two being alone at any point in the evening."

"He came into the room."

"The one you and I were sleeping in?"

"Yes."

337

"I see."

"And he knelt by my bed and whispered things to me. Sad little things. He wanted me to know the truth. I guess he thought it would make for a happier trip. I gave him absolution of course."

"And then you moved over and let him get into bed with you."

"That's correct," she said.

"And I was right across the room. A deep sleep it was indeed. And you two have been swinging ever since?"

"Here and there."

"I see."

"Yes," she said.

"What I don't understand are the logistics of the thing. How did you manage it?"

"We grasped at every fleeting opportunity. It was like the springtime of urgent love. While we were on the road it wasn't at all easy. Things picked up when we got here."

"What about Pike?"

"Guard duty," she said.

"And the first time was that night in Maine and I was right across the room."

"It was really quite funny, David. You were snoring like Lyndon Baines Johnson."

"I don't snore. I do not fucking snore."

What followed had its aspects of burlesque humor, a touch of stylized sadism, bits of old tent shows and the pie in the face. I swung my legs over the arm of the chair and pushed myself up over it and onto the floor. Sullivan got off the bed and we were both standing now. In her soiled torn trenchcoat she seemed to belong in a demonstration thirty years overdue.

"Wait here," I said. "I want to take leave of the others. Handclasp of manly comrades. We'll drink to destiny."

"And what will you and I drink to, David?"

"My health, of course."

I climbed into the back of the camper. Pike and Brand were

playing gin rummy. Pike was talking about the dingo dogs of Australia and he did not look up when I came in. I stood behind him, put my hands on his shoulders and squeezed very hard. Finally he had to stop talking.

"The lady wants you."

"What for?" he said.

"Room 211. You'd better haul ass, colonel."

He got up slowly and left and I took his folding chair, turning it around first so that my crossed arms rested on its back as I faced Brand across the small table. He was wearing a khaki fatigue jacket. I was wearing rugged corduroy trousers and a blue workshirt.

"She told me," I said.

"Who told you what?"

"Sully told me that you two have been playing doctor and nursey."

"So what."

"That took balls when you consider that we're old friends, you and I, and she was with me if not in name then certainly by implication."

"Balls help," he said.

"I've known her for years. You can't just move in like that."

"You knew her for years and I knew her for minutes. It comes to the same thing. These matters have to be assessed in the light of eternity."

"Let me tell you something. Latch on to this. Are you listening? She let you into her pants only because you're afraid to be a writer. Did you get that? My advice to you is re-up in the goddamn Air Force. Our weapons system isn't complete without you."

"At least I flew, buddy. You were some kind of grunt or file clerk."

"I wasn't even in."

"That figures."

"That figures, does it?"

"Damn straight," he said.

339

"Let's get out to where we'll have some room to move around in."

"Talk is cheap."

"That's a very original comment," I said.

We walked through a narrow driveway into the parking lot behind the hotel. Three cars were back there, front bumpers nudging a long squared-off log. Brand took off his jacket and threw it to the ground. I reached for the tattooed dogs on his forearm and began to pinch. He looked surprised and then yelled. Then he pinched the side of my neck. We held on to each other that way, pinching and trying not to grimace or yell. I was in great pain. I knew I could not take it for very long and I let go of him and kicked him in the shins. He pulled my hair. Then we stood facing each other.

"Why are we fighting over that ugly bitch?" I said.

"She's not ugly."

"Homely then."

"She's not even homely and you know it."

"She's homely."

"She is not," he said.

"Aren't you going to take off your glasses?"

We started to wrestle and he bit me on the shoulder. I got him in a headlock and then spun him to the ground over my hip. I didn't kick him in the ribs although it would have been the easiest thing in the world. Then, on the ground, he looked up at me fiercely and clutched his groin. It was a strange thing to do and I didn't know what it was supposed to mean.

I helped him up and we went out front. We shook hands and I told him he could have my car or sell it and keep the money; either way it was his. Then I went to the back of the camper and stole Sullivan's radio. I left it with the desk clerk and went upstairs. I told them Brand was waiting and we wished each other luck. Pike and I shook hands. Sullivan kissed me on the chin. When they were gone I packed my things in two suitcases, including the camera, which weighed only about seven-and-a-half pounds, and all the reels of tape and film. I decided to leave behind the tripod and tape recorder as well as a suit, a sportcoat and two pairs of shoes. I called the desk clerk upstairs and told him that everything was his and that it was more than enough to pay for repainting the room. He went away confused. Then I masturbated into the clean sheets, feeling an odd and emptying joy, the cool uncaring pleasure of those times when nothing is foreseen and all that is left behind seems so much dead weight for the ministrations of the minor clergy. I went downstairs and stuffed the radio into one of the suitcases. Then I took off on the first stage of the second journey, the great seeking leap into the depths of America, wilderness dream of all poets and scoutmasters, westward to our manifest destiny, to sovereign red timber and painted sands, to the gold-transfigured hills, westward to match the shadows of my image and my self.

PART FOUR

12

I am falling silently through myself. The spirit contracts at the termination of every passion, whether the season belongs to pain or love, and as I prepare the final pages I feel I am drifting downward into coma, a sleep of no special terror and yet quite narrow and bottomless. Little of myself seems to be left.

1) Intense solitude becomes unbearable only when there's nothing one wishes to say to another.

2) Saints talk to birds but only lunatics get an answer.

I have reached the point where the coining of aphorisms seems a very worthy substitute for good company or madness. Surely this account falls short of either. Too much has been disfigured in the name of symmetry. Our lives were the shortest distance between two points, birth and chaos, but what appears on these pages represents, in its orderly proportions, almost a delivery from chaos. Too much has been forgotten in the name of memory. There is no mention of the scar on my right index finger, the white medicine I took as a child, the ether visions of my tonsillectomy. In my mind the resonance of these distant things is sheer thunder, outlasting immortal books, long and short wars, journeys to other planets. In short I have not been cunning enough. I have taken the middle path, neither heaven nor hell, and no amount of self-serving research can persuade me that cunning does not grow its sharpest claws at the very extremes of consciousness. Not that this work has been engineered to no purpose. It is a fond object. I like to look at it, pages neatly stacked, hundreds of them, their differences hidden from the eye. Every so often I move the manuscript to another room in order to be surprised by it as I enter that room. It never fails to be a touching thing, my book on a pinewood table, poetic in its loneliness, totally still, Cézannesque in the timeless light it emits, a simple object, the box-shaped equivalent of the reels which sit in my small air-conditioned storage vault.

I've been studying the footage of late, hour after hour. There is a crippled beauty in some of it—Sullivan on the swing, all shadow and menace, a long dark heron wading through one's empty sleep. The Fort Curtis episodes are only a small part of what eventually became a film in silence and darkness. The whole thing runs nearly a week, the uncut work of several years. Viewed in the sequence in which it was filmed, the movie becomes darker and more silent as it progresses. There are the Fort Curtis segments. There are demonstrations, speeches, parades, riots. There is a vacation I took in Vermont, and people entering my apartment, and selected parts of a love affair. Then there are long unedited scenes in which friends and strangers declaim their madness to the camera. At this point I dispensed with sound. There are houses, all kinds of houses, everywhere I went. There are newspaper stands, store windows, bus terminals and waiting rooms. There are nuns, hundreds of them, so very black and white, perfect subjects in their long procession, soundless as beads passing through a hand. I returned to individuals briefly—women and boys in hospital corridors, deaf-mutes playing chess, people in tunnels. The true play could not be found in theaters. The true play was ourselves and we needed shadows on which to chalk our light, speed to conquer sequence, infinitesimal holes in which to plant our consciousness. I began to underexpose then, to become ever more crude, destroying shape and light, attempting to solve the darkness by entering it fully. There are museums toward the end of the movie, overcast scenes shot in marble halls, all empty, submarine in appearance, being crushed by darkness spreading from the edges of the screen, limestone kings barely visible, pleasant Flemish ladies in square frames, and then, finally, for a long time, there is nothing. I myself appear briefly at the very end, reflected in a mirror as I hold the camera during the first of the Fort Curtis scenes. These twenty seconds of film also serve as a beginning.

The movie functions best as a sort of ultimate schizogram, an exercise in diametrics which attempts to unmake meaning. I like to touch the film. I like to watch it move through the projector. This is my success. Sullivan and Brand, in their surgical candor, taught me to fear and envy the artist. (Brand, of course, as it turned out, was a writer of blank pages. That's how I think of him, definitely a novelist, by all means a craftsman of high talent—but one who chose words of the same color as the paper on which they were written.) I wanted to become an artist, as I believed them to be, an individual willing to deal in the complexities of truth. I was most successful. I ended in silence and darkness, sitting still, a maker of objects that imitate my predilection.

From this window I can see the ocean, far out, rocking in that blank angry sheen which foul weather sets upon all waters. Later I'll walk on the beach for an hour or so. If the weather has cleared by then I'll be able to see the coast of Africa, the great brown curve of that equatorial loin. But right now it is a pleasure to anticipate slipping once again (a paragraph hence) into a much more filmworthy period of my life.

There will be no fireworks when the century turns. There will be no agonies in the garden. Now that night beckons, the first lamp to be lit will belong to that man who leaps from a

347

cliff and learns how to fly, who soars to the tropics of the sun and uncurls his hand from his breast to spoon out fire. The sound of the ocean seems lost in its own exploding passion. I am wearing white flannel trousers.

Clevenger's paleolithic lavender Cadillac was equipped with air conditioning, deep-pile carpeting, padded instrument panel, stereo tape system and a burglar alarm. Behind the wheel he seemed a veteran jockey not at all awed by the magnificence of his own colors. He was about fifty, a small man with a neck of Playa clay traversed by wide deep ridges. Clevenger was a Texan. He had picked me up somewhere in Missouri where he had been visiting his sister and her family. When I told him I was heading nowhere special he had grinned and told me to get in. He kept grinning through most of Kansas and I could only guess that his own youth held some dry secret of thumbing days and freight cars and nights spent with song-less men in the crouched light of fires. We stayed at the most expensive motels and Clevenger ate steak and home-fries for breakfast. He was superintendent-in-chief of a test track for automobile and truck tires just outside a town in West Texas called Rooster. This was the last week of his vacation and he was seeing to some private business interests which were apparently fairly lucrative and certainly well spread out. After Kansas we tore off a corner-piece of southeastern Colorado and went charging across New Mexico. The journey was very boring. We kept moving toward the seam of earth and sky but never got there, and nothing was undiscovered, and time was confused. Jet trainers skimmed over the mountains and desert. The past returned in plastic. Ecological balances were slipping and things seemed not quite the sum of their parts. Troopers bulged with sidearms. There were neat reversals of the currents of history and geography; the menu in a frontier-style restaurant included a brief note pointing out that the main dining hall was a replica of the main dining hall at the famous Cattleman on Forty-fifth Street in New York City.

People fished, hunted, took their sons to visit the inevitable new military installation and talked about places like Phoenix and Vegas as if remembering some telescopically distant moment, some misty green leaflet of childhood on the planet Earth. All those days in fact were not far from one's idea of life on a lunar colony; everywhere we went Indians ranged across the landscape like workers thirsty for oxygen, men sent to move stones in a place which is nothing but stone. Kenneth Wattling Wild (of Chicago, River Forest, the U.S. Marine Corps, Leighton Gage College, Chicago, Insomnia and, no doubt, River Forest again) had once written:

> Death came in twos in the night
> with whisky vengeance on its breath.
> Our carbines lay by the river.

This too, then, moon and painted ponies, seemed the coming and going of time set free from whatever binds it. Literature is what we passed and left behind, that more than men and cactus. For years I had been held fast by the great unwinding mystery of this deep sink of land, the thick paragraphs and imposing photos, the gallop of panting adjectives, prairie truth and the clean kills of eagles, the desert shawled in Navaho paints, images of surreal cinema, of ventricles tied to pumps, Chaco masonry and the slung guitar, of church organ lungs and the slate of empires, of coral in this strange place, suggesting a reliquary sea, and of the blessed semblance of God on the faces of superstitious mountains. Whether the novels and songs usurped the land, or took something true from it, is not so much the issue as this: that what I was engaged in was merely a literary venture, an attempt to find pattern and motive, to make of something wild a squeamish thesis on the essence of the nation's soul. To formulate. To seek links. But the wind burned across the creekbeds, barely moving the soil, and there was nothing to announce to myself in the way of historic revelation. Even now, writing this, I can impart little of what I saw. The Cadillac averaged close to ninety and its windows were tinted bottle green for the benefit of Clevenger's sunbaked eyes.

But he never tired of driving. We stopped only to sleep and eat. He made quite a few phone calls, met some people now and then, and several times parked for a moment at the edge of a town and gazed with an appraising eye at vast pieces of real estate. But these delays were timed to coincide with the sleeping and eating stops, and we were always on our way again soon enough. Clevenger loved the road. It was a straight line of marked length and limits, and progress could be made upon it only in the most direct of ways; some snug lane curling through highest Bavaria would have destroyed his mind. He let me take the wheel only as a matter of form. When he was not driving he talked hardly at all and I thought the wheel might be his secret vice, the only circle in his life, and he was close to being lost without it. Time slipped forward and back, and nature was off-center, and I listened to the radios. We switched from car radio to stereo tape to Sullivan's world-shrinking portable. Sometimes I was able to work out a lively mix and statesmen or commercial announcers chanted beneath whoops of soul-rock. Clevenger got a kick out of that and would tickle the accelerator and jab an elbow into the padded door. Most of the time I stayed with the portable and the car was filled with the sounds of big beat, gospel, ghetto soul, jug bands and dirt bands, effete near-lisping college rock, electric obscenity and doom, wild fiddles of Nashville, ouds and tambourines and lusting drums, and then with night I would twirl the dials to hunt for jazz, and with luck I'd catch a scrap of catatonic Monk, or Sun Ra colliding with anti-matter, and some note would pin together pieces of the spreading night and it would all make sense for a moment, the mad harmonics bringing most of what was sane to those who ran with death, and we would head into the gulf of early light with that black music driving over me and I would feel a stranger in my love of it, for I did not run with anything.

At breakfast Clevenger eyed the waitress, a slow-moving woman wearing a white uniform and no stockings, a woman who knew so well the tensions of her own body, its points of firmness and elasticity, and how to make the most of walking and standing, that after a few minutes the uniform became more or less superfluous. Clevenger ordered his steak well-done and ran his thumb and index finger the full length of his cigarette before lighting it.

"Some women you lay," he said. "Some you screw, some you bang, some you hump. That there is a royal hump and a half. That is a camel ride to a place well below sea level. One-night stand to beat the band. That there is *stuff.*"

"It's the no stockings that gets me," I said.

"Only one thing better than no stockings. That's stockings. They get you coming and going. It's a good old world as long as the little baby girls keep growing up."

"When do you have to be back?"

"Three days," he said. "I have to sneak up on Phoenix first. Come on down with me, Dave. Wife'll be glad to have some company. She gets lonesome way out there. Coyotes and Mexicans. She's a San Antonio girl and if things turn the right way maybe I can get us back to San Anton. That's a real nice city. Little woman doesn't get along with my sister or I'd have had to take her along on this tour of ours. Everything works out for the best if you wait around long enough. Look at the legs on that thing. They are awesome. She is one awesome thing."

"I don't think I should tag along too far. I've already abused your hospitality."

"Hell, don't worry about that, Dave."

"I'm practically broke. I've got to make some kind of move."

"I can put you on for a while. Hell, you can drive a car. You come on down with me and take a look at the track. It won't pay much but at least you'll be making yourself some cash while you're deciding what your next move is."

"Maybe I'll do that."

"No maybes now. And from here on, keep your money in your pocket. No need for you to be laying out. I got everything in hand. We'll have us some belly laughs before this thing is over."

On his way to the toilet he said something to the waitress and she smiled, full mouth and narrowing eyes, a nice warm sendoff and maybe a sly ticket for a return trip. Then we were on the road again and Clevenger was never happier. That woman had started some rotary pool of low blood going, a fine mean leveling at the edge of his mood, and he talked well into the afternoon, cruising at close to a hundred and hunched forward around the wheel so that his bottom rode up slightly and he was sitting on his thighs. He told me he had two divorces to his credit, bobbing his head and flashing a victory sign. His first wife was part Mexican, part Apache, part Welsh, a slug or two of French Canadian. He was nineteen years old when he met her and she was the most beautiful thing he had ever seen. Their troubles began when she tried to bite off his right ear during an argument about another man. Clevenger pointed to the side of his head and I leaned over for a closer look; there was nothing very distinctive about the ear but I nodded anyway. His second wife was a salesgirl. She never bothered him. She spent all day at the five-and-dime selling toys and things. At night she cooked, cleaned, ironed and mended. Clevenger began to beat her.

I wore my magic plaid rallying cap. Clevenger pushed hard into Arizona. I asked him where the big Navaho reservation was and he said we were well south of it, which was fine with me. We ate lunch in a powder blue saloon and I went into the men's room and looked in the mirror. My hair, uncut since New York, had thickened considerably and I liked the way it was massed behind and below the hat, which I wore low over my forehead and cocked just a shade to one side. I hadn't shaved in two days but it looked all right. In fact I had been told several times in the past that blond stubble is rather attractive. I checked for dandruff. The next day we began the last leg to Phoenix.

"You have to keep them down," Clevenger said.

"Who?"

"Whoever's closing in on you."

We passed a young man on the road but he wasn't carrying a guitar and in any case it would have been impossible for Kyrie to have walked this far in so short a time. Beyond the windshield all the earth was pale green lymph as if something had gone wrong with the sun, leaving this invalid civilization submerged in aqua-light. Good wombs and bad wombs. The earth curved. I visualized my apartment then, empty and dark and quiet, furniture from John Widdicomb, suits from F. R. Tripler and J. Press, art books from Rizzoli, rugs from W&J Sloane, fireplace accessories from Wm. H. Jackson, cutlery from Bonniers, crystal by Steuben, shoes by Banister, gin by House of Lords, shirts by Gant and Hathaway, component stereo system by Garrard, Stanton and Fisher, ties by Countess Mara, towels by Fieldcrest, an odd and end from Takashimaya. We had lunch in a huge glass cafeteria that stood just off the highway; about a dozen trailer trucks were parked outside. After we ate I called my home number, collect, and listened to the phone ringing in the empty rooms. It was a sad and lovely experience and I was able to see dust settling on the tables and books and windowsills. Everything was still and I could walk through the rooms, touching the edge of the mantelpiece, turning the pages of a book left open on the coffee table. With my index finger I rubbed a thick line through the dust on the radio. I blew at the shower curtain and looked into the mirror above the wash basin and I listened to the phone ringing. I had been reading that book not too many weeks ago and it seemed possible that some small odd ether still clung to it, making an eternal moment of what had been a wet finger turning a page. Then the rooms were empty again, even in my mind. I was not there and nothing moved. There was only the sound of the telephone.

The truck drivers sat over their cups of coffee in a sort of contained delirium, men who had done a thousand times what had to be done, understanding it too well. We got going again. Clevenger, at the wheel, pointed to a group of ten or twelve small dwellings located in a shallow valley about three hundred yards off the road. They appeared to be huts of wood and clay. He slowed the car and pulled over.

"That's where they are," he said. "A year ago they were maybe three or four. Now I hear it's up to twenty."

"Who are they?"

"Bunch of kids. Younger than you. Living down there with the Indians. Hell, I don't know what they're up to. I hear they claim some kind of agrarian squatter's rights. That's government land they're on, so it's only a matter of time."

"I think I'd like to take a look. Do you mind?"

"It's a free country, boy."

"Maybe I should take my stuff. I've been enough trouble."

"Tell you what," he said. "You go on down and have your look. I'll run into Phoenix and pick you up soon as I can. Have two Jewboys to out-hustle. Take me no more than a couple of hours. Then we'll be on our way."

"I've been enough trouble, Mr. Clevenger."

"Get your ass on down there, son. And get used to calling me cap'n. That's what the boys at the track call me."

I slid down the embankment and walked across a field of flat stones and sagebrush. The huts were arranged in no discernible pattern and there did not seem to be any village square or center. A few people sat on the ground—two young men, a white girl holding an Indian baby. I sat next to one of the men. He wore no shoes or shirt and his pants were tan chinos cut off above the knees.

"Dave Bell," I said. "Just having a look around."

"I'm Cliff. This is Hogue. That's Verna and the baby's name is Tommy. Or is that Jeff?"

"That's Jeff," the other man said.

"So you're living with the Indians. What's it like?"

"It's the total thing," Cliff said. "It outruns all the other scenes by miles. We all live like persons. There's a lot of love here, although it gets monotonous at times."

"Are these Navahos or what?"

"These are Apache. Exiles from an Apache tribe about a hundred miles east of here. Misfits more or less. They refused to become ranchers like the rest of their people. There's only eleven of them here but we expect more to come. There's eighteen of us. We'd like to have more of them than us. It's an emotional factor."

"I don't want to sound like a critic at the very outset because you've probably had plenty of those coming around but I don't think I understand what you expect to accomplish."

"We don't expect to accomplish anything. We just don't want to be part of the festival of death out there."

"Here comes Jill," Hogue said.

She was very thin and seemed to be coming at us sideways in small skips and bounces. She couldn't have been more than seventeen years old. Her hair was reddish brown and there were several dozen muted freckles swarming about her nose. After introductions and further commentary, she offered to give me a tour of the village. I liked the way her gums showed when she smiled.

"I'm from Trenton, New Jersey," she said.

"I'm from New York."

"Neighbors!"

She wore a man's white shirt, tails tied around her middle, and blue jeans cut off above the knees. We went into one of the huts. It had a dirt floor with a carpet on it. There were several straw mats, a sleeping bag, some rolled-up blankets, a Matisse print propped against a wall, and that was it. A man with blue hair was asleep on one of the mats. It was hot and dark. We sat on the ground.

"Are you happy?" I said.

"We're all happy. This is the happiest place in the world. I mean that really seriously."

"Are the Indians happy?"

"It's hard to tell. They don't say much. But they must be happier than they used to be or else they'd go back to ranching."

"You're pretty young to be living like this, not that I'm criticizing. Did you run away from home?"

"My dad and I both ran away. Mom was driving us batty. It was psychorama twenty-four hours a day. I guess I love her and all but it got pretty bad. All she did was drink and smoke and yell things over the telephone to my father at his office. So then he stopped coming home from work. So then after that he came and got me at school and we sneaked my things out of the house when she was shopping and we got into the car and ran away. My dad's in Tempe now trying to start a dry-cleaning place. He comes out here on weekends to see me."

"Don't you get bored?"

"Anything's better than working for the death machine. We all try to dress the same way here. Simple and beautiful. But it's not like uniforms. It's just part of the single consciousness of the community. It's like everybody is you and you are everybody. Sex is mostly auto. You can watch someone doing something with himself or herself and then they can watch you do it. It's better that way because it's really purer and it's all one thing and you can do it with different people without anybody running for their shotgun like in the death factory out there. Sometimes it's not auto but mostly it is and it's two people mostly because two is still the most beautiful. I don't know what the Indians do."

"Look, Jill, I'm not a reporter or anything, so you don't have to tell me things that are private or sensitive."

"It's okay," she said. "I would tell you anything because you remind me of my brother. He was killed by the police."

"I'm sorry to hear that."

"It's okay. I loved him very much but I wasn't sad. You have to get beyond that."

"Who's that guy over there?"

"That's Incredible Shrinking Man. He sleeps every day at this time. At night he goes into the desert. He's the one that started this whole thing. He has so much love in him. It won't be long before they kill him too. He believes in the truth of science fiction. The cosmos is love. Something is out there and once we learn to welcome it instead of fear it, we'll find out that its mission is love. His name is the name of an old sci-fi movie. At night he goes into the desert to watch for UFOs. He's seen lots of them. We've all seen them. This is a good place for sightings. That's one of the reasons he started the community out here. The visibility is terrific. So then they'll kill him because he preaches love."

"I believe in the saucers."

"Almost everybody does," she said. "But people are afraid to admit things to themselves. If we can learn to welcome instead of fear, the whole universe will heave with love. But the festival of death is going on all the time. That makes it hard for some people."

"I knew a boy at college who did what you did. He left school just like that and went to live with the Havasupai Indians. He lost forty or fifty pounds."

"They're north of here. I think they're farmers and planters."

"I wonder if he's still with them. Leonard Zajac. A very brilliant boy."

"This is the only community that's sci-fi oriented."

"I know another guy who's walking to California," I said.

Incredible Shrinking Man rose to his elbow. He was wearing plaid bermudas. He was well-tanned and very muscular, dispelling the vague sense of undernourishment in the area. His hair reached down almost to his shoulders. We stood to shake hands and I realized he was about six feet eight inches tall, broad across his bare chest, lean at the waist. His grip was gentle. I found myself exerting pressure. Then we sat down again.

"This is an interesting thing you've got here."

"The locals fear us," he said. "What they don't realize is that we're much more conservative than they are. This is a very conservative settlement. We want to cleave to the old things. The land. The customs. The words. The ideas. Unfortunately wilderness will soon be nothing but a memory. Then the saucers will land and our children will be forced to embrace the new technology. If they're not prepared, if we don't prepare them, there'll be an awful lot of confusion. We have to learn to accept the facts of technology without the emotion it engenders, the death impulse. But soon big government will take this land from us and install silos and missiles and lasers to keep out the UFOs. Big government beeps out everything in the end. Screaming meemies wield all the guns. Pimps and brainwashers are gaining power footholds. The answer is indistinguishability. Become indistinguishable from your neighbor and his neighbor and his neighbor. The death circus is coming to town and benign totalitarianism is the only feasible response."

"I'm not a journalist," I said.

"Whoever you are, you're welcome. Everybody's welcome. Love lives in our own galaxy. We sing at nine."

"Jill said you've seen a lot of UFOs out in the desert."

"He calls them love-objects," she said.

"I've seen them by the score. Night things filled with love. But they won't land until the time is right. The thing is out there. Jupiter and beyond the infinite."

"I have my own theory about UFOs," I said. "They're not from outer space at all. They're from the oceans. The depths of our own oceans."

"Who pilots them?" Jill said.

"Dolphins."

"He's just kidding," she said to Incredible Shrinking Man.

She and I continued the tour. A few Apaches played cards inside one of the huts. The girl Verna was still holding the Indian child. A group of eight young men and women, all of them appearing a few years older than Jill, sat in the dirt playing a game of jacks. A boy of fourteen or so, an Indian, knelt at the fringe of the group; there were two fielder's gloves and a baseball on the ground beside him. I picked up one of the gloves, a very old Luke Appling model. I spat into the palm and pounded it a few times. The boy got up and we walked slowly past the last of the huts and started playing catch. At first we stood only thirty feet apart and tossed the ball easily back and forth, limbering up. Then we doubled the distance and began to throw a bit harder. Then he moved back another ten feet and started firing. It was dry and very hot at the rim of the desert. I felt wonderful. The boy had a strong and accurate arm. The glove was soft with use, not as well padded as the later models, and my hand began to sting. He moved still farther away and I tossed him some high flies, which he fired back on a line. I took off my shirt. The sun felt good and my face and neck and upper body broke into lavish sweat. He moved across the dirt and weeds, kicking up dust, purposely delaying his break for the ball so that he could make an over-the-shoulder or backhand catch. My hand hurt badly now and I could not recall feeling this good in many years. I continued throwing long high flies, first to one side, then the next, and the boy veered and cut and back-pedaled, always sure of his terrain, dodging the larger stones without taking his eye off the ball. Sweat was collecting at my navel and I would rub it off with my right hand and then rub my hand in the dirt and wipe off the sticky dirt on my pants and blow on my hand then, drying it further, and then lean back and heave another long arching fly into the mouth of the sun. All trace of lettering had long since vanished from the baseball.

We walked back to the village. I draped my shirt over my neck. Jill came toward us and the boy was gone. We sat on the ground and she put one finger to my chest and then touched her lips with it. We stared at each other for a moment.

"Why does he dye his hair blue?" I said.

"Vanity."

"To what end?"

"Vanity's end," she said. "It's silly for a person to repress his own vanity. Make love to your body and you kill the death inside you."

"There are certain inconsistencies here."

"I think his hair is beautiful. Why shouldn't he have blue hair if he wants to? Do you feel it threatens you in some way? Really seriously now, what harm is he doing? If you let yourself be what you want to be, physically and spiritually, you can kill a lot of the death inside you."

"I love to be instructed by the very young. It implies I'm not yet a lost cause."

"I could never instruct you," she said. "And I could never get mad at you. It's not just the brother thing either. You're so beautiful."

"And that's important, you think."

"Youth and beauty are always important. It's what the death police hate most. They want to kill us and fuck us at the same time."

"I admit he's a striking figure. I suppose the Indians think he's a god."

"The Indians think he's a fag," she said, and she giggled for a bit, then slapped herself on the wrist as punishment.

"Your gums show when you smile," I said. "It gives me an almost death-dealing pleasure."

"I got all shivery when I touched you before."

"Do it again."

"I better not," she said.

"Your eyes are hazel."

"Do you want to stay with us?"

"I don't know. Maybe I'd better keep right on going. I'm trying to outrun myself."

"Is this like a suicidal period?"

"I don't think so."

"If it is, my dad could probably help. He's a great guy. So

then my screamy mother takes her repressions out on him."

"Did you watch me while I was playing catch with the kid?"

"A-mazing."

"Baseball is so beautiful and lazy. It's our version of the café life. You sit there and nothing happens. I really love it. The season's underway now. If this were 1955 I could be sitting in the bleachers at the old Polo Grounds, watching the Giants play the Cubs. All around me there would be shirtless old men with sunken pink chests and their pants rolled up over their bony knees. What is it like? It's like a seashore at the end of time. Jill, your hazel eyes destroy me. It's nice sitting here. A spot of small talk with our dusty tea. Fatigue is such a luxury these days."

"You should stay," she said.

"Somebody's coming by to get me. I'm surprised he hasn't turned up yet."

"This is a part of the world," she said, "where people don't always turn up."

We walked back to the hut. Incredible Shrinking Man was standing out front, almost as high as the hut itself, wearing just the bermudas, his body a rich tempered tone of pennies, the blue hair hanging lank, strands of deep muscle extending along his arms. It was an astounding sight and as we approached I slid my shirt down off my neck and put it on. Later the Apache boy came for me and we took a sponge bath together behind his hut and then everyone gathered around several fires for hamburgers and corn, and a girl played a guitar and sang some western ballads, and still Clevenger did not come. In the darkness at the edge of the assembly I kissed little Jill and touched her softly beating hooded breast and she put her finger to my wrist. Incredible Shrinking Man walked into the desert for the feast of his infinity, white dwarfs and waltzing binaries, the first fictional inch of the space odyssey. Hogue, Jill and I settled down to sleep in the Matisse hut. A small fire burned. Hogue told of his life in Canada and Mexico, the search for gold, then God, then the perfect vacuum; his grandfather had prospected near this very site, a gunslinging man who was not averse to mule-meat, but his father, the all too timid issue of the panning days, had ended up in hardware. The three of us lay far apart. Soon the fire died and I thought she would come to me in the darkness, freckled Mescalero maid smelling of leather and sagebrush. But she did not come. And at dawn I woke to see Incredible Shrinking Man leaning into the hut, his naked body stained with the blood of the rattler he held in his hand. Jill got up and moved toward him and they went silently to whatever place they went for the ablutions of late and early man.

The Cadillac was waiting. We had just finished lunch and Jill walked with me toward the road. Clevenger stood outside the car, wearing new boots and smoking a cigarillo. Jill said goodbye at the foot of the embankment and I asked her to wait a moment. I got my suitcases out of the trunk, emptied both, and then filled one with almost all of my remaining clothes and slid it down to her.

"You can sell this stuff and get some food."

"Don't go," she said. "It's bad out there."

For the first time since I had met Clevenger we were heading east, south and east, and if he seemed less happy it might have been nothing more than the tight fit of new boots. He asked me to get his sunglasses out of the glove compartment. There was a revolver in there, a long-barreled thing, probably a .45, and I wondered how often he took target practice or in his mind fired from the speeding car, knocking off coyotes, redskins, small foreign automobiles. And now he was doubly screened behind stained windshield and sunglasses, bowed low in his cool church, and I knew this was why I was with him, to search out the final extreme, the bible as weapon, the lean hunt of the godfearing man for the child who confounded his elders. Clevenger drove with one hand.

"They ought to be drug out in the desert and horse-whipped."

"They're not bothering anybody," I said.

"That's government land they're on."

"So what."

"Hey boy, you got your back up, ain't you? Chip, chip, chip. I can't say I blame you. I did my best to get back last night but the wheelers were dealing and the dealers were wheeling. It was a right fine mess. Then there was this woman."

"It's okay," I said.

"Call me cap'n now."

"It's okay, cap'n."

"There was this woman. A pot of warm syrup. I hate like hell to have to be getting back. The goddamn punctured lung of America. But that's all right. We'll have us a pig-party. Hey, see that gulch over there?"

"I've never been to Texas."

"Where we're going ain't exactly Texas. It ain't exactly no place. See that gulch we just passed? That's a piece of local history, that spot. I get put in a good frame of mind just thinking about what happened there. Of course some people wouldn't think it was so damn funny."

"I'm listening," I said.

"Now this girl was about twenty-one years old. A sweet little coed. Spends a night with a married man. Goes home the next day and tells her mama and daddy. Don't ask me why. Maybe just to rub their faces in it. They decide she needs a lesson. Whole family drives out into the desert, right out to that spot we just passed. All three of them plus the girl's pet dog. Papa tells the girl to dig a shallow grave. Mama gets down on her hands and knees and holds the dog by the collar. When the girl is all through digging, papa gives her a .22 caliber revolver and tells her to shoot the dog. A real touching family scene. Make a good calendar for some religious group to give away. The girl puts the weapon to her temple and kills herself. Now isn't that a heartwarming son of a bitch of a story? Restores my faith in just about everything."

"This is the only country in the world that has funny violence," I said.

"And what do you think the parents are charged with? Now what do you think? Go on now, take a crack at it."

"Manslaughter?"

"Manslaughter, hell. Cruelty to animals. Intent to kill, maim or otherwise injure, or suffer to be killed, maimed or injured, or an accessory thereof, a damn dog. That beats my meat. That's the living dead end."

He howled then, the consummate reb yell, a two-syllable sound that was hog call, battle cry, the bark of the saved soul at a prayer meeting. I didn't understand Clevenger. There were shades to him which dimmed what I kept expecting to find. Literature. Movies. We cut across the scaly land and it seemed to glide a tongue among the bones of mules and greed, and all signs pointed to national monuments, to Organ Pipe, Casa Grande, Saguaro, Chiricahua, Gila, White Sands, loving attempts to embalm the long riddle of the cliff-dwellers, and we moved into evening, crest of the setting sun at our rear window, the tender menace of our land, freetailed bats in flight above the whispering huts of mystics and every unwritten death singing in the hills. Literature. I told Clevenger about Incredible Shrinking Man, his great height and brawn, the energy of his presence.

"I ain't seen the man yet who bullets bounce off of."

At some point in the night, sleepless, as I stood by a window overlooking a blue swimming pool, I remembered walking once past the Waldorf and St. Bartholomew's and the Seagram Building and then looking across the street to see a lovely girl in light green standing by the Mercedes-Benz showroom on Fifty-sixth Street. It was a summer evening, a Friday, and the city was beginning to empty. I crossed to the traffic island and paused a moment, watching her. She was waiting for someone. The violet twilight of Park Avenue slid across tall glass. Traffic slowed and the mild bleating of horns lifted a half note of longing into the heavy dusk. There was a sense of the tropics, of voluptuousness and plucked fruit, and also of the sea, a promise disclosing itself in tides of air salted by the rivers and bay, and of penthouse hammocks and huge green plants, a man and woman watching the city descend into the musical craters of its birth. And she stood by the window, not quite facing me, shapely and fair, all that elegant velocity bottled behind her, concealed torsion bars and disc brakes, the poise of fine machinery, and her body then, softly turning, seemed to melt into the rippling glass. That was all there was and it was everything.

"We'll be sucking hind tit if we don't get moving," Clevenger said.

He was putting on his boots in the dark. He had slept only two hours after driving close to four hundred miles and it was still deep night when we set out again. He said he had not slept at all the previous night, needing only a hot towel and shave, the bite of a crusty cigar, to keep his senses on target. I turned on the portable radio and we listened to the Reverend Tom Thumb Goodloe, a country singer and preacher shouting out of El Paso. Clevenger began to smile.

"Adams I say. Aldrich I say. Andrews, Armstrong, Bancroft, Barton, Bennett, Box, Brown, Bryan. Give me Calder. Give me Carpenter and I'm all right. Give me Cartwright, Cassidy, Cole, Cooper, Curtis, Dale, Dixon. I want Elliot on my team. Fowler sounds like my kind of man. I want Benjamin Cromwell Franklin. I want Calvin Gage. I want Albert Gallatin. I want Gant, Gillespie, Gray, Green, Hale, Hamilton, Hawkins, Hunt, Ingram, Jackson, Jennings, Jones, Kenyon, King, Lambert, Lane, Lawrence. Lewis I say. Lightfoot I say. Lindsay and Logan. Love, Marshall, Martin. Maxwell I say. McClelland, McCoy, McKay, Mercer, Mitchell, Moore, Nabers, Nash, Orr, Pace, Parker, Patton, Phillips. I want to hear the right-sounding names like Powell, Proctor, Reed and Reese. I want to hear Rhodes, Robbins, Rockwell, Russell, Sanders, Scott, Slayton. I want to hear the old-time names like Smith, Stilwell, Taylor, Thompson, Tindale. I want the good people on my side. Trask, Turner, Tyler, Wade, Walker, White, Williams, Yancey, York, Young. They were all there, every last one of them, raising the lone star standard. And by God there was a Goodloe too. Robert Kemp Goodloe. And I was not a stranger in my own land."

"What was that all about?" I said.

"He likes to read off some of the names they got scratched on one of the monuments over at the San Jacinto battleground cemetery. War with the Mexicans. Sam Houston. Army of the Republic of Texas. He likes to leave out all the foreign-sounding names."

"Plain talk of the plain people. Only a youth but a youth with a song. Only a poor native son but a son with a hymn in his heart. Dirt farmer and banjo player but all Texas is my home and I am not a stranger unto it."

"He's warming up now," Clevenger said.

"If you can't pronounce a man's name, that man is a stranger; and if he don't look you in the eye, he runs with danger."

"Nothing but hell, ain't he?"

"Soft white underbelly. Spread those words around and tell those good neighbors of yours to keep the ball rolling. Tell them you heard those words from out of the mouth of Tom Thumb Goodloe, the midnight evangelist, twenty-six years old and on his way to the glory road. Now what are those words? Those words are soft, white and underbelly. Spread them around, friends. We're too soft and too sweet and we got to bear down on all those people that blaspheme our Christian nation with their catcalling and their jibbering like an Islamic sect from out of the motion pictures. We got to blitz them, friends. We got to send our linebackers. Keeryst Jesus was not a stranger in his own land. He spoke the lingo. He ate the grub. He felt right at home. Now our fine engineer, Mr. Dale Mulholland, signals me it's time to do some singing and I ask each and every one of you out there to join along with me, right there in your beds or in your kitchens fixing a late snack or what all you're doing. Will you come to the bower? Those that know it raise their voices with me. Those that don't, should. But first we have to pause so's I can read this commercial message."

I didn't know what was so funny but Clevenger was driving all over the road and punching the steering wheel in glee. I changed stations, a wave of exhaustion coming over me as I slipped down into the seat. Ten minutes later a Spanish-speaking disc jockey signed off in a blur of static and a few seconds after that another voice traveled across the long night.

"Fools, pretenders, pharisees and knaves. Beastly here with the final hour of 'Death Is Just Around the Corner.' Some philosophical patter. Some strolls down lobotomy lane. An occasional pocket of dead air. It's just occurred to me, like jukes and jingoes, that you won't be needing my special form of truth much longer. Drugs are scheduled to supplant the media. A dull gloomy bliss will replace the burning fear of your nights and early mornings. You can look forward to experiencing a drug-induced liberation from anxiety, grief and happiness. Endoparasites all, you'll be able to cling to the bowel-walls of time itself. But I shall be missed. Pills and magical Chiclets are no substitute for the transistorized love which passes between us in the savage night. I pale with sickly forethoughts. But onward, chloroformed brutes, into the mysteries and mayhems. I ran into an old friend today, Lothar Nobo, the former George Jefferson Carver Eleanor Roosevelt III. No doubt the news has reached even the most barricaded among you that Lothar Nobo is currently the nation's chief spokesman for black manhood and pride, pending release of next month's top forty. I first met Lothar last year on the J. Edgar Hooverplatz in West Berlin where we were both attending the international book-burning fair. If I recall, he made a few rather demeaning statements to the press concerning the private parts of our esteemed head of state, H. C. Porny. But I don't want to talk about that. Suddenly I prefer to discuss more gentle matters. Enough of obscenity. My life is being overwhelmed by redeeming prurient value.

Everywhere I walk, I see the flowering of my nightlong labors. Now that history has absolved me, and with a vengeance, I think I'd like to go very far away—to the Aran Islands, to the Sahara, to some village high in the Himalayas. There to situate my stale body and well-paid mind against the wild dogs of nature. Sea, desert and mountain. What neo-saintly El Dorados of solitude. What amazement on my face when I emerge from my earth-covered wickiup to see not the diffident old gents and waxy ladies of Sixty-fourth Street but some tall Mephistophelean yak shambling through the snowdrifts. I spin my Harry Winston prayer wheel. Or I stand above the furious sea, urbane man of Aran, spitting in my own face. Temporal salvation. Alone, I might be able to sustain a serious thought or two. Pure mathematics of the desert. To be gone from this radioactive puddle. My skin is getting dry and flaky. My tongue is coated with isotopes. My extremities, all of them, are turning blue. All secrets are contained in the desert. Lines intersecting in the sand. Where you are and what you are. Bedouinism in all of its bedpan humor. Buckmulliganism in its bowl. An Irish Arab lives in my inner ear, announcing news, weather and sports. He is Jesuit-educated and wears the very best that dogma can buy. Speaking of clothes, all the eunuchoid trend-spotters out there might be interested to know that when I saw Lothar Nobo on Fifty-third Street this afternoon, right outside the Museum of Modern Commerce, he was wearing a braided Sassoon lion's mane, a speckled leopard-pelt jumpsuit, and a pair of king cobra elevated shoes. The shrunken head of a former Oakland policeman was dangling from the love beads around his neck. Lothar and I shook hands warmly and then he gave me the latest black power sign, locked pinkies and thumbs down, a form of greeting prevalent among the members of a nomadic tribe in south central Algeria who worship the mystical eye on the back of American dollar bills. Without further comment I'll now read the note which Lothar handed me at that time. Quote. I would like to take this opportunity to remind the white rapist imperialist power-hungry genocidal warmongers that they have exactly twenty-four hours to get out of Africa, Asia, South and Central America, the West Indies, Australia and New Zealand. Failure to comply with this order will result in a worldwide orgy of bloodshed that will make World War II seem like a Quaker picnic in New Harmony, Indiana. Unquote. Jungle and desert being built, rhetoric by rhetoric, in the dark crack of the dawn. Hammering out those bronze names. Also known as: Ahmed Abu Bekir. Halil Rassam. Shafik Bey. Imam el-Mahdi. Kwame Mwanga. Majid Said. Hassan Karami. Rashid Nimr. Muhammad Lateef. Mustapha al-Attassi. Dugumbe Ujiji. Ismail bin Salim. James Lumumba. Abdul-Rahman Alami. Yakoub Mahmoud. We were sailing along on Shafik Bey/ when a noise from off the port bow/took our breath away. My little ineffables, my trolls and trogs—you think there are noble sounds in these names of the desert. Bulrushes and scimitars. My bosom lightly trembles with the laughter of the angled Saxon. Which is what I am. Triplicate flesh of the graded sequence. Extract of the terminal afterthought. File child registered in the provisional substring. Picture transmitted by numerically shaded values. Standardized implementation of the coded tabulator. I am the inconceivable Mandrake. And I see we have to pause now for a recorded announcement of crucial importance to everyone within the sound of my voice. In the meantime, don't do anything detrimental to the national incest."

The test track was a nine-mile circle in the desert. It was sunrise and we were parked on an overpass watching the trucks and cars move beneath us. Clevenger said they rolled twenty-four hours a day, six days a week, all kinds of weather. Every so often one of the drivers falls asleep, he said; goes barreling off the road; turns over six or eight times; burns to death. Trucks don't bounce as much as cars but seem to burn better. Then he said it was time to be checking in at the office but first he took a turn around the track, nine very hasty miles, his final burst for the wire, speedometer quivering at 117. I wondered why he had come out here before going home.

In the office he showed me some schedules and gave me a brief run-down of the operation. He had twelve more or less steady employees; four were white, two black, six Mexican. The workload was informally organized in such a way that the Mexicans did most of the driving, the blacks most of the tire-changing, the whites most of the balancing and measuring as well as the checking of air pressure, temperature, tread loss and the rest. I told him I wanted to drive and change tires and he seemed to look at me in anger at all dumb-ass northern guilt and innocence, although his head did not move the slightest, nor his eyes; it was just the way it seemed. He checked his mail then and we did not speak for a long time. The cars and trucks went by and the land ran dead flat up to a bank of blue mountains far off. I said it looked like rain.

"Anybody who tries to predict the weather in Texas is either a stranger or a damn fool."

"Right," I said.

A man stood by the window drinking something hot from a paper cup and Clevenger went outside to talk to him. I called Warren Beasley at his home.

"For our cash jackpot of $840,000, can you identify the man or woman who was playing third base for the Philadelphia Phillies at the exact moment that James Mason walked into the sea to save Judy Garland's career?"

"I don't talk money without my lawyers," he said. "Who is this?"

"David Bell. I heard the show a couple of hours ago. I'm down here in the middle of nowhere. I thought you were kind of unfunny there with the black militant thing. Why shouldn't they have whatever names they want? Did I wake you up?"

"I couldn't sleep," he said.

"Anyway it was good to hear a familiar voice."

"I agree with you. I listened to it myself. Cheered me up considerably."

"I don't get you, Warren."

"It was on tape. I've been taping for the last three or four months. Doing it live was too much strain."

"I should have known," I said. "I really should have guessed. We're all on tape. All on tape. All of us."

"Sorry, Tab, if I upset that delicate circuitry of yours. But it's really more practical this way. I can tape a couple of shows at a time and take a day off now and then."

"It was better the other way, Warren."

"Only in the ontological sense. But I have to admit I haven't had one good night of solid sleep since I went over to tape. I think that's my wife's fault more than anything else. The first four were insomniacs. Consequently I slept like a baby all those years. My metabolism is based on subtle polarities. But the current bitch is always in the sack. She's like a serpent asleep in warm water. I'm helpless against this kind of power. And when I finally doze off for a few minutes I get the tapeworm dream, which I haven't had in years. Listen, Tab, come on over and have a couple of bloody marys with me. We'll sit by the bed and watch her sleep. She does a certain amount of finger-diddling every morning about this time. If you get over here real fast you'll be able to see it."

"Warren, I'm not home. I'm in goddamn Texas."

"When did this happen?"

"I don't know," I said. "I left about five weeks ago. I don't even have a job anymore."

"Look, she's starting."

"Goodbye," I said.

I went outside and Clevenger introduced me to two white men named Lump and Dowd. He said he'd get the women as soon as Peewee showed up. We went around to the garage. A small dump truck stood in the center of the concrete floor and dozens of tires were stacked against the wall. All over the place were weighing and measuring devices, rags, jacks, tire-irons, carburetors, rims, hubcaps, exhaust pipes. Lump carried in two cases of quart bottles of beer; he carried them one on each hip, a hand gripping the far edge of each wood and iron case. He and Dowd sat on a tire. Clevenger sat on a fender of the dump truck. I leaned against a bare section of wall. We started drinking. It was seven o'clock in the morning.

We drank straight from the bottles. The beer tasted awful at that hour of day but I said nothing and kept drinking. The others were drinking about twice as fast as I was. Dowd chugged half a quart and then said he'd best be getting outside for a kingsize piss and everybody laughed. We drank beer for about an hour, each of us in turn drawing laughter by standing in the huge square of the open garage door and pissing onto the gravel outside. When my turn came, there was both laughter and applause as if by this act I had joined them in some mythic union. I found myself pleased with their benedictions. Peewee showed up with a fifth of bourbon and we started passing the bottle around. Through a window I could see the cars and trucks circling the track, headlights off now. Clevenger went to the wall phone and spoke very softly and evenly for no more than ten seconds before hanging up. Dowd lowered the garage door.

The women arrived half an hour later. There were three of them, all Mexican. The young one wanted to know where Danny Boy was and Clevenger told her Danny Boy was in jail minus his right eye. Dowd took the fat one into the cab of the truck and she got on her back and pulled up her dress. His knee slipped off the seat and he fell over her leg and down under the dash. We were all laughing. He crawled out onto the running board and dropped to the ground, laughing and vomiting, one foot still hooked to the running board. Lump walked right over him, then opened his pants and got on top of the woman. Clevenger took off all his clothes, stepped back into his boots and told the young one to sit inside a truck tire that was standing against the wall. As she lifted her dress he got on his hands and knees and put his head inside. Peewee had the other one against the bare wall, dress up, biting her breasts which were not uncovered and trying to work his way into her. I dragged Dowd over to the back of the truck and when I was sure no one could see what I was doing I kicked him hard in the ribs. Then I finished off the bourbon and poured part of a bottle of beer on Lump's head and he laughed and kept going. Peewee began sliding down the woman's legs. Over Clevenger's rump the young one looked at me, picking her nose. Peewee was on the ground, curled around the other one's legs, biting, his pants not quite off. Lump came out of the cab, took off all his clothes and picked up a quart of beer. Clevenger came out from under the dress and got on top of the fat one in the cab. He told her to take off her dress but she wouldn't and he began to laugh. Lump threw the bottle at a wall. I saw Dowd crawling past and I helped him to his feet and pushed him toward the young one. He fell over halfway there. She was still in the tire and Lump went over and put his head under her dress. I kicked Dowd. Peewee had the other one's shoes off and he was putting one of her feet inside his pants. She looked down at him and laughed and then he laughed and she dropped on top of him and they lay together laughing and pulling each other's hair, biting, rolling from side to side. I couldn't get the garage door opened and I leaned my head against it, feeling myself falling and waiting to hit, wanting to, but somehow still standing, the door cold on my cheek. Clevenger was slapping me on the back and repeating the words *soft white underbelly* over and over. I turned and saw the fat one pouring beer all over Dowd. Peewee was standing now with a length of pipe between his legs and they all laughed. The young one was still inside the tire. Lump pissed against the wall. Dowd got up and put his arms around the fat one and threw up again. She punched him in the face, twice, hurting him, and everybody laughed. Peewee was out of his clothes now and he crawled over to the young one and put his head under her dress. Clevenger told me to watch out for the fat one. Her cunt had teeth in them. The fat one and the other one sat on the running board sharing a bottle of beer. Dowd, on the ground again, said it was time he was getting his. He lurched toward the two women, tried to get up, lost his balance and hit his head on the edge of the bumper. Lump was standing in his own piss. I went over to Peewee, grabbed his ankles and pulled him away from the young one. I dragged him along the ground on his belly and face. Clevenger poured beer on him. Then I went to the girl sitting in the tire, pushed her dress up around her hips and buried my face between her legs. Her thighs parted and then closed, wet against my ears, and I tried to put my tongue higher into her, feeling again as though I were about to pass out. She was patting my head. Someone pulled me away from her and I crawled toward the fat one, trying to take off my shirt, just my shirt. Clevenger got to her first and they went to the back of the truck and after a while managed to climb in. The other one pushed me to the ground, straddled me, unbuttoned my shirt and took it off, and began taking off my belt. I could see Dowd. He was still out but there was no blood. The woman had my cock in her hand and she was trying to put it inside her. I pulled her down to me and kissed her and she let go finally and just lay on top of me, moving from side to side and licking my face. Then she straddled me again and I realized she was pissing all over my belly and chest. She got up finally and sat on the running board and drank some beer. I pushed myself up to my knees and fastened my belt. Then I threw up. Lump was under the young one's dress. Peewee was on the ground smoking a cigarette. I crawled over to him and asked for a drag, although I hadn't smoked in several years. We sat next to each other sharing the cigarette. Clevenger eased himself down off the truck, took off his boots, got dressed and put on the boots. The fat one stood in the back of the truck and the other one handed the bottle up to her. Clevenger made a phone call. Lump came out of the dress and pissed all over Dowd. The young one sat inside the tire.

Then Clevenger left by a side door. I went after him and got my suitcase out of the car. He said he'd be back in half an hour. I watched him drive around the test track. He went around three times, almost twice as fast as the trucks and other cars. I looked at that huge circle of asphalt, nine never-ending miles, something left behind by a crazed or childlike people. It made me think of Warburton for a moment, his final memo, and I began to juggle the alphabet, to fit it together finally, three names from two, anagrammatized, a last jest from corporate exile. I went back to the garage and got my shirt. Then I ran across the track and across fifty yards of dirt and out the gate onto the road. Clevenger was still circling the track. I put on my shirt and walked for about half an hour. It started getting warmer. Dead coyotes were hung on wire fences. A car stopped for me then, an old Studebaker. The driver started up again before I had the door closed. He was a one-arm man wearing the dress blues of the United States Navy. Along the road and spread out across the desert were hundreds of oil drills, their black shafts stroking, triangular heads and lean frames, slave colonies of gigantic worker ants, the science fiction of prehistory and hereafter. Black smoke came gusting out of a refinery and covered the land and sky. I asked him where he was heading and he said Midland. On the radio Bob Dylan was singing "Subterranean Homesick Blues." We came out of the smoke and I asked him how long he had been in the navy. He appeared to be in his mid-twenties, a slight wincing man with the thin mouth and white-blond hair of a secret planner of bank robberies.

"You think I'm not navy because of the arm. You find me incongruous. That's always been my strength. I project a mystery that a lot of men and women have tried to unlock. But maybe the mystery is in themselves. You're wondering how I know so much about people. I've been places all my life.

I've been to China, one of the few. I'm a voracious reader. I studied at the sore bone in Paris. That was before the arm."

"No offense meant. I was just asking."

"Everybody's interested in the arm. There are other parts of me, deep down, that nobody has succeeded in reaching. I have an insatiable curiosity about people from all walks of life. The way to learn about people is to keep your eyes and ears open and your lips sealed. I roamed the streets of Paris like a cat. I was silent and watchful. Nobody messed with me. I carried a knife all through my Paris days. I had only one intimate friend, a writer-painter from Harlem. He was sleek and wiry. He was the coolest spade in Paris. He was the ace of spades. We were like two cats prowling the Left Bank. I carried my knife at all times. Mess with either one of us and the other'd cut your throat."

"What was his name?"

"Whose name?"

"The writer-painter," I said.

"You're being polite because you're afraid of me. Fear impels people to ask ingratiating questions. I've been noticing that for quite a few years. It's an intricate thing, fear. I've been making a study of it during my travels. There's a whole literature of fear in the libraries of the world, just waiting to be read and synthesized. It's the arm that worries people. Mystery is the white man's enemy. I'm one of the few with soul. Let me take a gander at what the hell you look like."

"How far is Midland?"

"I'm taking a gander," he said. "First billboard we come to I'll park this vehicle behind it. Then we'll see how much mystery you have. I'm hung. I'm hung like a fighting bull. I'm yea big. We'll see who's more man. Bigger gives it. Smaller takes. Them's the rules of the road."

"That's it," I said. "Let me out."

"Rejection is one of the banes of our time. People should never reject each other. You think this is nothing but vulgarism on my part. What I offer is more than merchandise.

Men have paid plenty for my sexual gifts and proclivities. But my mystery isn't for sale."

"Stop the car."

He slowed down and pulled over to the side. I grabbed my suitcase and got out. And then, a delighted child reciting a rhyme, a child remembering word for word some old lesson or torn bit of lore, he leaned toward the window and said victoriously:

"Good little boys do not accept rides from strangers."

A deaf-mute couple took me the next forty miles. They looked enough alike to be twins. I sat in the back seat next to a guitar. Then I rode a short stretch with a man who sold rat poison and had once been a delegate to a political convention. A former stripteaser picked me up then and took me into Midland. She used to play gin rummy with the Duke of Windsor. I got a room, shaved, showered, checked out and rented a car. I drove all night, northeast, and once again I felt it was literature I had been confronting these past days, the archetypes of the dismal mystery, sons and daughters of the archetypes, images that could not be certain which of two confusions held less terror, their own or what their own might become if it ever faced the truth. I drove at insane speeds.

In the morning I headed west along Main Street in downtown Dallas. I turned right at Houston Street, turned left onto Elm and pressed my hand against the horn. I kept it there as I drove past the School Book Depository, through Dealey Plaza and beneath the triple underpass. I kept blowing the horn all along Stemmons Freeway and out past Parkland Hospital. At Love Field I turned in the car and bought a gift for Merry. Then, with my American Express credit card, I booked a seat on the first flight to New York. Ten minutes after we were airborne a woman asked for my autograph.